DARK RISE

ALSO BY C. S. PACAT

C. S. PACAT

DARK RISE

Quill Tree Books
An Imprint of HarperCollinsPublishers

For Mandy,

I wonder if we both
needed a sister

PROLOGUE
London, 1821

"WAKE HIM UP," said James, and the hard-faced shipman promptly lifted the wooden pail he held and threw its contents into the face of the man slumped and restrained in front of them.

Water slapped Marcus, splashing him into consciousness, coughing and gasping.

Even dripping, chained, and beaten, Marcus had a nobility to him, like a knight-gallant in a faded tapestry. *The arrogance of the Stewards*, thought James. It lingered, like the stinking miasma of the river, though Marcus was manacled to prohibit all movement, in the bowels of Simon Creen's cargo ship.

Down here, the ship's hold was like the insides of a whale ribbed in wood. The ceiling was low. There were no windows. Light came from the two lamps that the shipmen had hung when they had dragged Marcus in here, perhaps an hour ago. It was still dark outside, though Marcus would have no way to know that.

Marcus blinked wet eyelashes. His dark hair fell into his eyes in dripping strands. He wore the tattered remains of the livery of his order, its silver star stained with grime and blood.

James watched the horror rising in Marcus's eyes as he realized he was still alive.

He knew. Marcus knew what was going to happen to him.

"So Simon Creen was right about the Stewards," said James.

"Kill me." Marcus's throat scraped with gravel, as though seeing James meant a full understanding of what was happening. "Kill me. James. Please. If you ever felt anything for me."

James dismissed the shipman beside him, and he waited until the man was gone, until there were no sounds but the creak of water and wood, and he and Marcus were alone.

Marcus's hands were chained behind his back. He was sprawled awkwardly because of it, unable to right his balance, thick chains binding him with no give to the four heavy iron brackets of the ship. James's eyes passed over the massive, immovable iron links.

"All those vows. You've never really lived at all. Don't you wish you'd been with a woman? Or a man."

"Like you?"

"Those rumors," said James evenly, "aren't true."

"If you ever felt anything for any of us—"

"You strayed too far from the flock, Marcus."

"*I beg you,*" said Marcus.

He said the words like there was a system of honor in the world, like all you had to do was appeal to a person's better nature and goodness would prevail.

The self-righteousness of it stuck in James's throat.

"Beg me, then. Beg me on your knees to kill you. Do it."

James hadn't thought Marcus would do it, but of course he did—he probably loved it, on his knees in an act of martyring self-sacrifice. Marcus was a Steward, had spent his life keeping vows and following rules, believing in words like *noble* and *true* and *good*.

Marcus moved awkwardly, unable to balance without his hands, finding a new posture within the chains with humiliating difficulty, his head lowering, his knees spreading on the planking.

"Please. James. Please. For what's left of the Stewards."

James looked down at that bowed head, that battered, handsome visage that was still naive enough to hope that there was a way out for him.

"I'm going to stand at Simon's side," said James, "while he ends the line of Stewards. I'm not going to stop until there's no one left to stand in your Hall, until the last of your light flickers and goes out. And when darkness comes, I'll be standing next to the one who will rule it all." James's voice was precise. "You think I felt something for you? You've forgotten who I am."

Marcus looked up then, eyes flashing. It was the only warning James had. Marcus pulled, calling on all his strength so that his muscles strained and bulged, flesh pitted against iron—

—for a single terrifying moment the iron groaned, shifting—

Marcus made an agonized sound as his body gave out. A laugh of relief bubbled up in James's throat.

Stewards were strong. But not strong enough.

Marcus was panting. His eyes were furious. Underneath that, he was terrified.

"You're not Simon's right hand," said Marcus. "You're his worm. His bootlicker. How many of us have you killed? How many Stewards will die because of you?"

"Everyone but you," said James.

Marcus's face turned ashen, and for a moment James thought he was going to beg again. He would have enjoyed that. But Marcus just stared back at him in thick silence. It was enough, for now. Marcus would beg again before this was over. James didn't need to provoke it. He only needed to wait.

Marcus would beg and no one would come to help him here on Simon's ship.

Satisfied, James turned to walk out up the wooden stairs that would lead him to the deck. He had his foot on the first step when Marcus's voice rang out behind him.

"The boy's alive."

James felt hotly resentful that it made him stop. He forced himself not to turn, not to look at Marcus, not to take up the bait. He spoke in a calm voice as he continued on his way up the steps to the ship's deck.

"That's the trouble with you Stewards. You always think there's hope."

CHAPTER ONE

Three weeks later

WILL'S FIRST GLIMPSE of London came before the sun rose, the forest of masts on the river jet-black silhouettes against a sky barely one shade lighter, joined by hoisting cranes, scaffolding, and every upright funnel and flue.

The docks were waking up. On the left bank, the first warehouse doors were unlatched and thrown open. Men were gathered shouting their names in the hope of being taken on for jobs; others were already in the shallow boats, winding rope. A satin-waistcoated mate called out a greeting to a foreman. Three children in rolled-up trousers had begun groping in the mud for a copper nail or a small piece of coal, a rope end, a bone. A woman in heavy skirts sat beside a cask calling out a day's wares.

On a river barge making its slow way along the black water, Will pushed out from behind roped-down barrels of rum, ready to jump down onto the bank. He was tasked with checking the ropes that tethered the barrels to stop any slippage, then looping crane tethers or just straining under the weight himself to unload cargo. He didn't have the ox build of many of the dock laborers, but he was hardworking. He could throw himself against ropes and haul, or help heft sacks into a cart or a boat.

"Pier's ahead, bring her in!" called Abney the bargeman.

Will nodded and took up a rope. Unloading the barge would be a morning's work, before they'd break for a half hour, the men sharing pipes and liquor. His muscles already ached with strain, but soon he'd find the rhythm that would carry him through. At the end of the day, he would be given a hard crust of bread with pea soup steaming hot from the pot. He was already looking forward to it, imagining the warming taste of the soup, feeling lucky to have fingerless gloves that kept his hands warm in the chill.

"Get those ropes ready!" Abney had his hand on one of the ropes himself, right near one of Will's knots, his cheeks ruddy with alcohol. "Crenshaw wants the barge clear before midday."

The barge sprang into action. Stopping a thirty-ton boat with nothing but currents and poles was hard in daylight, harder in the dark. Too fast and the poles would snap; too slow and they'd ram the pier, wood splintering. The lightermen sank their poles into the silt of the riverbed and heaved, straining against the whole heavy weight of the barge.

"Tie her up!" came the call, seeking to secure the barge before the unloading.

The barge slowed to a stop, barely rising and falling on the dark water. The lightermen sheathed their poles and threw out mooring lines to tie the barge to the pier, pulling on the ropes to draw them tight, then knotting the ropes further.

Will was the first to leap down from the barge, and he looped his mooring line around a bollard, helping those aboard draw the barge tight to the pier.

"The foreman'll be drinking with the ship's merchant tonight," said George Murphy, a big-whiskered Irishman, pulling rope alongside Will.

That was the subject that all the men on the docks talked about—work and how to get it. "Might offer more work when this job's done."

"Drink makes him swing, but it also makes him miss," said Will, and Murphy gave a good-natured snort. Will didn't add, *Most of the time.*

"I was thinking I'd try to catch him after, see if I can get hired on," said Murphy.

"Better than standing at the gate hoping to get called up for day work," agreed Will.

"Might even have the chance of a bit of meat on Sunday—"

Crack!

Will's head whipped around just in time to see a rope release from its tether, flying up into the air.

There were thirty tons of cargo on this boat, not only rum but cork, barley, and gunpowder. The rope whipping up through the iron rings released all of it, snapping canvas, barrels rolling, tumbling. Right toward Murphy. *No—!*

Will threw himself at Murphy, knocking him out of the way of the cascade, then feeling a teeth-jarring burst of pain as a barrel hit his own shoulder. Breathing heavily, he pushed himself up and looked at Murphy's shocked face with a rush of wild relief that the man was alive, with only his cap knocked off, revealing a head of flattened hair above his whiskers. For a moment he and Murphy just stared at each other. Then the full scale of the calamity dawned on both of them.

"Haul them up! Get them up out of the water!"

Men were splashing around, desperate to save the cargo. Will did his own splashing as barrels were pushed toward the pebbled shore. He ignored his hurt shoulder. It was harder to ignore the memory of the flying rope and Murphy in the way of the crash. *It could have killed him.* He tried to focus on the wreckage. How badly was the cargo damaged? Cork

floated, and the rum barrels were airtight, but saltpeter dissolved in water. When they crowbarred open the barrels of gunpowder, would they
find it ruined?

To lose a bargeful of gunpowder—what would that mean? Would
Crenshaw's business fold, his wealth floating in the river?

Accidents were common on the docks. Just last week Will had seen
a plodding draft horse shy unexpectedly as it pulled a barge along the
canals, breaking its ropes and overturning its boat. Abney had a story of
a snapped chain that had killed four men and sent a boatload of coal to
the bottom. Murphy had two missing fingers from badly stacked crates.
Everyone knew the daily reality: hazardous skimping, corners cut.

"A bloody rope's slipped!" swore Beckett, an older laborer with a
faded brown waistcoat fastened tight up to the throat. "There." He pointed at the broken tether. "You." He turned to Will, who happened to be
closest. "Get us some more rope, and a crowbar to open up these barrels."
He gestured to the warehouse with his chin. "And be quick about it. Any
lost time comes out of your pay."

"Yes, Master Beckett," said Will, knowing better than to argue.

Behind him Beckett was already ordering others back to their work,
directing the flow of sacks and crates around the dripping barrels on the
bank.

Will hurried toward the warehouse.

One of many large brick buildings that lined the foreshore, Crenshaw's
warehouse was filled with merchandise in barrels and crates, resting for
a night or two before it found its way into drawing rooms, onto dining
tables, and into smoking pipes.

Inside, the air was cold, and sickened with the stench of sulfur in
yellow bins, and hides in stacks, and barrels of cloyingly sweet rum. Will

hid his nose in his arm as a pungent whiff of fresh tobacco in stacks was obliterated by the throat-itching scent of rich spices he'd never tasted. He had spent a half day hauling crates inside a similar warehouse two weeks ago. The cough had stayed with him for days and been a nuisance to hide from the foreman. He was used to the foul smell of the river, but the fumes from the tar and the alcohol made his eyes water.

A laborer with a coarse, bright-colored handkerchief around his throat paused in his work stacking timber. "You lost?"

"Beckett sent me in to find some rope."

"Down back." He gestured with his thumb.

Will scooped up a crowbar that lay alongside a few older barrels and a heaped pile of lines smelling of tar. Then he looked around for a spare coil of rope that he could sling over his shoulder and take back to the barge.

Nothing here, nothing behind the barrels. . . . To his left he saw an object partially covered in a white sheet. Anything there? He reached out and tugged the dusty sheet, which slipped off and pooled on the floor.

A mirror was revealed, leaning against a cargo crate. It was made of metal, and it was old, an antique from an ancient era, before mirrors were made out of glass. Warped and streaked, it scattered his reflection in choppy glints across its metal surface, hazy glimpses of pale skin and dark eyes. *Nothing here either,* he thought, and was about to return to his search when something in the mirror caught his eye.

A flicker.

He looked around sharply, thinking that the mirror must have caught the reflected movement of someone behind him. But no one was there. *Strange.* Had he imagined it? The warehouse at this end was deserted, long corridors between stacked crates. He looked back at the mirror.

Its dull metal surface was tarnished with age and imperfections, so that it was hard to make himself out. But he still saw it, a movement in the mirror's hazy surface that stopped him in his tracks.

The reflection in the mirror was changing.

Will stared at it, barely daring to breathe. The dim shapes in the metal were re-forming before his eyes, into columns and wide-open spaces. . . . It wasn't possible, and yet it was happening. The reflection was changing, as if the room the mirror faced was a long-ago place, and there was no one to tell him not to come forward and look across the years.

There was a lady in the mirror. That was what he saw first, or thought that he saw, then the gold of the candle beside her, and the gold of her gleaming hair, caught in a single plait that fell over her shoulder and all the way down to her waist.

She was writing, illuminated letters on pages with rich colored borders and tiny figures fitted into the ornate capitals. Her room was open to the balconied night, with vaulted ceilings and a series of shallow steps that led out—he somehow knew—into the gardens. He had never seen that view before, but inside him was a memory of green evening scent and the dark movement of trees. He moved closer instinctively to see it better.

She stopped writing, and turned.

She had eyes like his mother. She was looking right at him. He fought the instinct to take a step back.

She was coming toward him, her gown unfurling behind her in a train across the floor. He could see the candle she held on its stalk, the bright medallion she wore around her neck. She was coming so close, it was as though they faced one another. He felt suddenly that all that separated them was the distance of an outstretched hand. He thought he must see his own face reflected in each one of her eyes, small as candle flame, a twinned flicker.

Instead, doubled, silver and new-minted in her eyes, he saw the mirror.

All the hairs rose on his arms, the strangeness of it prickling over him. *The same mirror . . . she's looking into the same mirror . . .*

A voice said, *"Who are you?"*

He jerked back, sudden, a stumble, only to realize—foolishly—that the voice had not come from the mirror; it had come from behind him. One of the warehouse laborers was staring at him suspiciously, a raised lamp in his hand. "Get back to work!"

Will blinked. The warehouse with its dank crates faced him, dull and ordinary. The gardens, the high pillars, and the lady were gone.

It was as if a spell had broken. Had he imagined it? Was it the warehouse fumes? He had the urge to rub his eyes, half wanting to chase the image that he had seen. But the mirror was just a mirror, reflecting the ordinary world around him. The vision in it had vanished: a fantasy, a daydream, or a trick of the light.

Shaking off the dazed sensation, Will forced himself to nod his head and say, "Yes, sir."

CHAPTER TWO

DAWDLING IN THE warehouse earned Will three weeks of docked pay and a demotion to some of the toughest work on the docks. He forced himself through it, though his muscles burned and his stomach cramped without food. The first three days were dredging and lifting, and then Will was put on wheel work, trudging to turn the warehouse's giant wooden cylinder with six much bigger men, his legs burning as the wheel's pulleys lifted giant casks eighteen feet in the air. He returned each night to his anonymous, overcrowded lodging house too exhausted to even think about the mirror or the strange things he'd seen in it, too exhausted to do more than tumble down onto the grimy straw pallet and sleep.

He didn't complain. Crenshaw was still in business. He wanted this job. Even at reduced pay, dock labor was better than the living he'd scraped when he'd first come to London. He'd spent days scrounging for scraps before he'd learned to pick up burnt-out ends of cigars, dry them, then sell them to dockmen as tobacco for pipes. It was those men who had said you could get unskilled jobs on the docks if you were prepared to work hard enough.

Now Will hefted the last sack of barley onto its pile, long after most of the other men had left at the bell. It had been a punishing day's work, double pace with no breaks, to try to make up for lost time when the barge came in late. The sun was setting, and there were fewer people on the foreshore, the last stragglers finishing up their work.

All he had to do was sign off with the foreman and he'd be free for the night. He'd head to the main street, where food sellers gathered to offer a bite to workers for the right price. A late finish meant that he had missed out on his scoop of pea soup, but he had a single coin that would buy him a hot potato in its jacket, and that would be enough to fuel him for tomorrow.

"Foreman's around front." Murphy indicated upriver with his chin.

Will scrambled to get there before the foreman left. He turned the corner, calling a goodbye to Beckett and the last of the workers, who stumbled off toward the public house. Crunching along the foreshore, he saw a chestnut seller in the distance crying his wares to the last of the dock laborers, his bearded face crimson with the fire shining through the holes at the bottom of his stove. Then he reached the empty pier.

That was when Will really looked at where he was.

It had grown dark enough that men had come out to light the grease lamps that coughed and spluttered, but Will had left those behind him. The only sounds were the slap of black water at the end of the pier and the distant calls of a dredging boat moving slowly from the canal to the river, netting whatever it could find. The pier was utterly deserted, with no hint of life.

Except for three men in a disused wherry half-hidden alongside the shadowy planking.

Will couldn't have said the moment he realized it, or what caused it. There was no sign of the foreman. There was no one within earshot to hear a cry for help. The three men were getting out of the boat.

One of them was looking up. Right at him.

They found me.

He knew it at once, knew the purposeful look in their eyes, the way they were spreading out to block his path as they climbed out of the wherry.

Will's heart jammed in his throat.

How? Why are they here? What had given him away? He kept to himself. He kept his head down. He hid the scar on his right hand with fingerless gloves. He had to rub at it sometimes to keep his fingers mobile, but he was very careful not to let anyone see when he did that. He knew from experience that the smallest gesture could betray him.

Maybe it was the gloves themselves, this time. Or maybe he'd just been careless, the anonymous boy on the docks not quite as anonymous as he'd hoped to be.

He took a step back.

There was nowhere to go. A sound behind him: there were two other men coming up to block his way, shadowy figures he didn't recognize. But he knew the coordinated way the men were moving, fanning out to block his escape.

It was sickeningly familiar, part of his new life, like seeing her lying on blood-soaked ground and not knowing why, like months of hiding without the first idea why they had killed her or what they wanted from him. He thought of the last word his mother had said to him.

Run.

He sprinted for the only way out he could see, a stack of crates to the left of the warehouse.

Jumping for the top of the crates, he pulled himself up desperately. A hand snatched at his ankle; he ignored it. He ignored the shaking, the heart-thundering panic. It should be easier now. He wasn't stupid with fresh grief. He wasn't naive, like he had been those first nights, not knowing how to run or hide, not knowing to avoid the roads, or what happened when he allowed himself to trust someone.

Run.

No time to sprawl when he landed in the mud on the other side. No time to get his bearings. No time to look back.

He pushed himself up and started to run.

Why? Why are they after me? His feet slapped on the wet, muddy street. He could hear the men shouting behind him. It had begun to rain, and he ran blindly into the wet dark, over slippery cobbles. Soon his clothing was sodden and running was harder, his breath too loud in his throat.

But he knew the warren of streets and smaller lanes that were in constant construction, a mess of scaffolding, new buildings, and new roads. He made for them, hoping to get far enough ahead to misdirect and hide, and let the men run past him. He ducked and wove between the planks and struts of construction and heard the men slow and fan out, looking for him.

I can't let them know I'm here. Staying very quiet, he slipped in between struts and then into a space behind a high scaffold that laddered up a half-built structure.

A hand grabbed his shoulder; there was hot breath against his ear and a hand on his arm.

No. Heart pounding, Will struggled desperately, and when a wet hand clamped over his mouth, he stopped breathing—

"Stop." The man's voice was hard to hear over the rain, but it made Will's blood run cold. "Stop, I'm not one of them."

Will barely registered the man's words, the sound he made muffled under the man's heavy hand. *They're here. They're here. They've caught me.*

"*Stop,*" said the man. "Will, don't you recognize me?"

Matthew? he almost said, recognizing the voice with a jolt the moment the man said his name. The outline of one of the men from the river resolved into a figure he knew.

He went still, disbelieving his eyes as the man's hand slowly lifted from his mouth. Half-obscured by the rain, the man was Matthew Owens, a servant of his mother's in their old house in London. Their first house, their first life, before they had moved to a series of different out-of-the-way places, his mother never telling him why, but increasingly anxious, wary of strangers, watching the road.

"We need to stay quiet," said Matthew, lowering his voice further. "They're still out there."

"You're with those men," Will heard himself say. "I saw you at the river."

It had been years since he had seen Matthew, and now he was here, had chased him here from the docks, might have been chasing him since Bowhill—

"I'm not one of them," said Matthew. "They only think I am. Your mother sent me."

A renewed burst of fear. *My mother's dead.* He didn't say it, staring at Matthew's gray hair and blue eyes. Seeing a familiar servant from the old household brought a child's desire for safety, like wanting to be soothed by a parent after cutting his hand. He wanted Matthew to tell him what was happening. But the tug of childhood familiarity hit the cold reality of his life on the run. *Just because I know him doesn't mean I can trust him.*

"They're right on your trail, Will. Nowhere in London is safe." Matthew's low voice was urgent in the shadowed space under the scaffolding. "You must go to the Stewards. The bright star holds, even as the darkness rises. But you must hurry, or *they* will find you, and darkness will come for us all."

"I don't understand." *The Stewards? The bright star?* Matthew's words didn't make any sense. "Who are those men? Why are they chasing me?"

Matthew took something from the pocket of his waistcoat as though it was very important, and held it out to Will.

"Take this. It belonged to your mother."

My mother? Danger and desire fought. He wanted to take it. The yearning was like a pain even as he remembered those awful final moments as she had looked up at him, her blue dress covered in blood. *Run.*

"Show it to the Stewards, and they will know what to do. They are the only ones left who do. They will give you the answers, I promise. But there isn't much time. I must return before *they* notice I'm gone."

There was that unfamiliar word again. *Stewards.* Matthew placed what he held onto one of the planks of scaffolding that separated them. He was backing away, as if he knew Will wouldn't take what he'd left while he was still there. Will gripped the scaffolding behind him tightly, wanting nothing more than to step forward toward the man whose gray hair and tattered black satin waistcoat were so familiar.

Matthew turned to go, but stopped at the last moment, looking back.

"I'll do what I can to throw them off your trail. I promised your mother I'd help you from inside, and that's what I intend to do."

Then he was gone, hurrying back toward the river.

Will was left with his heart racing as Matthew's footsteps faded. The sounds of the other men were fading with him, as though their search was moving on. Will could see the outline, the shape of what Matthew had left him. He felt like a wild animal looking at bait in a trap.

Wait! he wanted to call out after him. *Who are* they? *What do you know about my mother?*

He stared out into the rain after Matthew, and then all his attention returned to the small package on the scaffolding. Matthew had said to hurry, but all Will could think about was the object that lay in front of him.

Had his mother really left it for him?

He came forward. It felt like he was being pulled by a string.

The package was a small, round shape, wrapped in the leather tie that Matthew had taken from the pocket of his waistcoat. *Show it to the Stewards,* Matthew had said, but Will didn't know what *Stewards* were or where to find them.

Will reached out. He half expected those men from the docks to descend on him at any moment. He half expected this to be a trick or a trap. He picked up the package, his fingers numb with cold. Unwinding the tie, he saw a rusted piece of metal. He could barely feel its jagged edges, he was so cold. But he could feel its weight, unexpectedly heavy, as though it was made of gold or lead. Will angled it for better light.

And felt the shiver go through his whole body.

Roughly circular, twisted, it was an old, broken medallion. He recognized it. He had seen it before.

In the mirror.

A wave of dizziness passed over him as he stared down at the impossible in his hands.

The lady had worn this same medallion around her neck. He remembered the shine of it as she walked toward him, her eyes fixed on him as though she knew him. It had been shaped like a five-petaled hawthorn flower, and bright as new gold.

But its surface now was dull, cracked and uneven, as though years had passed—as though it had been buried and dug up, weathered and broken.

But the lady in the mirror was just a dream, she was just a trick of the light—

Turning it over, he saw that the medallion had writing engraved on it. It wasn't written in any language he knew, but somehow he could understand the words. It felt like they were part of him, like they came from deep inside, a language that had always been there, in his bones, on the tip of his tongue.

I cannot return when I am called to fight
So I will have a child

He didn't know why, but he started to shake. The words in that strange language blazed in his mind. He shouldn't be able to read it, but he could—he could *feel* it. He saw again the image of the lady's eyes in the mirror, as if she was looking right at him. *My mother's eyes.* Everything around him disappeared, until he could only see the lady, an aching sensation between them as they faced each other. *I cannot return when I am called to fight.* She seemed to say it directly to him. *So I will have a child.* He was shaking harder. "*Stop,*" he gasped, wrapping his hands around the medallion, willing the vision to vanish with all his might. "*Stop!*"

It stopped.

Will was left breathing shallowly. He was alone, the rain dripping from his hair, soaking through his cap and his clothes.

Just like the mirror, the medallion was ordinary again. An old, dull thing, with no hint of what he had just seen. Will looked up to the place where Matthew had disappeared into the rain.

What was it? What had Matthew given him? His fingers gripped the medallion so tightly the jagged edges cut into him.

The streets by now were empty. No one had heard his gasp at the medallion's vision. The men searching for him had moved on. It was his chance to get away, to run.

But he needed answers—about the medallion, and the lady, and the men who were chasing him. He needed to know why all of this was happening. He needed to know why those men had killed his mother.

Putting the medallion on its cord around his neck, he started running back through the rain, feet splashing in the mud. He had to find Matthew. He had to know what Matthew hadn't told him.

The streets whipped past him. The eyes of the lady in the mirror burned in his memory.

When he finally came to a stop, panting, he saw that he had come almost all the way back to the warehouse.

Matthew was sitting on a street bench, a few blocks from the river. The street was better lit than the ones he had come from, and Will could see that Matthew was wearing buckled shoes and pleated pantaloons with his white shirt and black waistcoat.

Will had so many questions that he didn't know where to start. He closed his eyes and drew a breath.

"Please. You brought me that medallion. I need to know what it means. The Stewards—what are they? How do I find them? And those men—I don't understand why those men are chasing me, why they killed my mother—I don't understand what I'm meant to do."

Silence. Will had spoken in a rush. Now, as the silence stretched out, he felt his need for answers transforming into a darker throb of fear.

"Matthew?" he said in a small voice. Though he knew. He knew.

It was raining hard, and Matthew was sitting out in it, oddly exposed. He wasn't wearing a jacket. His arms were slack in his drenched shirtsleeves. His clothes were sopping on his body. Water dripped from his unmoving fingers. The rain was pelting him, running in streaming rivulets down his face, into his open mouth, over his dead open eyes.

They're here.

Will threw himself—not along the road, but sideways toward one of the doors, a last desperate hope that he might alert the owner or find his way inside. He took the first blow at the outer gate. Before he could reach the door, a hand grabbed his shoulder; another closed around his neck.

No—

He saw the hair on one man's arm and felt the hot breath of another against his face. It was the closest he had been to any of them since that night. He didn't know their faces, but with clotting horror he saw one thing he did recognize.

On the underside of the wrist reaching for him, an *S* was branded into the man's flesh.

He had seen that *S* before, at Bowhill. Burned into the wrists of the men who had killed his mother. He saw it when he couldn't sleep, snaking into his dreams. It felt old and dark, like an ancient evil. Now it seemed to squirm over the man's skin in raised, moving flesh, crawling toward him—

Everything he'd learned in nine months on the run vanished. It was as if he were back at Bowhill, stumbling away from the house and the men who were chasing him. The rain had made it hard to see that night, and easy to trip and fall, scrabbling down banks and splashing through ditches. He hadn't known how long he'd pushed on until he collapsed, shivering and wet. He had wanted—it was stupid—his mother. But she was dead, and he was unable to go back to her because he'd made a promise.

Run.

For a moment, it was as if the S was reaching for him from out of a deep pit.

Run.

Thrown down hard onto his back on the soaking cobblestones, Will tried to push himself up, putting his weight on an elbow, and was shocked into gasping at the pain of his shoulder as his arm collapsed under him. They overmastered him immediately, though he used all his strength. He'd never had to fight before that night in Bowhill, and he wasn't terribly good at it. Holding him down, one of the men hit him methodically until he lay, reeling, on his back in his sodden clothes, breathing as best he could.

"You've had an easy life, haven't you." The man raised his foot to nudge at Will briefly with his toe. "A mama's boy, clinging to your mama's skirts. That's all done now."

When he tried to move, they kicked him, again and again, until his vision turned black and he stopped moving altogether.

"Tie him up. We finish up here, then take him to Simon's ship."

CHAPTER THREE

"OUT OF THE way, rat."

A thoughtless hand shoved Violet backward, shutting her out of the spectacle on the deck. Pushed and jostled, she craned her neck for a glimpse. She couldn't see much past the shoulders of the sailors, the press of their bodies thick with the smell of anticipation, brine, and sweat, so she scrambled up onto the ratlines, wedging her arm into the knotted rope to hold herself in place. Her first glimpse of Tom was over a crowd of caps and kerchiefs, the sailors encircling him on the deck.

It was Thursday, and Simon's ship, the *Sealgair*, was moored on the crowded river. Heavy with cargo, its main mast flew the three black hounds, Simon's coat of arms. Violet wasn't supposed to have snuck aboard, but she knew the ship from the work her family did for Simon, a great source of pride for them. The oldest son of the Earl of Sinclair, the man her family called Simon had his own title: Lord Crenshaw. He oversaw a lucrative trade empire on behalf of his father. They said his reach was farther than King George's, stretching out across the globe. Violet had glimpsed Simon himself once, a powerful figure in a rich black coat.

Today there were men with pistols guarding the railings, others barricading the pier. But everyone else was on the quarterdeck, the work of loading and securing cargo halted. From her perch high on the ropes, Violet could see the tense jostling among those crowded in a rough circle. These hard men were all gathered to witness one thing.

Tom was going to be honored with the brand.

He was stripped to the waist, his head exposed, his dark auburn hair falling about his face. He knelt on the planking of the ship. His bare chest rose and fell visibly: he was breathing quickly, in anticipation of what was about to happen.

The air of those watching was expectant—partly jealous too, knowing Tom had earned what was about to be given to him. One or two of them were drinking whiskey, as though they were the ones who would need it. She understood how they felt. It was like the ceremony was happening to all of them. And in a way it was, like a promise: *Do well for Simon, please Simon, and this is what you will get.*

A shipman came forward, wearing a brown leather over-apron, like a blacksmith.

"You don't need to hold me down," said Tom. He had turned back anything he was offered to help him deal with pain—alcohol, blindfold, leather to bite down on. He simply knelt and waited. The cord of expectation pulled tighter.

At nineteen, Tom was the youngest to ever take the brand. Watching, Violet swore to herself, *I'll be even younger.* Like Tom, she would do well in the world of trade, bringing back Simon her own trophies, and then she too would be promoted. *As soon as I get a chance, I'm going to prove myself.*

"Simon rewards your service with this gift," said Captain Maxwell. He nodded to the shipman, who moved to stand near a brazier of heated coals that had been brought out onto the deck. "When it's done, you'll be his," he said. "Honored by his brand."

The shipman pulled the branding iron out of the hot coals.

Violet tensed as though it was happening to her. The iron was long, like a fire iron, but with an S at the tip, so hot from the coals that it glowed red, like a moving flame. The shipman came forward.

"I swear this oath to Simon," said Tom, ritualistic words. "I am his loyal servant. I will obey and serve. Brand me." Tom's blue eyes looked right at the shipman. "Seal my pledge into my flesh."

Violet held her breath. This was it. Those with the brand became part of the inner circle. Simon's favorites: they were his most loyal follow-ers, and it was whispered they got special rewards—and more than that, Simon's attention, which was its own reward for many of them. Horst Maxwell, the captain of the *Sealgair*, bore the brand, which gave him au-thority even above his station.

Tom held out his arm so that the clean skin of his wrist was visible.

The only other time Violet had seen a man take the brand, he'd screamed and spasmed like a fish on the floor of a boat. Tom had seen that too, but it didn't seem to faze him. He met the shipman's eyes determined-ly, holding himself in place with his courage and his will.

Captain Maxwell said, "That's it, boy. Take it well."

Tom won't scream, Violet thought. *He's strong.*

The men were so quiet now that you could hear the lap of the water against the hull. The shipman lifted the brand. Violet saw a sailor turn his head, not wanting to look—less brave than Tom. That was what Tom was proving. *Take it, and show you're worthy.* Violet gripped the ropes tightly, but she didn't look away as the shipman brought the cauterizing brand to the skin of Tom's wrist.

The sudden burning smell was terrible, like seared meat. Hot metal pressed into flesh for longer than seemed necessary. Tom's every muscle bunched with the desire to curl around the pain, but he didn't. He stayed on his knees, breathing heavily in and out, his flesh trembling like an exhausted horse, covered in sweat at the end of its run.

A roar went up, and the shipman held Tom's arm aloft, hauling him to his feet and brandishing his wrist for everyone to see. Tom looked dazed, stumbling up. Violet saw a brief flash of the skin of his wrist, branded with the shape of an S, before the shipman quickly doused it with alcohol and wrapped it in a bandage.

That's how I'll be, thought Violet. *Brave, like Tom.*

He disappeared from her view, the crowd swallowing him in a wave of congratulations. She was craning her neck again, straining for any glimpse. Cut off, she went slithering down the ropes, trying to reach Tom through the press of men, even as she was shoved impersonally here and there, pushed back. She couldn't see him at all, though the sickly rich smell of cooked meat lingered. A painful grip on her arm wrenched her sideways.

"I told you to stay back, rat."

The man who gripped her arm had lank hair under a dirty kerchief, his beard a rash across his cheeks. He had the rough skin of a sailor, red capillaries like netting on his face. The manacle of his fingers hurt. She smelled stale gin on his breath and felt a wave of revulsion. She pushed it down and dug her heels in. "Let go. I've a right to be here!"

"You're an ugly brown rat who's stolen his better's clothes."

"I haven't stolen anything!" she said, though she was wearing Tom's waistcoat and trousers, and his shirt too, and the shoes that he'd outgrown. And then, humiliatingly, she heard Tom's voice. "What's going on?"

Tom had shrugged into a shirt, though the two buttons of the high collar were still undone and the front ruffle hung open. Violet had a clear view of him as space opened between them. Every eye was on them.

The sailor held her by the neck. "This boy's causing trouble—"

The sheen of sweat from the branding still on him, Tom said, "That's not a boy. That's my sister, Violet."

She saw the sailor react to that the same way that everyone reacted to it: with disbelief at first, and then with a new way of looking at Tom, as if they had learned something about Tom's father.

"But she's—"

"Are you questioning me, sailor?" Freshly branded, Tom had more authority than anyone on the ship. He was Simon's now, and his word was Simon's word. The sailor closed his mouth with a snap, releasing her instantly to stumble onto the planking. She and Tom faced each other. Her cheeks felt hot.

"I can explain—"

In London, no one guessed that Tom was Violet's half brother. They didn't look alike. Tom was three years older and didn't share her Indian heritage. He looked just like their father: tall, broad shouldered, and blue eyed, with pale skin and auburn hair. Violet was slight and took after her mother, with brown skin, dark eyes, and dark hair. The only thing they shared was their freckles.

"Violet. What are you doing here? You're supposed to be at home."

"You took the brand," she said. "Father will be proud."

Tom instinctively gripped his own arm, above the bandage, as though he wanted to grasp the wound but knew that he couldn't. "How do you know about that?"

"Everyone on the docks knows about it," said Violet. "They say Simon brands his best men, and they rise in the ranks, and he gives them all special rewards, and—"

He ignored her, talking in a low, urgent voice, glancing at the men nearby with tense concern. "I told you not to come here. You need to leave the ship."

She looked around them. "Are you joining his expedition? Will he put you in charge of a dig?"

"That's enough," said Tom as his face shuttered. "Mother's right. You're too old for this. Following me around. Wearing my clothes. Go home."

Mother's right. It hurt. Englishmen abroad didn't usually bring their bastard daughters with them back to England. Violet knew that from the fights between her father and Tom's mother. But Tom had always stood up for her. He'd tug one of her curls and say, "Violet, let's go for a walk," and take her out to a street vendor to buy her hot tea and a currant roll, while inside his mother shouted at their father, *Why do you have that girl living in this house? To humiliate me? To make me a laughingstock?*

"But you gave me these clothes," she heard herself say, and the words seemed small.

Tom started to say, "Violet—"

Later, she would think that there had been warning signs—the men on the pier—the tense looks of the sailors—the patrols with pistols—even the tightness in Tom's mouth.

Now the only warning was Tom jerking his head up.

A sudden jolt shuddered the ship, sending her stumbling sideways. Violet heard a shot ring out and turned to see the sailor who had fired it, white-faced, his pistol shaking.

Then she saw what he was shooting at.

Swarming over the side of the ship, up grappling ropes and planks, came men and women dressed in a white starburst livery. Their faces were noble, like something out of an old storybook. Their features were varied, as though they came from many different lands. They seemed to rise up out of the mist, and they didn't have modern weapons—they were armed like knights, with swords.

Violet had never seen anything like them before, like a myth brought to life.

"*Stewards!*" screamed a voice, jolting her out of her reverie, and chaos broke loose, the unfamiliar word spreading like wildfire. *Stewards?* Violet thought, the old-fashioned moniker ringing in her ears. Tom and Captain Maxwell reacted as if they knew what it meant, but most of Simon's men were just running for weapons or drawing pistols and immediately starting to shoot at the attackers, the deck filling with thick smoke and the choking smell of sulfur and saltpeter from the guns.

Violet was knocked back and saw everything in a jumble. Three of the attackers—*Stewards*—swung up around the bowsprit. One of them closer to Violet leaped the rail with freakish ease. Another pushed one of the half-ton crates out of her way with one hand, which was impossible. *They're strong,* Violet thought with shock. These Stewards in their white starbursts had a strength and speed that wasn't—that *couldn't* be— natural, as they evaded the first round of pistol shots and started to fight, Simon's men letting out screams and cries in the smoke as the Stewards began to cut them down—

She felt Tom's hand close on her shoulder.

"Violet." Her brother's voice, strong. "I'll cut them off here. I need you in the hold to protect Simon's cargo."

"Tom, what's happening? Who are these—"

"The hold, Violet. Now."

Swords. No one used swords anymore, Violet thought, watching in shock as a male Steward with high cheekbones calmly hewed down the ship's bosun, while a female Steward with blond hair ran her blade through the chest of one of the sailors with guns.

"*Find Marcus*," the blond Steward ordered, the others fanning out, obeying her authority.

Tom was stepping out to face them.

Violet needed to go. The deck was a jumble of sight and sound, the fighting pushing closer. She was rooted to the spot.

"Simon's Lion," said the blond Steward, while another beside her said, "He's just a cub."

Lion? thought Violet, the strange word echoing in her, even as she realized they were talking about her brother.

Tom had picked up the branding iron and was holding it like a crow-bar. Amid the gunfire and the swords it looked foolish, but Tom stood out in front of the others, facing down the line of Stewards, as though he was willing to take them on alone.

Tom said, "If you know we took Marcus, you know you're not invincible."

The blond Steward laughed. "You think one Lion can stop a dozen Stewards?"

"One Lion killed a hundred like you," said Tom.

"You're not like the Lions of old. You're weak."

The Steward's sword flashed a silver arc. It was fast—so fast. Violet saw only an instant of shock on the blond Steward's face before Tom smashed the sword out of her hand, then drove the crude iron bar through her chest. Then he was pulling out the bar and rising to face the others.

Tom wasn't weak. Tom was strong. Tom had always been strong.

Violet stared at him. There was blood on Tom's face, blood on the iron, blood spattered over the white of his shirt, turning it red. With his auburn curls a halo around his head, he did look like a lion.

He threw her a single look.

"*Go*, Violet. I'll follow you down when I can."

She nodded blindly. She went, scrabbling backward, then ducking and running across the planking, as the ship shuddered again as though it had been hit. Above her, the rigging swayed and shook. A barrel rolled uncontrollably across the decking. More gunfire; Violet raised her arm to her mouth so that she didn't choke on smoke. Her heel skidded on blood. She glimpsed Captain Maxwell loading a pistol, then careened sideways to avoid three of Simon's men struggling with a Steward, before she made it through the haze into the hold.

Relief, as the hatch closed—there was no one here. The sounds from above deck were muffled, shouts and cries and the muted crack of gunshots.

She tried not to let it feel like the doors to her father's study closing, shutting her out after Tom was led inside.

Stewards, Tom had called them. They had called him *Lion*. That word was beating at her like blood. She remembered a younger Tom bending a copper farthing in half with his fingers, telling her, *Violet, I'm strong, but you can't tell anyone*. His strength was a secret they kept between themselves, but now it made her ordinary brother seem like he was like the Stewards, strange and otherworldly.

Lion.

She kept replaying the moment that Tom had killed the blond Steward, red blood on the iron bar.

She had not believed Tom capable of killing anyone.

Her hands were shaking. It was stupid. Locked up tight in the hold, she was the safest person on the ship. She squeezed her hands into fists to stop it. That worked, a little.

She needed a weapon. She looked around herself.

The *Sealgair*'s hold was a cavernous space, with thick beams near the stairs, and crates, barrels, and containers extending to the back of the ship. A long line of lamps hanging from hooks overhead disappeared into a darker area, like the black interior of a cave. There, she could see only distant shapes, half-draped canvas and huge wooden bins.

This was Simon's cargo, part of a steady stream of goods that he brought back from his trading outposts. They said Simon was a collector, and that his trade funded the unusual objects that he brought back from around the globe. Tom had been rewarded with the brand for procuring one of them, something rare and hard to find. Violet could only guess what strange items lay inside these crates. An uneasy chill passed over her, as if she shouldn't have come down here. As if there was something here that shouldn't be disturbed.

She stepped off the last of the stairs. In this murky lamplight, it was hard to remember that it was sunny outside. Crates loomed on either side of her, anonymous shapes that flickered in the lamplight, appearing to shrink and grow. Despite the snatches of light, it was cold—cold as the river. The *Sealgair* was low in the water, weighed down by the cargo. Outside, rather than towering above the river, prow tall as a building, it lay near level with the pier, accessible by ladders. Down here, she was submerged.

Moving deeper into the hold, she found herself sloshing through water. *Water?*

It was ankle deep, and cold, with the dank, repugnant smell of the river.

"Who's there?" said a tense voice.

A splash as she turned, her heart racing at words in a place she had thought was empty.

A boy of about seventeen, in a torn shirt and ripped breeches, was chained up in the darkness of the hold.

CHAPTER FOUR

THE BOY WAS clearly a prisoner, chained to the heavy beam behind him, irons so thick they looked more like anchor chains than restraints. Under the tangled dark hair, his pale skin was bruised and mottled, old bruising and fresh, in a pattern of purples and yellows. He'd been beaten, more than once. The shoulder of his torn jacket was dark with blood, his shirt marked and stained, hanging open to show that the bruising covered his body.

She stared with cold, creeping horror. Why was there a boy her own age chained in the hold of this ship? In her mind's eye, she saw again Tom pulling the iron bar out of that woman's chest, red with blood.

"What's happening?"

The boy had trouble standing upright as he spoke, his weight on the wooden beam. He was breathing shallowly, as if even that was difficult, and trying to hide the effort, like a wounded creature trying not to show that it was in pain.

"The ship's under attack."

"By who?"

She didn't answer that. She told herself that if Simon had a boy down here, he must have reason for it. He must be a prisoner or—or a petty thief, an urchin criminal, the paid flunky of one of Simon's merchant rivals.

She told herself that the boy had brought this on himself. He must be dangerous.

The boy wore the tattered clothing of a dock laborer, but with high cheekbones and a certain intensity in his dark eyes, he didn't quite look like one. His eyes were fringed by long dark lashes that might have been pretty in a less battered face.

"You don't have Simon's brand," said the boy.

Violet flushed. "I could have." Fighting down the impulse to grip her own wrist where the brand would be. "If I wanted." She flushed harder, feeling like she had been tricked. She realized that as she was observing him, he had been observing her.

"My name's Will," he said. "If you helped me, I'd—"

"I don't have the key," she said. "And I wouldn't help you even if I did. This is Simon's ship. He wouldn't have you here unless you crossed him."

"He's going to kill me," said Will.

Everything seemed to stop. She could hear the sounds of fighting as she looked at the boy's bruises, the dried blood on his face and shirt. "Simon doesn't kill people." But as she said it, she felt a pit opening up underneath the words, no longer quite certain of anything.

"You could find the key," said Will. "I could slip out during the fight. No one would ever know you were the one who—"

"Check every inch of the hold." A man's voice. They both jerked their heads toward it.

A woman answered him, "If Marcus is here, we'll find him, Justice."

Will realized at the same moment she did.

"Hey!" called Will. "*Over here!*"

"No—!" She spun around to shut him up—too late. The two came striding around the corner.

Stewards.

It was her first time seeing them up close, in full armor and white livery with a silver star. Will's eyes went wide.

The first of them was a tall man who looked like he might be Chinese. He was even more imposing than the others, wearing an expression of purpose and concentration. *Justice.* Beside him was the woman who had spoken. She was a similar age to Justice, perhaps twenty, her voice containing the hint of a French accent. They both wore the same white surcoat over silver armor. They both had the same cut of hair: shockingly long for a man, half pulled back from their faces with a tie, to then fall loose down their backs.

They both had swords. Not the thin whippy cutlasses that brigands still sometimes used to overrun barges on the river, but two-handed broadswords, the kind that could cut a man in half.

Her thoughts raced to her brother. *Tom.* She remembered how easily the Stewards had killed Simon's sailors, cutting through their bodies like butter. If two of them were down here, what was happening above deck?

Violet was grabbing a broom handle and stepping forward to stand in their way before she knew what she was doing.

Her heart was pounding. Facing her, the Steward called Justice was overwhelming, not only handsome but radiating nobility and power. Violet felt small, insignificant. She stayed where she was anyway. *Tom was brave,* she thought. If she could slow them down, even for a moment, she could buy her brother time above deck. Her eyes met Justice's.

"It's not Marcus," said the French Steward, holding Justice back by the arm. "Simon's keeping prisoners down here. A girl and a boy. Look."

"If you let me go, I'll give you anything you want," said Will.

Justice looked past Violet toward Will, and back again. "We'll help you," said Justice. "We'll help both of you. But right now it's not safe on deck. You have to stay down here while we clear this place out—"

"Clear it out?" said Violet. *He thinks I'm a prisoner, like that chained-up boy.* Her hand tightened on the broom handle.

"Justice. There's something else down here." The French Steward had taken a step away from the three of them into the dark of the hold, with a strange expression on her face. "Not the prisoners, something—"

Justice frowned. "What do you mean?"

"I don't know, can't you feel it? It's something dark and old, and it feels—"

Violet could feel it. It was the same sensation that she'd had coming down into the hold, like there was something down here that she didn't want to go near, and she was closer to it now than she had been on the stairs.

She knew that Simon brought artifacts back from the digs he had scattered across the empire. She had even seen some of them, sneaking after Tom on the days he did business on the docks. Pieces of armor in iron caskets. Strange chunks of stone. The broken-off limb of a statue. Simon's operations were a constant stream of digging and taking. What if the item Tom had procured was here, what if it was what was causing her to feel—

"It's the reason for all the guards," said Justice grimly. "It's not Marcus they're protecting, it's something on this ship—"

A pistol shot rang out from the stairs.

Everything after that happened in a jumble. *"Get down!"* Justice shouted, throwing himself between her and the pistol. She was enveloped by his warmth, his body curving over hers protectively. She felt him jolt, with a sound of pain through gritted teeth. When he pushed her back a second later, she could see the red stain blossoming on his shoulder.

He'd been shot. He'd been shot protecting her. Violet stumbled backward into a crate, staring.

A Steward had just saved her life.

The French Steward had drawn her sword. "They're coming."

Justice drew his sword alongside her, ignoring the bullet in his shoulder. "We kill Simon's Lion, then strip the cargo from this ship."

Tom. She didn't have time to react. Another pistol shot burst half the wood from the corner of a cargo crate—the fight was suddenly in the hold. Simon's men were reloading and taking aim at the Stewards, while others struggled on the stairs, a tangle of bodies and the slash of swords. One of the hanging lamps was smashed sideways, a short-lived burning arc that extinguished itself in the water, making visibility harder.

She had to get to her brother. She pushed off the crate and took her first steps, only to look down and find that the water level was now up to her knees. The dark swirl of it was tugging at her legs, swelling in at a disturbing speed.

That isn't right. There shouldn't be water in the hold, and it shouldn't be this deep, knee height and rising.

She looked up at the cargo. She felt that cold sense of dread again, as if there was something dark and terrible down here with her. Her eyes fixed on one crate, chained down the way the others weren't. As soon as she looked at it, the feeling of aversion became almost overpowering. That crate—that was it.

There's something else down here. It's something dark and old, and it feels—

"You're not going anywhere, Steward."

She jerked around to see Tom, standing silhouetted in the entrance to the hold.

Alive. Tom was alive. A rush of relief and pride almost overwhelmed her. His shirt was slashed open, and he was covered in blood, holding the iron bar. But he was her brother, and he was going to win the fight for Simon and her family.

"Where's Marcus?" said Justice.

Tom came down the steps, iron bar at the ready. "I've killed the others."

"You're going to tell me what you've done with Marcus," said Justice. "Or I'll cut down everyone on this ship—then find him anyway."

"You won't get past me," said Tom.

Tom's strong, she thought. *Tom will show him.*

But as the two young men came together, it was immediately clear that if Tom was strong, Justice was stronger.

He came in under Tom's iron bar, and with a single blow sent Tom flying in an arc across the hold, into the heavy beams of the ship. The impact took out the support struts near the stairs, pulverizing the wood, and sent huge beams crashing in a collapse that came smashing down, exploding crates open in the dark depths of the hold.

And that single crate, the one that she had seen and not wanted to go near, was knocked from its stack to crash down onto the planking.

No—

A wave of sick horror rolled over Violet as the crate shattered, a choking, tangible feeling, as if something terrible had been released into the hold. She didn't want to turn her head and look at it. One of Simon's men nearby whitened visibly, as if the wave of sickness from the crate had hit him even more strongly. A moment later, he swayed, his skin mottling. She made herself turn and look.

There's something else here, and it feels—

She saw people staggering, vomiting, collapsing into the water, then she lifted her eyes further—

—like it's trying to get out.

It looked plain except for its black hilt, and its long, carved black sheath. It was a sword that had fallen out of a smashed container, and now lay tumbled on the edge of a crate. The fall had exposed a single sliver of its black blade, the rest of the sword still quiescent in its sheath.

The wave of revulsion she felt at that glimpse of black blade was like nothing she had ever felt before. *Sheathe it!* she wanted to scream, knowing immediately that it was the source of the roiling sickness. In the next moment, she saw arcs of black flame leaping out from the blade, striking the hull and pulverizing it, letting in a new rush of water. As she watched, the flame struck one of Simon's men, and he vomited up black ichor, as though his internal organs had rotted through. *Sheathe it! Cover it!*

But no one could get to it without risking the black fire.

Around her people were screaming and scrabbling to get to the exit, panicking as the black flame flared like unholy lightning, killing anyone it touched. Others were simply trying to get as far away from the sword as they could, whimpering and hiding behind crates that wouldn't save them when the black fire struck. All the Stewards were dead.

Only Tom and Justice were still fighting, locked in battle like two titans. In the black light of the flame, Justice hauled Tom up out of the water, silhouetted for a moment, hitting Tom hard enough that he reeled, then hitting him again, and again.

Tom! The water was up to her waist and rising—Violet was wading to reach them, pushing hard through water as the black flame arced nightmarishly. It was very dark, most of the lamps jostled out and much of the cargo now floating, like nighttime icebergs.

She didn't have a weapon; she just threw herself bodily at Justice, knocking them both backward into the water. There was a ringing crack as the sharp corner of a floating crate hit the base of Justice's skull. His hands instantly went slack, and he floated, facedown and unmoving.

Violet was already splashing toward her brother.

"Tom!" she called out. "Tom!" Tom's face was white, unconscious—but he was breathing, and she could get him out of here. *Alive*, she thought, cradling Tom in her arms. But for how long?

She looked up desperately for a way out.

And saw the boy. *Will.*

He had the sword in his sights and was trying to get to it, rather than cowering back from the flame. He was going to try to sheathe it, she realized as her skin prickled over. The same idea that she had abandoned as impossible. Her first instinct had been to save her brother. Will's had been to save everyone.

He was making gritty, determined progress. Straining against his chains toward the sword looked like straining against a battering force, and he was injured and weak. *He's going to make it*, she thought in stunned disbelief, even as she squirmed at the thought of what it would be like to touch that horrifying weapon. At what might happen to Will. She had seen men collapse and vomit up black blood. What would it do to someone who touched it?

Will's outstretched hand was six inches from the sword when he hit the limit of his chains.

He can't reach it.

He couldn't close the gap, his whole body straining. Unable to get to him, she remembered the moment when he'd begged her to unchain him. She had refused. She had damned them all: Will, Tom, even the captain, she thought. They were all going to die here in this hold.

And then she saw something that shouldn't have been real. The sword hilt began turning toward Will, rotating until it faced him. Then, from one blink to the next, it was in his hand, as if it had jumped the six inches into his grip. *That isn't possible.*

As soon as he had it, he drove it back into its sheath.

Everything stopped; the flame went out. The sickness ended, leaving her gasping. In the new ringing silence, the moans and sobs of the terri-fied survivors were suddenly audible, along with the rushing sound of water and an ominous groaning from the hull.

Violet was staring at the boy in disbelief. *He pulled it to him. He pulled the sword to him with an invisible hand—*

The boy was shaking. Curled over the sword, his eyes opened full of agonizing struggle, as if it was taking everything he had to keep it sheathed. Just for a moment, he looked right at her.

"I can't hold it!" he said to her. The sword was fighting him. "Go!"

"Throw it!" she said. "Throw it into the river!"

"I can't!" said Will, the words forced out through pain. He looked like he was barely holding on. "Get everyone out!"

At the look in his dark eyes, she understood what he was telling her. If she could clear the ship, he would hold the sword here as long as he could. As long as he had to.

She nodded and turned.

"Go!" she said, roughly shoving at one of the stupefied men until he stumbled toward the stairs. The hold was a wrecked space rapidly filling with water. The exit was still half-blocked; three of Simon's men were pulling desperately at the giant wooden beam that jammed it. At least a half dozen others were gasping and coughing, dragging themselves through the water, while several closer to her were clutching on to crates, just staring at the boy, their faces slack and eyes wide.

Others were dead. She had to get everyone out. Had to force her way around the lifeless bodies with Tom, pushing others through the water toward the exit. Some of the bodies were bloated and disfigured, as if the black flame had twisted them. She didn't want to look at them. She saw a

Steward floating facedown, and with a jolt recognized Justice's black hair, floating in a dark corona around his head.

"Go, there isn't time!" She grabbed another man by the shirt and hauled him forward. She couldn't bear to be in here another moment, couldn't stand to be near the repellant sword. Following behind the last of the staggering, drenched men, she took up Tom's body and heaved its awkward wet weight up the stairs, until she finally emerged out of the hold onto the deck.

The first touch of fresh air on her face was miraculous. It was like the sun breaking out from behind clouds, after the stifling, fetid wetness of the hold. Above her, the wide-open sky. For a moment she just drank it in.

And then she saw the deck. The black flame had penetrated here too, parts of the deck scoured as though burned with lashes of fire, its plank-ing shattered and uneven. There were screams from the riverbank, shouts, people pointing. A terrible groaning of wood behind her, and she spun to see the mast was falling—a second later it smashed onto the deck, sending rope and bits of planking flying, the whole ship starting to tilt.

She ran. Below her feet, the deck was sloping. The *Sealgair* was going down. Cries of "Take the rope!" and "Jump!" from the foreshore didn't help her, not with Tom to drag across the deck. And then—

"*Tom!*" Captain Maxwell's voice was calling her from the railing, and she felt a rush of thankfulness. She stumbled gratefully toward him as his hands took the weight of Tom's body from her, pulling him down a makeshift gangway toward the pier, with her following, until finally she stepped onto dry land.

Relief, so great she wanted to dig her fingers into the dirt and pebbles of the foreshore, as if to prove to herself that it was real. That she had done it. That she was here.

She sank to her knees, next to where Maxwell had laid her brother.

"*It's all right, we've got him.*" She heard that as if from a distance. "*Tom, come on, Tom,*" Maxwell was saying, and Tom chose that moment to cough and start to come around. "Violet?" he said in a roughened voice. "Violet?" and Maxwell answered, "*She's right here, Tom.*" As if from far away, Violet could hear Maxwell saying to her, "You did well, getting him off the ship. Simon will be pleased when he hears all you've done."

Simon will be pleased. And that was what she had wanted. To impress Simon, to be like Tom.

But she just sat there, wet, exhausted, and dripping, on the foreshore next to them.

It should have been finished, but she knew it wasn't.

The bank was thronged with men and women shouting, crying, crowding around those plucked from the water and staring across at the *Sealgair.* She heard voices exclaiming *I saw it, black flame,* the murmurs across the crowd in all the languages of the docks, *miracolo, merveille.*

"*There was a boy who took up the sword . . . ,*" a voice beside her was saying, and with a shock, she recognized the man who had called her a rat as he'd dragged her by the scruff of the neck. He'd been saved, just like all the others. She thought of the boy in the hold, his bruised face. She wondered which of these men had beaten him, who he had also saved. He had saved everyone on the ship. But not himself.

She stood up.

The *Sealgair's* bulk was listing in the water, untethered. Gangplanks had fallen away, and there was a gap of more than ten feet of water between the hull and the pier. The gap was widening.

She knew what she had to do.

For so long all she had wanted was to prove herself—to Tom, to her father, to Simon. But there were some things more important than that.

Violet took the ship in her sights, ran, and jumped.

It was like jumping back into hell, after having made it out the first time. The *Sealgair* was a deserted wasteland. It groaned dangerously, the mast broken, the deck cracked, planking splintered and protruding. Cargo barrels were smashed and scattered. Half of a ripped sail was hanging across the deck.

She swallowed down horror as she descended the stairs into the hold. Images of black fire played behind her eyelids—she expected it to burst out at her at any moment. But inside, the hold was dark, and almost fully flooded, water pouring in to swirl ice-cold at her chest. She pushed through it, half swimming, past the overturned crates, past the wreckage and signs of the fight.

The boy was still chained, and alone now, in the watery hold. He was breathing carefully, staying quiet in the dark with his head up, as if, even alone, he was trying not to show he was afraid.

He was still holding the sword, but she saw that he had found some way to lock it into its sheath, the same mechanism that must have restrained it before the crate burst open.

"You can let go of it," she said. His knuckles were white where they gripped the sword. "Let it go. Let it go down with the ship."

After a moment he nodded and threw it, and she watched the gleaming, wavy length of it sink into the water.

Around her, the hold was dripping, the water at chest height and rising. It was not long now before the rushing water filled every last space of air and dragged the *Sealgair* under. When she looked at the boy, she could see in his eyes that he knew he had no way out, chained to a drowning ship. He looked back at her with his dark eyes. "You shouldn't have come back here."

She said, "You said to get everyone out."

She had pushed through the heavy water until she stood facing him. She could feel his desperate hopelessness, despite the wry half smile that he managed through his shallow breathing.

"You don't have a key," he said.

"I don't need a key," said Violet.

And she reached into the water and took hold of the chains.

Lion, the Stewards had said. And no one ever realized they were siblings, but Tom was not the only one with strength in his veins. She heaved.

The wood splintered, the iron screamed and came free, and for a moment the boy just stared at her, and they were looking at each other with a kind of wonder, and a recognition as though across a chasm. In the next moment, as she took his weight on her shoulder, the boy—Will, she recalled—collapsed against her, sliding into unconsciousness in her arms.

He was lighter than Tom, and easier to carry, so thin that he seemed underfed, a fragile casing to hold enough strength to try to save a ship. His face was hollowed, cheekbones too sharp, new bruises blossoming under the pale skin. A flash of fierce protectiveness made her determined that she would get him out to safety, no matter how difficult it might be to fight their way to shore.

"Here!" called a voice from the stairs. There was another shuddering jolt from the ship, which was listing sideways, so that the whole hold was on a diagonal. "This way!"

She made her way toward the voice, pulling gratefully through the water.

Then her stomach swooped and sank as she saw who had called out to her.

His collar was torn and bloodstained, and he was soaking wet, even the tendrils of his hair dripping, so that the bright insignia of his Steward's star was barely visible. But he was alive and breathing. He had stayed here—or no, she realized, as she looked at his face. He had returned here to fulfill a promise. Just as she had.

"Take my hand," said Justice.

CHAPTER FIVE

"MISS KENT." THE man spoke to Katherine directly, though her guardian aunt and uncle were not yet in earshot, still stepping out of the carriage with her younger sister. "I'm afraid that Lord Crenshaw has been delayed. There has been an incident on the docks."

"An incident?" said Katherine. "What happened?"

She stood in her best new dress of white sprig muslin as the luggage was being brought down from the carriage. Her aunt's maid Annabel had spent hours testing different hairstyles on Katherine, before deciding on one that arranged gold ringlets on either side of her face, with a delicate pink ribbon to bring out the fresh blush of her cheeks and the wide blue of her eyes.

"One of my lord's ships went down in the Thames."

"Went down!" said Katherine.

Aunt Helen said the words in a shocked voice. "Is he all right?"

"My lord is unhurt. It was a cargo ship. He wasn't aboard. He sends his regrets that he can't be here to show you the house."

The house. Their new house, provided by her fiancé, Simon Creen—

Lord Crenshaw. The oldest son of the Earl of Sinclair, Simon was the heir to a title and a fortune. His father owned half of London, it was said. Annabel had later whispered, *The expensive half.*

"Not at all. We understand completely," said Aunt Helen. "Please, show us in."

Are you sure? Aunt Helen had said to Katherine, taking both her hands and sitting on the small sofa with her, on the day Lord Crenshaw had proposed to her.

At sixteen, Katherine had not yet been out in society, but her aunt and uncle had arranged some small visits of the most respectable company, in the hope of improving her prospects. Though she was the daughter of a gentleman, Katherine and her sister were both orphans without a fortune, and Katherine had known for a long time that her family's future depended on her ability to make a good match. But that her chances as a young girl in reduced circumstances were slim.

A remarkable beauty, were the words Mrs. Elliott had said, peering at her through her bifocals. *It's a shame she has no fortune or connections.*

Katherine remembered Lord Crenshaw's first visit as a whirlwind of preparations, pinching her cheeks to give them color, her aunt assuring her that it was proper to have no jewelry, and Annabel peeking out from beside the window curtain at the arrival of the carriage.

"It's very grand," Annabel had said. "Shiny black wood, with a driver and two footmen dressed in such fine clothes. There's three black hounds on the carriage door—what a noble family crest—and gilding on the sides." Annabel drew in a breath. "Now he's stepping out. Oh, Miss Kent, he has such a handsome look!"

Now as she was escorted to the large columned doorway of the fine London terrace, Katherine decided she had never been more sure of any- thing. The terrace was in beautiful proportion with its elegant facade and

rows of high, evenly spaced windows. It looked like a house where only
the most refined family would live. Behind her, the carriage man gave a
flick of his whip and a "Hya!" and the carriage was moving away to the
stables behind the house, because it was appropriate that a grand town
house like this should keep an equipage.

She turned to the man, who was Mr. Prescott, one of Lord Crenshaw's solicitors. Mr. Prescott had a distinguished, lined face with gray
hair under his tall hat. She asked him in the doorway, "Did Lord Crenshaw ever live here?"

"Yes, indeed. He stayed here often as a young man. Over summer, of
course, he lives at Ruthern with his father. He takes a house on St. James's
Square when he is in town."

Ruthern was the family estate in Derbyshire. Lord Crenshaw had
described its rolling green grounds, the southern aspect with its lake and
arched walking paths where you could stroll in summer. Ruthern eclipsed
any of Lord Crenshaw's town houses and housed the priceless artifacts
he brought back from around the world. She found herself imagining its
ivy-mantled walls and its corbeled bell turret, and how it must feel to
walk around an estate knowing it was your own.

"So he did live here," said Katherine, almost to herself.

The solicitor smiled. "He has had it redone for you. It was far too
masculine to suit a young lady."

Stepping into the wide hall with its marble floors, Katherine loved
it immediately. She could see the morning room with a delicate frieze and
pretty cornices, the perfect place to sip a little breakfast of hot chocolate.
The drawing room opposite had a beautiful classical fireplace with fluted
sides, and she glimpsed a Broadwood piano, surely installed so she might
sit and play after dinner. The staircase rose to a second floor, where her
bedroom would be, and she already knew it would be charming, with

delicate silks framing the windows and bed.

"I liked our old house," said Elizabeth.

"Elizabeth!" said Aunt.

Katherine looked down. At ten years old, Elizabeth was a pale girl with flat, dun-colored hair and very dark, strong eyebrows.

"We're going to be very happy here," Katherine told her younger sister, touching her hair. She spared a thought for their cozy home in Hertfordshire with its comfortable furniture and old-fashioned wood paneling. But Lord Crenshaw's house surpassed it in every way.

The night of the proposal, she had stayed up in bed with Elizabeth talking about the future that had opened up for her—for all of them. "We'll be married at St. George's Hanover Square. I'd have it happen at once but Aunt Helen says we must wait until I turn seventeen. After that we'll live at Ruthern, but we'll come up to London for the Season. He'll keep a house for Aunt and Uncle, and you may stay with them or with us as you wish. Though I hope you would choose us! You'll have a governess, one you like, and he's going to settle a dowry on you, so your chances of a good match will be higher too. Oh, Elizabeth! Did you ever think we'd be this happy?"

Elizabeth had frowned at her with her stern monobrow and said, "I don't want to marry an old man."

"You'll be rich enough to marry whoever you want," Katherine had said, hugging her sister affectionately.

"I apologize for our youngest," Aunt now said to Mr. Prescott. "The house is extraordinary."

"You must of course meet the staff," said Mr. Prescott. "Lord Crenshaw has made every arrangement."

There were a lot more staff than Katherine had been expecting. There was a housekeeper, a butler, and footmen for the main house; a cook and kitchen staff for the kitchens; a groomsman, driver, and stable hands in the mews; and curtsying maids of different types that Katherine didn't follow.

Her aunt greeted each of them, asking a series of questions pertaining to the running of the household. Katherine was delighted to learn that she was to have her own lady's maid, Mrs. Dupont. Mrs. Dupont was a young woman with dark hair in an elegant style perfect for a lady's maid in a household of means. With the name Dupont she might be French, thought Katherine with excitement, having heard a French lady's maid was the truest sign of refinement. Mrs. Dupont had no French accent but she immediately endeared herself to Katherine by saying:

"Oh, you're even more beautiful than they said, Miss Kent! The new styles will look so well on you."

Katherine was very pleased by that, imagining the dresses that she would have. "You had heard me described?"

"Lord Crenshaw speaks of you often, with the highest praise."

Of course, Katherine knew Lord Crenshaw thought well of her; she had seen it even in their first meeting, his eyes on her, heavy and assessing. At thirty-seven, he was old enough to be her father, but there was no sign of gray in his hair, which he wore natural in a classical style, the same dark brown as his eyes. And her aunt's maid Annabel had assured her that he cut a very fine figure for a man of older years. Katherine could imagine him on horseback, or surveying his grand estate, or commanding his household of servants.

Lady Crenshaw. That idea was still new, and never failed to come with a little thrill. She would attend balls and house parties, and host elegant gatherings, and there would be new dresses every season.

She was just thinking that she might be able to wear a little more jewelry now that she was a young lady engaged, when Mrs. Dupont gestured to nearby stairs. "Upstairs, your room is—" The motion caused her dress sleeve to shift a little.

"What happened to your wrist?" said Katherine.

Mrs. Dupont quickly pulled her sleeve down. "I'm sorry, Miss Kent. I didn't mean for you to see that."

Katherine couldn't help staring. On Mrs. Dupont's wrist there had been a burn mark in the shape of an S. Katherine forced her eyes away, feeling oddly unsettled. Mrs. Dupont couldn't help it if she had a blemish on her wrist, and it was wrong to feel queasy about it. But it wasn't the burn itself that disturbed her, Katherine thought. It was something about the S. . . .

"How did the ship sink?" Elizabeth's voice.

Mr. Prescott turned toward the young voice, and so did Aunt and Uncle. Katherine was opening her mouth to hush Elizabeth again when her aunt said, slowly:

"It is strange for a ship to sink in the river, isn't it?"

The servants looked at her and then looked at each other. Mr. Prescott didn't answer at once, but he looked troubled, as if there was something he was reluctant to say. Katherine's attention caught and held. They knew something. All of them knew something she didn't.

"What is it?"

"There are rumors that there was foul play," Mr. Prescott said after a moment, as if this were a trifle. "Or an attack by one of his rivals. Lord Crenshaw has men looking for a boy he believes is responsible."

"A boy?" said Katherine.

"Yes, but not to worry," said Mr. Prescott. "We'll find him soon enough."

CHAPTER SIX

COMING TO SLOWLY, Will forced himself not to stir. He could feel the prickle of mattress straw beneath him, his nose full of its smell: cut hay left sitting in the field too long; the musk of all the other bodies that had lain on the mattress without airing; stale beer. An inn room, maybe. And he could hear voices—

"I've never seen anything like that before." A girl's voice.

"No one has." Quietly. "I did not know that anyone could sheathe the Corrupted Blade. But whatever the boy did, it appeared to exact a price."

Will kept very still. *They're talking about the sword. They're talking about that sword on the ship.* Simulating sleep, he carefully cataloged what he could of himself and his surroundings. He wasn't chained up. The bruising and cuts from the beatings throbbed, and his hair was still damp, but the chilling cold from the river was gone. He recognized the voices. A man and a girl.

"Who—who is he?" The girl, sounding a little hushed.

"I only know that Simon wants him, and he's hurt."

"He just fainted. I didn't hit him or anything." The girl, a bit defensively. "When he wakes up—"

"He's awake," said Justice.

Will opened his eyes at that, to find Justice's steady gaze was on him. His jet-black hair framed a face of startling nobility. Will remembered him from the ship, the shearing power of his broadsword as he plowed through rising water. He had cut through the men on that ship like hope.

"Now we must decide what we do," said Justice.

Justice was wearing a long brown cloak that covered his strange garments, but he still wore a sword. Will could see it distorting the shape of his cloak. Justice looked even more incongruous in a grimy room with cracked plaster walls than he had on the ship, like heroic statuary in an unexpected setting.

Behind him, the girl—Violet—slouched, boyishly handsome, with a fierce, scowling look. It was Violet who had come back for him. Will remembered that clearly. Her impossible strength felt like a secret that had passed between them: the connection they had shared in their joint experience of the extraordinary.

But the way they were both looking at him was new—wary, as though he were something dangerous and they didn't know what he might do. It sent him right back to that night at Bowhill. The attack, his mother's desperate words to him as she died, being hunted by those men every waking moment since and not knowing why. Not knowing why anyone would try to kill him—only seeing that look as the knife drove toward him—

Will pushed himself up on the bed, ignoring the blanching pain, the dizzy spin of the floor. "I need to leave."

The door was to his right. It was the only way out. The windows were all closed, each black-lacquered shutter locked with a heavy wooden latch. The thick plaster walls muffled most of the sound, but he could hear murmurs drifting up from beneath the wooden floor. This was almost certainly the upstairs room of an inn—his heart started to pound with the old fear.

The first rule, hard learned, was to stay away from inns, because the roads and public houses were watched.

"It's all right. We made it off the ship," said Violet. "You're safe."

"None of us are safe," said Justice.

He was coming forward—it was all Will could do not to flinch. Justice came so close he felt the air stir as Justice's brown cloak swirled and settled. His eyes on Will were searching, tracking over the marks and bruises on his hands and face, then looking into his eyes.

"But I think you know that better than any of us," said Justice quietly. "Don't you?"

Will felt exposed. He felt *seen*, as he had not since he started running. These two, they knew Simon wanted him. They might know more . . . might know the answer to the question that gnawed at him. *Why? Why did he kill my mother? Why is he after me?*

After all, they were part of it: part of the world of the mirror, the medallion, and the terrifying burst of black flame. Justice's physical feats on the ship had not been natural. He had thrown a young man from one end of the ship's hold to the other, as impossibly strong as Violet, who had wrenched chains apart.

Either one of them was strong enough to tear him in half. But what scared Will was not their strength, but the idea of what they might know about him.

"I don't know what you mean." He kept his voice steady.

"Here," said Justice, instead of answering. "Drink this."

Justice unhooked a thin silver chain that hung from his waist where a monk might wear a rosary. It was a single piece of white chalcedony, set at the end of a chain, and it was worn smooth like a beach pebble.

"It's a relic of my Order," said Justice. "It helps those who are hurt."

"I'm fine," said Will, but Justice was taking the battered tin cup from the table along with a pitcher of water. Dangling the chain, Justice poured the water so that it ran down the chain over the stone, into the tin cup.

"They say that after the Battle of Oridhes, our founder used this stone to tend the wounded. Their number was so great that its jagged edges were worn smooth by the water—as happens with every use, and perhaps its power diminishes as well. Yet it is still a marvel to those who know nothing of the old world."

When the water hit the stone, it sparked and glittered like the clearest spring water gleaming with new sunlight. Will felt the same prickling that he'd had when he'd looked into the mirror. *A marvel*, Justice had called it. Justice handed him the cup, with the stone at the bottom and the silver chain hanging over the side, and Will found himself taking it, even though he had meant to turn it aside. The glints from the stone reflected up onto his face like sunlight.

He lifted it to his lips, cool and perfect. His dizziness receded, as did the bone-deep weariness he had felt since the ship. And though there was no miraculous knitting of cuts, the worst of the pains from the beatings seemed to fade a little, so that breathing was easier.

"These are rooms at the White Hart," Justice said. "And you're right. We can't stay here long. Simon will be searching every lodging house, and he has more than one way to find a person."

"I told you. I need to go." Will tried to rise. Justice shook his head.

"You can barely walk. And you're mistaken if you think the streets of London are safe. Simon's eyes are everywhere. Only the Hall is beyond his reach. We must wait until nightfall and then find a way to cross."

"The Hall?" said Will.

Justice said, "I don't think the two of you have any idea what you're caught up in."

Will looked instinctively at Violet. She had a tumble of dark curls in a boy's cut, her brown skin scattered with a sprinkling of freckles across her nose. In boy's trousers, jacket, and waistcoat, she was dressed similarly to him, although her clothes were of far better quality.

The two of you . . . Will didn't know what had forged this uneasy association between her and Justice. The last thing he remembered was attempting to take a step with his arm around Violet's shoulders, and feeling weakness wash over him. Before that, Justice had been fighting against Simon's men, while Violet had been fighting for them. Now Violet was hanging back near the shuttered windows looking tense, while Justice had come forward past the room's only chair and table, his attention all on Will.

"Then tell me," Will said.

"Here's what I know," said Justice. "Simon was searching for a boy and his mother. For seventeen years, he bent his whole attention to finding them. He watched the roads, the lodging houses, and the ports in this country, on the continent, and beyond, to the farthest reaches of his trade empire. And for seventeen years, the boy's mother evaded him, always staying one step ahead. Until nine months ago, when Simon found and killed them both."

Justice leaned forward, fixing Will with his gaze.

"Then last night as I watched Simon's ship from a hidden vantage, I saw his Lion shouting orders in the rain, while men holding flaming torches brought a prisoner on board under cover of darkness. I thought that prisoner was my shieldmate, Marcus, but it wasn't. It was someone else."

Will's breathing was shallow. "I don't know what any of that has to do with me."

"Don't you?" said Justice.

And Will thought of months of hiding, and before that years of fear in his mother's eyes.

"Though I can't summon the Blade, I have fought many dark and dangerous things," said Justice. "And Simon is the most dangerous of them all. If he has turned his eye to you, then you will not escape him by hiding."

Violet broke in, shattering the moment. "This isn't possible. Simon's a trader. You're talking about him like he's . . . Simon's ruthless, but so is every man on the docks. He doesn't kill women and children."

"Do you really think all of this concerns the simple dealings of trade?" said Justice. "You've seen the brand on the wrists of Simon's men. You've seen the unnatural strength of the one Simon calls his Lion."

"Lion—you mean," Violet said, "you mean that boy. The boy you were fighting."

"The boy who took you both captive," said Justice.

You both? Will's eyes jerked helplessly to Violet, whose flush darkened—guiltily. Violet wasn't a captive. Violet had gathered up that boy Lion in her arms and pulled him from the sinking ship.

Justice doesn't know. The realization hit him fully. Violet worked for Simon, and Justice didn't know. Justice had brought her here believing she was Simon's captive.

It made sudden sense of their strange alliance. In a rush, Will understood the nervy tension in Violet, as well as Justice's calm trust in her—the way he turned his back to her as though she was no threat. In the dark chaos of the hold, he must not have seen who had knocked him out.

Justice had no way of knowing that Violet had left him floating face-down and unconscious, ignoring him to instead save Simon's Lion.

Will remembered waiting alone and exhausted, the black water swirling at his chest. He had sheathed the nightmare sword, but he had had no way off the ship, chained to one of its heavy beams. He had thought it was over. He had thought that all his running had led him to a dark dead end that would seal him up with water.

He had looked up to see Violet's face on the stairs. She had waded forward and put her hands on his chains. And he had woken up here, when he had not expected to wake up at all.

"That's right," said Will, without hesitating, "the boy who took us both captive." He deliberately didn't look at Violet, his eyes on Justice.

"Simon's creature," said Justice, with distaste. "Sworn to serve him, as a Lion always will. It's in his blood." Will felt rather than saw Violet react to those words.

"You know," said Will. "Don't you? You know what connects all these"—*marvels*, he might have said, using Justice's word, or he might have used his own, *horrors*—"all these strange and unnatural things."

—a lady in a mirror with eyes like his mother; a sword on the ship that spewed black fire; Matthew pressing a strange medallion into his hand; his dead eyes staring as the rain soaked his clothes—

"I can't tell you all of it," said Justice, lowering his voice. "Even to my Order, much is shrouded in mystery. And some tales are too dangerous to tell, even in daylight."

"I've—seen things. I know Simon isn't a good person," Will said. "No one good burns their name onto their men."

Justice was shaking his head. "Did you think the S that he brands into the flesh of his followers stood for 'Simon'? For 'servant,' perhaps, or 'submission'? That S is the symbol of something older, a terrible sigil with power over his followers that even they do not fully understand."

"A symbol of what?" said Will.

Justice just looked back at him. *He knows*, Will thought again. His heart was pounding. That S had felt ancient, evil and rapacious, as if it, even more than the men who bore it, was hunting him. He felt right on the edge of understanding, as if something vast and important lay just outside of his reach.

After a long moment, Justice pulled the chair forward and sat, half-shadowed by the dim light of the shuttered room, his heavy brown cloak settling around him.

"This is as much as I can tell you," he said, and the shadows of the room seemed to gather in close as he spoke.

"Long ago," said Justice, "there was a world of wonders—of what you and I might call magic. Great towers and palaces, fragrant gardens, and marvelous creatures."

It was like the words of a familiar story, yet it was one Will had never heard before.

"In that world, a Dark King rose, growing in power and killing those who stood in his path."

The light from the room's only candle flickered, obscuring the planes of Justice's face.

"It was a time of terror. The Dark King's shadow spread out across the lands. Armies broke against his power. Cities fell to his hordes. Heroes gave their lives to hold him back just for a moment. The lights of the world went out one by one, until there was only one light left, the Final Flame. There, those on the side of Light made their last stand."

Will saw it, an island of light surrounded by a vast expanse of darkness, and over it all rising a great and terrible power wearing a pale crown.

"They fought," said Justice, "until the earth was scoured. They fought for their own lives and for all the generations that were to come. And with a single act of great sacrifice, the Dark King was overthrown."

"How?" Will was caught by it, as if he were there, battered by the fighting, tasting the ashes and flame.

"No one knows," said Justice. "But his defeat came at a terrible cost. There was nothing left of that world. The survivors were too few, and the world fell to ruin. Years passed, and all that had been was lost to the silence of time, grass growing over the fields where armies once fought, palaces no more than a scattering of stones and the deeds of the dead forgotten.

"And gradually humanity took up residence, and built cities, and knew nothing of what had come before. For that world is our world, with all its wonders gone, except for fragments, like this stone, which time will take too, until even it is worn away into nothing."

Justice held up the white chalcedony, which swayed like a slow hypnotist's watch at the end of its chain.

A *remnant*, thought Will, *of a once-great world.*

"And Simon?" said Will. He felt half-dazed, like one blinking out of a dream, almost surprised to find himself in an ordinary inn room and not looking out at the vistas of the past.

Justice gazed back at him with dark eyes.

"Simon is descended from the Dark King, who swore to return and retake his kingdom," said Justice. "Simon works to bring him forth and restore him to his throne."

It was as if a chill wind pierced him, turning Will cold.

Simon works to bring him forth . . .

The words rang in his mind, like his fear of what lay beyond the locked shutters, Simon's men killing his mother, then hunting him down with that S on their wrists and trying to kill him too.

An ancient world, a Dark King—it ought to have been impossible. But he could feel that presence in its pale crown as if it were right here with them.

As the white chalcedony swung on its chain, Will knew somehow that it was not the only remnant. The Blade on the ship had been another. A terrible weapon unearthed by Simon for a deadly purpose. He shivered at the memory.

"None of that is written in any of the history books," said Will, shaken.

"Not all that is written has passed," said Justice, "and not all that has passed is written." Justice looked troubled. "My Order are all that's left who remember. Only we keep the old ways, and it is no accident that the Dark King reaches his hand across time now, when our numbers dwindle."

Justice's coat slipped back from his left shoulder, and Will saw two things at once. The first, that the fabric of Justice's sleeve was red with blood from wrist to shoulder. Justice had taken a bullet to protect Violet, thinking that he was saving her from Simon's men.

The second was the symbol on his livery, torn and grimy but visible. It was a silver star, its points of varying lengths, like a compass rose.

The bright star holds, he thought.

"You're a Steward," he said.

He was suddenly conscious of the medallion that he wore under his shirt. Simon's men hadn't taken it, uninterested in a dull, warped piece of old metal.

"It's our sacred duty to stand against the Dark," said Justice, "but if Simon succeeds, we will not be enough. The last time that the Dark King rose, all fell before him. The only one powerful enough to stop him was—"

And Will felt the knowledge pushing at him, like it was part of him—

"—a Lady," said Will.

He remembered her in the mirror, ancient and beautiful, but with the same determination in her eyes as his mother. He remembered the jolt of familiarity, and the shock when their eyes had met, as though she recognized him.

His stomach twisted. "She looked at me like she knew me."

"You *saw* her?"

"In a mirror." Will closed his eyes for a moment, feeling the warm metal against the skin of his chest. Then he made his decision. "She was wearing this."

With unsteady fingers, he unbuttoned his coarse shirt and took out the battered medallion. It swayed on its leather tie, engraved with the words in that strange language, which now took on a new meaning:

I cannot return when I am called to fight
So I will have a child

Justice had gone very still. "Where did you get that?"

Will thought of his mother's old servant Matthew, his sightless eyes, the rain soaking his clothes. "It belonged to my mother."

Justice let out a breath. Will wanted to ask a question, but in the next moment Justice's hands clasped around his own on the medallion and pressed it back to his chest.

"Show it to no one else." He seemed shaken, and that more than anything convinced Will to quickly tuck the medallion back in his shirt and do up the buttons again.

"I must take you to the Elder Steward. I came to that ship searching for my shieldmate, Marcus, and have stumbled on something beyond me." Justice's eyes were serious. "But I swear to you: I will protect you. My sword is yours, and by my life I will not let Simon take you." Justice closed his eyes briefly, as though even he might be afraid. "Though I think, having had you in his grasp, he will tear London apart to find you again."

You must go to the Stewards, Matthew had said. Justice was offering an-swers. Justice understood what he faced. Justice was the only person he had met who was fighting against Simon. Will found himself nodding, once.

Justice said, "It's not long till sunset. Once it's dark, the three of us can make for the Hall."

"The three of us," said Will, and thought again of this strange alli-ance of three, forged in water and black fire. He turned to look for Violet.

But the girl had gone.

CHAPTER SEVEN

VIOLET PUSHED OUT onto the street, her heart pounding.

Outside, there were just the regular sounds of London: the clop of hooves, the barks of an overexcited dog, the cry of the evening newspaper, "Fine *Evening Mail!*" A stagecoach trundled past on spoked wheels. A boy darted in front of a water cart, and the driver called a perfunctory "Watch it!" after him.

She blinked at the normality of it. It was nothing like the inn room she had left—the boy on the bed with the dark eyes, and the man who dressed like an ancient knight and talked about the stirrings of a bygone world. Magic and dark kings . . . Will had listened to Justice's stories like he believed them. And she—even she, remembering the black fire on the *Sealgair*, watching the bruises fade from Will's face as he drank water poured across the surface of a stone—for a moment, she had started to believe.

Justice had talked about Tom like—

Like he was a monster. Like he'd hunt a woman down and kill her. Like he served a dark power, and did it willingly. A horror rose up in her. *Simon's creature. It's in his blood.* She remembered Tom splattered in blood driving an iron bar through a woman's chest on the *Sealgair. Long ago, there was a world that was destroyed in its battles against a Dark King . . .*

A burst of laughter to her left. A cluster of young men in rough-spun shirtsleeves passed her, still slapping each other on the back at the tail end of their joke. Violet let out a breath and shook her head.

The street was just a street. There were no men out searching, no shadowy figures sent by Simon. Of course there weren't. Those stories were just stories. This was England, where everyone knew magic wasn't real, and there wasn't any King except George.

She hurried on.

Her brother would be at Simon's warehouse. He'd insist on working with his first coughing breath, still dripping river water. He would see her and throw his arms around her, as glad to see her as she'd be to see him. He'd ruffle her hair, and things between them would be the way they used to be.

No one needed to know that she had helped Will escape.

She slipped skillfully through a piece of broken boarding into a loading yard. She had grown up on these docks, where she had often scavenged odd jobs for herself. Some nights, she had snuck out of her house to sleep high up among stacked crates, or just to sit, gazing out at the ships, their lights bright. Now, clambering up a stack of cargo, she looked out at the river that was like a second home.

And went cold.

It looked like the site of an explosion. Great tracts of riverbank were gouged and burned where they'd been lashed by ropes of black fire. Ruined, dripping cargo lined the foreshore. The pier was smashed and twisted, the lapping water clogged with splintered wood.

On the bank, dockers strained at a winch crane. A team of men had roped four draft horses in heavy collars and were calling "Heave, ho!" as they hauled. A wave of horror passed over her.

They were dredging the river for the Corrupted Blade.

No, no, no. The thought of that thing back in Simon's hands made her stomach churn. The cold, trapped terror of the hold swept over her as she remembered Simon's man vomiting up black blood.

They were going to find it. The search spanned the full length of the docks. Simon's men were manning barges with nets and long poles, and somewhere down there the Blade was waiting, the corrupted horror of its presence barely held back by its sheath.

—black fire tearing a hole in the hull, the men around her rotting from the inside out—

Staring out at the wreckage now, she saw the scale of what the Blade had done. Simon collected objects, she recalled sickly. She thought of Simon's archaeological digs, his trade outposts, his empire spread across the world all to drag things up out of the earth and back to London. Like the Blade, full of dark power that could tear a ship in half.

I don't think the two of you have any idea what you're caught up in, Justice had said.

"Capsized," she heard from the gathered crowd on the bank, trying to fit natural explanations to the sight, when nothing natural had done this. "Burst pump" and "Freak weather."

She tore her eyes from the wreckage. The bank swarmed with onlookers held back by Simon's dockers. She glimpsed a few distinctive jackets, quay guards from the Thames River Police. A flash of auburn hair amid the crowd on the bank—

Tom.

She was scrabbling down from the crates the instant she saw him.

Staying out of sight, she maneuvered through the dredged cargo, glimpsing Tom greeting the *Sealgair*'s Captain Maxwell. As the two men walked, she followed the distinctive glint of Tom's hair.

They stopped on the far side of a few stacks of cork. There was no one else around, just her brother and the captain talking in low voices—perfect for an inconspicuous homecoming.

Violet stepped out, opening her mouth to say *Tom* when she heard—

"—thirty-nine dead in the attack, but there are no more bodies in the water. The boy is missing."

"And the girl?"

The auburn-haired man wasn't Tom. It was her father.

Some child's instinct stopped her in her tracks, the sight of her father's back and shoulders conjuring up guilt, as though she might be in trouble. Hastily, she stepped back, finding a shadowed space between the piles of cork.

"Where is Violet, Maxwell?" Her father's shoulders were taut, his voice clipped in the way it became when he was controlling himself.

"There's no sign of her," said Maxwell.

"Search again. She has to be found."

"Mr. Ballard—I saw her jump back onto the ship—I don't know how anyone could have survived—"

"She can't be dead," said her father. Violet was taking a step forward, opening her mouth to say *I'm right here*, when her father said, "I need that stupid mongrel back alive."

Violet stopped, the words like a slap. She felt everything go very still and soundless, as if every particle of air had been sucked away.

"Tom may be of Lion blood," her father said, "but he can't come into his true power without killing another like him. I haven't kept that bastard girl in my house, humiliating my wife and jeopardizing my social standing, only to have her die before time."

Violet felt her back hit the cork before she realized she had moved. Her fist shoved hard into her mouth to hold back the sound that tried to get out. She was staring at her father.

"We'll keep looking," Captain Maxwell was saying. "If she's out there, we'll find her."

"Then do it. And for God's sake, don't alarm her. Tell her that her brother has been asking for her. He's sorry he had harsh words for her, he misses her. She'll do anything for Tom's approval."

She was stumbling back blindly. Barely aware of her surroundings, she wasn't thinking about being caught. She was just trying to get away, her limbs clumsy with horror.

She pushed through the stacks of cork and didn't hear the voices approaching, footsteps coming right for her—when a hand grabbed her and pulled her to safety behind some crates.

Scant seconds later, her father and Captain Maxwell rounded the corner, passing right by the spot where she had been standing.

In the dim space between crates, she was staring at Will's shocked face.

"Let go! Let go of me, you don't have any right—!"

"I heard," said Will. "I heard what they said." She felt hot, then cold. He had heard. He had heard the words that made her shivery sick. The feeling of exposure was horrible. "You can't go back to them."

He was holding her by the shoulders, pressing her back into the crate. She could push him off, shove him away easily, if she could just stop shaking. She was strong enough. If she could just—

"Why are you here?" she said thickly. "If they find you—"

"They're not going to find me."

"You don't know that."

"If they do," said Will, "we'll go together."

"Why would you—"

"You saved my life," said Will.

He said it simply. She remembered that Simon had spent years tracking him down, then had chained him to a post on a ship filled with unnatural cargo. Yet he had followed her here.

"Everyone who has ever helped me is dead," said Will. "I didn't want that to happen to you."

She stared back at him. He had come all the way back into Simon's stronghold. And he'd heard. He'd heard the words that had turned her life into a lie. *Tom can't come into his true power without killing another like him.* Her father wanted to kill her. And Tom—did Tom know? Did he know what their father planned to do?

"Come with me," said Will.

"He's my father," she said. If she could just stop shaking— "And Tom. Tom's my brother. The Lion."

As children, she and Tom had done everything together. Their father had always encouraged their closeness, as he'd encouraged her presence in the house. *She's the same blood as Tom,* he'd say. She felt sick.

She remembered how normal the day had seemed, before her ordinary world had been shattered, Stewards and Lions and a sword that spewed black fire.

No, not normal. Tom getting Simon's brand burned into his flesh. The smell of it like cooked meat, and a boy beaten and chained in the hold.

"What Justice said—" She made herself ask it, through chattering teeth. "Do you think it's true?"

"I don't know," said Will. "But whatever's happening, we're both part of it."

"Is that why you want me to come with you?"

"I want answers, like you. And I tried running. The things that are happening . . . I couldn't get away from them. I couldn't run from what was part of me. Neither can you."

"They're my family," said Violet.

Will said, "Simon took my family from me too."

She didn't know him. With the bruising mostly faded, he looked different—like a clerk, if a clerk were all cheekbones and intense eyes. His dark hair and too-pale skin were half-hidden under a cap, and his faded blue jacket was torn at the shoulder.

"Stewards hate Lions. You didn't hear them, on the ship." On the ship, before Tom killed them. "Whatever I am, I'm not welcome."

"You don't have to tell them what you are," said Will. "No one knows what you are except you."

She realized it then. She was going to follow him, this boy she'd barely met. "He's here, isn't he? Justice." Justice, who hated Lions. Justice, who had fought her brother and almost killed him. Justice, who might kill her too, if he knew what she was. "You're going with him to the Stewards."

Justice, who had taken a bullet for her in the confusing crush on the ship.

Justice, who thought she was Simon's captive and Will's friend.

Will nodded once. "I have to know. What I am. What Simon wants with me."

Will had lied to Justice for her. Will had come back here to help her. They had stumbled into this together, and he was right. She wanted answers. Violet closed her eyes.

She said, "Then I'm going too."

Darkness had fallen, but there were lights on the river, and lamps and torches flaming on the banks where the work of salvage was still going on. It gave them both cover to creep around in.

Will *was* good at hiding. Slipping in and out of shadows and gaps, he had a skill born of necessity: discovery for Violet had only ever meant a box on the ears; discovery for him meant capture and death. He knew how to move, where to put his feet, when to stay still.

They had to reach the other side of the pier, through stacks of crates, and stuffed sacks and long lines of lumber. There was no sign of her father, but twice she heard voices that sent her heart into her mouth, and once they had to cram themselves into a space between bins while Simon's men patrolled.

Justice was waiting, a cloaked figure indistinguishable from the shadows until Will pointed toward him with a silent tilt of his chin. He had stayed back to deal with Simon's guards while Will came in to find her, she realized. He was likely the reason they had seen so few patrols: he had cleared them out.

As he emerged, Violet felt a shiver of fear, remembering Justice's strength on the ship. He had thrown Tom around like he weighed nothing, then survived a blow to the head that had set him floating facedown in the water. Even now his hand rested protectively on his sword, an old-fashioned weapon like his old-fashioned clothes and his old-fashioned way of speaking.

If he knew what I was—

"Good" was all Justice said, with a nod. "We must go."

He didn't ask her where she'd been, just seemed glad that she was safe. They set off with Justice in the lead. She found herself staring at him, at his jet-black hair that was straight where hers was curly, his upright posture that seemed to radiate authority, the seriousness of his warm brown eyes.

"It's dark enough now that we can try to cross without being seen. If we can make it past Simon's patrols—"

There was a sudden commotion from the bank, and all three of them jerked their heads toward it.

"Something's happening," said Will.

The clatter of a carriage, the sound of voices from the river—but more than that, there was a shift in the air that she felt but couldn't quite name, like the build-up before a storm. She could almost taste it, dangerous, electric.

Justice's expression changed. "James is here."

CHAPTER EIGHT

WILL TURNED.

James. He didn't recognize the name. But he could hear the tension in Justice's voice. Simon's men seemed to feel it too, waiting in tense clumps on the bank. *James is here.*

The carriage was arriving like a processional, announcing itself with the sound of hooves, wheels, and the clink of harnesses. There were three men riding before it, each wearing a single piece of broken armor atop their riding clothes. It gave them an unnatural look. They felt wrong, their sunken eyes unblinking, their faces death white. They cantered ahead of the carriage, like the obverse of Stewards.

The carriage itself was black, high-gloss lacquered wood, drawn by two black horses with arched necks and flared nostrils, their eyes hidden by blinkers. On the doors and carved into the wood were the three black hounds that were Simon's coat of arms. The curtains were drawn; you couldn't see inside.

Driving right down into the crowd, it only stopped where packed dirt became the pebbled foreshore. Two carriage men leaped down from their seats with a spring. They opened the carriage door as for some lord in the high street, and that was when James stepped out onto the river-bank.

The air changed, lifting like the breeze in a long-ago garden.

It's you, Will thought, as though they knew each other.

Palaces fallen to ruin, grass grown over the fields where armies fought, a world with all its wonders gone, except for fragments, glimmers that left you breathless.

He was beautiful. A golden beauty, he might have been carved from fine marble by some master, but there was no one in the world who looked like this.

A shiver of fear rippled across Simon's men—a strange reaction to James's young, lovely face. His youth itself was a small shock: James was a boy of about seventeen, Will's own age.

Will found himself moving closer, ignoring the reaction of Justice behind him, until he was right at the edge of the wet crate. Will heard one of the sailors say, "It's him. Simon's Prize." Another answered, "For your life, don't let him hear you call him that." The fear among the crowd winched tighter.

James strolled forward.

All activity had ceased with James's arrival. The men who had gathered around the carriage fell back, opening up a path for him. Will recognized one or two of them from the hold of the *Sealgair,* and realized with new fear of his own that there were no lingering bystanders. Those few who remained were Simon's men down to the last. There were brands under those shirtsleeves.

The crunch of James's boots on the pebbles of the foreshore was loud.

The riverbank was illuminated near the carriage by a row of torches that flamed on poles and lanterns that men held aloft, their faces flickering.

The river behind them was black, with a choppy glinting path of moon-light on its surface from the high three-quarter moon above; the sky was clear. The occasional sound was distant: a muted splash, the far-off ring of a bell.

James's cool blue eyes surveyed the damaged chaos of the bank. His elegant silhouette embodied the fashion of the times: his golden hair brushed in a fashionable part, his jacket with its taut waist, the fine fabric of his trousers with their glove-like fit, his long shiny boots.

"Mr. St. Clair," Captain Maxwell of the wrecked ship greeted him, bowing deferentially, even nervously, though James was likely more than thirty years his junior. "As you can see, we've dredged almost all the car-go. Some of the larger pieces can be salvaged. And of course the—"

"You lost the boy," James said.

In the pin-drop silence, his voice carried. Will felt his stomach flip at the confirmation that they cared more about him than about the ship or its cargo.

"Who was in charge?"

James's mild question was met with silence from the men. The only movement was the lapping of the water on the foreshore, a soft in-and-out, like the waves of the sea.

"No, Tom, you don't have to—" said a voice, and Tom was ignoring it, pushing past the men in the crowd to step out and stand in front of James.

"I was," said Tom.

Violet's brother. Will hadn't seen him since the attack, Violet dragging him unconscious out of the hold. Tom looked recovered, and even wore a new set of clothes, though his good brown waistcoat did not match James's exquisite tailoring and his sleeves were pushed up roughly, as if he'd been doing the kind of physical labor that was beneath his station. In front of the men, Tom dropped to one knee, so that James was looking down at him. James's eyes passed over him, a long, unhurried look.

"Bad kitty," said James. His voice was not quite pleasant.

Humiliated red flooded Tom's face.

"I accept any punishment Simon wants to give me."

"You let Stewards board the ship," said James. "You let them kill your men. And now the one thing Simon wants is in Steward hands."

Another voice cut across the riverbank. Will saw Tom's father stepping forward. "The boy's only been missing a few hours. He can't have gone far. And as for the attack—if it had just been Stewards, Tom could have fought them off. It was the boy who—you saw what he did to the ship. We weren't warned. We had no idea that the boy was—that he could—"

"Your son's best quality," said James, "is that he doesn't make excuses."

Tom's father closed his mouth with a snap.

On one knee, Tom looked up, his hands fists, his face determined as he made his pledge.

"I'll find him."

"No. I'll find him," James said.

The gathered men were uneasy, shifting in the repressed silence. The three too-pale men swung silently down off their horses, their single black pieces of armor faintly repelling. Those left on the banks were shooting nervous glances from them to James and back again. Will felt it too, a strange pressure growing in his chest.

James merely peeled off his gloves.

The three men took up positions around James, as if guarding him from interruption. Their livery was emblazoned with Simon's three black hounds, but it was the single piece of armor they each wore that made Will queasy. The pieces were different, as if the three men had scavenged different parts from the same armor suit. Pitch-black and metal-heavy, they emanated *wrongness*, like the chalk-white faces of the men and their staring, sunken eyes.

One of the gathered dockmen handed James something—a patch of frayed blue fabric. James closed his newly bare fist around it. Will realized with a shiver that it was a bloodstained scrap of his own jacket.

Then James went very still.

It was so quiet now that Will could hear the flaming of the torches. Behind him, Tom's father yanked Tom off his knees and pulled him backward as if out of the way of danger, and the watching men were shrinking away from James as well, like singed paper curling back from a flame.

Will could feel—*something* happening. Like words whispering, *I will find you. I will always find you.* Like a metal gauntlet closing around flesh. *Try to run.* Behind him the flame light illuminated the faces of the men. They were terrified.

"Will," said Justice.

It jerked him out of the moment, his heart pounding. He heard the urgency in Justice's voice and was surprised to see fear in Justice's eyes, reflecting that of the men on the docks, as if they knew what was to come.

"We have to go. Now."

The stirrings of a breeze were kicking up dust and scraps in whirls of air by James's feet. The torch on the pole closest to James flickered and went out like a snuffed flame on a wick. The wind rose; it wasn't the wind. It was something else.

"We have to go. We have to leave before—"

Before James gathers his power.

He could feel it, a tang in the air. He felt an almost mesmerized desire to stay and watch James do it. And a desire to see if he could stop him.

Was there a way to stop magic?

Will looked past Justice to a winch crane that stood out near the river, repurposed to haul goods from the water. Those manning it had paused their work when James arrived. The crate it held was dangling in the air, still dripping.

It was dripping quite close to James.

Beside Will towered the pile of salvage from the *Sealgair*, a high stack of beams, which included long thick interior logs and two sections of the main mast. Tied with rope to prevent them rolling.

Will put his hand on the rope knot.

If the beams rolled, they would knock the brace from the winch crane and send the crate crashing down to hit James, or close enough to distract him.

Will's heart was pounding. He knew how to tie ropes and untie them. He knew how to alter knots to make them slip.

Before Justice could stop him, he tugged at the fibrous knot of rope and pulled it open.

"*What are you doing?*" Justice grabbed his hand back from the rope, but Will was barely aware of it, his eyes on James. *Show me what you can do.*

The first beam swung out before it rolled, missing the crane and splashing into the river. It was the second beam that hit, knocking the brace from the crane winch, which spun violently, releasing the whole length of its chain in a tumbling crash and rattle of noise.

High above, the crate plummeted.

James's head jerked around toward it—as the released chain flew upward—as the crate plunged—James flung out his hand and the crate abruptly stopped, frozen unnaturally in midair by his gesture.

It was a display of power beyond anything he had dreamed. For all Justice's talk of magic, the sight of a boy holding a ton crate suspended in midair with nothing more than his will stole the breath out of Will's lungs. He had wanted to test it—to see it. Now he had.

Got you, Will thought with a twist of excitement. James was visibly struggling to control the crate, his chest rising and falling, his outflung arm trembling.

Everything had stopped: the wind, the sense of rising danger—it had all cut off the instant James's concentration had swung to the crate.

Simon's men were stumbling back, frightened of the crate above them, the open, unnatural display of power. A second later James swept his hand sideways, and the motion flung the crate violently away, smashing it into a thousand harmless splinters on the bank.

James looked up. His blond hair was mussed, and he was breathing unevenly. He looked spent. But his eyes were furious, full of barely repressed emotion.

With those deadly blue eyes, he looked right across the docks at Will.

"They're here," said James.

"Go," said Justice.

They ran—scrambling over the crates and boundary walls toward the street. Justice ran swiftly, and Violet kept up with him, sure-footed, sailing over the detritus of the shipyards. Will struggled to match them.

His last glimpse of James had been to see him sharply giving orders to the three men with the disturbing pale faces, who had mounted smoothly, their dark horses wheeling and turning in Will's direction.

Now he could hear hoofbeats, and when Justice pulled them all out of sight into a doorway for a moment, Will fought to catch his breath.

"Who are those men?" said Will, chilled by their too-pale faces and sunken, unblinking eyes. "They're dressed like Stewards."

"Those are no Stewards," said Justice grimly. "They're Simon's creatures. . . . He calls them the Remnants. Each of them wears a piece from an ancient suit of armor, once worn by a member of the Dark King's Inner Guard. Simon excavated the armor near a ruined tower in the Umbrian mountains, at a small village called Scheggino." Justice kept his voice low. "The Remnants used to be men. The armor changes them. Do not let them touch you."

Will shivered, thinking of that ancient guard, rotted away underground until all that was left was a few fragments of his armor. He didn't want to think about that armor being worn by someone else, or that remnants of a dark guard might be hunting him.

The hoofbeats were louder. The moon passed behind a cloud, and they used the cover to run across the open street, toward the mouth of another, smaller and narrower. But there was no way to outrun a mounted guard. Will scoured the street for a place that a horse couldn't follow, a doorway or an opening that would not also be a dead end, a trap—

"Here!" called Justice, using the hilt of his sword to break open the lock of a small loading yard. Inside was an old hauling cart, its owner gone for the night. But the cart remained, with its workhorse still in part-harness. Justice strode inside.

"Can you ride?"

Piling into the yard, Violet and Will looked at its single, shabby inhabitant, neck lowered past bony shoulders, hooves splayed.

"An old cart horse?" said Violet, with disbelief.

Justice put a hand on the horse's neck. He was a poorly kept gelding, his black coat shoddy, his mane muddy and clumped. "He is a cart horse, but his breed traces its line past the Middle Ages. His ancestors were warhorses. He has heart, and he will run."

And indeed, there was something in the tone of Justice's voice that seemed to stir the horse. When Justice touched him, the horse lifted his head.

Will looked at Justice and Violet. Justice was offering him the horse because he believed Will was somehow important, and that he would make better time on horseback than on foot.

He also knew that Violet and Justice could get away if Will rode out on horseback, drawing the Remnants away from them.

The Remnants would chase him. Simon's men always chased him. They'd ignore Violet and Justice and come right for him. He thought, an old cart horse, against the three fresh glossy steeds he'd seen wheeling on the riverbank.

"I can ride," said Will.

Uncoupling the horse from the cart shafts, Justice looked up, his hands on the buckles. "We'll split up and meet at the Hall. The three of us."

Will nodded as Justice led the horse out by its bridle.

"You'll need to cross the Lea," said Justice. "It's three, maybe four miles from here—at least half of that through open countryside. After that, it's the Abbey Marsh, treacherous going for horses. The abbey was torn down a hundred years ago, but the gate still stands. Make for the gate."

The gate, thought Will, fixing the idea of it in his mind.

Justice used the top three inches of his sword to cut through the longer driving reins of the cart's bridle, then tied them off, shortening them enough for makeshift riding reins. As he did, Violet touched Will on the arm, drawing him away to one side.

"I know you're only agreeing to ride alone to keep them from coming after us," said Violet.

Will looked quickly at Justice to make sure he hadn't heard. "They'll follow me no matter what I do."

"I know that, I just—" She broke off.

He wondered if she was concerned about being left alone with Justice. He was opening his mouth to reassure her when she reached out and knocked his shoulder with her fist, a gesture of solidarity.

"Good luck." It was all she said, brown eyes serious in her boyish face. Unused to fellowship, Will nodded wordlessly.

There was no saddle, and no stirrup to push himself up with, so Violet made a stirrup with her hands and Will took hold of a clump of mane and hoisted himself up and onto the horse's warm, broad back.

Justice was at its neck, murmuring to it in a strange language. Will found he could understand the words: "*Run, as your ancestors ran. Do not fear the darkness. You have greatness within you, as do all your kind.*" The horse tossed his head as if something in him was responding; his black mane was tattered but he had a brave look in his eye. Looking up at Will, Justice said, "Ride fast. Do not look back. Trust the horse."

Will nodded.

Skittish with new energy, or alarmed at the darkening of the shadows, the horse was hard to hold. Will had ridden in his youth with his mother, but never bareback with only makeshift reins. He drew in a shaky breath, then he drove the horse out into the center of the road and called out.

"Hey!" he called. "Hey, I'm here!"

The three men rounded the corner on horseback, and Will's skin went cold. The Remnants were like the vanguard of a nightmare. The shadowy ground beneath them seemed to move—hunting dogs were sliding in and out of their horses' legs like a roil of snakes. This close, the single piece of armor each Remnant wore gave them asymmetric silhouettes: one wore a gauntlet; one a shoulder piece; and one a broken shard of black helm that covered the left side of his death-white face. The sight of them was like looking into an open tomb.

They were just men. Just Simon's men. But even as Will told himself that, a Remnant stopped in front of an ivy-covered wall, and the dead of its eyes seemed to spread to the vine where the Remnant's armor brushed against it, the green leaves withering, desiccating and darkening, the blackness spreading like rot. *Do not let them touch you.*

Sensing these cold fingers of danger, his own horse reared up on its hind legs and let out a cry, then sprang off down the cobbled stones of the road. Will clutched on, his heart pounding.

Ride fast. Do not look back.

He didn't have much of a head start, but he knew the best paths, and he gained at first. He kept off the straight roads, where his slower horse would be at a disadvantage, turning instead into the twisty lanes he'd traversed on foot. His pursuers lost seconds pulling up and turning, and their swarming dogs clogged up the narrow spaces. It gave Will hope that he could stay ahead.

But the straggling outskirts of the shipping district quickly gave way to open countryside. In the distance, Will could see the outline of sparse cottages. To the north, the low smocked windmill was a collection of strange dark shapes. To the south was Bromley Hill, a shallow rise scattered with black trees and a lone farmhouse.

In front of him was a mile of flat commons, with nowhere to hide until the river.

He burst out into the open with the dogs streaming behind him, their baying a terrible, hungry sound. Bred to rend flesh and bring down large prey, the hunting dogs snapped and snarled toward the vulnerable legs of his horse. And even on the muffling grass, Will could hear the threefold thundering of the Remnants, shaking the ground.

They were gaining. His horse was not a hotblood built for sprints across a flat. But its great heart gave its all, driving its heavier body on. *"Run!"* he called out to it. *"Run!"* His words were snatched away by the wind, but he felt his horse respond and gather itself beneath him, felt its stride stretch out longer.

Run, as your ancestors ran. Do not fear the darkness.

Trust the horse.

They raced across the flat, barely two strides ahead. He didn't even hear the water before it was suddenly looming in front of him, a rushing black channel, as far across as a wide street, cut into a dark grassy bank with an unknown drop. *Cross the Lea,* Justice had said.

His horse launched chest first into the river. Will felt the bottom drop out from under him and the shock of freezing water as the horse swam with head extended, hindquarters lower than its churning shoulders. He clutched two handfuls of mane, clinging to the horse's slippery neck and back.

He looked back, a single glance, and saw the shearing spray of water as the Remnant in the shoulder piece galloped powerfully into the river. In front of it, like a stream of rats, the dogs were swimming, clambering over each other to reach him. "Up!" Will called. "Up!" His own horse heaved itself up onto the opposite bank, its haunches bunching as it propelled itself for the final leap up the bank slope.

He thought he'd see his destination then. *Cross the Lea, then make for the gate,* Justice had said. He thought he had made it, that reaching the gate now really was possible.

But when his horse crested the bank slope, Will turned cold at what he saw.

There was no gate, only endless flat marshland, where long streaks of black water flowed around islands of grassy earth. A vast, harrowing landscape full of sucking mud and slimy ground where a horse's hoof would sink or skid.

He had no choice but to drive his horse into it. He tried to keep to dry land, avoiding the glinting water between the patches of long grass. The footpads of the dogs were lighter, and they raced over the top of the marshland without miring. As his tired horse labored in the swampy earth, the dogs swarmed toward him, narrowing the gap.

The gate, he thought. *Make for the gate.* But there was no gate; he was alone on an empty marsh with the three Remnants behind him closing in.

How close were they? Could he hold a lead and find his way to cover? Will twisted his head, risking a second look behind him.

The gleaming black gauntlet was stretching out, about to close on him.

Will hurtled himself sideways. His horse screamed and veered with him; the reaching hand closed on air. A second Remnant reached out before he'd even righted himself. He could feel the hot breath of a third's mount to his right. If he looked sideways, he would see them drawing alongside him.

He called on his horse one last time, a new sound of hooves swelling and breaking around him, his own breath sobbing with the need to escape. His horse gave its last burst of strength as he looked up through the haze and saw that the sound of hooves was not coming from behind him. It was coming from ahead.

Out of the white curling mist rode the Stewards.

A charge of light: twelve Stewards on white horses were galloping hard toward him. They wore the star and carried winged spears like lances, their silver armor glinting in the moonlight. Will gasped as they swept past him, heading right for the Remnants in their black armor.

"*Back, darkness!*" he heard the foremost Steward call, raising a staff with a stone set in its top that seemed to radiate a shield of light. "*The Dark King has no power here!*"

Will turned his horse in time to see the rushing dark of the Remnants seem to hit the barrier that the Stewards drove before them—and break, like a wave smashing against unyielding rock, the horses of the Remnants rearing and cowering back, the tendrils of the dark vanishing.

"*I said back!*" said the Steward as the three Remnants whipped their horses, trying to rally. Unable to pass the barrier, the Remnants were forced to drag at their horses' mouths with their reins and turn to canter impotently back to the river. Reduced to faltering whimpers, the dogs milled uncertainly with their tails between their legs before finally following the riders, silent shadows moving along the water's edge.

The Stewards were swerving, surrounding Will, twelve radiant white horses circling around his exhausted black gelding, who trembled, its neck and haunches lathered in sweat.

"You have trespassed on Steward lands," said their leader, a Steward with a commanding voice and a jagged scar stark across the brown skin of her left cheek and jaw. She was hardly older than the others, but marked out by the insignia that she wore on her shoulder, like a captain's badge. "You will tell us the interest those dark creatures have in you before we escort you out of our territory."

"A Steward sent me," said Will. He thought of the three Remnants riding back to London, where Violet and Justice were alone and vulnerable. "He's still in danger. You have to help him—Justice."

"What do you know of Justice?" said another voice. A younger Steward in pristine armor was pushing forward, his eyes full of hauteur. "Have you taken him? Have you taken him the way that you took Marcus?"

The young Steward dismounted, and in the next instant was pulling Will off his horse. Wet and sopping, Will slid off and hit the ground. "*Cyprian!*" the Steward captain called, but the young Steward ignored her, grabbing Will and pulling up his sleeves roughly. Will barely realized what he was doing until Cyprian made a stymied sound when only Will's thin wrists were revealed.

"I don't have Simon's *brand*," said Will, revolted.

Cyprian didn't seem to believe that, his hands pushing up over Will's wrists as though searching for the truth. In the next second, he took hold of Will's shirt and ripped it downward. The wet, abused fabric tore open, jerking Will forward. The medallion swung away from his body, exposed. Will let out a cry and clutched at the medallion while his other hand braced in the mud.

When he looked up, he saw Cyprian's immaculate silver armor and his drawn sword.

The Steward captain's expression changed. "Where did you get that?" Her eyes were fixed on the medallion, which dangled on its leather tie.

Justice had warned him not to show it to anyone. Now all these milling Stewards had seen it. He hesitated for a moment, unsure what to do.

"My mother," said Will, remembering the familiar face of her old servant Matthew, holding the medallion out to him in the rain. *The bright star holds, even as the darkness rises.* He pushed himself up to his knees in the mud. "Her old servant gave it to me. Matthew." Matthew's dead eyes staring sightlessly in the rain— "He told me to come here, and to show this to you. He said it belonged to my mother."

His eyes met those of the Steward captain. The look on her face was one of shock, with a flicker of fear. "We must take him to the Elder Steward." Her words echoed Justice's, but she said it as an order to the others.

The other Stewards looked stunned, sharing glances that were openly disturbed. Cyprian gave their feelings voice.

"You can't mean to take him inside the walls," said Cyprian. "Captain, no one not of Steward blood has ever stepped into our Hall."

"Then he will be the first," said the Steward captain.

"And if it's a ruse? What better way to get inside our walls than to play a victim evading capture? Our most sacred oath is to protect—"

"Enough," said the Steward captain. "I have made my decision. What will be done with the boy now is not for you but for the Elder Steward to decide."

Cyprian shut up at that.

"Bind him," said the Steward captain, wheeling her horse. "And take him into the Hall."

CHAPTER NINE

WILL TRIED TO get her to listen. "Justice is still out there." The Remnants galloping behind him, the outstretched gauntlet reaching for him— "There's a girl with him—both of them are in danger—those things that were chasing us—" Black rot spreading across the leaves of a vine— "I saw a vine wither when they touched it—"

"Justice knows his duty" was all the Steward captain said, ignoring him as Cyprian stepped forward. "Tie his wrists, novitiate," said the Steward captain.

Will had to force himself not to jerk back as Cyprian lashed his wrists together in front of him. His horse had no saddle to bind him to. Instead, Cyprian tied his ankles together by a length of rope that passed under his horse's belly, so that if he slid off he would be dragged. Will gripped his horse's mane awkwardly, his lashed wrists making it hard to move his hands. His black gelding was roped to the white horses of the others, and they set off in a procession of twos, six Stewards ahead of him and six behind.

Being restrained made Will's heart pound in his mouth, a fine sweat breaking out over his skin. If they were attacked, he couldn't run. If they were surrounded, he couldn't fight. He clutched his horse's mane with every instinct at screaming alert, the marsh stretching out, a shadowy, alien landscape, the pairs of Stewards like strange glimmers in the dark.

The captain rode ahead, her expression forbidding. *Leda,* the others had called her. The discipline in her bearing reminded him of Justice and was echoed by the others in the procession. But she lacked Justice's warmth, her eyes impassive on the marsh ahead.

Cyprian was too perfect, riding straight-backed in garments that seemed to repel the mud of the marsh. He was one of two Stewards who were younger than the others—Will's age—and he and the girl were dressed differently too. Their surcoats were silvery gray instead of white, and their armor was simpler, like that of a Steward in training. *Novitiate,* the captain had called him.

Will's tension rose as they rode through the night. His mother's old servant Matthew had told him to come here, but what if Matthew had been wrong? What did he really know about these knights who rode white horses and called themselves Stewards? Will wanted to believe that he was riding toward answers, but he felt as if were traveling to a strange, unknown country, leaving everything he knew behind.

As they rode in a long column, Will could hear all the night sounds of the marsh, the rhythmic creak of frogs, the soft, distant splashes of small creatures, and the wind over the grassy water, its gusting sound like the roll of ocean waves. The occasional calls of *"All clear!"* and *"Ride on!"* rang out from the Steward captain at the head of the column.

And then he saw it with a shock, rising out of darkness in the thin moonlight.

"Hold formation and stay close," said the captain, halting for a moment as they crested a grassy slope. "We're taking him across." She urged her horse forward.

The gate, Justice had said.

A broken arch, standing alone on the ruined moor—it was a gate to nowhere, lit by the moon. It stood out starkly against the sky. A few tumbled stones might have formed part of a long-ago wall, but had long since fallen into the water.

Will's skin prickled with the strangest sense of recognition as the line of white-clad Stewards rode toward it through the dark. He felt like he knew it—like he had been here before—but how could he?

"What is this place?" he said.

"This is the Hall of the Stewards," said the captain, but there was no Hall, just a lone arch on the vast, empty marsh. It made him shiver that they were riding toward a Hall that didn't exist, or that had long since crumbled to ruins, with only a single archway left.

Something had stood here once, long ago—

Before he was ready, the captain was driving her horse forward. At the head of the column, she was the first to pass through the arch, and to Will's utter shock, she didn't emerge on the other side. Instead, she vanished.

"What's happening?" Will's heart was pounding at the impossibility of what he had just seen. A pair of Stewards disappeared through the arch, and the column was still moving forward. Will was seized by the dizzy feeling that there was something important through that arch that was just out of his reach. Another pair of Stewards vanished, and Will was certain that he could hear the sound of hooves striking stone, echoing as if from a tunnel or chamber. But how could that be when there wasn't any chamber, just the grass and mud and wide-open sky?

Wait, he wanted to say, but in the next moment, he was riding under the arch himself.

He felt a lurch, and a momentary prick of panic when he didn't come out onto the marsh on the other side—instead he found himself riding under fragments of ancient stone and giant pieces of masonry. Disembodied, they scattered the earth and filled him with awe.

And then he looked up, and caught his breath at what he saw.

An ancient citadel, gleaming with a thousand lights. It was monumental and very old, like the huge pieces of stone around him. Ancient battlements stood high, a second arch over an immense gateway, and behind that soaring towers. Parts of it were a ruin, but that only increased its strange, aching beauty. It was like glimpsing a wonder that had passed from the world and that—once this citadel was gone—would be lost forever.

The feeling that he knew this place swept over him again, though he had never seen it before. *The Hall of the Stewards* . . . The words rang like a bell that made something in him tremble.

"No outsider has ever passed through our gates," he heard a Steward say behind him, jolting him out of his reverie. "I hope the captain knows what she's doing, bringing you here."

He looked back and saw the others riding in single file. Behind them he could still see the marsh on the other side of the arch, covered in grasses. He blinked, the ordinary patch of marsh at odds with the extraordinary sight in front of him.

Is this what Justice meant? An ancient world that was destroyed, except for remnants. . . .

High above the citadel, a giant flame burned like a shining beacon that defied the night. It was set atop the walls, lighting the gates and showing off the splendor of the citadel. And if the walls were old, the flame was new, leaping like young gold. *The bright star holds*, thought Will, and the trembling sensation grew stronger.

"Open the gates!" came the call, and on the walls above, two Stewards on either side of the gate began pulling the chain rope—not with a crank or a lever, but with their own unnatural strength—and the huge portcullis began to rise.

Passing through the gates, Will felt dwarfed by the size and wonder of the place. He saw a vast courtyard of ancient stonework, four enormous columns each broken at the top, reaching up into the empty sky. The great staircase leading to the first of the buildings was intact, stone steps rising from the courtyard to a set of immense doors. It must have been a place of great wonder at its height, and even now it was still beautiful, as the bones of a ruined cathedral are beautiful, conjuring its past in elegant remnants of stone.

And then he became aware of the stares, the shocked reactions as the Stewards on the walls saw him. Whole groups of Stewards in the courtyard stopped and stared. In their old-fashioned white livery, the Stewards suited this ancient place as monks suited a monastery. Will felt like an intrusion in his muddy clothes, an ordinary boy on a black horse. Every eye was on him.

The Steward captain ignored them, dismounting in a smooth motion.

"Cut him down," she said, and Cyprian pulled a knife from his belt and slashed the rope that bound Will's ankles, so that he could be yanked off his horse. This time when Will hit the ground he kept to his feet, though his bound hands unsettled his balance and he stumbled a little.

"Take the horses," the captain told the others, and they dismounted and took up the horses' reins with the deference of squires, leading them away.

Will's horse screamed, showing the whites of his eyes and rearing up out of reach as a Steward tried to take his bridle. He was refusing to leave Will. "Easy. Easy, boy," Will said, his heart feeling tight as the horse that had carried him so bravely now fought to stay with him. "You have to go with her." He felt his horse's warm breath and the velvet brush of its muzzle as it hesitated uncertainly. He wanted to put his arms around its neck and hold it close, but couldn't, his wrists tied. "Go," he said with a pang of loss. He watched the Steward finally lead his horse away, and felt utterly alone.

Pale in the moonlight, the citadel rose before him in giant arches and immense white stone. Looking at it, Will felt as if every great human building was just an echo of this splendid form, trying to re-create something half-remembered, with tools and methods too crude to ever capture its beauty. *Once those walls were fully manned,* he thought. *And the citadel blazed with light.* And then he shivered, not knowing where the thought had come from.

A pair of Stewards were coming toward him; in their white tunics they had the look of monks on their way to speak with the abbot, though Captain Leda in her silver armor looked more like an ancient painting of a celestial knight.

"Captain, we were not informed that a new Steward had been Called—" The Steward who spoke was a man of perhaps twenty-five years, his red hair worn in the Steward style.

"The boy is not a new Steward." The captain spoke brusquely. "He does not have Steward blood. We found him on the marsh, being chased by Simon's men."

"An outsider?" The red-haired Steward's face whitened in shock. "You have brought an outsider through the gate? Captain—"

"Call everyone into the great hall," said the captain, as if he hadn't spoken. "Now, Brescia. Do not tarry."

Brescia, the red-haired Steward, had no choice but to obey. But Will could see the fear and disbelief in his eyes, as around them the shock rippled outward. *"An outsider?"* he heard. *"An outsider in the Hall?"*

It made his skin prickle. He'd wanted answers, but hadn't had the first idea of the enormity of all he might encounter, and he hadn't realized how radical Justice had been in sending him here.

"You will be brought before the Elder Steward," the captain said to Will. "It is she who will decide your fate. I go now to prepare a way for you. Cyprian, hold our prisoner in the north antechamber until I give the signal to bring him into the great hall."

Cyprian's look was challenging. "My father will not like this. You know our rules. Only those of Steward blood are allowed inside our walls."

"I will deal with the High Janissary," said the captain.

Cyprian did not seem pleased by that, but his obedience was immediate. "Yes, Captain."

A grip closed on Will's arm, hard as a tourniquet, as Cyprian took hold of him and propelled him toward the wide steps of the main entry.

To his surprise, Cyprian did not seem to possess the supernatural strength of the other Stewards. He was strong, but it was the normal strength of a young man. Will remembered the captain calling Cyprian *novitiate*. Did that mean the Stewards were not born with their strength, but gained it later?

Three pairs of Stewards accompanied them inside. They walked in perfect unison, precise and graceful. Roped between them, Will felt like a mud lark flanked by pairs of white swans. With his hands tied behind his back and still weak from the ship and two days without food, he wasn't a threat, but the Stewards had spears drawn as if he were dangerous. He suddenly felt that he had stepped into a world that was much bigger than he was, full of practices that he didn't understand.

They brought him into an antechamber with a high arched ceiling.

The Stewards took up positions, two at each of the chamber's two doors, while the other two stayed close to him with Cyprian.

"The great hall is ahead," Cyprian said. "We wait here until Leda gives the signal."

But as time dragged on, the tight knot of Will's concern wasn't just for what lay ahead; it was for Justice and Violet, who were still out there somewhere with those men in their strange pieces of armor and their dozens of dark hounds. By now the Remnants would be all the way back to London, and Justice and Violet might be anywhere.

"What about my friends?"

It was the wrong thing to ask. Cyprian stared back at him with the hauteur of a young knight. His olive skin and dark hair were paired with high cheekbones and green eyes. He had the kind of Mediterranean looks that might have come from anywhere from Egypt to Sicily, and a Steward's nobility, combined with an almost too-perfect posture and livery.

But his green eyes had turned utterly cold.

"Your *friend* Justice is the reason my brother is missing."

"Your brother?" said Will.

"Marcus," said Cyprian.

Marcus? Will's eyes widened in recognition of the name, but before he could ask about it, the call came from the far end of the antechamber, summoning him at long last into the great hall.

Huge double doors opened on a hall of columns that seemed to stretch forever. Dressed in white and silver, pairs of ceremonial Stewards guarded the doors, their armor polished to a gleaming shine. Entering at spear point, Will looked up and caught his breath at the scale of it, conjuring up structures he had seen only in paintings or book engravings. Like the

Great Pyramid at Giza, it was an ancient place so monumental it had out-
lasted the civilization that had built it.

He felt very small as he was brought forward, his footsteps echoing,
the magnitude of the hall overwhelming him. The ceremonial Stewards
arrayed in their dress armor seemed too few, filling only a tiny portion of
the space. Awe slowed his steps as he approached the center.

Rising from the dais at the end of the hall, there were four towering
thrones of pure white marble. Beautiful and old, they seemed to glow in
the reflected light. They were made for figures greater than any human
king or queen, in command of ancient armies and grand, forgotten courts.
Will could almost see the majestic figures moving back and forth, bringing their business before their rulers in this hall.

But the thrones were empty.

Below them, on a small wooden stool, sat an old woman with long
white hair. She was the oldest person in the great hall, her olive skin
wrinkled as a nectarine stone, her eyes filmy with age. Her clothing was a
simple white tunic, her white hair tied back in the Steward style. A man
who Captain Leda addressed as High Janissary stood beside her, dressed
in blue, not white, a heavy silver seal visible around his neck. He was
flanked by two dozen Stewards in silver armor with worked star detail-
ing, bearing short capes over white surcoats.

And a muddied figure was kneeling in front of them.

Will's heart leaped. It was Justice, his livery stained, his forearm
resting on his bent knee, his head bowed. And Violet—Violet was with
him, held between two Stewards, with her hands tied in front of her.
She was splashed with mud up to the waist; likely their journey over the
marsh had been on foot.

He was so relieved to see her—to see both of them—that he almost
forgot what was happening around him, but the prick of a spear driving

him forward brought him sharply to attention.

"This is the boy you sent to us," the High Janissary said to Justice. "Violating our every rule and selfishly endangering our Hall."

"He's more than just a boy," said Justice. "There's a reason Simon wants him."

"So you claim," said the High Janissary.

Will's stomach flipped. He felt like he was on trial, but he didn't know why or what for. He could feel the attention of every Steward on him as the four empty thrones stared down at him like empty eye sockets.

"So I saw," said Justice. "He sheathed the Corrupted Blade. He called it to his hand and put out the black flame."

"That isn't possible," said the High Janissary as the Stewards broke out into a ripple of comment. "Nothing can survive once the Blade is drawn."

Will shivered, because those words felt true. A single sliver of the Blade peeking from its sheath had been enough to destroy Simon's ship. Will remembered the instinct he'd had to re-sheathe it, knowing somehow that if it got free, it would kill everyone on board.

"Simon had the boy chained and under heavy guard," said Justice. "When I saw him take up the Blade, I guessed at why. But I didn't know for certain until I saw what he wore around his neck."

"Around his neck?" said the High Janissary.

Justice looked up. "Will. Show them."

Slowly, Will opened his torn shirt and drew out the medallion.

He didn't understand its importance; he only knew that giving it to him had been the last thing his mother's old servant Matthew had done. Will held it out, no more than a dull, warped piece of metal, once shaped like a five-petaled flower.

Not everyone in the Hall seemed to recognize it, but the High Janissary's face whitened. "The hawthorn flower," said the High Janissary.

"The Lady's medallion." At that, there were shocked cries from the Stewards lining the Hall.

"Marcus always believed the boy survived," said Justice.

"Anyone can put on a necklace," said the High Janissary.

Before anyone else could speak, Leda knelt swiftly at the dais, her head bowed and her right hand held as a fist over her heart. She mirrored Justice's posture, and she seemed to add her voice to his.

"High Janissary. Simon's Remnants were riding with two dozen hounds over the marsh, chasing the boy into our territory. Simon wanted him enough to risk sending the Remnants deep into Steward lands." She drew in a breath. "This may be the boy we've been searching for." There were gasps at that.

"Simon would like nothing more than to infiltrate our Hall," said the High Janissary, his mouth thinned. "That is the way of the Dark, is it not? They worm their way in, taking the guise of a friend. Simon probably gave this boy the medallion and told him to show it to us."

Justice was shaking his head. "There have been rumors that Simon had resumed his search, believing the boy was alive—"

"Rumors planted by Simon. This boy you have plucked from the docks is a spy, or worse. And you have let him inside our walls—"

"Come here, my boy."

The old woman on the stool spoke to him in a kind, conversational voice. Her eyes were on him, her face framed by her long white hair. Will stepped forward hesitantly, aware of the others falling silent as she indicated for him to take a seat on a small three-legged stool alongside her.

Up close, he could feel her presence, which seemed warm, steadfast, and wise. She spoke as if the hall had disappeared and they were sitting comfortably together in front of a small hearth fire. "What's your name?"

"Will," he said. "Will Kempen."

He felt a reaction from the Stewards behind him, but the only reaction that seemed to matter was from the old woman.

"Eleanor Kempen's son," she said.

All the hairs rose on his body. "You knew my mother?" And suddenly he remembered being in the White Hart with Justice and Violet and feeling *seen*. His heart was beating rapidly.

"I knew her. She was brave. I think she would have fought until the end." And Will, who had been there at the end, felt a tremor begin deep in his body that he had to clamp down hard to still.

"You have a powerful advocate in Justice," the old woman said. "He is the strongest of us, and he does not often make requests of the Hall."

The old woman was looking at Will as though she was seeing more than his face, and Will remembered Justice speaking of a Steward who could help them, a Steward who held all their ancient wisdom, and he realized—

"You're the Elder Steward," Will said.

"You're safe here, Will," she said. "We are Stewards. Our sacred duty is to stand against the Dark."

"Safe," said Will. *None of us are safe.* He remembered Justice saying those words.

The Elder Steward's snow-white hair matched her white garment and the giant white marble columns that rose to the vaulted ceiling. When she gestured to the great hall around her, she looked like she belonged in it.

"This is the Hall of the Stewards. Once it was the Hall of Kings. It has had other names too. The Undying Star, it was called once, and its beacon the Final Flame. Long ago it was the last stronghold in the battle against the Dark King." Her voice conjured up ancient vistas as she spoke. "Now its glories are faded, and its sun has almost set. Yet it holds, as we guard the long twilight against the oncoming dark. Simon may have greater strength outside, but no one can challenge us inside these walls."

Will remembered the Stewards driving back the darkness as they galloped in a line of white across the marsh. They had been assured in their power on their own lands, the Remnants cowering before them.

Justice had told him about this place. *The lights of the world went out one by one, until there was only one light left, the Final Flame. There, those on the side of Light made their last stand.* A light that had stood against the dark, at the very end of the world.

This was it, Will realized with an awed shiver as he looked around at the giant ancient columns and the four empty thrones. Still standing centuries later, when its people were dust and silence, and its stories were forgotten.

But if this was the last stronghold, that meant all that Justice had said was true, and he was standing in a hall that had seen the final battle. *The one place the Dark King couldn't conquer.* That thought flickered through him.

"It feels familiar to you, doesn't it," said the Elder Steward. "As if you've been here before."

"How did you know that?"

"New Stewards feel like that sometimes too," she said. "But Stewards are not the only ones who have walked these halls."

Will felt again the overwhelming sense that he was surrounded by the ghost of a place he knew but that no longer existed, as if he looked upon the bones of a great ancient beast that would never roam this world again.

"Why do I recognize it?" he said, the crowding of his mind with half memory almost painful. "The Lady with the medallion—who is she? It has something to do with my mother, doesn't it? Why was Simon chasing us—chasing me?"

The Elder Steward's eyes were on him. "Your mother never told you?"

His heart was pounding, as though he were back at Bowhill with his mother's eyes staring at him. *Will, promise.*

"She told me we left London because she was tired of it. Each time we left a place she said it was just time to move on. She never told me about magic or a Lady."

"Then you don't know what you are."

The Elder Steward was looking at him with such a searching gaze that he felt as if she could see into him. As if she could see everything. As if she could see Bowhill, his stumbling run through the mud, the accident on the docks in London, Matthew giving him the medallion, and the moment on the ship when he had reached for the Corrupted Blade.

When he had entered the great hall, Will had felt as if he was on trial. Now it was as though his very self was being weighed by the Elder Steward, and he was suddenly desperate not to be found wanting.

Please, he thought, not even certain what he was pleading for, only knowing that her approval was important to him.

Finally, the Elder Steward sat back on her stool.

"We have not taken in an outsider since magic first warded the Hall," said the Elder Steward, seeming to make a decision. "But I offer you sanctuary here if you wish to take it. If you stay with us, you will find the answers you seek . . . though you will have much to learn, and you may come to wish you had never sought the truth. Dark times lie ahead." And then, after another long look, her eyes warmed. "But even in the darkest night, there is a star."

Will looked at the grandeur of the Hall around him, with its honor guard of snowy Stewards. Outside, Simon waited, the relentless chase, the howling dark, no person to be trusted, no hiding place safe. He looked up at Violet, who was standing tense and nervous, with her hands still bound. And he drew in a breath.

"My friend too?" said Will.

"Your friend too," said the Elder Steward, with a half smile.

"Elder Steward, you cannot believe that this boy may be—that he is—" The High Janissary had stepped forward in protest, but the Elder Steward held up a hand and stopped him.

"Whatever he is, he is just a boy. The rest can wait until he's rested."

"This is a mistake," said the High Janissary.

"Kindness is never a mistake," said the Elder Steward. "Somewhere in the heart it is always remembered."

Violet scrambled up as Will approached, and he found himself looking at her and Justice, their familiar faces in this unfamiliar place.

"I'm glad you made it," said Violet.

"You too," said Will.

"Justice almost sprained something trying to get to the Hall after you."

In all the time Will had been running, there had never been anyone who cared if he made it. He looked at Violet's boyish face, her young man's clothes, and the new tense way she held herself.

There was so much he wanted to ask her, about her own escape with Justice and how it was to be here so far away from her family. But he couldn't do that with Justice himself standing beside her. She seemed to understand that, glancing briefly at Justice and then back at Will, and nodding slightly. Will turned his own gaze to Justice, to whom he owed so much.

"Thank you," said Will, "for arguing for me."

"I told you that you would find welcome here," said Justice, with a small smile. "The Elder Steward has asked the janissaries to escort you to your rooms."

"Rooms?"

"I think you are tired," said Justice, "and still bruised from your capture, and you have gone a long time without rest. Let us offer you the
protections of the Hall." He gestured.

Two girls wearing robes of the same blue as the High Janissary's were
waiting. Like the Stewards, they had a noble, otherworldly look. One
was pale and freckled with hair the color of a dry wheat husk. Her name
was Sarah. The other girl was taller, and her skin was a darker brown
than Leda's. She had the sort of profile that looked sculpted, and wore a
blue pendant around her neck. It was she who spoke.

"I am Grace," she said. "I am a janissary to the Elder Steward. She has
ordered rooms prepared for both of you."

Will looked back at Violet. Both of them were covered in mud, and
he realized Justice was right: they were both exhausted. When Violet
nodded, he also gave his assent.

Grace took them up steps worn from centuries of footsteps, a slow,
spiraling journey upward through a section that felt oddly uninhabited. He
saw only glimpses of strange courtyards, corridors, and chambers, many of
them fallen to ruin. Around him, the faded beauty of the Hall was like the
long red of sunset, before the last of the light goes out of the world.

Grace had an assurance of belonging as she escorted them up. Notic-
ing that the wall was curved, Will wondered if they were now inside
one of the towers he had seen when they rode through the gate. He felt
again that sense of entering a world that was bigger than he had imagined. Grace stopped at a landing, in front of a door.

"They say that in ancient times guests used to stay in this part of the
Hall," Grace said. "But Stewards do not take in outsiders, and this wing
was left empty. The Elder Steward asked for it to be opened up again.
This will be your room." She nodded to Violet as her counterpart stepped

forward with a bristle of iron keys on a chain, producing one to fit into the lock.

Violet hesitated on the threshold, turning back to look at Will. He imagined that she'd be looking forward to sloughing off the mud of her trek over the marsh, even as the prospect of staying the night with the Stewards felt momentous. Instead, she was delaying. "Is Will's room nearby?"

"Right alongside yours," said Grace.

"All right, then," Violet said, drawing in a breath and giving a thank-you nod.

Will said, "Until morning." And with a last look back at him, she disappeared into her room.

Will turned back to Grace, who gestured to the other janissary to proceed up the stairs. The three of them moved on, around the curving wall.

"And this room is yours," Grace said.

They had come to an oak door silvered with age that swung open with the key. "The Elder Steward bids you to rest and recover," said Grace, and with that the two janissaries left him to step into his new room alone.

It couldn't have been more different from his overcrowded lodgings in London, where boys slept on the floor with barely space to stretch out in. Despite the Elder Steward's kind words, Will had half expected a prison cell, or a wintry, abandoned ruin. He walked in disbelieving as the door closed behind him.

Above his head, the stone ceiling arched in ribbed vaulting, each panel colored with faded blues and silvers as though it had once been painted. The arches met at a carved stone star. There were large windows that looked out on the walls, and a huge stone fireplace with a high mantel.

Someone had lit the fire and left a lamp glowing on the small table beside an old-fashioned bed. The bed looked soft and warm, and there was a sleeping shirt for him to change into. A flannel, a basin, and a silver ewer of warm water were laid out by the fire for him to wash if he wished, and when he went to pick up the lamp, he saw that there was a small stool on which lay a plate of supper: fresh brown bread, soft white cheese, and a tumble of ripe grapes.

His mother must have yearned for a place like this, where she would be safe from the men who were chasing her. Where the Stewards were there to drive the dark back. *She's the one who should be here.* But she had never made it inside these walls. She had chosen to take him and run instead, until she couldn't run anymore. He lifted his hand to the medallion that he wore around his neck.

A glimmer from the window caught his eye.

Walking over to it, he saw again the gleam of that giant flame on the far-off walls, shining like a light in the window, promising home. It was the beacon, tended by Stewards even through the night. *The Final Flame,* the Elder Steward had called it. Kept lit for centuries, it had burned to the last, when it was the only light left.

For a moment he could almost see it, the armies of the Dark converging on the Hall and the single light on its walls, shining, defiant.

Will stood looking out at it for a long time.

Later, when he had washed, put on the sleeping shirt, and eaten the small repast down to the crumbs, he lay in bed with the Lady's medallion skin-warm against his chest. After a while, his thoughts became a dream in which he walked these halls long ago, with the Lady beside him. She turned to him with his mother's eyes, but her face warped and changed.

And where the Hall had been, he saw nothing but a great darkness, and above it rose a pale crown and burning eyes of black flame. They drew closer and closer, and he couldn't run. No one could run. The black flame rose to consume him, and then to consume everything.

Gasping, Will woke and lay staring up at the carved stone star, and it was a long time before he managed to go back to sleep again.

CHAPTER TEN

VIOLET WOKE TO the sound of bells and a drifting morning chant. The chant was melodious, a monastic choral weaving in and out of her sleep. But something about it didn't make sense. The language was unfamiliar. It wasn't Latin. It sounded older. And why could she hear monks instead of the shouts and calls of London traffic? Then in a rush it all came back to her.

Tom can't come into his true power without killing another like him. Her father's cold, matter-of-fact voice, and her decision to trek at night across marshes with the Steward called Justice, who hated Lions and had tried to kill her brother.

She was inside the Hall of the Stewards.

Pushing up in bed, she saw a strange, high-ceilinged stone room, with a carved mantel fireplace and arched windows set deep into the stone. The occasional calls she could hear were from outside, where Stewards patrolled the walls. The chants drifting in the windows were Stewards in some morning ritual.

She was surrounded by Stewards, and every single one of them wanted to kill her.

In London, the kitchen would be preparing breakfast: hot porridge, bacon, eggs, or buttery fish. Her father would be the first down to the table. And Tom—

Did Tom know she was missing? And then, more frightening: Did Tom *know*? Did he know why her father had brought her to England— what he had planned to do?

"Don't be afraid," Justice had said to her last night, misinterpreting her expression as she had stared up stunned at the lights of the Hall. "No creature of Simon's has ever set foot inside our walls." She had instinctive- ly put her hand on her wrist, remembering her longing for Simon's brand only that morning. *No creature of Simon's . . .*

Escorted in past walls ablaze with flaming torches, she had found the Hall already buzzing with an outsider's arrival—Will's. They had reacted in shock to Violet too—the second interloper. Overwhelmed, she had been only dimly aware of High Janissary Jannick, demanding, "What of the others?"

Justice had dropped to one knee, head bowed, right hand a fist over his heart in a formal, old-fashioned pose.

"There was a Lion," Justice had said. "The others are dead."

They hate Lions. She had seen the High Janissary's look of detestation at the word. And the cold, chilling thought in this strange place: *What would they do to me if they knew I was one?*

She pushed out of bed. Her small room didn't have the grandeur of the great hall, but the strange, faded beauty of the place was more visible than it had been last night: the remnants of frescoes; long ribs of the curved ceiling; the archway leading to the balcony.

From outside, she could hear rhythmic calls and disciplined responses of a large group moving through military exercises in perfect unison.

And then she saw something that made her stop, her heart speeding up.

A Steward's uniform was lying out on the chest at the end of her bed.

Not the surcoat and chain mail that Justice wore, but a silvery-gray tunic
with a similar cut, and the star blazon on the chest, along with wool
leggings and soft boots—the clothing that the Stewards wore when not
armored for battle.

It had been laid out here for her, like the bed shirt she had put on last
night. She looked over at her own clothes, a dank pile of dried mud by
the fireplace. She couldn't wrestle back into them and didn't particularly
want to. But—

She picked up the tunic. It was clean and light to the touch, made
of some fabric she'd never encountered before, with embroidery around
the star blazon. She could see the tiny, exquisite stitching, and when she
pulled it on over her head, she found it fit her perfectly. Cinching her belt
and pulling on the leggings and the boots, she was aware of an ease of
movement that even trousers and a jacket didn't offer. It felt like putting
on clothing made just for her.

Turning to the wall mirror, she was shocked by the transformation,
the clothes giving her that same androgynous appearance of a medieval
knight that the Stewards possessed. She was suddenly a fighter of the
ancient world, proud and powerful. *I look like one of them.* She could almost
hear the battle horn, feel the sword in her hand.

If her father saw her in these clothes—if Tom saw her—

"It suits you," said a voice behind her, and she jerked around.

Will spoke as he swung onto her balcony, dropping soundlessly down
from the railing. He was wearing an identical copy of the Steward livery.
The clothes had the same androgenizing effect on him that they had on
her, highlighting his striking bone structure, though his dark eyes were
too intense for him to look pretty.

"I don't usually wear skirts," said Violet, with a tug at the tunic,
which was skirted below the belt to mid-thigh.

"Me neither," said Will, echoing her gesture. Tentatively, they were smiling at each other. The silver tunic suited him too, she thought. She didn't tell him that. She didn't tell him how glad she was to see him. She remembered him lying for her at the White Hart, taking her side against Justice though she barely knew him.

"Thank you," she said. "For telling Justice that I was"—she felt strangely shy to say it—"your friend." She drew in a breath. "If they find out Tom's my brother, I don't know what they'll do."

Will looked so different in the Steward clothes. They transformed him from the bruised, bloodied wastrel in Simon's hold to a young man whose looks suited this strange, ancient place. It reminded her that he was a stranger, who had called a sword to his hand.

She didn't know him. She still felt wary. But he hadn't turned her in to the Stewards. He had lied for her when he didn't have to.

"So you're really—like Tom?" said Will quietly. "A Lion?"

She said, "I don't know. I've always been—"

Strong.

As children, she and Tom had done everything together. She even shared Tom's cast-off boy's clothing, a habit that Tom's mother had disliked, but her father had thought of fondly.

Or so she'd thought.

Tom can't come into his true power without killing another like him.

"I never heard the word *Lion* until yesterday. But you heard my father. He thinks one Lion has to kill another. That's why he—" *Why he brought me here from India. Why he raised me. Why he kept me in the house even though Tom's mother hated me—*

The full truth of it hit her, breathing sharply difficult. Her family planned to kill her, to sacrifice her for Tom to gain power, and she couldn't ever go back to them.

She remembered when her father had sat by her bed for five days and nights when she'd gotten sick, telling the physician, *Whatever it costs. I need her to recover.* She thought of all the times he'd stood up for her to Tom's mother, all the times he'd reassured her, told her she was special—

He'd brought her home to kill her. He'd kept her there to kill her. His caring, his concern, none of it had been real.

"The Stewards won't find out," said Will. "I won't tell them."

Shaken by her thoughts, she looked over at him. He said it with the same calm certainty he'd had on the docks, as if when he made a promise, he kept it. She might not know him, but they were alone in this place, the two of them. She drew in a steadying breath.

"You were right," said Violet. "The Remnants—those three men on horseback—galloped right past us. They only wanted you. Justice and I waited until they were gone, then crossed the river on foot."

Step where I step, Justice had said, picking a careful path across the marsh. Any time she hadn't followed his footsteps exactly, she had found herself up to the waist in mud, scowling at Justice's outstretched hand ready to haul her back up. In the distance, they had heard the eerie baying of the hounds, and once they had glimpsed the Remnants in their ancient armor on the horizon, galloping over the bridge. "We saw them riding west back to Simon." Streaming across the land with hounds. She had been surprised at the sharpness of her own relief that Will wasn't with them.

"To tell him where I am," said Will.

It was darkly shocking. Violet shivered at the thought of Simon turning his attention to the Hall. She had a vision of those black hounds swarming across the Lea, baying as they surrounded that lonely, broken arch on the marsh.

"Why does Simon want you so badly?"

Her words hung in the air. It was something she had wanted to know since she had stumbled upon him in the hold of the *Sealgair*. Why would Simon capture a dock laborer, have him beaten and chained up? Will looked different now that he was bathed and out of his ragged London clothes, but he was still just a boy.

"I don't know. But you heard the Elder Steward. It has something to do with my mother." Will looked at the palm of his right hand, which was crossed over with a long white scar. He rubbed a thumb along it, as if unconsciously.

It was more than his mother. It was something to do with *him*. With what he was. The Stewards had reacted to him with a mixture of awe and fear. Justice had been the same, going to his knees in front of Will the instant he had seen Will's medallion. Different forces were converging on him, closing on him like a vise.

Before she could ask him about it, Will moved to the window and said, "Have you noticed? You can't see London from the windows."

"What do you mean?"

"You can't see London. You can just see the marsh, disappearing into a kind of mist. It's as if this place is hidden away inside a bubble."

That didn't make sense. Distracted, she came to stand beside him. And every hair on her arms stood on end at the sight.

There was no sign of London, and the purple marshes faded to a distant blur. She remembered standing on those empty marshes, the arresting ruined arch against the sky. The Hall of the Stewards hadn't appeared until she had ridden through that arch. Before that it had been invisible. The utter strangeness of that moment struck her anew. She hadn't thought about what it would look like from the inside. It really was as if they were in a bubble; a pocket; a hidden fold in the world.

"Does that mean that the gate is the only way in and out?" said Violet, tension in her voice. It made that lonely arch on the marsh seem even stranger. And made her feel trapped. "What happens if you tried to get out another way? If you climbed one of the walls and kept walking?"

"Your path would bring you back to the wall," said Justice, from the doorway.

Violet jolted, turning. Her heart raced at the idea of what he might have heard her say. *Tom . . . Lions . . . her family . . .*

"Good morning," said Justice.

He was a tall, arresting figure in the doorway. His long black hair was half pulled back from his face in a tight bun, the other half falling down his back. His white Steward surcoat gleamed.

The sight of him made her every nerve come screaming to alert. Where his old-fashioned livery had been incongruous in London, here he fit, part of the otherworldly nature of this place. But he was still a threat. He had attacked her brother; he had attacked Simon's ship. Her heart was thundering.

He brought me here because he didn't know what I was. If he knew—

"Why is there only one way in or out?" An edge to Violet's voice.

"The gate protects us," said Justice. "Ancient wards hide this place from the outside world, so that a stranger on the marsh can walk around the gate and even pass through it, and never find the Hall. But you may come and go freely."

"So—we can leave any time we want?" said Violet.

"You are our guests," said Justice. "You may leave if you wish, to return to London, or simply to ride on the marsh. . . . But if you come back, you will need a Steward to escort you through the gate, as it will only open for one of Steward blood."

Return to London. A sharp stab, pain and danger. She couldn't go back to her family, not to visit, not ever. She forced herself not to show what she was feeling on her face, not with Justice standing before her, gazing at her with his warm brown eyes.

It was Will who stepped forward. "Neither of us have business in London." He didn't look at Violet but kept his voice steady. "For now, we'd like to stay."

Relief, even as the tension of maintaining the lie stretched out in front of her. When Justice turned back to the door, she and Will quickly met each other's eyes, and she felt the renewed reassurance of his presence on her side.

"We live lives of simplicity and order, but I think there are some benefits to life in the Hall." Justice gestured for them to follow him. "The Elder Steward wishes to see Will but is not quite ready. While you wait, I can show you something of the Hall. Come."

Violet hesitated. Was it safe? The feeling of being on enemy territory was sharp. But she was curious too. She followed Justice out into the corridor.

A fortress the size of an ancient city greeted her. Violet caught her breath at the scale of the place that stretched out around her; she had never seen or imagined anything like it. Huge stone carvings made them tiny as they descended wide-set stairs that looked out onto views of interior courtyards. She caught glimpses of abundant gardens where blossoms rioted, while berries and apples and peaches fruited all together out of season. The length of one hallway had a ceiling covered with interweaving coats of arms. It was beautiful, like a forest canopy. Another was crowned with stars carved into the stone where the apex of arches met.

"We call it the Hall, but it is really an entire citadel," said Justice. "Much of it has fallen into disrepair. The western wing is off-limits, and parts of the north are closed as well. There are whole sections and rooms where Stewards have not walked for centuries."

In the distance, she could see the high outer wall, where pairs of white-clad Stewards patrolled, while three young men dressed in blue passed them. The simplicity and order that Justice had spoken of was all around them. Everyone here had a purpose, moving amid the beauty and tranquility of the Hall as though they belonged to it.

"This is the eastern wing of the Hall, where we live and train. Stewards rise at dawn and eat after the morning chant. You have missed the morning meal, but the janissaries have set aside some food for you both."

They entered a room with a large wooden table, where she could glimpse what looked like kitchens. She hadn't expected anything as simple as breakfast, but the moment that she saw the baskets and linen-covered foods on the table, she was suddenly ravenous.

"Janissaries?" she said, sitting down opposite one of the linen parcels and beginning to unwrap it. She breathed in the smell of fresh-baked bread.

"The life of a Steward is strict. We seek perfect discipline, train continuously, and take vows of self-sacrifice and celibacy." Justice sat opposite her but did not eat; if what he had said was true, he had broken his fast hours ago, at dawn. "Not everyone with Steward blood wishes to become a Steward. Nor are all those who wish to become a Steward capable. Those who lack the desire or who fail the tests become honored janissaries, not Stewards. They wear the blue, while Stewards take the white."

"Like Grace, and the young men we saw . . . ," said Violet. She remembered Grace showing her to her room, and the three figures they had just passed in the halls. The janissaries had looked as otherworldly and ethereal as Stewards, but they had dressed in blue, not white, and they had not carried swords. Her own tunic was a silvery gray, like those of the novitiates. *Gray, blue, and white*, she thought. *Novitiates, janissaries, and*

Stewards. "Janissaries made this for us?"

Justice nodded. "Janissaries keep the knowledge of the Hall; they are scholars and artisans. They tend to the libraries, the artifacts, the gardens. . . . It's janissaries who craft our weapons, write our histories, and even weave our clothes."

Violet looked down at the tunic she wore. The light silvery-gray fabric seemed like it had been woven by magic, not by human hands. The artistry of the janissaries was beyond anything she had ever seen.

And when she took her first bite of the breakfast, it had the same quality. It was simple fare, but more sustaining than any food she had ever tasted. The freshest bread, wrapped in a linen cloth and still steaming. Bright yellow butter newly churned, and the sweetest honey. There were six red apples in a bowl, and when she tasted one, it was more freshly rejuvenating than the cool, crisp taste of water in a forest stream on a hot day.

"It's as if I always thought food should taste like this, but it never did," said Will.

"Some of the magic of the old world still lingers here," said Justice. "You can feel it in the food we harvest, the water, even in the air."

It was true. Violet felt refreshed after only a few bites of the warm bread, and the honey melted on her tongue. Was this what the ancient world had been like? The colors brighter, the air cleaner, the food more delicious?

She thought about her family again, eating their breakfast in London. Did they know about this place? They knew what Stewards were. Tom had recognized them on the ship. And Simon . . . Simon knew about the Hall. His Remnants had chased Will here, until the Stewards had driven them off. But did they know about its magic, its bright-tasting food, the quality of the air?

She felt the pang of wanting to share all of this with Tom but knowing that she couldn't, and fearing that he had known it all along and kept it from her.

What else hadn't he told her? What else didn't she know? As Justice took them out into a series of gardens, Violet saw Stewards and janissaries working side by side tending the plants and the soil, sharing the menial tasks of the Hall. She realized that she was seeing traditions that had been carried out in just this way for hundreds of years. An entire world hidden away, that no one on the outside would ever see.

Especially not a Lion.

Justice pointed out the armory and then the stables and told Will that later he might visit his horse. But Violet barely heard him, overwhelmed by the realization that she and Will were the first to witness any of it, to breathe the air, to taste the food. . . . Stewards had lived and died here over centuries, following their rules, keeping traditions alive when no one else knew they were here.

"Why do you do all of this? Why not live a normal life outside the walls?"

Justice smiled—not an unkind smile, but a smile of acknowledgment, as if she had asked him the most important question.

"Look up," said Justice.

High above them on the battlements burned a brilliant beacon, its flames reaching impossibly high into the sky. She had seen it blazing in the dark last night, when she had passed through the gate with Justice.

The Final Flame.

"Magic sustains it," said Justice. "Magic from before our time. From a distance, it looks like a bright star burning in the sky. The symbol of the Stewards."

Looking up at it, she imagined she could feel the heat of its flame. As she did, Justice came to stand beside her.

"The Flame is our purpose," said Justice. "When the Dark King swore to return, we swore to prevent it, no matter how long our Order had to stand at the ready. We have kept that vow for centuries, holding the knowledge of the old world, quashing his Dark objects where we find them, and preparing for the day when we would fight. In that way, we keep the Flame alight."

As she looked at the Flame, she imagined the Stewards of the old world swearing that vow. Had they known what it would mean for their descendants? That they would live apart from the world for centuries, waiting for a day that might never come? Generations of Stewards, rising each morning to their mission, holding to their traditions, living and dying while the Dark King lay silent?

"Outside, the world sleeps like an innocent who is not afraid of the dark," said Justice. "But in here we remember. What has come before will come again. And when it does, the Stewards will be ready."

Like a single flame burning, they had carried light of knowledge across the centuries. *The Undying Star*, the Elder Steward had called it. *The Final Flame*. But the spark of light that the Stewards had tended all these years was even more fragile than she had thought.

If the Stewards had ever faltered, ever allowed themselves to drift from their mission, the past would have faded out of memory, and the Dark King could have returned to an unknowing world.

No one would have seen him coming. No one would have known how to stop him.

The past would have risen to overwhelm the present, and all the battles fought, all the lives given to defeat the Dark King, would be as nothing. He would rise again, and all he had to do was wait, until the world forgot him.

That thought stayed with her.

"Now come," said Justice. "I will show you the heart of the Hall."

They entered the great hall through its giant doors. What had been a vast, torchlit cavern by night was by day transformed into a cathedral of light. Sunlight streamed in from high windows, creating huge beams of light that reflected off the many white columns, like a dazzling forest of white trees rising high and bright.

Violet saw the four empty thrones high on the dais. Now that she had a sense of the history of this place, she wondered for the first time about the figures who had once sat there. *The Hall of Kings*, the Elder Steward had called it.

"What happened here?" Violet said, looking around at the magnificent structures of stone. "How did this place survive when everything else was lost?"

Justice followed her gaze up to the empty thrones. Each one was different, and carved with a unique symbol. A tower; a faded sun; a winged serpent; and a flower she had never seen before.

"Long ago, there were four great kings of the old world," said Justice. "The Hall was their meeting place, a nexus of sorts. But as the Dark King rose, the four kings faltered. Three made a bargain with the Dark King and were corrupted, and the fourth fled, his line lost to time. It was the Stewards of the four kings who stood against the dark in their stead, part of the great alliance who joined the final fight."

"The Hall of Kings became the Hall of the Stewards," said Violet.

Justice nodded. "The Stewards swore when the battle was done that they would keep guard against the Dark King's return. Humans were growing in number, and the last remaining magical creatures of

that world spent what was left of their power to hide the Hall, shroud-
ing it in wards and magic. Now we Stewards serve in secret, and those
who have the Blood of Stewards are Called from across the world to
join our fight."

It explained why many Stewards seemed as if they were from other
countries, if they had come here from across the world as their kings had
once done. Violet had heard different languages spoken in the Hall, particularly when the Stewards had gathered in knots to discuss her arrival
with Justice. She remembered that she had also heard Stewards with different accents, like the French Steward on the ship.

"It's said that in our darkest hour, the Stewards will Call for the
King, and the line of Kings will answer." Justice smiled a little ruefully,
as if even to him this was just a story. "But for now, we stand because we
are the only ones left. And we hold to our vows—to guard against the
Dark, to watch for signs, and to remember the past—as Stewards have
done for centuries."

She couldn't help wondering what had happened to those ancient
kings. They had left the fight to the Stewards, who had taken it up loyal-
ly, holding to their duty for far longer than anyone might have imagined.
What had made the kings turn from the fight?

Around her, the Hall took on a new importance, and as they walked
through its forest of marble columns, she thought about the kings and
queens who had lived in here, glimmering, majestic beings who surpassed
humanity in power and beauty.

Then she turned and saw a face.

It was floating midway up the wall and staring at her. She let out a
sound and stepped back.

A second later, she saw that it was only an etching. Tarnished and
faded, the face of a lion was staring back at her with liquid brown eyes.

It was carved onto the old, broken piece of a shield that hung on the wall like a trophy.

"What is that?" she said.

"The Shield of Rassalon," said Justice.

The Shield of Rassalon. That name echoed in her, stirring something deep. The lion seemed to look right at her. She reached out to the stone beneath the shield, where strange writing was carved into the wall. Time had half eroded its words.

Violet's fingers brushed the words, tracing the cool stone, her heart pounding. "What does it say?"

"We Stewards have lost most of our knowledge of the old language," said Justice, "but I'm told it says, '*Rassalon the First Lion.*'"

Violet jerked her fingers back as if singed. She was staring at the lion with its great mane and liquid eyes, her pulse racing.

The First Lion . . .

"The Stewards have few artifacts of the old war," said Justice, "but this is one of them. Here the Shield of Rassalon was broken."

She couldn't help staring at the lion on the shield, her mind racing with a thousand questions.

Who was Rassalon? Why had the Stewards fought him? How had he come to fight for the Dark King? *This shield . . . what is it? What am I caught up in?*

The lion seemed to gaze back at her. She imagined Stewards with spears encircling an animal that bled where it was pierced in the side.

Stewards had been fighting Lions since the great battles of the old world.

"Excuse my interruption, Justice." A girl's voice jolted Violet out of her reverie. She recognized Grace, the janissary who had shown her to her room the night before. "The Elder Steward is ready to see Will."

CHAPTER ELEVEN

HEART POUNDING, WILL followed Grace down a long corridor, deep into the Hall.

The architecture changed around them, the archways lower and narrower, the shapes of the carvings different, the walls thicker. A stillness hung over everything, as if no one ever came to this part of the Hall.

They reached double doors set at the end of a passageway. Will stopped, aversion keeping him back. He felt as if he was about to enter a tomb, a place that should not be disturbed. *I don't want to go in there.* But Grace pushed the doors open.

The room was circular with a domed ceiling, the gray stone old as the immovable rock of a mountain. In the center was a stone tree, carved to reach the ceiling.

The tree was dead, desiccated and blackened, as if a living tree had ossified centuries ago.

Will shivered with a shock of terrible familiarity; he knew this place, but somehow all he knew was gone, replaced by the strange, desolate presence of the dead stone.

The Elder Steward was waiting beside the tree, a solemn figure in white. High Janissary Jannick stood beside her, his unpleasant eyes as unyielding as the stone. His blue janissary robes looked wrong, a splash of color in the gray room like life disturbing the dead. The doors closed behind Will and he was alone with them.

With each step forward Will's sense of familiarity grew. He could almost see what had been here before, a phantom vision just out of reach.

"What is this place?"

"This is the Tree Stone," said the Elder Steward. "It is the oldest and most powerful place in the Hall. But it is also a place of great sadness, where Stewards rarely come."

Will knew the Elder Steward and the High Janissary were both watching him. But he couldn't take his eyes off the Tree Stone. He *knew* it, he remembered it, or almost remembered it, like a word on the tip of his tongue, except that what he remembered was different from what was in front of him—

"You sense something from it," said the Elder Steward, "don't you?"

The High Janissary made a scornful sound. Will barely heard him, his attention fixed on the Tree. It was as if he was standing in the dark, where there should be—

"Light. It shouldn't be dark. There should be light—"

"The Tree of Light," said the Elder Steward, her eyes on him. "It was called that once."

"A guess," said High Janissary Jannick.

"Or else he really does feel it," said the Elder Steward.

He could feel it. Except that he was looking at its absence, like looking at a wasteland and knowing it had once been a forest, where she had walked among the trees.

"She was here, wasn't she?" said Will, turning to the Elder Steward, his heart pounding. "A long time ago, the Lady was here and the Tree was alive—"

It was more than alive; it was bright.

Who was she? How had he seen her in the mirror? She had felt so real, when this place was long dead. He lifted his hand to the medallion under his tunic. The Tree of Light was a hawthorn tree, like the hawthorn medallion he wore around his neck. *A hawthorn tree was the Lady's symbol.* How did he know it had once shone with light?

"It died when she did," said the Elder Steward, nodding. "It's said her touch will bring it back to life, and make it shine."

Will looked up at the Tree, its dead branches like skeletal remains in an empty landscape.

"Put your hand on it," said the Elder Steward.

His stomach twisted. He wasn't sure he wanted to. The Elder Steward and High Janissary Jannick were looking at him as though it was a test.

He reached out and placed his palm on one of its cold granite branches. He could feel it, worn smooth by the passage of time. No light shone or green shoot stirred. It was dead, like everything in this place.

"You see? Nothing," said Jannick.

Will glanced at the High Janissary, who was staring back at him with a mixture of scorn and contempt.

"Ignore him," said the Elder Steward. "I want you to try."

"Try?" said Will.

"Close your eyes," said the Elder Steward, "and try to find the Light."

He wasn't sure what she meant him to do, but he could feel the weight of her expectant gaze. Will drew in a deep breath and closed his eyes. Under his hand the stone was cracked and weathered with time and felt cold. He tried to silently will the Tree to light up, but it was like trying to will stone to fly. Simply impossible.

The Elder Steward stepped forward and spoke again gently, as if he had not understood.

"No. You're looking in the wrong place. The Lady made the Tree Stone shine, but the Light wasn't in the stone. It was in her."

Will closed his eyes again. He could feel the tension, the sense of importance from both the Elder Steward and the High Janissary. *In her.* He tried to imagine that there was something inside him that was waking up. His memory was starting to churn. He remembered the Lady, staring out at him from the mirror. He remembered his mother's face, white with fear. *Will, promise.*

He didn't want to remember. He didn't want to unearth the past, the pain slicing through his hand, the breath sobbing in his bruised throat as he stumbled across the muddy hill, his mother's last words ringing in his ears. *Will—*

Will wrenched open his eyes. There was no light. Not even the faintest glow. The High Janissary was right. The Tree Stone was dead and cold, and whatever was needed to bring it to life, it wasn't inside him.

"He's not the one we seek," High Janissary Jannick was saying. "He doesn't have the Lady's power. This is a waste of time."

The Elder Steward gave a small, almost sad smile. "And yet, the Lady made her promise."

"The Lady?" The High Janissary shook his head scornfully. "Where was the Lady when Marcus was taken? Where was the Lady when my wife was killed? Where was the Lady when my son—" He bit down on whatever he had been about to say, as though he couldn't bear to let it pass his lips. His face was white.

"Jannick," said the Elder Steward gently.

"The Lady is dead, Euphemia. We are the ones who have to fight.

Not a boy who lacks skills or training. I won't waste my time on a fantasy," said High Janissary Jannick, and he turned and stalked out of the doors.

Will was left alone with the Elder Steward in the quiet chamber. Her long white hair framed her kind, wrinkled face. The name Euphemia suited her, though he had never heard it spoken before. With the Tree Stone dark and dead-looking beside her, Will felt like he had let her down.

"It is not your fault," said the Elder Steward. "He's a good man. He adopted Cyprian and Marcus when they most needed a father, and raised them as his own. But he doesn't trust outsiders. He hasn't since his first son died six years ago."

"I'm sorry," said Will, looking back at the Tree Stone. "I tried, I just—"

"Jannick is right," said the Elder Steward. "You lack training. You're not ready." The Elder Steward looked into his eyes as if she was searching for something. "But which of us is ready for what life asks us to face? We don't choose the moment. The moment comes whether we will it or no, and we must make ourselves ready."

"Ready for what?"

For a long second, she just continued to look at him. "Justice has told you some of it."

In the inn of the White Hart in London, Justice had told him about an ancient world that fell to darkness. A few days earlier, he wouldn't have believed it. But he had seen black fire tear apart a ship, and a girl his own age use her bare hands to break open chains.

"He said that there was once a Dark King who tried to rule," said Will, "but that he was stopped by a Lady."

Her. She. He knew so little about her, but he yearned to know everything. The glimpse he had seen of her in the mirror—she had looked at him like she knew him, like they were connected. She had looked at him with eyes like his mother. He drew in a breath.

"They loved each other, and she killed him," said the Elder Steward, "somewhere far to the south, near the Mediterranean Sea. We don't know how she defeated him, only that she did. She was the only one who could."

He had so many questions. But churning at the heart of them all was, why? Why had Matthew pressed the Lady's medallion on him? Why had Justice brought him to the Hall? Why had the Elder Steward told him he was the one the Stewards were seeking? Why did the Stewards look at him the way they did, with fear, awe, and hope?

"You think I'm her, somehow."

The Elder Steward gave a slow nod. "You have her blood, passed down to you from your mother. And the Blood of the Lady is strong." The Elder Steward's voice was grave. "Strong enough to kill an ancient king. That is why Simon seeks you out." She looked at him. "He is trying to return the Dark King. It is his one desire . . . the thing he seeks above all else. Under the Dark King's dominion, dark magic would be returned to the world, humans slaughtered and subjugated as the past is brought into our present. Simon wants to stand over it all as the Dark King's heir. And the Blood of the Lady is the only thing that can stop him."

"My mother . . . was meant to kill the Dark King . . . ?" said Will.

Later he would think back on it as the moment when he had understood, all the pieces fitting together into a picture he didn't want to see.

His mother's destiny—

Now his mind flew back to Bowhill, kneeling beside his mother as her blood soaked into the ground. The realization swept through him: his mother's last words to him, her death, and the reason for it, the reason for everything that was happening to him. *Will, promise.*

Will's fingers closed over the medallion. He remembered the Lady looking right at him through the mirror. He remembered his mother gasping, *Run.* He felt his fingers start to shake, and clamped down on it, clutching the medallion tighter.

"Eleanor stopped Simon once before, years ago," said the Elder Steward. "He killed her sister—Mary, your aunt—in his first attempt to return the Dark King. But those were his early, clumsy efforts. He is much closer to his goal now. And with Eleanor dead, he believes nothing stands in his way." The Elder Steward held his gaze. "Except you."

"Me," said Will, grappling with the immensity of it. "But I'm not—I can't—"

Oh God, he could see the Lady's eyes on him, like his mother's eyes, staring up at him. *Will, promise.* She had known. She had known. All those months, all those years of running—

He had known that his mother had been—

Afraid.

He had just never known what it was she had been afraid of.

"You are Blood of the Lady, Will," the Elder Steward said. "And she fights the Dark King still. Through you."

He stared at the Elder Steward, feeling the cold emptiness of the stone room, the black branches of the dead Tree like cracks in the world.

"I can't fight the Dark King." The Tree seemed to mock him, proof that he couldn't do what they wanted. "I don't have her power." Unconsciously, he clutched at the medallion. It dug into the scar on his hand.

"Look down at the medallion," said the Elder Steward. "You can read it, can't you? You know the words of the old language. Even if you don't understand why."

He looked down at the words carved into the warped surface of the metal. It was true that he could read them when he shouldn't be able to, when they were written in a language that he had never seen before.

I cannot return when I am called to fight

So I will have a child

It was a message sent across time. A message to him, he thought, feeling his skin chill. The Lady had carved it meaning for him to read it. It had been passed from hand to hand, countless times over centuries. And it had made its way to him, as she had meant it to.

In the mirror, she had looked at him like she recognized him.

"My mother," said Will, struggling to process all of this. "She knew?"

"Many have borne the Blood of the Lady," said the Elder Steward, "but only one will find themselves facing the final fight. And the final fight is almost upon us. Those of us with the Blood of Stewards feel it too."

You feel it . . . The way she felt it . . . He thought of his mother in those final moments, the desperation as she had looked into his eyes.

"It is different to train your whole life to face a threat that might never come than it is to begin to see the signs, the portents that the Dark King's return is almost here." The Elder Steward's face was serious with purpose, and he could only feel the hard edge of the medallion in his hands. He was trembling.

"The signs?" he said.

"You've met James St. Clair," said the Elder Steward. "You've seen what he can do?"

Will nodded.

"James is not a descendant of the old world as you are." The Elder Steward paused, her eyes shadowed. "He is a Reborn, one of the most frightening portents. In the final days, the Dark King ordered that his greatest generals, servants, and slaves be killed, so that they could be reborn with him, and usher in his reign. His deadliest fighter was called the Betrayer. They say he was the brightest symbol of the Light, until he betrayed his own kind to serve the Dark King. He became the Dark King's most ruthless general, a merciless killer known for his beauty, his blue eyes and golden hair."

"Are you saying—"

"James isn't merely a descendant. He is the Dark King's general, reborn into our time. He is young now, but when he grows into his power, he will be more terrible than you or I can imagine, for he is not one of us. He is not human, and he is here with one purpose only, to herald the way for his master—"

A powerful shiver went through Will, and all the shadows in the room seemed to deepen and rise as she said—

"—Sarcean, the Dark King; the final eclipse; the endless night, whose dark reign will bring about the end of our world."

Sarcean.

The name struck like black fire, like something he'd always known that came blazing back to life until it threatened to overwhelm him. He remembered the crude *S* burned into the wrists of Simon's men, and the words that Justice had spoken at the inn of the White Hart.

That S is the symbol of something older, a terrible sigil with power over his followers that even they do not fully understand.

Sarcean.

He saw again a shadow reaching out of the past, spreading out over London, over Europe, over a world that had no defenses because it had forgotten. In his vision, then as now, the lights went out one by one until all was dark and still.

He'd stop it if he could, he thought. He'd stop it from happening again. He'd prove to his mother that he—

"What do I have to do?"

The Elder Steward didn't answer him at once, just looked at him with searching eyes.

"You said Simon was close," said Will. "You said my mother stopped him in the past, but that now he was almost at his goal. How?" He could see in her eyes that there was something she didn't want to tell him, and he was suddenly desperate to know. He focused on Simon as someone he could fight, something he could do.

"Simon has acquired something," said the Elder Steward after a pause. "Something he's needed for a long time. Call it the last piece of a puzzle that he is trying to solve. . . . We are working to get it back before he can." She would not say more. "The Stewards are here to stop Simon. At all costs, we will fight to prevent him from returning the Dark King." Her eyes on Will's were steady. "But if we fail, you must be ready."

"Ready." Will felt a cold understanding settling in him, a terrible truth that he couldn't push out of his mind. *Will, promise.* For that was the last part of it, the final realization in his mother's eyes. "You mean to kill him. That's what you think I have to do. Kill the Dark King before his new reign ends this world."

"Ready to face an enemy unlike any you have ever seen," said the Elder Steward. "One who will seek to turn your mind to darkness, to sway you to his cause, even as he ends this world to make way for his own. A relentless force seeking out any who oppose him, extinguishing every last spark of light and hope, unto the very ends of the earth."

The Elder Steward picked up the wall torch. "Look. I know you can read the words they wrote." She held the torch aloft, illuminating the dark above the giant doors. High above, there were words crudely chiseled in the stone.

Will turned cold, only half hearing the Elder Steward as she spoke.

"These doors mark the entry to the inner fort. It is the oldest and strongest part of the Hall.

"But these words were written above every door in every fort, in every town. These are the words the people saw as they barricaded themselves in when their outer walls were breached. As they waited in the dark . . . their last cry, their greatest fear . . . even as their doors broke open, and they faced what was on the other side."

Will could almost feel it, the fear as the people huddled together. The torchlight flickered over the words.

He knew what it said. He could read the ancient script that the people of the old world had carved in rock as they huddled together in the dark.

He is coming.

CHAPTER TWELVE

"YOU'RE LOYAL TO him, aren't you," said Justice.

He meant Will. Violet flushed. "He saved my life." *A stranger saved my life the day I learned my family planned to kill me.* Will might be a stranger, but he was the only one here who knew what she was. He knew, and he had stood by her side.

After a long, studying look: "Come with me," said Justice, seeming to make a decision. "There's something I want you to see."

Violet's palms felt clammy as they made their way toward the eastern side of the Hall. Being alone with Justice made her nervous. It was the powerful strength of his presence, and the omnipresent danger of what he would do if he found out she was a Lion.

Rounding a corner, she heard the same faint metallic sounds of sword fighting that had drifted into her room this morning. They drew her forward, past a row of columns to a wide-open arena.

She saw perfect rows of young fighters. There were perhaps two dozen novitiates. They all wore the same silvery-gray tunics Violet and Will had been given, embroidered with the Steward's star, and skirted to mid-thigh. They all moved in unison, a pattern of sword movements that flowed one into another, identical. She watched, entranced, as their swords lifted gracefully, then arced to the right.

One boy was astonishingly better than the others, his long hair flying around him as his sword sliced the air. She thought she recognized him. *Cyprian*. The novitiate who had accompanied Will into the great hall.

She couldn't take her eyes off him. He was strikingly handsome, the way a statue is handsome, nose, eyes, and lips all in faultless symmetry. But it was the way he moved, embodying the ideal Steward, that made her yearn to be like him, to fit somewhere as well as he fit, to find a place where she—

"*Halt!*" called Cyprian.

The novitiates instantly stopped, their sword tips held out with unwavering precision. She was the interruption, she realized suddenly. They were all looking at her. She fought the instinct to take a step back.

"What are you doing here, outsider?" Cyprian's voice was cold. He crossed the training courtyard to confront her, his sword still in his hand. "*It's that girl*," she heard one of the novitiates say behind Cyprian. "*That girl who came from outside.*" "Are you here to spy on our training?"

She flushed. "I heard you from the corridor. I didn't know I wasn't allowed to watch."

"Steward training is private," said Cyprian. "Outsiders don't belong."

"I brought her here," said Justice, arriving behind her. "She is our honored guest, and there is little harm in her watching you practice."

"Shouldn't you be out looking for my brother?"

That stopped Justice completely.

"It is the Steward way to offer aid to those in need," Justice began, his voice gently chastising. Cyprian was uncowed.

"You're barely half a Steward, walking around without a shieldmate.

You've made a mockery of our Order with your mistakes and your reck-lessness."

"That's enough, Cyprian," said Justice, his voice hardening. "You may be foremost among the novitiates, but you do not yet have the authority of a Steward."

Cyprian accepted the reprimand without lowering his eyes.

"Justice might think you can be trusted, but I don't," he said, his eyes holding Violet with a cold look. "I'll be watching you."

"Do not let Cyprian disturb you. He has striven his whole life to please his father, and High Janissary Jannick does not take well to outsiders."

Justice had brought her to a room that had the look of a disused train-ing hall, its walls hung with old arms and armaments. He spoke kindly, but standing alone in a room with Justice was not reassuring. Instead, the tense sense of danger returned tenfold. In his white livery, Justice was a fighter in a place made for fighting, part of this space filled with the ghost of battles from an ancient past. Cyprian's words jangled in her head.

"Why did you bring me here?" Violet tried to keep the tension from her voice.

She could still hear the sounds of the novitiates training, though they were distant. They were a reminder that she was here under false pre-tenses. She had the sudden fear that Justice was going to tell her that she couldn't stay in the Hall. Will's insistence that she was his friend—that he wouldn't go anywhere without her—had only brought her so far.

Sent back to London, she would have nowhere to go. She waited tensely. But Justice didn't answer her question directly.

"This is the room where I trained for many years when I was a boy." Justice walked forward with an air of nostalgia.

"You trained here?"

"I practiced the drills here whenever I had time to spare," said Justice. "That was when I first came to the Hall."

"Came?" said Violet.

Justice nodded. "Cyprian is one of the few born to the Hall. Most Stewards are Called. It happens around the age of seven, sometimes earlier." She remembered him saying that those of Steward blood were Called from across the world. Cyprian's parents must have been janissaries, since Stewards took a vow of celibacy. "For those of us who are Called, the Hall is like a place we've always known, and everything here makes a kind of sense," said Justice. "Your friend Will felt that way too. He is Blood of the Lady, as I am Blood of the Stewards. We share a connection to the old world. You, on the other hand . . . You are the first true outsider to come into the Hall."

Outsider. Cyprian had called her that. He thought she was an ordinary girl brought here from London. He was wrong. She had her own connection to the old world. Just not one that she could ever tell Stewards about.

"Is that why you showed me those fighters?"

"I showed you the fighters so that you could see our mission," said Justice. "Relics of the old world still exist. The Corrupted Blade, the Shield of Rassalon . . . Stewards scour the world for any surviving objects from those times," said Justice. "Pieces kept by unknowing collectors, excavations that uncover fragments of the past. . . . Where we find his Dark artifacts, we destroy them or lock them away to prevent them from doing harm. When we must, we battle evil unleashed from such objects, or awakened in archaeological digs that delved too deep into the past.

"But the real fight is coming," said Justice. "Your friend Will stands at the center of a great battle. He may be all that can hold the Dark King back."

"What does that have to do with me?"

To her surprise, Justice went over to one of the racks, took out one of the long silver swords, and held it out to her, hilt first.

"Here."

A sword. Like the ones the novitiates had been using when she had watched them training. Her heart began to beat faster at the purposeful way he was proffering the sword.

He meant for her to take it. She did, gingerly testing its weight. She had never held a sword before and was surprised at both the solidity and the heft of it.

And then, disconcertingly, she was looking at him over its length.

"You heard the word *shieldmate*," said Justice. "Stewards do everything in pairs. We take a partner when we take our whites. Someone to fight beside and protect."

"That's what Marcus was to you? A shieldmate?" said Violet.

"That's right."

She looked into Justice's warm brown eyes, remembering how desperately he had looked for Marcus on the ship.

"You could be that for your friend," he said.

Violet curled her hand around the hilt and lifted it. She shivered with the same sense of destiny she had felt when she had put on the Steward clothes, a connection to the past, as if she held a sword in an ancient battle.

She thought of Will, then of the sequence she had seen the novitiates practice. She tried to replicate it, stepping forward and arcing the sword to the right. She could feel how awkward it was: new to her body, the motion did not flow easily. This was a crude copy. She didn't have the grace of the Stewards. She finished the first movement frowning, knowing she could do better.

But when she looked up at Justice, she saw that she had surprised him.

"You did that from memory?"

She nodded.

"Try the second movement."

This time, as she began the slow arc, he brought his own sword up to meet hers in a countermovement, as if they were clashing in a stylized battle. "Now the third." His sword met hers again, this time on its downward stroke. Then he began a slow, sweeping attack that aimed at her neck, and she found herself lifting her sword into the fourth movement—which was somehow a perfect block to his attack. It was her turn to show surprise.

"We train for the opponent that we will face," said Justice, responding to her expression, "when the day comes that we are called on to fight."

Justice in his Steward garb faced her with a sword in his hand. Their blades came together again as she executed the fifth movement, and Justice became that opponent. The beautiful, abstract sequence suddenly had a purpose. She found herself looking at Justice across naked steel. Her heart was pounding, and not from exertion.

"Relax your hands. You don't need to grip the hilt so tightly."

It was unnerving to mimic fighting him, yet thrilling at the same time. *You tried to kill my brother.* Another movement. *Stewards killed the first Lion.* Another. She remembered her Lion brother, Tom, blocking a Steward's sword with an iron bar. Right before he drove it through the Steward's chest.

"Less weight on your front foot."

It felt terrifying, and right. She had dreamed of taking part in the battle, just never thought she'd be training to fight against Simon.

"Blade tip higher. Hold it steady."

The sequence was relentless. Her arms had started to hurt, and her tunic was damp with sweat. Cyprian had made this sequence look easy. Justice, moving with her in counterpoint, made it look easy.

Three movements left.

Why couldn't a Lion fight for the Light? Why couldn't she find a place here? She was as strong as any Steward.

Two movements.

"Your friend carries a great burden," said Justice. "If he is what the Elder Steward believes him to be . . . When the darkness comes, he will need a protector. Someone who'll stand by him. Someone who'll defend him. Someone who can fight."

One.

"*I can fight.*" She gritted out the words, and with a surge of determination she finished the final movement. Chest heaving, she looked over at Justice in victory.

"Good." She felt a rush of success. "Now do it again."

Justice stepped back, lowering his sword.

"Again!" she burst out.

He called a halt hours later. Dripping with sweat and trembling with exhaustion, she looked up at Justice. Her vision was hazy, her limbs at the edge of their endurance. She was barely able to lift her sword.

"Your movements are crude. You are not a Steward. You do not have our training," said Justice. "But you have the heart, and I will teach you."

She stared at him—he was a Steward, her father's enemy.

But she didn't have to follow her father. She could forge her own destiny. She tightened her grip on the sword.

"Then teach me," she said.

Utterly exhausted, she was barely aware that it was evening. Training over, she wanted nothing more than to collapse, pouring herself onto the bed in her room. But she found herself instead walking back into the great hall.

At this time, there was no one else here, just those ghostly white pillars stretching off into the dark. Her footsteps echoed, too loud. The raised dais emerged out of the gloom, the four empty thrones staring down at her.

They had the look of a majestic tribunal, reigning supreme over all brought before them.

But they weren't the reason why she was here.

The broken piece of shield hung on the wall. She stopped in front of it and looked up at the face of Rassalon, the First Lion.

The lion seemed to gaze back at her. His visage looked so noble. His great mane curled in proud metallic whorls around his face, his eyes serious above the triangle of his nose.

He almost seemed like he had something to say to her. *What is it?* she thought, suddenly wishing she could talk to him too. *I'm not betraying you by training with the Stewards. It's what you would do too,* she thought. *Isn't it?* How could something as honorable as a Lion have fought for the Dark?

As she had not dared to do before, she now reached out and touched the lion's face.

A sound behind her. She whirled, heart pounding.

Cyprian.

He had come from late practice just like she had, still armed and wearing his fighting tunic.

"Are you following me?" she challenged him.

He'd been training all day too, but he looked irritatingly perfect, without a single hair out of place, as though hours of sword work was easy for him. She was too aware of the dirt smudged across her forehead and the sweat tendrils in her hair.

I'm stronger than you, she thought defiantly. But her heart was hammering guiltily. Had he seen her touch the shield?

"What are you doing in our hall?" His hand was on the pommel of his sword.

"I'm just walking. Or isn't that allowed?"

He looked over at the shield, then at her. "That's the Shield of Ras-salon."

Her heartbeat spiked higher. She couldn't explain what had brought her here, the connection she felt to the ancient creature.

Violet flushed. "I don't care about an old shield."

Cyprian's mouth curled unpleasantly. "Whatever you're hiding, I'm going to find it out."

It wasn't fair. *Born to the Hall*, Justice had said, and he looked it; he fit here better than she had ever fit anywhere. Nerves transmuted into prov-ocation. "Trying to toady up to your father?"

Instead of answering, Cyprian looked back at the shield, as if he was looking right back into the past, his posture straight and his eyes steady.

"Lions are servants of the Dark," he said. "Do you want to know what Stewards do with them?"

"What?" she said, and his answer made her turn cold.

"We kill them," said Cyprian. "We kill all of them we can find."

CHAPTER THIRTEEN

"JUSTICE SAID THAT you fought James," said Emery.

About sixteen years old, with long brown hair worn in the Steward style, Emery was a shy-looking novitiate Will had seen training with Cyprian. He had just approached Will with his two friends Carver and Beatrix standing behind him, and was waiting wide-eyed for Will's reply.

"Not—exactly," said Will carefully.

On his way back from requisitions, Will was carrying two extra tunics, a cloak, and a pair of tall fur-lined boots. The tunics were light, but the cloak and boots he had been given were soft, warm, and made for winter. They each had astonishing artistry, as if spun from threads of silvery moonlight or the softest, most delicate cloud.

"But you did see him?" said Emery.

He was wearing a gray-silver tunic like the ones that Will held in his arms. He talked about James as if Will had encountered a mythical creature, like the Hydra or Typhon.

James is a Reborn, Will reminded himself. A living piece of the old world. The Stewards spent their lives studying the histories and trying to glean what was forgotten from the artifacts that they collected, keeping the ancient traditions as best as they could remember them. He could see the awe in Emery, like that of a researcher face-to-face with his subject.

"What was he like?" said Emery. "Did he talk to you? How did you get away?"

"Emery," said Carver, curbing the younger boy's questions. Then, to Will: "I hope these questions do not plague you. We do not spend much time with outsiders. And the Reborn to us is a figure of legend."

Carver was the oldest of the three novitiates, perhaps nineteen years old, with dark hair and the serious voice of one who did not talk much. Though he was taller than the others too, by almost a head, he had a quiet look.

"It's all right," said Will. Then, to Emery: "James was on the docks. I distracted him just long enough that we could get away. Justice told us to run, and he was right. Even with a head start we almost didn't escape. But it wasn't James who chased us; it was three men with pale faces and sunken eyes, each wearing a piece of black armor."

"The Remnants," said Emery, wide-eyed.

"Then it's true. Simon really is on the rise." Beatrix's voice had the trace of a Yorkshire accent. Will knew that many novitiates were born outside the Hall, but it was still strange to think of them being Called from anywhere as ordinary as Leeds. "It's why they moved up the date of your test." She said it to Carver.

"There might be many reasons for that," Carver said.

"Test?" said Will.

"To become a Steward," said Emery. "He's going to pass his test and take his whites and sit with the Stewards at the high table."

"That is not certain," said Carver. It was his turn to flush. "The test is difficult and many fail. And there is no shame in becoming a janissary."

"And you? Will you be training with us?" Beatrix's attention was on Will.

"No, I'm—" Will hadn't let himself think about the days ahead that had been planned for him, and it became real only as he said it. "I'm training with the Elder Steward."

He saw the eyes of the novitiates widen. *Training in magic.* The unspoken words hung in the air. The way the novitiates reacted made him realize that magic was something out of myth to them too. They'd had the same look in their eyes when he'd talked about James.

The idea of training made him nervous, at the same time that he felt drawn to it, glimmering with promise. It took on a greater weight when he saw how the novitiates reacted to it, as if he was about to embark on something beyond their understanding.

"I've never heard of the Elder Steward taking a student," said Beatrix.

"Not even Justice," said Emery.

"You have been given a great honor." Carver broke the spell of reverence with a nod of acknowledgment. "Stewards and janissaries alike seek the council of the Elder Steward. She has knowledge that no others possess, and if she is training you, it is for a purpose. She is the wisest and most powerful Steward in the Hall."

Justice had said that too. Will remembered the way the Elder Steward had looked at him the night he had come to the Hall, as if she was seeing right into his heart. He wanted to make sure he never let her down.

"Any advice?" said Will.

"Don't be late," said Beatrix, as a frowning trainer called out to them with a sharp word, and the three novitiates went hurrying off to their own lessons.

"To train someone in magic . . . that has never been done here before." The Elder Steward's eyes were serious. "Not by a Steward. Not by anyone since the last of the old cities fell and magic went out of the world."

Will came into the Tree Chamber, the dead branches of the Tree like cracks, making him shiver. He looked over at the Elder Steward, a figure of snowy white beside the black Tree, holding a single candle.

"Stewards do magic," Will said. The Stewards on the marsh had driven the Remnants back with an invisible shield. He remembered the black hounds fleeing before it, remembered the pale faces of the Remnants cowering back.

But the Elder Steward shook her head. "Stewards use artifacts from the old world. We have no magic of our own."

"I saw Stewards conjure a light." His memory of the white light on the marsh was vivid. "On the marsh. A shield of light to drive back the Remnants—" It had been bright and fierce, and it had seemed to envelop and protect the Stewards, pushing the creatures chasing him back.

"Stewards who patrol outside the gate carry stones with them," said the Elder Steward. "We call them ward stones, but in truth they are pieces of the Hall's outer wall, which has its own power to repel invaders."

"Ward stones?"

He thought of the strange, invisible barrier that enclosed the Hall, hiding it from the outside world. Could twelve Stewards riding in formation create a shield by carrying stones from the Hall?

"The strength of the ward stones fades the farther they get from the wall, but they have some power all the way to the banks of the Lea." The Remnants and the swarm of dogs driven back across the river . . . "All the Stewards' magic comes from such artifacts. We use what remains, though artifacts of the old world are few, and we cannot remake or repair what breaks or is lost. There is no one left who remembers those skills." The Elder Steward smiled sadly, her eyes on the dead branches of the Tree. Then she looked back at Will. "But your power is different. . . . It is part of you, in your blood."

My blood. Those words still filled him with a sickening unease. It made him even more determined to do this, and even more frustrated that he couldn't.

But there was one other time that he had seen magic. And it had not been an artifact; it had been raw power, summoned with the glitter of dangerous blue eyes.

"James can do magic," he said, and that stopped her.

"You're right. But he is a Reborn. His knowledge is innate. Or perhaps Simon sat with him like this, with old books and rumors, not realizing he was training a creature far more powerful than he was himself, taking a deadly chance with what he might unleash." She looked at Will, a long, steady look. "No Steward would train a Reborn."

"Why?" said Will.

"Out of fear that they would use their power for evil and not for good," said the Elder Steward. "And that they would become something that could not be either stopped or controlled."

The idea of Simon training James made something twist in his stomach. Beginning his own training felt like following James, but starting years late. He wanted to catch up to him, even as the idea of James as a Reborn brought its own disturbing fascination.

"The books in our libraries have crumbled, and been rewritten, and crumbled again. Nothing remains in the old language, which you might have been able to read. We have only snippets, in Arabic, in Ancient Greek, in Old French." The Elder Steward gestured for him to walk with her to the other side of the room, where she carried her candle to a stone table with two chairs. "Together, we will walk these ancient paths that have not been trodden in centuries. And today we begin here. In the place where magic once flowed, let magic come again."

Will looked up at the dead Tree. It was so large that its branches stretched over them, like black cracks in the sky. It seemed like a testa- ment to everything that he couldn't do: a piece of the dead world that he couldn't bring back to life. He had touched it and felt no spark in it, or in himself.

"Ignore the Tree." The Elder Steward brought the candle forward and put it on the small table. "We begin where light already exists. With a flame." She sat at one end of the table and nodded for him to sit at the other.

Slowly, he sat. The candle lay between them, but he was still too aware of the spreading branches of the dead Tree overhead.

"The power to stop the Dark King lies within you, Will," she said. "But you are right about James. If you want to fight the Dark King, you will have to first fight him."

She was so certain, when he felt nothing but churning doubt. James hadn't seemed to need anything more than concentration to make the air crackle. But if Will had magic, it lay beyond his reach.

What if I can't? he thought. He remembered James with his hand out- flung, the crate hanging in the air above him. *What if I don't have that power?*

He drew in a breath. "How?"

"With light," she said. "Look at the candle, and try to move the can- dle flame."

He sat in front of the candle. It was smooth and cream colored, made of beeswax, not tallow. The flame was an upright lozenge, bright and steady. Will looked at it and thought, *Move.* Nothing happened, no matter how much he wanted it to. Once or twice, he felt a wild stab of hope. *Did I do it?* But the candle's few shifts and flickers were due to air currents, not because of him.

"As you did with the Tree Stone," said the Elder Steward, "reach beneath the surface. Look for a place deep inside."

Deep inside. He kept his eyes on the candle flame, *willing* it to move. It was a foolish feeling, like trying to look more intensely out of his eyes, or tense up the back of his head.

He had failed to light the Tree. But this was just a single spark. A flame. He closed his eyes. He tried to picture the flame in his mind, to make it not just an image but a true embodiment of the flame. Distantly, he was aware that he was shaking. If he could just—

Will opened his eyes, gasping. Nothing. The candle was steady. Not a single flicker.

The Elder Steward was gazing at him. "There was a sword on the ship. A weapon that spewed black fire. Justice said you called it to your hand. What happened?" she said softly.

"I didn't want those people to die."

"And so you summoned the Corrupted Blade."

He didn't want to talk about that. "I wasn't trying to do it. It just seemed to come to me."

"The sword had words in the old language carved into its sheath. Do you remember what they said?"

He remembered the faint markings on the sheath, carvings that he'd felt under his hands, but—

"I couldn't read the inscription. It was worn away." A jet-black sheath with markings worn by time and the touch of a hundred hands.

"The Blade was not always corrupted," said the Elder Steward. "It was once the Sword of the Champion."

"The Champion?" said Will.

The Elder Steward's face was warm in the candlelight, turning the white of her hair and her tunic to soft gold.

"Called Ekthalion, it was forged by the blacksmith Than Rema as a weapon to kill the Dark King. It's said that a great Champion of the Light rode out with it to fight him . . . but could do no more than draw a single drop of the Dark King's blood. That's all it took to corrupt the Blade. You've seen its black flame. That is the power contained in a single drop of blood from the Dark King."

She leaned forward as she spoke, and Will almost felt as if the Tree and the stones in the room were listening.

"But there is another story," she said, "that one with the heart of a champion will be able to wield Ekthalion, and even cleanse it of its dark flame. If you had been able to read the inscription, you would have seen the words that once shone silver before the blade turned black. *The Sword of the Champion bestows the power of the Champion.*"

"I'm no champion," said Will. "I didn't cleanse the blade."

"And yet it came to you."

"And now Simon has it."

The Elder Steward sat back, and to his surprise she gave a small smile.

"But you do not need Ekthalion to defeat the dark," she said. "Even those who think themselves powerless can fight with small acts. Kindness. Compassion."

"The Stewards fight with swords," said Will.

"But our swords are not what make us strong," said the Elder Steward. "The true power of the Stewards is not our weapons. It is not even our physical strength. It is that we remember." And something in her eyes seemed ancient. "When the past is forgotten, then it can return. Only those who remember have the chance to stave it off. For the dark is never truly gone; it only waits for the world to forget, so that it may rise again."

She looked at him with a grave expression.

"I think there is great power in you, Will," she said. "And when you learn to wield it, you must make your own choices. Will you fight with strength, or compassion? Will you kill, or show mercy?"

Her words stirred something inside him. He could feel it, even though his mind wanted to shy away. He didn't want to look at it. But he forced himself to, and when he did, it was there. Not power. But something else.

"A door," said Will, because he was overwhelmed by the feeling. "There's a door inside me that I can't open."

"Try," said the Elder Steward.

He looked deep inside himself. He was standing in front of a giant door made of stone. He tried to push on it, but it didn't move. He could feel somehow that it was sealed tight. And there was something on the other side.

What was behind the door? He pushed at it again, but it didn't budge. He tried to think of the Stewards' battle and all that depended on his success. *Open!* he thought, straining to try to move it, shift it, anything. *Open!*

"Try," said the Elder Steward again, and he threw everything he had at it, every particle of strength—

"*I can't,*" he said, frustrated to his core. It seemed to taunt him, no matter how he pummeled at it, no matter how he pushed and strained—

"That is enough for today," said the Elder Steward as Will came gasping up out of his reverie. He didn't know how much time had passed, but when he looked at the candle, it had burned down almost to a stub. "I believe you need something to focus your mind. Tomorrow, I will begin to teach you the chants of the Stewards. We use them to still our inner turmoil, and to focus our concentration."

She rose, still speaking, and Will stood with her, thinking of the drifting Steward chants that he heard each morning. He knew they were significant, but had not understood their purpose before now.

"The chants have been handed down to us across generations," said the Elder Steward. "They have shifted and changed over the centuries, but they were once used by those with magic in the old world, and I believe they will still have some power. Come."

She moved to the other side of the table and picked up the candle. Then, as if weakened, she swayed, and the candle dropped from her hand. Will rushed to pick it up, then stepped in to support her. She leaned on him gratefully.

But for a moment, he had the strangest impression that the candle hadn't dropped from her hand; it had instead dropped *through* it. He shook his head to clear it.

"Are you all right?"

"Just tired," she said with a smile, her hand on his arm solid and warm. "One of the effects of getting old."

"Will!" called Emery, waving him and Violet over to his table in the dining hall.

Novitiates began their morning chants at dawn, and the first bell rang an hour before that. They ended their training at sunset. Downstairs in the dining hall, rows of novitiates sat at long tables, set for an evening meal. Sitting with Violet in the chairs Emery had gestured for them to take, Will found himself famished, as though his exercises with the Elder Steward had worked up a great appetite.

Violet tore open a warm piece of bread, while Will helped himself to a generous portion of hot potage, thick with barley and leeks. The first spoonful was warm, comforting, and heartening, and he had soon eaten it down to the bowl, never having eaten better.

Several of the novitiates at surrounding tables gave Emery strange looks at his friendliness to the outsiders. Emery didn't seem to care and had shifted so that Will and Violet could sit with him, alongside Beatrix and Carver.

"You're dressed differently," said Will. Emery and his friends were not wearing their usual novitiate tunics, but were instead dressed in the kind of garments that were worn under armor.

"We're going outside the gate," said Emery. "With the Stewards, on patrol. Tonight."

He said it as if it was uncommon. "Novitiates don't go outside the walls often?" said Will.

"No, hardly ever. That is—the best go, sometimes." *Like Carver,* thought Will. Or Cyprian, who had been riding outside when Will had met him. "But for us, it's an escalation of our training. We're going to ride along the marsh to the Lea, then north as far as the coppices on the Flats."

It was funny to hear Emery talk about the River Lea as if he was describing a mission to an exotic location. Will supposed that to novitiates who had lived most or all their lives inside the Hall, the outside world must seem a strange place. He tried and failed to imagine Emery or his friends on the streets of London.

"Do you know why they're sending you out now?"

Emery shook his head, but then leaned forward to speak almost secretively. "Everyone's saying the Stewards are preparing for something big," he said. "They want the novitiates to be ready . . . as ready as we can be. It's why Carver's test was moved forward."

"You said it yourself," said Beatrix. "Simon is on the rise. The Reborn has come into his power. And—"

"And?" said Will.

"And you're here," said Beatrix.

Will flushed, feeling the eyes of everyone on him. He knew what the Stewards thought . . . that he was Blood of the Lady. They thought he could kill the Dark King. But when he thought about what he was supposed to do, all Will could remember was the dead Tree, and the unmoving candle flame.

"It's like the alliance of old," said Emery. "All of us fighting together."

Will's stomach turned. *I can't,* he thought. *I can't be what you need.* He didn't want to say that, with all of them looking at him.

He felt Violet's shoulder leaning slightly into his, and was grateful for the silent gesture of support. He drew a steadying breath.

"When is your test?" Violet asked Carver.

"In six days."

"And it's early?"

"I'm nineteen. Novitiates usually test a year later. Unless their blood is very strong."

Carver's quiet, serious manner was different from the strong certainty of Beatrix and the shy, naive friendliness of Emery. The three of them were a tight-knit group, and he seemed like the steadfast presence that kept them together.

"Who will your shieldmate be?" said Violet.

Carver shook his head. "I haven't been told that yet."

"You don't choose?" said Will. He was surprised that such an important relationship was assigned rather than chosen. "I thought it was—a deep connection." It didn't make sense. Wasn't a shieldmate a partner for life?

"We're paired by our elders," Carver said to Will. "The connection comes later."

That seemed like a risky way to gain a life partner. What if you didn't like your shieldmate? The Stewards he saw in the Hall were always in pairs. They bedded down together, ate together, patrolled together.

Perhaps Stewards were so dutiful that they accepted any shieldmate. Or perhaps after they were matched together, some kind of bond was formed.

"I wondered if it might be Cyprian," said Carver, "but he isn't testing for another month."

Will looked over at Cyprian. He was sitting two tables down, with a group of novitiates Will didn't recognize. Straight-backed and perfectly attired, he had the quality of a Steward about him already. But Cyprian was sixteen, and Carver had said novitiates usually took the test at age twenty—

"He's three years younger than you," said Will.

Carver nodded. "He'll be the youngest to take the test since the Elder Steward."

"So who will get stuck as Cyprian's shieldmate?" said Violet, as if she couldn't imagine anyone wanting to be. But Carver answered her question seriously.

"Probably Justice."

"But—he *hates* Justice!" said Violet as Will's mouth fell open in shock.

"They're the best," said Carver, as if this explained everything. "They assign Stewards of equal strength together."

Later, Will talked to Violet in his room.

"The Stewards are preparing for something," said Will. "A mission. I wonder if it has to do with the object the Elder Steward told me about? The one Simon took."

The Elder Steward had said Simon had taken possession of an artifact that he would use to return the Dark King. But she had refused to say what it was. Why?

"You think they're going to try to retrieve it?"

"Maybe."

Violet was sprawled across his bed, still in her training clothes. She had dropped her sword on the floor when she had collapsed down, exhausted after her evening drills with Justice. Will had pushed his own practice to one side when she came in, looking away from the candle and rubbing his tired eyes.

He picked up her sword. It was heavy; the simple act of holding it was difficult. But it took his mind off the unlit candle and his failure to make progress. Violet had tried staring at it with him earlier before she gave up. Now he tried one of Violet's sword movements, and almost lodged her sword in the bedpost.

"Not like that, thrust up, like it's going under an armor plate," she said, when she had finished wiping her eyes. He shook his head and replaced the sword.

"Your family worked for Simon. What do you know about him?"

"He's rich," said Violet. "Stupidly rich. My father has done business with his family for almost twenty years. He has offices in London, and a trade empire that stretches all the way across Europe. He also has digs all around the Mediterranean, in Southern Europe, and Northern Africa." She paused and thought for a moment. "His family estate is in Derbyshire . . . it's miles from London. It's supposed to be very grand, but he hardly ever invites people to visit there."

Will's mind fixed on that one detail. "He has family?"

Violet shrugged. "A father. And a fiancée. I heard she's beautiful. He's rich enough to marry whoever he wants."

Simon. Will tried to picture him. The man he had thought so much about since Bowhill—the man who had changed the course of his whole life. Was he frightening? Commanding? Sinister? Cold? He was the Dark King's descendant. Was he like the Dark King? Did he look like him? Have his traits? Had something been passed down to him across the years?

"I've never even seen him," said Will.

He knew so little about Simon, even after everything that had happened between them. He had only a scattering of impressions: The kind of man who would brand his servants. The kind of man who would order others to kill. The kind of man who wanted to return the past to the present, heir to its terrible king.

"I have," said Violet. Will's eyes flew to her face. "He came to see my father, and he met Tom too, in my father's office. I wasn't allowed to join them."

"What was he like?"

"I only caught a glimpse of him—I was watching from the stairs. A shadowed figure in rich clothes. Honestly, what I remember most was how my father was acting. He was so toadying, maybe even . . . scared."

"Scared," said Will.

His mother had been scared. Years moving from one place to another, of hurriedly packing, looking over her shoulder, until Bowhill, where Simon's men had found her after she had stayed too long.

Violet clambered up onto her elbows.

"Have you ever noticed that there are no old Stewards?" said Violet.

"What do you mean?"

"They die," said Violet. "They die in battle, like they died on Simon's ship. There are old janissaries. But no old Stewards."

She was right. The only old Steward in the Hall was the Elder Steward.

"It's the price they pay," said Will, thinking of Carver and the other novitiates. "They all believe the Dark King is coming, and that it's their duty to stop him."

"What happens if Simon attacks the Hall?"

"You can fight and I'll flicker the candles," said Will.

And she let out a shaky breath, stopping to punch him in the arm as she rose to pick up her sword.

"You spoil him," said Farah.

Will had come to the stables before his lesson to see the black cart horse, carrying an apple he'd saved from his breakfast as a thank-you for the horse's courage. When the black horse saw him, he cantered over to the railing tossing his head, then whinnied softly and whuffled the new apple up from Will's hand. Will rubbed his neck, the strong curve of muscle under the satiny fall of his black mane.

Farah was the stablemaster, a Steward of about twenty-five years. Her brown skin was streaked with dust from her work in the training yard, and her hair was tied all the way up. She had come over from the stalls, only a few Stewards and janissaries at work this early.

"He helped me," Will said softly, feeling the warm, strong arch of the horse's neck beneath his hand and remembering their race across the marsh. "He's brave."

And perhaps there *was* something in the food or the air here, because the black horse had changed in even a short time: his neck was arched, his black coat had grown glossier, and there was a gleam in his eye that hadn't been there before. He was beginning to look like a battlefield steed, one that could lead a charge.

"He's a Friesian," said Farah. "One of the ancient breeds . . . made for war. Brave, yes, and powerful enough to carry a knight in full armor. But the days of the warhorse are gone. Now Friesians pull carts in the city. Does he have a name?"

"Valdithar," Will said, and the horse tossed his head and seemed to respond to the name. "It means *dauntless*." The word from the language of the old world came to him instinctively.

When he looked up, Farah was looking at him strangely.

"What is it?" said Will.

"Nothing, I—" She broke off. And then: "It is a long time since that language was spoken in this place."

Valdithar. The black horse seemed to grow taller, as if the name had made him more himself.

Will came back to the stables every morning. He loved to brush Valdithar until his coat shone and his mane was a black waterfall. Once or twice he went out to ride with the novitiates, and the Steward horses they rode were a strange delight. Graceful, otherworldly creatures, with silvery-white coats and high, flowing tails, they had the arresting beauty of a Pegasus. Farah said they were descendants of some of the great horses of the old world, the last herd of their kind. In motion they were as mighty as a wave crest, as light as foam, as intoxicating as spray from the ocean.

But Will secretly preferred Valdithar's powerful earthy gallop, and he was pleased that Valdithar held his own among them, a single black gelding in a herd of white.

When Farah took him to ride outside the walls—safe with pairs of Stewards carrying ward stones—the Steward horses transformed the marsh into a place of wonder. They were fine as the mist that blanketed the marsh in the early morning, running so lightly over the watery earth it seemed like they never touched it. Watching them, Will's breath caught in his throat, as if he had glimpsed the old world. This was why he was trying to move the flame: to preserve what was left from the danger that was coming.

He kept training.

But always that door within him remained stubbornly closed. He visualized it over and over in every possible way: it opening gently; it bursting open; battering at it; throwing himself against it; heaving at it with all his might. Once he strained so hard that he came out of the trance gasping and shaking. But despite his sweat-drenched clothes, there had been no change in the flame.

"That's enough for today," the Elder Steward said gently.

"No, I can keep going. If I just—"

"Will, stop. We don't know what the strain will do to you. This is an unknown path for us both."

"But I almost had it!" He spoke thickly, frustrated.

"Rest and sleep," said the Elder Steward. "Return tomorrow."

CHAPTER FOURTEEN

"WHAT DOES HE have to do?" said Will.

There was a tense, expectant hush that hung over the crowd, every eye fixed on the lone figure in silver who stood on the sawdust with only a sword in his hand.

All the Stewards, janissaries, and novitiates in the Hall had gathered to watch the test, filling stands that ringed what must once have been a great amphitheater. Its arches and columns had crumbled, but it still conjured up a past of mighty contests. The anticipation was a sharp metallic tang, like the sound of a sword unsheathing.

Will sat with Violet and a handful of others, and he asked his question of Emery and Beatrix, who were perched taut on the edge of their marble step, because the lone figure on the sawdust was their friend Carver.

"We practice triten—sword patterns," said Emery, answering Will's question. "He has to finish three triten to pass; any less is a failure." Emery drew in a nervous breath. "You know his test is a year early. Most novitiates aren't ready until they turn twenty. But Justice was eighteen. And of course everyone thinks—" Emery broke off.

Will followed Emery's glance across the amphitheater and saw Cyprian sitting beside his father, the perfect straight-backed novitiate. This was a test Cyprian would take at sixteen, a prodigy. Will could see Cyprian's future in this ceremony, his shining excellence eclipsing quiet Carver, no one doubting that he would pass his test and become a Steward like his brother.

"Carver can perform the triten as quickly or slowly as he likes, but if the tip of his sword falters, he will fail," Emery said.

It didn't seem like very much. Will had seen Violet practicing the Steward sword patterns in their rooms night after night. Most novitiates had mastered them by the age of eleven or twelve. After that, it was just the endless Steward quest for perfection.

"That's all? He just has to complete three of the Steward patterns?"

Emery nodded.

Will looked back at the arena. On the sawdust, Carver was walking forward to face the Elder Steward, who sat on a simple wooden stool at the front of the stands. He wore armor, his surcoat the silvery-gray color of the novitiates. He knelt in front of the Elder Steward in a traditional bow of respect that Will had seen Justice and other Stewards perform, fist over his heart. *He has been training for this day his whole life,* Will thought.

"You seek to wear the star," said the Elder Steward. "To join the Stewards in their fight against the Dark."

"I do," said Carver.

"Then rise and prove your strength," said the Elder Steward, her touch to his shoulder a benediction.

Carver stood.

Two Stewards emerged from one of the archways, carrying a metal casket between them with poles like a palanquin.

Will didn't know what to expect as the two Stewards came toward Carver, lowering the metal casket to the ground, but in the next moment the Stewards were pushing back the latches of the casket and throwing it open.

Wrong. That was what Will felt the moment the casket opened. Inside lay a metal belt made to fit around the waist. Seeing it made Will sickeningly uneasy. It reminded him of the armor pieces that he had seen the Remnants wear on the chase across the marsh, the gauntlet reaching out for him. *Don't touch it!* he wanted to stand up and shout. His fingers curled as he gripped his seat.

Before he could say anything, the Stewards drew the belt from the casket with metal pincers and put it around Carver's waist.

The effect on Carver was immediate. He almost staggered, his skin turning gray. Carver was wearing plate armor. The metal belt wasn't touching his body. But Will had seen Dark objects kill people even at a distance, like the sword and its black fire. The belt didn't need to touch Carver's skin to affect him.

"What *is* it?" said Violet.

"It's a belt made with a sliver of metal from a Dark Guard's armor," said Beatrix.

"Like the Remnants," said Violet.

"Not as strong," said Beatrix. "It's not a full armor piece. That would kill him. But it's strong enough. Most who fail the test go to their knees right away."

Carver stayed on his feet. And when the two Stewards moved away and back, Carver drew his sword.

That was when Will realized that the test was not the triten.

It was control. To stay a Steward in the face of the Dark. To hold to your mission. To fight.

Will's heart was pounding as Carver began the first of the triten, the amphitheater utterly silent. He could hear each footstep Carver took as part of the sequence, his sword cutting the air, arcing down from left to right. The belt around his waist was like an anchor stone, and he was soaked with sweat.

The second triten—he must have drilled it thousands of times since childhood. Will recognized the movements, had seen Violet perform this same sequence only last night. It was longer than the first, and now Will could hear the exhalations of breath as Carver completed each motion. By the time he finished the second triten, it seemed impossible that he could continue. He looked like he could barely stay on his feet. The entire amphitheater seemed to hold its breath—and they kept holding it in the long pause. Will saw the moment when Carver gathered himself to begin the third.

"What if he falters?"

"He won't. His blood is strong," said Beatrix.

Words of faith from his friend. Carver's gray skin had mottled, and a thin trickle of blood was running from his nose. He kept going, movement after movement. It was like watching a man keep his hand in the fire while the skin burned away. But Carver's sword arm never faltered, and he completed the final movement with a steady blade.

The amphitheater erupted in cheers. "Carver!" Emery and Beatrix leaped to their feet, shouting with pride. On her seat at the edge of the arena, the Elder Steward smiled. The two Stewards in the arena quickly came forward and took the belt from Carver's waist, hurriedly locking it back up in its casket. Carver, to his credit, did not drop to the ground with exhaustion but instead made his way forward to face the Elder

Steward and knelt for her a second time. He managed to make it seem like a graceful movement, rather than a collapse. The Elder Steward looked down at Carver with kind, proud eyes.

"You've done well, Carver," she said. "Now it is time."

Six Stewards emerged from the archway, dressed differently from the other Stewards in the Hall. They wore Steward whites, but long robes in the manner of a janissary, instead of the usual Steward short tunic. Most surprising of all was the insignia they wore on their chests: a cup, carved with four crowns. Will had never seen a Steward wearing anything like it. He had thought that all Stewards wore the star.

They walked in twos, paired as Stewards always were. The cup on their tunics gleamed, bell-shaped. It gave them a strange, ceremonial significance. Carver rose and accompanied the six Stewards in a processional through the archway and out of sight.

"What's happening?" said Will.

"He's going to the drink from the Cup," said Beatrix. "It's our Order's most secret rite. He will take his vow, drink, and return with the gift of strength."

"The Cup?" said Will.

"The Cup of the Stewards," said Beatrix. "The source of our strength."

So this was where Stewards gained their supernatural strength: from a cup. It explained the six Stewards and the insignia they had worn on their chests. They must be the Cup's attendants or guardians. But what did it mean for a novitiate to drink? Will's mind filled with questions. "How does a cup give him strength?"

"No one knows. No novitiate or janissary has ever seen the rite. Even the vow is secret. Only those who pass the test know what it is. But it's said only those with the strongest Steward blood can withstand the great power bestowed by the Cup. It's why there is a test. You have to prove your strength of will before you drink."

Will's eyes swung back to the archway at the end of the arena. "You mean he risks his life?"

Stewards already gave up so much. They lived lives of self-sacrifice and dedication only to die young in battle, while the janissaries lived out full lives, marrying and having children. Of the hundreds of Stewards in the Hall, only the Elder Steward had taken the whites and lived to old age.

He thought of Carver's quiet dedication, his humility, and the courage that he had shown wearing the belt. He wondered how many hours Carver had practiced, learning to hold his concentration through utter exhaustion.

"Look, he's coming back," said Emery. "There!"

A new cheer went up from the stands as Carver emerged from the archway, and Emery and Beatrix clasped each other in an outpouring of happiness for their friend. *"He's done it!"* Will heard one of the novitiates exclaim behind him. *"Carver's a Steward!"*

Carver was all in white, transformed as if from a chrysalis. His eyes were quietly proud and happy. But the biggest change was in his manner, and Will felt a sense of wonder at the difference in him, the new quality that he shared with the other Stewards. It was an inner radiance, as though he'd entered the chamber in gray and come out forged by the Cup into radiant white.

As he stood in the arena, a young woman Will didn't know stepped forward and took both Carver's hands in her own. She looked only a year or two older than Carver, but she wore Steward whites, and her long brown hair was worn in the Steward style. They each spoke ceremonial words meant for each other and for the gathered crowd. A *shieldmate vow*, Will realized with a shock as she spoke in a clear voice.

"I will watch for you," she said, "and you for me, and we will fight the darkness for each other."

"Do you think they'd ever let an outsider take the test?"

Violet stood beside him, the two of them alone on the balcony. The courtyards below were aglow with light, the Stewards gathered in celebration as the music of some ancient stringed instrument drifted through the leaves. Will could almost glimpse the beauty of the Hall at its height, the sights and sounds conjuring up long-ago pageants or the floating lights of a festival.

When he looked over at Violet, her eyes were wistful. She looked like a young Steward hopeful, he thought. Hours of drills with Justice had given her the sword-straight posture all Stewards had. She had learned their tritens and their focused meditations and could sit perfectly still in stress positions for hours. But she wasn't allowed to train with them or take part in any of their ceremonies.

"You need Steward blood to drink from the Cup," said Will. That was what Beatrix had told him. Only those of Steward blood could withstand the Cup's power.

"They only drink to give themselves strength," said Violet. "I'm already strong."

He knew what she was really asking. *Do you think a Lion could ever be a Steward?*

"I think if you took the test you'd pass," said Will. Her eyes flew to him. "You'd never let some belt defeat you." She drew in a breath, then gave him a crooked grin and knocked his shoulder with her fist.

He meant it. She seemed born to be a warrior of the Light, with her fierceness and her dedication.

He was the one who couldn't light the Tree Stone, who spent hours with the Elder Steward with nothing to show for it but dead branches, like cracks spreading through the firmament.

A sound nearby made them both stop and turn, not wanting their words to be overheard, but it was only Carver and Emery on the staircase, taking a private moment of their own.

"I'm proud of you." Emery's voice. Will could see the faint pale gleam of his tunic in a nearby alcove.

"For a moment, I thought I wouldn't make it. But I kept hearing Leda's voice: 'Steward, hold to your training.'"

Emery said softly, "I wanted to take my test at the same time that you took yours. I always hoped that—I might be your shieldmate."

"Emery—"

"I'll train hard. So we can be Stewards together."

"There's no rush," said Carver. "I—take your time. Don't rush for me, Emery. There isn't—"

"Will, Violet!" said Beatrix, waving to Carver and Emery too, and breaking the moment for all of them as she approached. "Let's go join the others outside." Violet stepped forward, but Will hesitated.

"Will?" said Violet, looking back at him.

"You go," he said to her. "I'll come down later."

After a moment she nodded, then turned and went down to the courtyard. He watched her follow the novitiates out, and then join up with Justice. Will stayed on the dark, quiet balcony alone, looking out at the revelry below.

He could see the Stewards and novitiates like glints of light, the music still drifting upward to his balcony, but it felt distant, like the occasional murmur of laughter or words that he couldn't catch. The air here was crisply cold, the balcony lit with only the blues and grays of moonlight. He drew in a long breath.

A battle was coming, and these were the people who were going to fight. These people against the Dark. He had seen how seriously they took their duty. Carver had fought through agony to show his mastery over the Dark influence. In only a month, Cyprian would take the same test. At sixteen, he would become the youngest Steward to drink from the Cup.

The Lady's medallion was around Will's neck. He could feel its tangible weight. He reached up and closed his fingers over it, remembering that his mother's old servant Matthew had died to give it to him. *You must go to the Stewards*, Matthew had said. He had believed in Will's destiny, his part in the upcoming battle.

"You're not celebrating with the others," said the Elder Steward.

She arrived as a companionable presence, quietly climbing the stairs to the balcony. Her eyes were kind as she looked out with him at the celebrations below. A distant burst of laughter drifted up to them, and he glimpsed Carver, white flowers around his neck, speaking to his new shieldmate. Will's fingers tightened around the medallion.

"Everyone says Carver took his test earlier than he should have," said Will.

She looked at Will, acknowledging his words. "His test is a year early. I ordered it brought forward, though it greatly increased the chance that he might fail."

"Why?"

"I won't lie to you. Your training is very important. We have very little time. You must succeed in summoning your power." Her attention turned back to the soft glow of lights below. "As for the Stewards, we will need all our forces at the ready."

"You think Simon's about to make his move," said Will. "No, it's more than that, isn't it. There's something you aren't telling me."

As the far-off sounds of the revelry filtered up to them, he saw secrets in her eyes.

"You should go down and celebrate with the others," she said. "Time is short. Enjoy these moments of high spirits while you can."

CHAPTER FIFTEEN

HE WOKE TO Violet tugging his shoulder. "Something's happening."

He came groggily out of sleep, and she'd already hauled him half out of bed, propelling him stumbling through a mess of bedding toward the window.

She was right. There was something happening on the walls. He could see the cluster of Stewards gathered in the dark without torches. He thought he glimpsed the figure of Jannick, the High Janissary. "Come on. We can find out what's going on." Violet thrust his novitiate tunic toward him.

The halls were deserted: it was the dead of night. Outside, they crouched in the frozen cold behind a cart, hidden in the dark. Will could see the High Janissary waiting in his long blue robes, and beside him, the smaller, thinner figure of the Elder Steward in her white cloak. There were six other Stewards gathered with them, including Leda the captain. All of them had their eyes fixed on the gate.

White horses and their white-clad Steward riders appeared like visions in the archway. A *secret expedition*, thought Will. He had seen

Stewards return from missions before, but never in the dead of night, while the heads of the Order waited for them in the dark without torches. As he watched, he saw that the returning Stewards were badly injured, two slumped in the saddle, the other three barely riding upright. And of two dozen white horses, only the first five bore Stewards. The other horses were riderless, carrying gray sacks that were the wrong shape for packs.

Leda rushed forward to take Justice's weight as he slid down from his horse in obvious pain. She lifted a flask to his lips, administering the waters of Oridhes. Others were doing the same to help Stewards covered in blood. Will looked again at the riderless horses and realized to his horror what he was looking at.

The gray sacks were not packs. They were wrapped bodies.

"Marcus?" said Jannick, and Justice, looking more defeated than Will had ever seen him, shook his head.

"So you came back without him," said a voice. Will turned to see Cyprian standing on the steps to the Hall. He must have woken up and come to see what was happening. But Cyprian wasn't creeping around hiding behind carts like Will and Violet. He had come like a blazon to challenge Justice directly. His lip curled. "Again."

"Cyprian," said High Janissary Jannick, stepping forward. "This isn't the time."

"But of course *you* survived. You're good at surviving while you leave my brother behind—"

"I said that is enough, Cyprian—" said the High Janissary.

"No," said Justice, pushing himself up out of Leda's hold to stand by himself. "He deserves to hear."

Justice's face was gray with fatigue. There was blood soaking through his white surcoat. Will felt his stomach turn over. What could have done this to a squadron of Stewards?

"We found the convoy transporting Marcus," said Justice. "It was right where our information had said it would be." Justice's expression changed. "But it wasn't carrying Marcus. It was bait for an ambush. James was there."

James, thought Will, his skin prickling, all his attention fixing on the name. He felt the way he had at the river, when he had seen James for the first time and been unable to look at anything else.

"The Betrayer," said Cyprian, in a hard new voice. "He did this?"

"A mist had come down in the valley," said Justice. "It gave us the perfect cover. We saw the convoy, four carriages bearing Simon's coat of arms. We thought we had him."

Will imagined Stewards riding down into the mist-wreathed valley, ghostly white shapes descending on the four shiny black carriages.

"We were mid-charge when our front riders just—lifted out of their saddles," said Justice. "They hung in midair, and their bodies started to jerk. In front of our eyes, their bones snapped, and their flesh tore. I saw Brescia's armor crumple like paper."

Stewards hanging limply, suspended in the mist, their bodies cracking and contorting into unnatural shapes. Horrifying and impossible, but Will had seen James lift a crate with invisible power. Why not lift a body, move it, break it to your will?

"It was chaos, screams, careening horses smashing into each other. I called for a retreat, but it was too late, that invisible force let loose among us. There was no way to fight it. We barely returned with our lives."

"But you did return. No one else was captured?" Jannick's clipped voice.

Justice nodded tightly. It was obvious that to return and bring home the bodies had cost him something, in lives, in pain. But he had done it.

They can't fight magic. The Stewards, with their supernatural strength, could outmatch any fighting force in the world. But they couldn't fight what they couldn't see.

That's why they need me. They think I can.

Will's stomach twisted as he thought of his failed lessons, his inability to light the Tree Stone or shift the single candle flame.

The Stewards are losing to Simon. They're safe in here. But out there . . . he's grown too powerful.

Leda had taken Justice's weight again, his arm over her shoulders. She beckoned Jannick over, glancing around to make sure they were out of earshot. Then she spoke in a low voice. "High Janissary, if we don't free Marcus soon, he—"

"Not here," said Jannick.

Will followed Jannick's gaze and saw a huddle of shapes in the doorway, a small group of other novitiates who had crept out after Cyprian and were watching. Will made out Emery, wide-eyed and pale, and Beatrix, still in a bed shirt with a blanket wrapped around her shoulders.

The Elder Steward stepped forward. "All of you to bed. We have wounded to tend to here."

Cyprian and the other novitiates were escorted away, leaving Will and Violet hidden dangerously close to where Jannick and the Elder Steward were standing. He tried to stay very still, barely breathing.

"The Betrayer toys with us." Jannick kept his voice low, but it was thick with disgust.

"He knows we will do anything to get Marcus back," said the Elder Steward.

"I blame myself. I'm the one who—the Betrayer. I had him. And he slipped out of my grasp. Now Simon has the power he needs to pick us off one by one—"

"We stand between him and the one thing he wants," said the Elder Steward.

Will shivered. She was talking about him. She believed that Will could stop the Dark King. Based on what? A few words of old language and the image of a lady in a mirror?

"You cannot blame yourself," said the Elder Steward to Jannick. "You could not know what the Betrayer would become when you—"

She broke off, stumbling slightly on the uneven cobblestones. Jannick immediately rushed to her aid, taking her arm and letting her lean her weight on him.

"Euphemia—"

"It's nothing. A missed step."

"Are you certain?"

"Yes. I'm certain." She smiled at Jannick, a reassuring hand on his arm. "I'm certain, Jannick. There is no need for concern. Now come. Let us speak further."

The last of the survivors had dismounted, and the Stewards in the courtyard had started to untie the gray sacks, others leading away horses who had forever lost their riders. The Elder Steward spoke at last. "Leda. Justice. Follow us."

Will exchanged glances with Violet. Their agreement to follow the Elder Steward was unspoken. Soundlessly they slipped out from behind the cart, waited until the way was clear, then followed the others.

The High Janissary's office was deep in the Hall. Glimpsing it through a sliver in the door, Will saw that it was filled with books, even the desk strewn with manuscripts and scrolls. Jannick's role as High Janissary meant that he oversaw all the work that the janissaries did in the Hall, and that included its scholarly aspect, the teaching of history, the keeping of records. Through the crack in the door, Will could hear the low voices.

"This the first time that James has taken on a squadron," Justice was saying. "Last year he could not have won that fight. He gets stronger with every day. . . . He is coming into his true power. And he knows it. He goaded us into that battle, confident he could win."

A woman's voice that might have been Leda's answered, but Will couldn't quite hear what she said. He glanced at Violet and the two of them moved closer to the door.

"Every year, there are fewer of Steward blood born to the Hall," said Justice, "and fewer still of Steward blood Called here from outside. We have so few novitiates, and of those barely a handful strong enough to drink from the Cup and become Stewards. Cyprian, yes. Beatrix— Emery, perhaps. But the others—"

Jannick frowned. "What are you saying?"

"Soon there may not be enough of us left to fight."

"That is Simon's intention?" said Jannick. "To pick us off one by one?"

"Clearing the way for his master," said the Elder Steward.

There was an awful silence as her words sank into all of them, and Will could almost feel the tension rise in its wake.

"Are there no janissaries who have the strength to drink from the Cup?" Leda's voice. "Many who wear the blue yearn to take the white."

"If I was strong enough to drink from the Cup, I would be a Steward already," said Jannick. "But I'm not. I cannot drink, and nor can any of weaker blood. It is too dangerous."

"There is still the boy," said the Elder Steward.

"The boy! He is nothing, shows no sign of any talent. No spark of power. The line of the Lady died with his mother."

"Perhaps it's time to tell the others," said Justice. "The truth. About Marcus. About Simon's plans. The novitiates and the janissaries deserve that much warning—"

"And break our sacred oath?"

"If the others knew what was really happening—"

"If they knew, there would be panic, chaos. And then how would we—"

Jannick broke off. Will felt a prickle of unease.

"Did you lock the door?" Jannick said.

"I thought so," said Leda.

"*Go*," mouthed Will, and he and Violet were pushing and pulling each other to get quickly out of sight. They ended up huddled behind a column, having turned several corners until they were deep in the Hall.

Staying silent though they were breathing hard from the run, they waited for footsteps to recede.

"It's worse than they've told us," said Will, when they knew they were alone. "Simon's getting stronger and they don't have a way to stop him." *Not even me*, he thought, and the words seemed to hang in the air even though he didn't say them.

"Will—" she began.

"The High Janissary is right," said Will. "I can't use magic. In all this time I've never lit the Tree or moved the flame."

"You stopped the sword on Simon's ship. I saw it."

"The Stewards are fighting for their lives," said Will. "They think I can help them. But what if I'm not—what if I can't—"

"You are. You will."

"How do you know that?"

He looked over at her. Her hair had grown long enough that she had started to wear it in the Steward style, and it gave her the appearance of one of them.

"I don't know. I feel it," said Violet. "You fit. Even more than the

Stewards. It's as if these halls were built for you, the same feeling that I get when I hear the Elder Steward speak, or learn one of the old legends. It just feels right somehow."

She was the one who fit. She had mastered the sword drills the novitiates practiced; she ate with them and talked with them; they had accepted her presence, seeming to forget that she lacked Steward blood. She looked like a warrior of old, walking the halls in her old-fashioned clothes.

"My mother could have done it," said Will. "She had a toughness. . . . I can see it when I look back at what she did, at what she—"

"You're her son," said Violet, and Will drew in a shaky breath and curled his fingers around the scar on his palm. He nodded once.

They pushed up and saw that the room they had come to was old and broken-down, with a huge fallen column running through its center, chunks of stone still lying near its shattered portion, even though it looked like the column had fallen centuries ago. The architecture here was different from that of the main citadel and reminded him of the ancient style of the rooms near the Tree Stone.

"Which part of the Hall is this?" Violet took a step out into the room.

"I think we're in the western wing." *The forbidden part of the Hall,* thought Will. "Do you think we'll be in trouble for coming here?"

"Not if they don't find us."

"Be careful where you tread," said Will as he looked down at dust that hadn't been disturbed in a long time.

It was dark, so he doubled back and returned with a torch from one of the wall sconces behind them, and they moved from room to room, looking at old carvings and frescoes. They saw a door made of stone too thick to push open. There was an inscription carved across it. Will found himself staring up at the words.

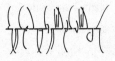

"*Enter only those who can,*" read Will with a shiver, only to find Violet looking at him with a strange expression.

"You can read it?"

He nodded.

"How?"

"I don't know. I just can." He remembered Farah's reaction to hearing him speak the words. She had just stared at him, though she had never asked him about it. The truth was that speaking words in the old language made him feel strange in the same way the Hall's familiarity made him feel strange. Like there was something he ought to remember and couldn't, a phantom at the edges of his vision. "It's like something I've always known."

"'Enter only those who can,'" quoted Violet.

"We can't get in. It's solid stone."

"So?" said Violet. Shouldering him out of the way, she put her palms on the stone. Then she used her strength to push at the door.

To his amazement, the door opened, with a low, echoing sound. The torch he held allowed them to see in the blackness that there were steps that led downward.

Violet had a hint of smugness in her voice. "They think only Stewards are strong enough to get through this door."

"Where *are* we?" said Will.

He lifted the torch, as they descended the steps into a dark underground chamber. Moving forward, they were a small circle of light.

Around them was illuminated a ghostly library, with shelves stretching three or four stories high, disappearing up into the dark. The books were bound in leather but were so ancient that the leather had faded to white. Their spines were bleached like bones, so that the room looked half grave-yard. *Alicorni*, read the black ink written on the spine of one; *Prefecaris*, said another. They walked through the vast chamber, which had the still-ness of a tomb.

"These were animals," said Violet in a soft, shocked voice as they entered a second room. Here they were surrounded by remnants of beasts: a handful of scales far too large to have come from any snake, a claw that shone like glass, an immense beak, a scattering of strange-looking teeth, hooves, bones, internal stones. Will saw a few fragments of hunting equipment, a spear tip, two hooks, part of a trident. On the wall above hung a horn meant to be brought to the lips to sound a single note. *A horn*, he thought, *to summon animals that no longer exist.*

Holding the torch aloft, he led the way into a third room. This one was filled with artifacts. There were stones mounted on the walls that showed pieces of carved inscriptions. He saw part of a bell. Half of a mar-ble statue, its white arm outstretched. A disembodied arch that was not part of the room but had been brought in from somewhere else.

"What is this place?" said Violet, her voice hushed.

Will said, "This is what's left."

His skin prickled as he realized it, the eerie statues and pieces of ar-chitecture around him all that remained of a lost world.

There were fragments of weapons: a hilt with no blade; a knob of ivory; a halved helm; a gauntlet like the one he had seen wither leaves on the vine. *What of the great armies who fought to protect the world?* But he knew the answer. *Gone. Gone like the traces of footsteps after a storm.* There were more poignant items: a phial in shards; a drinking bowl; a child's comb.

At the far end of the room, a beam of moonlight was filtering down from the ceiling, and it struck a stone plinth, as if what lay there was precious and rare.

Will could read the words:

The horn all seek and never find.

On the plinth lay a lacquered wooden box open to show the white horn of an animal he knew only from myth. It was longer than both his arms outstretched, a pearlescent spiral that whorled from a thicker base to a sharp pointed tip. Unlike the other artifacts in the room, it shone, like a spear of light. Clean and untarnished by dust or time, it was like a bolt to the heart.

"A unicorn," said Violet in a soft, awed voice, and he remembered that she was a Lion.

She was reaching out.

"It looks like humans sawed it off. . . ." Her fingers touched the wide base of the horn that was smooth and then spiked and jagged, as though it had been partway sawn and then snapped off.

Like a tree stump, Will thought, and a vision overwhelmed him, a battlefield charge of white horses like a crashing wave, some of them bearing armored riders with flashing swords, others with their long horns lowered like deadly spears. They were charging into an oncoming rush of black shadows, and Will's heart was pounding knowing they wouldn't survive but were charging anyway, impossibly brave. There was an answer here, as somewhere in the distance he heard Violet say, "Will."

He looked up, but not at her. At a black archway cut into the stone of the wall. There was another room.

He took his torch and walked toward it, drawn as if by a force. He could hear Violet behind him, saying, "Will? *Where are you going?*" He ignored her. There were steps leading downward to a room that was smaller than the others, and pitch-black.

It wasn't an ordinary darkness; it was tangible and surrounding, eerily darkening the torch rather than being lit by it. Violet raced down the stairs after him, then stopped short at the bottom, as if the thick, stifling dark repelled her.

There was something else here.

That's what the Steward had said on the ship, moments before the Corrupted Blade had cracked open its container. This felt the same, but thickly worse, as if whatever was here was darker and more dangerous than the black flame of the Blade could ever be. But he was drawn to it too, as if he sensed a presence that called to him. He took another step forward.

Will could feel what repulsed Violet, a roiling wrongness. Yet he couldn't stop. His heart was pounding. Every answer sought seemed to lie in the promise of what hung in the air before him.

It wasn't the Blade. It was something else.

It looked simple at first. A piece of black rock. As if suspended, it hung right in the center of the chamber, rotating slowly. He raised the torch to look at it, but the light had no effect.

It was so black that it seemed to suck all the light out of the room. An endless void, a terrible hole that wanted to consume everything in the world. It called to him as a chasm calls to one who might throw himself over, bringing him right to its edge and whispering to him to jump.

He wanted to touch it. He reached out his hand, and as his fingertips brushed its surface he felt a terrible stab of cold. He gasped as the shock of it went through him. He saw a vision of the four empty thrones of the Hall, but there were four resplendent figures sitting in them, great kings in bright, shining robes. But as he watched, three started to change, their faces sloughing off, their bones turning transparent, until they were horrific shadow versions of themselves. And then he saw a figure rising above them all, with a pale crown and eyes of black flame—

"Stop!"

He gasped as a hard grip on his arm wrenched him back, and he found himself staring instead at the face of the Elder Steward, her eyes flashing and stern. Her hands were on his shoulders, holding him back. "You must never touch it. That stone is death." Her voice was as unrelenting as her eyes, an expression he had never seen her wear before. "Even the briefest touch will kill."

He blinked, and looked around the chamber. He felt like he had been snapped out of a dream, or a spell. The Elder Steward had come in behind them, sweeping past Violet, who was looking on from the stairs with concern.

"Kill?" he said dazedly. The Elder Steward's hands on his shoulders made him feel warmer. Her presence had the opposite effect of the stone. She seemed to emanate a reassuring warmth, like the fire of a welcoming hearth. Near her the torchlight was brighter.

He looked back at the suspended stone. He could have sworn that he had touched it . . . hadn't he? He could still feel the chill of its cold, see those figures transforming in their thrones. Had he imagined it? He had an overwhelming urge to place his palm against the stone to make sure.

"That is why we keep it locked away, where no one can enter," said the Elder Steward, with a rather pointed look.

Still half caught up in the stone, it was a moment before Will recalled that he and Violet weren't supposed to be in this chamber. He flushed. "We were just—"

"Yes, I know. The two of you have a habit of being in places that you don't belong." But her tone was friendly. With a kind hand on his arm, she began to steer Will back toward the archway where Violet waited. Violet immediately drew in close to the circle of light from the Elder Steward's torch, as if it were a sanctuary that sheltered all three of them from the stone.

"What is it?"

Will turned for a last look at it, the flame from their torch touching its surface and disappearing utterly, as if falling into endless depths. He could still feel its pull, not wanting to look away.

"That is the darkest and most dangerous object we possess," said the Elder Steward, her own eyes growing troubled again as she followed the direction of Will's gaze. "That is the Shadow Stone."

"The Shadow Stone . . . ," said Will.

The words sent their shiver down into him. He remembered the white horses galloping into an army of roiling black shadows, the last, desperate charge of the light.

The Elder Steward nodded. "You once asked what happened to the four kings."

The thrones. Those four empty thrones. *Long ago, there were four great kings of the old world,* Justice had said. *It wasn't always the Hall of the Stewards. It was once the Hall of Kings.*

"Justice said that three of them joined the Dark King," said Will, "and the fourth fled and was lost forever."

"That is only part of the story," said the Elder Steward.

Surrounded as she was by the broken stones and displaced architecture of the old world, her words took on an extra weight.

"The three made a terrible bargain. They swore to serve the Dark King in exchange for power. He granted them strength beyond that of any human for the span of a single mortal life. But on their death . . . they transformed. They became monstrous creatures of shadow utterly obedient to the Dark King's will."

"Creatures of shadow . . . ?"

"Insubstantial as the night. Unable to be touched. No wall could keep them out. No warrior could fight against them. You cannot strike a shadow; your blade would pass through its form like smoke. But a shadow can strike you . . . strike you down and kill you. It made them invincible."

The Shadow Kings . . . He could almost taste it, dust, death, and horror: an endless darkness that would swallow them all. The circle of light where the three of them stood felt suddenly very small.

"How were the Shadow Kings stopped?"

"No one knows," said the Elder Steward. "But they are trapped in that stone. And they must never be allowed to get out."

In his vision of the Shadow Kings he had seen an even more terrible figure, rising above them all. The Dark King, the King of Kings, greater than any shadow, wearing his pale crown. It was as though the Shadow Kings walked before him, clearing a path for their master. And suddenly Will understood why they could never be let out. A moment later, the Elder Steward spoke the words.

"They are one of the portents," said the Elder Steward. "They will herald the return of the Dark King."

Like James, thought Will, and shivered. The Elder Steward searched his face for a long moment, and then continued, her eyes grave.

"Simon seeks to conjure a shadow of his own. It is the first step to returning the Dark King," said the Elder Steward. "The Dark King made many such creatures. They swelled the ranks of his armies, invincible on the battlefield. Only the most powerful magic users could fight them.

"If Simon managed to conjure even a single shadow, it would be a devastating opponent, and with magic all but gone from the world, no mortal now alive could stand against it.

"But the Shadow Kings were far worse. Faster, stronger, and with a deadlier desire for destruction. The Shadow Kings led the army of shadows on their nightmare steeds. They broke the defenses of the great cities of Light, and spread the dark across the lands, for neither might nor magic could stop them. A single shadow might seem terrifying to us, but they were nothing to the merciless horror of the Shadow Kings.

"If they get out?" said the Elder Steward. "Night will fall forever, and in the darkness He will rise, a final eclipse that will end our world."

"It's Marcus," said Will.

They were back in his room; its circular walls and the orange light from the lamps felt safe and familiar after the eerie depths of the rooms beneath the Hall.

Will spoke with his heart racing. He had barely been able to hold the words back until he and Violet were alone. Now, as she clambered onto the bedcovers where they sat together so often, it spilled out, blurted with urgency.

"What do you mean?"

"The reason why Simon's close to returning the Dark King. Marcus knows. He knows how to conjure a shadow."

Violet's eyes went wide. They had spent so many nights together in her room or his, Violet with a sword and him with a candle, practicing their separate lessons. It all seemed so naive now that he'd guessed the truth.

Will said, "You heard the Elder Steward. She said that conjuring a shadow was the first step to summoning the Dark King. Simon must be trying to get the secret from Marcus."

Stewards were strong, but how long could they hold up under torture? And if the Stewards couldn't fight James, how could they fight a shadow that no weapon could pierce? *You cannot strike a shadow . . . But a shadow can strike you.*

"How desperate they all are to get him back," said Violet slowly. "All of the missions beyond the wall, sacrificing dozens of Stewards—"

Will couldn't stop seeing that vision of the three Shadow Kings on their thrones, great and terrible creatures, subservient to one greater than all of them, the Dark King, who seemed to tower over their thrones like a god over the heavens.

Simon was the Dark King's descendant. Simon wanted a shadow army of his own.

And if he learned from Marcus how to conjure it . . .

He will rise. The final eclipse.

It made sense of all the tense looks, the broken-off conversations, the fear that underlay them. The Stewards were scared. But they were riding out anyway. To their deaths. Their Order had lasted for centuries, guarding the secrets of the old world, so that if the Dark King ever returned, someone would remember, and be there to stop him.

"They have to get Marcus back. It's the only way to stop Simon." The Stewards believed that they were now in the final days, with Simon right on the cusp of returning the Dark King. "But they can't," said Will. "They can't even *find* him."

And if they couldn't get Marcus back, Simon would unleash that terrible darkness, that cold . . . Will felt it down to his bones.

"How do you rescue a man you can't find?" said Will, looking up at Violet.

Abruptly, Violet pushed herself up off the bed and stalked to the window, which looked out at the gate. It wasn't dawn yet, so the view was still dark, the only points of light the torches on the battlements and the bright flare of the Final Flame.

"Violet?"

She seemed to be struggling with something. Her silhouette at the window had changed since their first days here. She was still boyishly slender, but constant training had broadened her shoulders a little. She held her head higher too, and her posture was straighter.

When she turned back to face him, her eyes were very dark, as though she was torn by a painful choice.

"They can't find him," she said. "But maybe I can."

CHAPTER SIXTEEN

SHE MET WILL in the east courtyard at dusk.

Her stomach was roiling with nerves, her senses on high alert, even as she tried to stay calm. The thought of what she was about to do made her feel sick, nauseous and feverish, as if chills had set her teeth chattering. She forced it down, determined to go through with this. It was her chance to make a difference, to show the Stewards she could do what was right. *I can do this.*

In the end, it was simple.

The Stewards needed to find Marcus, and she had access to Simon's inner circle that no one else had.

I can do this. I can prove myself. I can fight for the Light.

The Stewards couldn't know. She couldn't tell them, *I can find Marcus because I'm a Lion.* But if she went home to her Lion family, she could find out where Simon was keeping Marcus before he told Simon how to conjure a shadow.

Will was leading two white Steward horses, beautiful creatures with arched necks and delicate fluted noses. Violet had stolen two sets of

Steward whites from the washroom. It had been her idea to sneak out in secret, to keep the Stewards from finding out where she was going.

Will had argued against it. "You can't. You can't go back to them."

"My father's one of Simon's closest confidants," she had said to him, feeling the ugly truth of it. "I know that if I go back home, I can find out where he's keeping Marcus. I can sneak into my father's office, get access to his records. . . ." She had lowered her voice to a whisper. Talking about her father in the Hall made her nervous. She half expected the Stewards to burst in, forcing her to the ground, shouting, *Lion.*

If they ever found out what she was—

"Your father wants to kill you," Will had said. "Remember? He needs to kill a Lion so Tom can come into his power."

"I can handle my family," she'd said.

Can you? a voice in her mind had niggled back at her. But she'd squashed it down. She had a chance to help the Stewards, and she was going to do it.

A Lion doesn't have to fight for the Dark, she thought. *And I'll prove that.*

"You're the one who shouldn't leave the Hall," she had said to Will. "It's you Simon's after." In her mind the three hounds of Simon's crest were like the swarm of black dogs that had hunted Will across the marsh. Simon wanted Will badly and wouldn't stop until he had him.

"If Marcus tells Simon how to conjure a shadow," said Will, "it won't matter where I am. Are you sure you can't just tell them?"

Tell the Stewards. Tell Justice. *I'm a Lion. Tom's my brother. The boy who killed all your friends.* Her stomach clenched.

"I can't. You know what they'd do to a Lion. They'd lock me up"—*at best*—"and then we'd lose our chance to find out what Simon has done with Marcus."

They quickly put on the white Steward uniforms she'd stolen and mounted the two Steward horses. Then they rode to the gate looking as much like Stewards as possible.

They had chosen dusk because the dim light would further disguise their faces. Stewards guarded the gate against entry; they didn't police those who left the Hall. Even with these precautions, she still felt her pulse racing. As they approached the gate, a thousand worries rushed in. Had she worn the Steward whites correctly? Was she tall enough to pass as a Steward? Would Leda take a second look at her face? Would they somehow guess what she was?

Lion, Lion, Lion . . .

Leda, on duty, raised her hand from high above on the walls. Will raised a hand in reply. Violet sat up straight and did her best to adopt Cyprian's haughty manner: the perfect Steward, shoulders square, back straight, chin up.

Then to her astonishment they were through; she felt that lurch of crossing the threshold of the gate, and they were suddenly out on the marshes, breathing the fresh, crisp air and looking out at the world.

There was no sign of Simon's men on the ride, just the splashes and sounds of insects and birds, and the darkening light of dusk on the marshes.

A single glance behind her as they rode showed the broken arch on the marsh, that lonely image set against the sky. It was as if the entire Hall had disappeared, or been nothing more than a dream. If it weren't for her clothes and the white horses, she might have thought she had imagined all of it.

No going back now.

Not wanting to look like ancient knights in London, they stopped before the river to change their clothes. Expecting to feel like herself again, Violet was startled at how scratchy and uncomfortable Tom's cast-offs felt after the light fabric of the Steward tunic. She squirmed and frowned, like they didn't fit. Then she and Will rubbed mud into the white coats of the Steward horses, a determined blotting. The Steward horses looked utterly affronted, but at least they looked a little more like horses and a little less like two radiant beams of light.

Crossing the Lea at an upstream bridge, Violet let herself begin to look forward to seeing London again. Alongside the nerves, she thought of all the things she had missed. The taste of hot chestnuts in a cone of paper, or a buttery baked potato bought to keep her hands warm. The bright laughter of a puppet show on a corner. The grand carriages and top hats spilling out around a theater or hall.

And then she saw it on the horizon.

London was a shock, an ugly, clumped scar upon the land. The closer they got, the uglier it was. The countryside turned into torn earth and dirty, squalid houses, streets clogged with people, donkey carts, stage-coaches, trudging drovers, boys, thieves, idlers, and every sort of person that could be squeezed into its confines. It was an assault on the senses after the tranquility of the Hall.

When they dismounted, her foot sank into vile, squelching muck. A moment later she found herself coughing. A thick, choking miasma hung over the houses, woodsmoke and the smells of people and sewage from the river. She wanted to press her forearm to her nose to block out the stench, bile rising. Had it always smelled like this? And the noise: the clamor was so loud, voices shouting, drivers yelling, a discordant clutter that was too much for the ears. She was jostled, people pushing her out of the way, their shoulders slamming into hers, as though she couldn't quite find the right pace to keep up with everyone, instead at odds with them.

They had returned to the White Hart, reasoning that if Justice had brought them here, it would be a safe place for Will to stay while Violet searched for Marcus. A boy took their horses with more deference than she had expected. Looking at Will, she was surprised to realize that he looked different. The Stewards had always had something otherworldly about them, and Will had that quality now too—the way he carried himself, his posture straight, his movements purposeful, as though the squalor of London didn't touch him. She glimpsed herself in the inn window and was shocked to see that she looked just like him: knightly, even in her London clothes.

A woman threw a bucket of slops out of a window and Violet sidestepped, Steward-fast. Her stomach twisted as she realized what she had done—would instincts like that give her away to her family? Would they see a Steward when they looked at her? Would they know?

As she had hidden her Lion self from the Stewards, would she now have to hide her Steward self from her family?

New sounds and smells hit her as the inn door opened, a wave of shouts and bellowing laughter, and the smell of thick gravy, molding straw, and stale beer. She walked into a loud, raucous scene, hard to make out in the dim haze of the interior.

"This way, good sirs," the innsman said, and she had never had a "good sir" or "good miss" before. She and Will ordered two mutton joints with gravy and received a little bob of the head from the innswoman. It wasn't just her reflexes; it was a difference in bearing. Something in her was changing the behavior of others.

She chose an out-of-the-way table where she and Will could sit without being seen, and kept one eye on the door, alert for the possibility of danger.

"People never call me sir," said Will, leaning in to whisper across the stained wooden table. In the dimly lit corner of the inn, they were seated across from one another.

"Me neither. They call me boy, or scamp."

"Wastrel."

"Wretch."

"You there."

Or worse. "London—it's . . . different than I remember." She couldn't quite bring herself to say what gnawed at her: *I'm the one who's different. London hasn't changed.* It had been three months in the Hall. Only three months? How could three months have turned her into a stranger in her own city?

"Louder and more crowded, with no morning chants," said Will. She managed a weak smile.

Two mutton joints were plopped down onto the rough wooden table in front of them. She looked down into the greasy, congealing mess and felt sick. It smelled rank, gray and brown, the plate encrusted with grime. She forced herself to take a bite and it was thickly tasteless, its different textures unpleasant, this part gluggy, this part chewy, this part rough. She forced the swallow down. She didn't feel the wondrous revitalization that came after a bite of Steward food, the crunch of a fresh pea pod, or the sweet tang of an orange plucked from the tree. It just made her stomach heavy.

A burst of raucous laughter to her left made her head jerk around, a group of men slamming their tin mugs down on the table. Behind them two men jostled each other, unwashed, unshaven figures slopping beer onto the blackened straw. Her eyes darted from them to the figure near the door, shouting for the innsman. She felt jumpy, on edge. She looked back at Will uneasily.

"We haven't been recognized," he said.

"It's not that. It's—" She struggled to put it into words.

"They don't know," said Will, and she nodded slowly as he cut to the heart of it. "They don't know about the old world, about the shadows, about any of it. They don't know what's coming."

Her skin prickled, because that was it: the unnerving part, all this chaotic life, it was unknowing, and therefore vulnerable. "No one's warned them," she said. "No one's told them a fight's coming." They were just living their ordinary lives. But worse than that: "Even if someone told them—"

"They wouldn't believe it," said Will.

She nodded. These people—there was a battle raging and these people didn't even know it. They didn't know the truth, just like she hadn't known it. In the whole inn, only she and Will knew about the Dark King's threat.

She felt the loneliness of the Steward mission for the first time: to be the only watchers, the only ones who remembered the past, who knew the dangers of what was coming. . . .

More than that. The Stewards had always seemed so detached—so separate from the world. They kept to the ancient ways in the Hall, and it kept them in the ancient world, as if they had never really left it. Year by year, the world outside changed, but they stayed the same, growing more and more apart from people's lives beyond the Hall.

If she stayed with them, would there be a time when she couldn't return to the outside world either?

She already felt it. A separation from the people around her, based on a knowledge of what was coming, as though she had one foot in the ancient world.

Will said, "What are you going to tell your family?"

She pulled her gaze from the squabbling patrons. Her family weren't naive or unknowing, like the men and women sitting in this tavern. They knew the fight that lay ahead. And they had arrayed themselves on the Dark King's side.

"I used to sneak out at night all the time," Violet found herself saying. "Come back at breakfast. Just plonk myself down at the table and ask for some toast. My father would pretend he didn't know I'd been gone."

"Part of you wants to go back to them." Will said it in a quiet voice.

"Wouldn't you?" she said.

Will looked down at his scarred palm. "My mother and I, we moved around a lot. I never really got to know people. She kept us to ourselves." He looked up and smiled, a wry expression. "I've never lived somewhere like the Hall of the Stewards. I've never had somewhere that was safe, to depend on, and to protect." She couldn't look away from his straightforward words. "But there's a part of me . . . My mother and I didn't have much, but we had each other. We were family."

Family. Tom was still there in her heart, underneath all the painful fears and doubts. The Tom who she looked up to, the Tom she had striven to emulate, before she knew about Lions.

She knew what Will meant because she had felt it herself, the devotion to one person who she had believed would always be there for her, and the safety of that feeling.

"Would you go back to that?" Violet looked again at the others in the inn and tried to imagine being one of them again. "To not knowing?"

"I can't." Will pressed his thumb into his palm. "I thought my life was normal, but I know now that it wasn't." He looked up, his eyes very dark. "My mother was scared. Always on edge, always looking over her shoulder . . . She was trying to protect me from the truth. The truth about who I was and what was happening." The scar that ran along the fate line of his palm was mirrored on the back of his hand, as if it had been run right through. "I can see why she did it, and a part of me might even want to go back to it, but I can't. Not now that I know what she knew."

I thought my life was normal, but I know now that it wasn't. Violet thought about her childhood, indulged by her father, doing as she pleased, without rules or schooling.

She'd thought that was normal too. But something had been wrong the whole time.

"I'm glad I know," she said, making the decision suddenly and with stubborn pride. Better a Lion than a lamb to the slaughter.

"We both get to choose our family," said Will. She flushed slowly. She felt suddenly, fiercely protective of him, remembering his strange determination and his loyalty. He'd come back for her when no one else had, and he was here with her now, despite the danger.

"I should go soon," she said gruffly. "I don't know how long it will take." She had to find out the information they needed either from Tom or her father.

"I'll be here waiting."

"Don't get into any trouble."

"What trouble could I get into?" said Will.

CHAPTER SEVENTEEN

KATHERINE WAS PUSHING her toe back into her shoe at Martin's as the strange man entered, strode over to Mrs. Dupont, and whispered something in her ear.

She had just been fitted for the most perfect pair of slippers: white silk, each with a tiny pink embroidered rose. They would match exquisitely with the gifts that Lord Crenshaw had sent: beautiful day dresses of sprig muslin with high, tapered waists and delicate puffed sleeves; white silk gloves with six embroidered buttons; a necklace of pearls that was just the right accompaniment.

Now, however, Mrs. Dupont was approaching with a small frown on her face. The man who had whispered in her ear was waiting by the door. Katherine hadn't heard what he had said, except maybe she had seen him mouth the words *the boy*.

The boy?

"If you'd wait here, milady," said Mrs. Dupont. "I'll be back in a moment."

"But what—" Katherine began, but Mrs. Dupont had already left, striding out of the door of the shop.

It left Katherine standing awkwardly. She remembered Mr. Prescott saying something about a boy. What was it? *I'm sure Mrs. Dupont will be back shortly.* Moments ticked past. She could see the curious looks of the shop owner and his assistant. She flushed, imagining their disapproval. No young lady should be seen in public without a chaperone. Especially not the young fiancée of a man like Lord Crenshaw. Even the idea could ruin a reputation, and Katherine knew that she was watched by many who were prone to gossip.

Lord Crenshaw was spending a great deal of time in London recently—for business, but rumors of his beautiful fiancée were everywhere, Mrs. Dupont said, and everyone knew Katherine was part of the reason.

Katherine had liked the idea that she was talked about, that she would be glimpsed on this outing. Already invitations had begun to arrive at the house, though of course any social engagements were heavily curated by her aunt. A shopping trip had been allowed because she would be chaperoned by Mrs. Dupont and a valet, with their driver waiting with the carriage outside.

But now she was alone.

Uneasy thoughts of *scandal* and *impropriety* made her clasp her hands inside her sable muff. She wasn't supposed to be seen in town alone. How long until people started talking? She couldn't wait here; people were staring. She would wait in the carriage, out of sight of prying eyes, and safely accompanied by Lord Crenshaw's valet and driver.

She stepped out of the shop onto the crowded pavement, and her stomach sank, pulled down by the first tendrils of panic.

The carriage was gone.

The street looked cold and anonymous. She looked desperately around for any sign of the carriage, but it was nowhere to be seen. Its absence was strange and frightening. Where was Mrs. Dupont? The carriage couldn't really have left her here, could it?

But it had. They had all left her. The reality that she was alone on the streets of London made her skin chill. A terrible sense of being abandoned swept over her. Worse than the threat to her safety was the threat to her reputation. If anyone knew she had been out without a chaperone . . . Katherine was starting to panic, all the stories of young girls ruined by foolish indiscretions rushing into her mind.

As if enacting her worst nightmare, the shop owner emerged from the shop, and she realized that gossip was about to fly from his shop to the homes of every client he had in London—

"Cousin," said a voice, a hand in hers steadying her.

She didn't have a cousin. She didn't know that voice. She looked up in confusion.

The boy who had taken her hand had a striking, high-cheekboned face, dark eyes, and a tumble of dark hair. It was the sort of face you couldn't drag your eyes away from, that would have been startling even if you saw it across a room. He was attractive in a breath-catching, Byronic way, like the electric feeling of clouds gathering in a storm.

She felt a startling, instant connection, her eyes meeting his. He raised his brows, asking silently if she would play along. He was offering to pro-vide her with the perfect chaperone: a male relative. He had even said the word cousin loudly enough that passersby could hear.

She felt herself flush at the thought that this young gentleman—for he was a gentleman, surely—had seen her predicament and come to her rescue.

"Thank you, cousin," she answered, just as loudly.

Looking back at the shop front, she saw the owner relax and retreat inside, as though a minor mystery had been solved.

"'Cousin'?" she whispered, once the shopkeeper had gone. "We don't look a thing alike!"

"I wasn't sure I could pass as your brother."

Who is he? She was gazing at him. She couldn't shake that feeling of connection. His actions in coming to her rescue were both impudent and chivalrous, of which she was meltingly aware.

She could feel the warmth of his hand beneath hers. Except for the one or two scrupulously respectable acquaintances selected for her by her aunt, she had not met anyone in London, certainly not any attractive young men. Her heartbeat was behaving oddly. *What would Lord Crenshaw think if he knew a young man had taken my hand?*

"Where is it we're going?" he whispered back conspiratorially.

"My fiancé's carriage was supposed to be waiting for me." She said the word *fiancé* very intentionally. He didn't ask, *And where is your chaperone?* He didn't ask any questions about her situation, which was a sign of his gentlemanly manners, she thought. "We were returning home right away."

"And it's gone?"

"Yes, I—it's—yes."

"Then I'll find you a coach, Miss—"

"Kent," she offered.

"Miss Kent," he said.

The weather, which just that morning Annabel had described as "chancy," chose that moment to change from chilly into cold wet drops that fell from the sky. The young man was perfectly gallant. He immediately stripped off his jacket for her to hold over her head, so that she was shivering but dry as he stepped out into the busy road to hail down a hackney.

As she watched, he procured a coach while the rain utterly soaked him, the passing wheels of a carriage splashing mud across his boots and trousers. The hackney coach pulled up with its mismatched horses, one dull brown, one a dirty white color. Escorting her to it, he quickly gave up his jacket altogether, laying it down so she could sit on its dry lining to preserve her dress from the muddy seat. They clambered in together. The coach driver gave a flick of his whip, calling, "Walk on!"

Inside, she felt safe at last. She was on her way home, and the threat to her reputation was over. The rain had turned the carriage windows into a blur of liquid. Enclosed inside its bubble, she was dry and warm. The young man opposite her was soaked, his wet shirt transparent and clinging, his trousers ruined with mud. His garments were secondhand, but had been repaired so exquisitely the eye barely noticed. He looked like an aristocratic young suitor, his obvious breeding belying the clothes. She was struck again by his vivid good looks, the fall of his dark hair like the subject of a romantic painting.

He was gallant enough to say, "This is an adventure."

"May I ask your name?"

"Kempen," he said. "Will Kempen."

"I hope I'm not taking you too far out of your way, Mr. Kempen."

He was looking back at her with evident curiosity, though he had been too much of a gentleman to ask her any questions. So when he merely said, "Not at all; I'm happy to accompany you," Katherine found herself relenting, telling the whole story in a rush.

"The truth is, Mrs. Dupont—she's my lady's maid—was out with me, but a man came into the shop while I was being fitted for some shoes."

Martin's was one of London's most exclusive shoemakers, and Katherine had been looking forward to the excursion all week. Until Mrs. Dupont's disappearance, the outing had exceeded her expectations. She had been measured, then looked at delightful samples, with Mrs.

Dupont pointing out the most fashionable ones, telling her, *Lord Crenshaw thinks the color pink suits you.*

"He wasn't one of our servants. I'd never seen him before. He came and spoke to her. I don't know what he said, but she seemed to think it was urgent, and left right away!" The disturbing feelings of earlier came back to her, that sense of being abandoned. "And then, when I came out to look for the carriage, it had gone. Mrs. Dupont must have taken it, or—all I can think is that my fiancé called them away on business, not realizing I was with them."

"Your fiancé?" said Will mildly.

He was gazing across at her. Droplets of water still clung to the hollow of his throat and wet his waistcoat and shirt. But he had a way of ignoring the discomfort, as if it was all just part of the adventure, that of course he'd get drenched rescuing my lady from a social dilemma.

Looking back at him, it was easy to forget the disturbing feelings of earlier. It was occurring to her that this whole thing was rather dashing. Will looked just like the sort of handsome young lord's son she had always imagined asking her to dance at a ball. *I always knew I'd meet you,* came the thought, out of nowhere. Of course, her aunt wouldn't approve. This was one of those "unnecessary youthful experiences" her aunt wished her to avoid.

One she never thought she'd have. She was conscious of her own pulse.

"Lord Crenshaw," said Katherine. "Do you know him?"

The words were conversational. "I've heard of him. He owns ships, doesn't he?"

"Yes, that's him." Of course, everyone knew of Lord Crenshaw.

Will spoke with polite interest. "And he collects antiquities—or is that his father?"

"They both do. But Lord Crenshaw has a passion for it. They say he dredged the whole Thames in summer just to recover a sword that he wanted." Katherine liked the wealth and power this displayed. Annabel had later said it was the talk of the town. An extravagance that only a man of his fortune could afford.

"Did he find it?" said Will.

"Apparently. Annabel—that's my aunt's maid—she said that—"

"Whoa!" came the call from the coachman outside, and she broke off as the coach pulled up at the address she had given.

"Oh! We've arrived," she said.

She suddenly realized that it was the last she would see of her rescuer. This had not been a meeting at a ball where he might leave a card and come to call on her family a week later. This meeting had been a secret, a glimpse of a life she didn't have, and it would not be repeated. She felt again that connection to him, and the excitement of their adventure. She wasn't ready for it to end.

"I can't allow you to leave without replacing your jacket. It's the least I can do."

She could see his splashed, muddy trousers very plainly, and could only imagine the sorry state of the jacket that would be revealed when she stood up.

Will demurred. "That isn't necessary—"

"I insist. You're soaked. And covered in mud. And your hair is ruined. And—"

Carefully, he said, "I don't think your family would be thrilled to learn that a young man had escorted you home."

She flushed. That was true. It would be a scandal. The very scandal that he had accompanied her to avoid. If her aunt knew she had spent time with a young man, it would mean a lifetime of disapproving looks, not to mention losing every remaining freedom she had. Certainly, she couldn't introduce Will to any of them.

"Then you can wait for me in the stables while I bring you the clothes." She lifted her chin. "Tell the driver to go around the back," she said. Perhaps Will realized that she wouldn't be denied, because he opened the coach window to shout the instruction out to the driver.

They pulled up near the entrance to the mews, and she could see at once that her own carriage had not returned. Mrs. Dupont was still unaccounted for. But her aunt and uncle would be at home with her sister and the servants. She would have to be careful. She showed Will the back way in through the mews and stables that allowed you into the garden— and from there into the house.

The stables were dry and warm, smelling of fresh hay, and they ran in through the rain. She accumulated a few droplets on her hair and bonnet, but it was nothing she couldn't shake off, and she was home now, out of harm's way.

"It's a lovely house," Will said. He was looking past her into the dark leaves of the garden.

"We only came here in January. We used to live in Hertfordshire." She kept her eyes on the lit windows of the house as she said it.

"I was the opposite. My family used to live in London, but we left for the country."

He pushed his hand through his hair, forcing out the water. Something about the casual nature of the gesture made her flush. She had never been alone with a boy her own age before. Their eyes met, and he looked amused, making the situation like a joke shared between them.

"Wait here," she said, and went out toward the house.

Inside, the full impact of what she was doing reasserted itself. This was Lord Crenshaw's house. The servants were Lord Crenshaw's servants. She had ringed herself in with Lord Crenshaw's walls, and into it all she had brought someone she shouldn't. A young man whom she'd only just met, taking a risk she should never have taken.

Her heartbeat accelerated wildly as she entered the back parlor. Was that footsteps? She stayed very still inside the door. After a few seconds of silence, she took a first step inside.

"What are you doing?" said a familiar voice.

"I was just speaking with the coachman." Katherine turned calmly.

Elizabeth was standing in the parlor, frowning. "That's not the coach-man." And then: "It's a strange boy you've brought back to the house."

"He's a friend," said Katherine.

"You don't have any friends," said Elizabeth.

Katherine drew in a breath. "Elizabeth. He helped me, and it messed up his clothes. I'm getting him some new ones. It's just polite, but you know the kind of trouble I'd be in. You can't tell anyone."

"You mean it might mess up *the engagement*," said Elizabeth, with particular scorn.

That was true. But Katherine felt excitement rather than nerves. The threat of discovery was low, she thought. It felt more as if she and Will were in an adventure together. "That's right."

"He's getting you in trouble. I don't like him."

"You don't like anyone."

"That's not true! I like Aunt. And our old cook. And Mr. Bailey who sells muffins." Elizabeth spoke slowly, thinking the list through with care. "And—"

"I ran into him by chance and promised that he'd be safe here. Would you have me break my word?"

Her little sister was a very upright person, a stickler, even, for the rules, and this point of honor was digested, albeit with difficulty.

"No," said Elizabeth, scowling.

"No. So stay quiet and don't say anything."

Will looked up when she entered with the jacket, half-changed in long trousers and socked feet, with the shirt she had left out for him untied and the neckcloth still draped over his shoulders, a state of undress she had never seen before in a man.

She had earlier brought him a towel to get dry as well as the clothes he was now wearing. She would have liked to have sat him down in front of a fire with Cook's hot broth, but she couldn't light a fire or risk the kitchens. The enclosing walls of the stables would have to be their sanctuary, with its nose-tickling hay smell and the occasional soft sound of the horses. He lifted the edge of the neckcloth.

"Whose clothes are these?"

"My fiancé's," she said.

She saw him go still in a way that she liked. He didn't look like Lord Crenshaw in those clothes. He looked younger, her own age. Her heart was beating fast. It wasn't that he might be dangerous—he *was* dangerous. If she was found with him here, it would ruin her. It would ruin not only her but her entire family. She could hear the distant sounds from the house, see the lights from the windows. Each sound was a threat.

Does your fiancé know that you spend time alone with other men? He didn't say that, though she could feel it between them. Instead, he said carefully, "He's taller than I am."

"And older," she said.

What was she doing? She had brought him here to replace the clothes he had wrecked on her behalf. But now that they were alone together, it felt like having the dashing son of a lord ask her for a dance at one of the outings her aunt insisted she was too young to attend.

Despite what he'd said, Lord Crenshaw's clothes fit him perfectly, and he looked good in them. *Better than Lord Crenshaw*, whispered a treacherous voice. She'd imagined a suitor just like this. The draped neckcloth gave him an unconcerned, slightly rakish look. Her eyes were drawn to it.

She said, "I'll tie that for you. I used to do it all the time for my uncle. Come here."

He came forward in the same slow, careful way that he had spoken. She reached up to his neck and he pulled back instinctively. "Are you shy? I've seen a man before." She lifted her chin. "I grew up in a family with boys." She was lying.

"Cousins?" he said.

She took up the ends of the neckcloth. She knew that her looks were considered her greatest asset—her looks, after all, had procured the engagement with Lord Crenshaw. But youth and a sheltered upbringing had meant that she had never been feted as a beauty, nor yet even had the kind of social engagements that would put her in the company of suitors—at least not until Lord Crenshaw had made himself known to her family. And Lord Crenshaw's admiration had come at a businesslike distance. Now she got to see, gratifyingly, at close quarters, the effect she had on a young man of her own age, as Will's dark eyes went even darker.

She was less prepared for his effect on her, how hard it was to concentrate on tying the neckcloth over the consciousness she had of him, his breath moving the thin, fine fabric of the shirt, the one lock of hair that fell down over his forehead.

"If he knew about this, I suppose my fiancé would kill you."

Another conversational remark. She didn't look up. But she was attuned to his reaction, imagining—or was she?—that he was controlling his breathing too.

"Then I hope you won't tell him."

She straightened the last of the neckcloth now in its simple tie and made certain to adopt a casual calm as she stepped back. "There."

As he settled the jacket on his shoulders, she realized in a rush that it was a mistake—a mistake to have dressed him in Lord Crenshaw's clothes. That vital quality he had that drew the eye was transformed into a blaze, the clothing remaking him into a powerful young lord, and Lord Crenshaw had never looked like this, for all Annabel's assurances that he was just what a fine suitor should be.

"I'm in your debt," Will said.

Instead of demurring that it was he who had helped her first, she said: "Then answer a question."

His hands went still over the last of the jacket buttons.

"All right."

"Tell me who you are really. Where are you from? Who is your family? I thought you might be incognito."

"If I were hiding who I was, I'd hardly admit it."

It was all he said. The faint sounds of the horses were loud in the silence, the dust particles from the hay drifting slowly through the air. She realized that he'd said everything he was going to say, though she'd brought him back here and given him clothes. She spoke in a rush, frowning and sounding—she didn't care—a little like Elizabeth. "You're not going to tell me any of it!"

Will was shaking his head. "You've been kind," he said. "Kinder than I thought. You shouldn't be part of this. I'm sorry. I thought I could—I was wrong. I was wrong to—"

"To?"

There was a sudden loud sound, the unmistakable crunch of wheels on new-raked gravel, coming right toward them.

"It's the carriage," said Katherine.

"You should go out and meet them," said Will. "I'll go out the back way."

"But—" *Will I ever see you again?* was a plaintive cry she didn't want to make. There wasn't much time. She would pretend that she and Mrs. Dupont came back together, which would save her own reputation and Mrs. Dupont's. She lifted her chin. "The jacket is a loan."

From his eyes as he took her hand, she knew that he understood her meaning. "Then I'll have to return it."

He didn't kiss her hand the way Lord Crenshaw had done. He just bowed his head over her fingers, his words a promise that they would meet again.

She walked out into the courtyard to meet Mrs. Dupont.

CHAPTER EIGHTEEN

"—AFRAID IT'S TOO late for callers—" said the housekeeper as the door opened, but then her eyes went wide. "*Violet?*" and then, "Mr. Ballard! Mr. Ballard!"

Violet found herself pulled into the hall amid a flurry of activity, the house waking, doors opening, footsteps clattering, and voices raised all at once.

"Violet!" she heard. It was Tom's voice. She saw his familiar blue eyes wide with shock and recognition. She was immediately in his arms, his hug warm and safe. "Oh God. I thought you were dead. I thought you were—" She found herself clutching him in turn, like a lifeline. "They said you jumped back onto the ship—"

"Tom, I'm sorry. I didn't think—"

"It's all right. You're safe. You're home."

His strong, solid embrace was real, and she gave herself over to it, eyes closed. She had last seen him looking dead and pale on the riverbank, but now he was here, warm and alive. She let herself feel it, the relief of return, the wash of gladness at the genuine concern in his eyes. Nothing mattered but her brother.

"Violet?" she heard again, this time in a different voice.

Over Tom's shoulder, she saw the figure on the stairs, his stern features and graying auburn hair, a dark brown robe over his sleeping clothes. She drew back from Tom's arms slowly.

"Father," she said.

All she could see when she looked at her father was him standing on the docks coldly ordering Captain Maxwell to track her down. *I haven't kept that bastard girl in my house only to have her die before time.* The housekeeper chose that moment to shut the door, and Violet jumped. Her heart was pounding. The trellis wallpaper seemed to crowd in around her as her father approached, and she had to force herself not to step back. *He's going to know,* she thought. *He's going to know I'm here to spy on him.* At the same time, she told herself, *You have to do this. You have to find Marcus.* A reminder of her mission.

She let him embrace her and looked up at him with faked smiling relief.

He was smiling back down at her and saying, "Welcome home, my child."

Violet sat in the downstairs drawing room, a blanket wrapped around her shoulders and the remains of supper on a tray in front of her. Her brother sat next to her on the settee. Their father had drawn up a chair after ordering the servants to relight the fire and the candles and bring down some hot tea, sliced bread, and leftover meat cuts from dinner.

"Eat first," he'd insisted, after her injuries were tended, and she had done as she was told, having to feign the hunger, swallowing each bite determinedly. She looked up when she was done with the last of the bread and knew, with a twist in her stomach, that she couldn't avoid things any longer. She drew in a breath and said the words of the story that she had prepared:

"I'm sorry. I couldn't stop them. They took the boy."

"The boy?" her father said.

Violet was looking at Tom. "You told me to protect the cargo. I thought you meant him. That boy. The boy who was chained up in the hold."

"Go on," said her father, after a moment.

"The ship was sinking. The boy would have drowned. I went back and broke his chains . . . I thought I could carry him out. And then *they* came. They took us both."

"Stewards," said Tom. The way he said it was the way Justice said *Lions*.

"That's what they called themselves," she said. "Men and women in old-fashioned clothes. But they were—they weren't natural—they were—"

"Is the boy alive?" interrupted her father.

She had prepared for this too. "I don't know. He used the distraction and escaped." It was close enough to what they knew already, but ambiguous enough that it muddied the waters. "He wasn't natural either. At least, I thought I saw . . . What was he?"

Tom and her father exchanged looks. Instead of answering her question about Will: "The Stewards are enemies of Simon," said Tom. "And they hate our family."

"Why?"

Tom opened his mouth to answer, but their father cut him off with a small gesture. "There are some things you need to be told, but not until you're rested. It's a long story that shouldn't be heard late at night, half-exhausted." He smiled at Violet. "What's important right now is that you're home." His hand came down to rest heavily on her shoulder, squeezing it a little.

Tom took her upstairs to her room. Alone with him, she found her heart pounding, her mind crowding with all the things she wanted to say. How much she had missed him. How scary it was to have found out he was a Lion . . . and that she was one too. He was the only other Lion that she could talk to, and she had a thousand questions. About Rassalon, about the Dark King . . . all of them stopped in her throat.

"I'm sorry." It was Tom who spoke, the words a blurt, the moment they were alone. "I'm so sorry. I kept thinking that I was the one who had told you to go down into the hold. You wouldn't even have been on the ship if it weren't for me. You saved my life, and the last thing I said to you was—"

Go home. It had lodged in her like a knife.

"You were trying to protect me," said Violet, taking in a shaky breath. "You tried to make me leave. You knew it was dangerous—that's why you said—" *You're too old for this. Following me around. Wearing my clothes.* It had hurt. Now she saw his curt words in a different light: Tom nervy, watching the horizon, knowing what was locked in the hold.

Tom said, "You're my sister."

She wished suddenly, painfully, that she could just tell him. That she could tell him all of it and have him believe her. Looking into his open, honest face, she thought, surely if he knew what their father was planning— what he really wanted to do to her—if she could just tell him—

"I thought about you every day," she said. "There was so much I wanted—to tell you—"

"You can tell me now. I want to hear all of it," he said. "Violet, I thought you'd died. I kept replaying the attack, trying to imagine a way that you'd survived."

He couldn't know, could he? He couldn't know that she was the sacrifice, that he was meant to kill her?

"I—" she said as he reached out to put his hand on her head as he'd always done.

She almost reared back. The black, curling *S* burned into Tom's wrist. Her breathing shallowed at having it that close to her. *The Dark King's sigil*. Did Tom know what it really meant? Did he know what Simon was trying to do, what he was trying to unleash, a shadow that could not be fought? As she looked at the dark swirl of that brand, she felt the painful gap between them, how utterly she could not come home.

"We'll talk in the morning," she said with a smile. "Hot rolls with currants, like we always do."

"All right. But I'm here if you need me."

"I know," she said.

He ruffled her hair, a gesture as familiar as breathing. "Good night, Violet." And he was gone.

She stayed in her bedroom doorway for a long time after he disappeared down the hall. He looked just like she remembered, young, handsome, and tall. She'd only ever wanted to be like him. He was the image in her mind that had always made her strive.

"You."

Violet jerked around and saw the cold eyes of Tom's mother. Louisa Ballard was a woman of forty-one years, too thin, but very well-dressed. She wore her dark hair in a respectable dropped bun, and her well-styled dresses were proper for a woman of her age. Her lips were narrow as she frowned. The look she gave Violet was one of inflexible hostility.

"How dare you come back here."

Violet drew in a painful breath. For a moment, Violet had thought . . . but any ridiculous fantasy that Louisa's words might be a ploy—cruelty to

force her out for her own safety—was gone. This was no ploy. This wasn't
Tom trying to get her off the ship because he knew she was in danger.

She doesn't know. She just hates me.

She wondered what would happen if she told Louisa the truth. *Your
husband brought me to England to kill me. He raised me so that when I was old enough
your son could slit my throat.* Louisa thought Simon was a respectable gentleman who oversaw his father's trade company. She didn't know anything
about Lions or ancient worlds.

"The only good thing you ever did was leave," said Louisa coldly.
"But you were too selfish to stay away."

"Yes, Mrs. Ballard," said Violet, keeping her eyes on the floor, while
her nails bit into her palms.

Inside her room, she closed her door and pressed her back to it. This
was just life, she told herself. Just life. She looked around at the room,
alone among all these objects that she'd thought meant she belonged.

As soon as the house was dark and quiet, she pushed back her bedding,
quickly donned her shirt and trousers, and padded on socked toes into the
hall.

Her father's office was at the end on the left. She made straight for
it. If there were papers, contracts, ledgers, anything that might help the
Stewards find Marcus, they would be in that room.

She had snuck out at night before. She knew to avoid the creaking
third floorboard and to keep to the far wall so her shadow wouldn't be
seen below the door. She moved swiftly and before long was outside the
office door, putting her hand on the doorknob.

It was locked.

A lock wouldn't usually have stopped her. She could break a lock. She
could break the door. But if she did that, there would be no more pretend-

ing. Her father would know right away what she had done. And what if the information she was looking for wasn't in the office? She couldn't give herself away before she learned where to find Marcus.

She was grudgingly turning from the door to filch the housekeeper's set of keys, when she heard a low, male laugh from the opposite end of the hall.

She froze. It was coming from Tom's room. He was in there with someone.

With who? Tom doesn't have visitors this late at night. . . .

She approached silently, not wanting to be discovered. The door was ajar. There was a crack of light visible, and she could glimpse a sliver of the bedroom interior. She held her breath and peered through the crack of the door.

A handful of lit candles and the flickering embers beneath the mantelpiece provided the light. Tom sat in the armchair by the fire, and there was another boy relaxed on the Axminster rug at Tom's feet, his head resting on Tom's thigh.

Devon. Violet recognized him at once, one of Tom's friends, whom she disliked. Devon was the clerk of ivory merchant Robert Drake, and sometimes worked as a runner for Simon. A pale, unpleasant boy, he had the look of ivory that had faded, an old lady's dusty cameo brooch, all one color. Lank white hair hung down over his forehead. He usually wore a cap, but tonight he'd taken it off, revealing a grimy bandana that held his hair in place. His white eyelashes were too long.

Violet stared at Devon's sallow complexion, his eyes that were only one shade darker than translucent water. Devon was often lingering around on Simon's business, a colorless parasite. It was how Tom had met him. He attached himself to people as he'd attached himself to Tom, and now he was talking in that unpleasant voice.

"—I wouldn't tell anyone that she's back. Simon likes his Lions loyal. If he thinks for a moment that your family can't be trusted—"

"Violet's not a liability. She's my sister. Simon will see that she's an asset. She saved me on that ship."

"If you're wrong again, James will fit you with a collar and a little bell."

A snort. "I'm not worried about James."

"You should be. He's the golden boy. The only Reborn Simon has in his pseudo-court. More than a Reborn. He was the Dark King's favorite, and now he's following Simon's orders . . . you think that doesn't give Simon a thrill?"

"You've got a head full of intrigue," said Tom, sounding amused. "You think there's a spy behind every curtain and a dagger in every sleeve."

Devon turned, kneeling up between Tom's legs and facing Tom directly. "And you're a Lion; you think everyone is loyal. I have something you can use for leverage. James is coming to see Robert at dawn. Alone. And he's *never* alone. Simon must want something kept utterly secret, to send James out by himself. We can find out what it is."

"If Simon wants it kept secret, it ought to be kept secret," Tom said.

Devon leaned forward, sliding his palms up Tom's thighs. "You're not the slightest bit curious what Simon has planned?"

"Violet."

She spun. Her father was standing at the end of the hall, a raised candle in a holder in his left hand. He gave her a warm smile.

"My dear. What are you doing up?"

"I couldn't sleep," said Violet, smiling back at him. Her heart was pounding. Very deliberately, she did not look toward her father's office door, only a few yards away. "I thought I heard voices."

James, she thought. *Simon's planning something and he's sending James out alone.*

I have to tell the Stewards—

"Tom's doing some late-night work with Robert Drake's young clerk," her father said. "Nothing to worry about."

"Oh! Of course. I was just—"

"I thought you might be sneaking out," said her father with another smile before she could finish. "The way you used to, down the hallway, then out of the side window in the scullery." She felt cold hearing that he knew her secret route. "I'd hate to see you leave when you've only just come home."

Keeping her voice light, she said, "I just couldn't sleep."

Her father motioned down the hall toward the stairs, a friendly gesture. "The truth is, I couldn't sleep either. I know you have questions. And you're right . . . it's time I answered some of them."

She told herself, *He doesn't know I was snooping. He doesn't know anything.* Her heart was still pounding. She had to keep behaving as though she were innocent. She nodded, conscious of the fact that they were walking away from the locked office as he led the way down the stairs, holding the candle. She was careful not to look at it or give any sign that it was why she was here.

"I think you know already that what I'm going to tell you has something to do with our family," her father said. "Louisa doesn't know about any of it, and Tom only knows a part." It was very dark; the candle made shadows leap out before them, then shrink back as they approached.

"A part of what?"

"Something like this can't be told. It can only be shown." Her father stopped at the third door at the bottom of the stairs and gestured for her to enter.

It was the India room.

Violet had been four years old when her father had sailed with her for

England, and she had few memories of her life before then. Tom, who was three years older, remembered India far better. He told stories about their home in Calcutta, not far from the arched gates of Government House. Violet didn't like hearing them. She'd pushed them away, feeling a knot of unfairness that it was his to talk about, not hers. She didn't like to think about that country.

Her father often took guests through the room, pointing out the cabinets from his time in Calcutta, the large map of the city, the paintings of princes and ladies in gardens and under mango trees. Those were the times that she was most encouraged to make herself scarce. Her family's pride in their connection to India was conditional on her not being there.

Now she looked around at the paintings of nobility, the bronzes of deities, the hangings of delicately painted cloth, and saw a collection of faces staring back at her, displaced and unfamiliar. She took a step forward. Everything went dark, the light of the candle blotting out.

Click.

She knew. Even as she whirled around. The sound of the door locking was like the sealing of a tomb. *No.*

"Father?"

No.

"Father?"

She twisted the handle—nothing. She rattled the door—nothing. Feeling rising panic, she pushed her shoulder against it—it didn't even budge. She was pounding on the door with her fists. "Father? Let me out! Let me *out!*"

Not a dent, not a shift—even her voice sounded muffled. A *lion cage,* she thought, panic shoving into her throat. Her father had had this room built after his return from India. Months of construction—a room ready to hold the artifacts he'd brought home with him—

A room ready to hold me.

And she had walked into it, like a fool, and was trapped here.

There had to be another way out. It was pitch-black; she realized with a chill that the room had no windows. She had never noticed that before. She forced down the rising panic. *Think.*

She took a deep breath, moved back, and then ran at the door, hitting it with all her strength. The impact snapped her teeth together and sent a burst of pain through her shoulder. She gritted her teeth and tried again. And again. No effect. The door was papered to make it look like part of the wall, but under that, it was made of metal, thick as slabbed stone.

She tested the floor—it was stone. She beat the walls, but there was no weak spot. She piled furniture to reach the ceiling, but her thumping fist made no more sound than a palm slapping rock.

Panting with exertion, she dropped back to the floor. As she took a step, her foot hit a kitchen bucket next to the largest cabinet. Horror climbed into her throat. The bucket had been left for her. Proof of her father's cold planning.

She thought of the family upstairs. She was at the door again calling out "Tom! Tom!" even as she could tell from the muffled quality of the sound that her voice would not be heard unless someone was right outside. When she cast about the room, the objects in it seemed suddenly menacing. Dark shapes loomed, outlines as if of fellow prisoners, a wall full of faces.

Her groping hands found a painted vase, and she purposefully smashed it so that she could grip one of the shards like a knife. If she couldn't get out, she could be ready when her father came in.

It would be her father, and not Tom. She told herself that. She clung to Tom's words that she'd overheard, defending her to Devon. Tom wouldn't hurt her. Not of his own free will.

How would her father make Tom kill her? Would he be forced to do it? She couldn't envisage it, an involuntary sacrifice out of a storybook, with her and Tom both resisting. Whatever happened, she would go down fighting.

She dropped to her knees by the door, sharp shard of porcelain at the ready, and waited for the door to open, still believing that her brother would come to help her.

A sound from the other side of the door.

"Tom?" she said, scrabbling up.

Footsteps; they seemed to stop right outside the door.

"Tom, please, I'm in here."

She put her palms flat against the door and pressed her mouth as close to the seam as she could get.

"Tom, can you hear me? Tom, I'm locked in!"

"It isn't Tom," came the cold reply.

"Louisa." Violet's stomach plummeted. She let her forehead rest against the door, eyes closed. But she tried in a casual voice: "I've locked myself in. Can you let me out?"

"You haven't locked yourself in," said Louisa. "Your father shut you in there, and I'm certain you deserve it."

What could she say? If Louisa had already heard a story from Violet's father, nothing that Violet could say would be believed. Especially not the truth. *I'm Blood of the Lion. This room was built to hold me. He's been waiting until I was old enough so that Tom could kill me and take my power.*

"It's just a misunderstanding," said Violet. "If you open the door, I'll explain."

"Explain?" said Louisa. "If it were up to me, you'd stay in there. You're a selfish creature who causes nothing but harm to this family."

She could feel the cold door under her palms and where her forehead leaned against it. She had been in here for hours, and was already feeling weak. Louisa hated her. Her father thought of her emotionlessly as a sacrifice. Her one ally in the house had been her brother, but Tom's friendly obliviousness could not help her now. Violet drew in a breath.

"You're right." Violet made herself say it. "You're right. I'm selfish. I came back thinking this was my home. But it isn't."

The silence was deafening. She made herself keep talking.

"I don't belong here. That's what you've always said, isn't it? I'm not wanted except as a kind of—" She couldn't say it. "It was all just pretend. I was never really a part of this family. And Tom—" She thought of him holding her in the hallway, the way she'd felt safe in his arms. "Tom's better off without me."

The silence continued. She forced out each painful word.

"So I'll go. I'll go and I'll never come back. It won't be like last time. I'll stay away. You'll never have to see me again. None of you will. I'll leave, I swear." She drew in a shallow breath. "If you just open the door."

This time the silence went on for so long that she realized there was no one on the other side of the door. Louisa had gone. She'd left Violet here, in this dark room, talking to herself. Violet stood back from the door and just stared at it, feeling the dark loneliness of the room sink into her.

And then the door opened.

"He should have left you in the dirt in Calcutta." Louisa's cold eyes staring at her were full of dislike. Violet felt the clawing desire to laugh, but it probably would have been a croak. Instead, a bitter, transactional silence passed between them. It was the closest they had ever come to understanding each other. Violet ducked her head and hurried out.

She couldn't go out the way she knew—through the window in the scullery—so she slipped out a side window, dropping to the ground soundlessly. She had made it as far as the street when she stopped, a little breathlessly, to look back at the house.

It was so familiar, a window light shining upstairs, and some smoke trailing upward from the stove fire chimney. Soon Cook would begin making breakfast, and her family would eat together. Violet's last meal with them had passed without her even knowing it. Her final goodbye to Tom had been that ghostly feeling of his fingers in her hair.

She remembered her first needlework lesson. Her governess had suggested she embroider the word *mama*, which she had done with her crooked stitches, presenting it to Louisa. Louisa's face had changed. She'd snatched the embroidery and thrown it into the fire, and the governess had been dismissed. Violet had told Louisa the truth. She wouldn't come back. She didn't have a family, just a dream that had existed in her head.

It was late when she finally made it back to the inn, the grimy, impersonal place where she had left the horses. The raucous sounds of the downstairs tables, crowded with men slopping drinks and calling for more, hit her ears as she entered. She sidestepped around them to reach the narrow wooden stairs. Climbing with exhausted legs, she made it to the small room where she and Will had agreed to meet.

She wanted nothing more than to lie down on the bed with her forearm over her eyes and rest, but she knew she had to ride back to the Hall. They only had until dawn to find and stop James. She pushed the door open.

Will was waiting by the window, though there was little chance of seeing anything through its dim pane.

"Violet!" Will turned when she entered, eyes wide with relief.

"I've got what we need," she said. "We have to go."

From the cold, half-eaten meal on the sill, he'd been watching for her at the window for hours. She took in the uncomfortable stool where he'd been perched, his face all but pressed to the window.

"What are you doing?" She could see where he'd tried to wipe the window clean for a better view.

"I was worried about you," said Will.

It made her feel warm, like she wasn't alone. Like maybe, in that room, she hadn't been alone after all. Feeling suddenly awkward, she punched his shoulder lightly.

It wasn't until they were saddling their Steward horses in the stables that she noticed the immaculately fitted jacket, with its snug waist, and dark trousers.

"And what are you wearing?"

"I had to borrow these." He made a face, but she had to admit that the clothing made him look dashing, the tall standing collar setting off his high cheekbones and the fall of his dark hair.

"Borrow, or steal?"

"Borrow. It's not important." Swinging up into the saddle, he tugged a rein, turning his horse out onto the road. "Come on, we have to go."

CHAPTER NINETEEN

"HERE!" A WAVE of relief washed over Violet seeing Stewards ride out to greet them. "We're over here!" It felt so good to see the white tunics and the silver stars, pale shapes in the night. She counted two dozen mounted Stewards cantering over the dark marsh in pairs, with Justice at the head of the column.

Back in London she had told Will everything that she had overheard. "James will be alone with the ivory merchant Robert Drake. We can take him unawares, before he has a chance to use magic."

"He can lead us to Marcus," Will had said, grasping it instantly as she nodded.

The window to act was small. They had ridden back to the Hall in haste. Now Justice's face was a welcome sight, the words spilling over her lips.

"Thank God," Violet said as the Stewards reined in, surrounding them in a loose circle. "We don't have much time. We found a way to find Marcus, but we have to act before dawn."

Nothing happened. Violet looked for some sign that the Stewards had heard what she'd said, and saw only blank faces. A moment later, twelve of the Stewards dismounted, their spears out.

"Didn't you hear me? I said that we've found a way to find Marcus. But we have to go—now—"

Their faces stayed blank. She recognized the Stewards; they were people she knew. Carver and Leda were on horseback. Justice was one of the dozen of the Stewards who had dismounted.

"What is it?" she said, a prickle of cold going down her spine. "Why aren't you listening to me?"

"Because you're a Lion," said Cyprian, reining in his horse next to Justice, his eyes utterly cold.

Her stomach dropped, like a terrible pit.

"Don't get close," a voice said to her left. "She's strong." She heard a sword unsheathe.

"Violet—" said Will, in warning.

They knew.

They knew what she was. A Lion, descendant of Rassalon.

She saw it on all their faces, her worst nightmare come to life. With a flash, Cyprian's expression made sense. He must have seen her leaving the Hall and reported it to the Stewards. *I'll be watching you.* Had he followed her to her house? She could imagine him saying in his superior voice, *She's a Lion. Tom Ballard's sister.*

"Wait," she said. "I'm on your side. James will be alone at dawn. You'll have a chance to capture him."

Nothing.

"I'm telling you that I found out how to get to James. You can use him to find Marcus. That's why I went back. To help you."

The circle of spears was closing in. She swung around, but there was nowhere to go. Desperately, she searched the hostile expressions, looking for someone to listen. "Justice. You know me. Tell them."

But the familiar face that she knew from hours in the training hall was shuttered and cold.

"Stay back, Lion," Justice said.

Something horrible twisted in her stomach. She looked at the size of the converging force. Two dozen Stewards, half with spears closing in, the others on horseback with crossbows at the ready.

Did they think that she could fight two dozen Stewards? With no weapon?

They did. She could see the spear tips. All pointing at her.

"She's telling the truth. If you want to find Marcus, you'll listen," said Will, stepping forward.

All it did was swivel some of the crossbows from her to him.

She said, "You don't have to do this—I'm one of you—I—"

Two more Stewards had dismounted. They were carrying a heavy piece of iron, solid and old, with strange carvings. Manacles, she realized. They were so thick they looked like stocks. Something in her went cold when she saw them. The ground was crumbling under her feet. "Listen to me. Listen to me! We only have until dawn—"

"Take her," said Justice.

There was a blur of motion to her left—she heard Will struggling, already in Steward hands. "Stop this, she's telling the truth! She risked her life to find out how to help you—!"

"Will!" she cried out as one of the Stewards simply hit Will to stop him talking, a sword pommel to his temple. Will went limp in their arms at once, knocked out.

She panicked, swinging at the Steward who came at her from behind. She wasn't thinking—sending him flying with her full strength to crash into a line of his compatriots. She dodged one spear, then snapped the next. There was a metallic crunch as she drove her fist into the stomach of a third Steward, hard enough to cave a deep dent into his armor. Hard enough that the Steward felt the punch and doubled over, reeling. Hard enough that it hurt her own fist, the burst of pain distracting her so that she didn't see the swing to her head—

Blackness burst over her vision. She was forced to the ground, hard. With a wrench, her arms were pulled behind her and the heavy manacles closed over her wrists. Immediately she felt weak, hazy, as if the manacles had robbed her of her strength. They felt solid and immovable in a way she had never experienced, and could almost taste in her mouth. She was still saying "*Listen to me, James is going to be there at dawn, you need to get there before him*—" as her head was shoved downward, her cheek pressed to the wet, peaty earth.

Had she survived her family only to be killed by the Stewards? Justice was standing over her, his sword drawn. Her heart tightened at the thought that he was going to execute her, right here in the muddy dirt.

Nothing happened. Everyone was still, and staring. An eerie silence hung over the empty marshland. Will was a motionless shape on the ground, and strewn around Violet were the bodies of at least nine fallen Stewards, some injured, others unconscious.

Of the dozen who remained, she saw Leda wipe a thin line of blood from her mouth, and behind her, Cyprian held his sword in a white-knuckled hand, eyes fixed on her. She could hear the words that the Stewards were saying in horror and disgust. *Unnatural* and *Lion* and *old world* and *Rassalon*.

"That's enough." Justice cut the talk off, stepping forward. "Take them both to the cells."

———

As soon as Violet descended the stairs, she felt sick. If the manacles had weakened her, the cells left her nauseous and barely able to stand, as if the prison were in her head.

The Stewards dragged her into a barred cell, ignoring her pleas, just as they'd ignored her on the marshes, listening to nothing that she had to say about James, or how little time was left.

Deep in the rock, the only light came from the two torches outside. The bars threw shadows into the cell, crisscrossing the ground, a repeating iron lattice. She could feel in its stupefying effect on her that this place had been built to hold powerful prisoners, perhaps creatures of the dark in that ancient war. The cell walls were black, unnerving and wrong. They weren't made of stone; they were made of something more like obsidian, gleaming and carved over with long, curving script that looked like the writing of the old world.

But whatever fell creatures had once been imprisoned here, the black honeycomb of dizzying cells were now all empty, except for the one directly across from her own, where Will lay, pale and breathing shallowly, unconscious but alive. Laying Will's body out on the stone in a pair of manacles that matched hers, the Stewards had locked the bars and filed out, all but one of them, who had remained, standing outside her cell.

"Justice," she said.

He was still wearing his armor, white and silver. His handsome face was framed by his jet-black hair, half tied in its twist, the rest falling straight down his back.

"You'll be kept in this cell," he said. "You won't be let out. The High Janissary is meeting with the council now to decide your fate."

My fate. She felt those words in her bones. She thought of a lion hunt—the great beast speared in five places. As she looked into Justice's impassive face, she felt a terrible chill.

"But you'll tell them I'm on their side. You'll tell them I went to London to help them."

Her words fell into a cold silence. *He's looking at me,* she thought. *But he's seeing something else.* It made them strangers, suddenly. She felt utterly locked out, searching his face through the bars for any hint of its old expression.

"Justice?" His face didn't change.

"When the decision is made, they'll take you in chains to the Hall."

It was hard to breathe. "And do what?"

"You're a Lion," said Justice. "You'll be killed to stop you from hurting people."

She felt dizzy, breathless. "You can still get to James," she said. "He'll know where Marcus is being held. He's Simon's favorite. You can stop James and save Marcus."

"The Stewards will not be lured out to another ambush. Whatever you sought to gain by infiltrating our Hall, it's over."

"If you don't stop Simon now, you might not get another chance. He's strong and he's close to achieving his plans—"

"You're the Dark King's servant. It's in your blood."

"Justice, you know me," she said. "Not a Lion. Me. Violet."

"You will follow the Dark," said Justice. "Unless we prevent it. That's what Stewards are. We're the last protectors. Against creatures like you."

She barely heard the dull clang of the door as he left. She couldn't breathe; the pain was immense. She remembered another door closing, beating on it with her fists until they were raw. This was worse, her future shutting down, leaving her in the dark.

She thought, *My father had a lion cage and the Stewards have one too.*

Her world, all her dreams, narrowed down to this cell, her false lives stripped away to show the truth: she wasn't wanted. Justice looked at her and saw a Lion, and he was going to kill her. *How dare you come back here.*

Louisa's words wormed around in her head.

Her father's smiles, her brother's fond words, Justice's steady-handed guidance, it had all been lies.

No, that wasn't true. Her family had lied. Justice had been honest. He had told her what he felt about Lions from the start.

"Violet?"

She scrabbled up toward the bars, and in the cell opposite hers she saw Will, pushing himself up onto an elbow. She felt so stupidly glad to hear his voice, to see him alive and awake. He looked weak, and the hair on the left side of his head was clumped with dried blood. Before he managed to sit up, he said, "Are you all right? Did they hurt you?"

"I'm all right." She swallowed the feeling, his first thought being for her. "They hit you over the head."

"I know," he said, his weak returning smile making it a kind of joke. She watched him sit all the way up, then pretend he preferred not to stand, rather than show that he couldn't. She swallowed again. "How long have we been down here?"

"Not long. An hour. Maybe two."

"An hour! James will get away."

His frustration touched on her old feelings, the desire she had had to beat on the walls, *Hey! Listen to us! Let us out!* Alongside that was a spiraling hopelessness. They were trapped down here in this pit while outside, dawn was coming, and with it their one chance to stop James.

"It's my fault." Violet drew in a painful breath. "They wouldn't believe anything after they found out I was a Lion. They think I've got bad blood. That I'm destined to serve the Dark. That's why we're down here."

"Then they're fools," said Will.

He pushed himself up to his feet, though it obviously cost him. He came all the way forward to the bars of his cell. His hands manacled behind his back, he had to lean his shoulder against the bars. It was probably the only thing holding him up.

"I don't care what they say. You're good and you're true. Whatever happens, I won't let them hurt you."

She looked at his pale face with its tumble of dark hair. The blood at his temple—it was because of her. The manacles forcing his arms painfully behind his back—because of her. She was the reason they were here, the reason the Stewards wouldn't listen. She was a Lion by blood, her family served Simon, her brother was his creature.

"How can you trust me? I'm one of them."

"You came back for me," said Will.

Their first meeting; her monumental decision to jump back onto the sinking ship; and the way that he had looked up at her, bruised and chained. He hadn't expected anyone to come. Maybe no one ever had before.

She looked at him now through two sets of bars that seemed to symbolize all that separated them: different futures; different fates. He was the hero; she was the Lion who didn't fit anywhere.

"They'll let you out." She could feel how true it was as she said it. "You're Blood of the Lady. They need you."

"I don't care. I won't leave you."

Did he mean that? With the bars between them, their friendship felt like it was being forced apart, and yet it was the thing that was holding them together. He was in here with her, when outside there was a bigger fight.

She said, "You have a destiny."

"So do you," he said. "It's what we make it. You and me. We'll fight Simon together."

Together.

She felt his faith cutting through all doubt. His faith in her. It was like a flame piercing the dark. She looked at his bruised face, his unwavering gaze, and could see why people would follow him. She could see why people followed the Lady.

"Now, if we're going to stop James, we need a way out of here," Will said, as though the topic was settled.

She drew in a shaky breath and nodded. She didn't say any of the words of gratitude that crowded in her, what it meant to her right now to have a person on her side. She just followed his lead, looking around at the cell that confined her.

"There are no cracks, seals, or windows. It's only the barred door."

"It's the same in my cell. You can't bend the bars, or break open the door?"

She shook her head and gave voice to the nausea she'd had since she'd first set foot down here. "These cells—I feel—" She couldn't describe it. *Weak*, she might have said. *Dizzy*. "The manacles, the walls . . . it feels like—" *Like cotton in my head*, she might have said. *Like a weight on my chest. It's hard to think, or move, or do much.*

"I feel it too."

She looked up at him and realized that his struggle to stand was not due to the cut on his head; it was because of the black stone of the cell. It was affecting him just as much as it was affecting her. More.

"You mean you can't just"—a faint attempt at humor—"magic the door open?" Even saying it, she felt a roil of unease. The thought of anyone trying to push past this compulsion made her sick.

"Even if I knew how, I feel what you feel. Blocked. No, trapped. Except it's not in my body. It's in my head."

"Then we wait for someone to come," said Violet, "and get out the old-fashioned way."

"We don't have much time if we want to have any chance of stopping James—"

There was a sound at the top of the stairs, the metallic screech of the heavy iron door opening. Will broke off and swung around toward the noise.

Her heart started to pound as she imagined a squadron coming to take her to the hall, and then she saw a familiar shadow thrown across the floor.

"Cyprian," said Violet.

Of course it was him, descending the stairs in his gleaming livery. He'd put her in here, always sneeringly against her. He'd come to see her behind bars, to relish her being exactly where he'd always thought she should be.

"My father has made his decision," said Cyprian. That arrogant, up-pity voice.

"You coward," she said to Cyprian through the bars. "You and your father both. Why don't you come into this cell and face me without all the bars and chains."

He didn't take the bait. He just stood in front of her cell, a too-handsome figure in his novitiate tunic, his eyes passing over her slowly.

"What you said about James? No one believes it." A familiar sneer on his lips. "The Stewards won't act on the word of a Lion. They're readying the great hall. That's what my father decided. They're going to kill you."

"So you've come to gloat," she said with a disgusted breath.

"No," said Cyprian. "I've come to get you out."

"—What?" she said.

It was like putting her foot on a missing step, the ground vanishing out from under her. Violet stared at him.

Cyprian lifted his chin. She suddenly saw the way his chest was rising and falling, and that he was standing there as if pushing himself hard into discomfort.

"Every mission to rescue Marcus has failed. The Stewards don't know where he is, or how to get him back. Maybe you were lying when you said you had a way to find him." Cyprian drew in a final breath, then pulled something from his tunic. "But maybe you weren't."

It was a key. It was a *key*. Her eyes fixed on it, hope flaring. Behind Cyprian, Will was at the bars of his cell.

"You're really going to disobey the Stewards to help us?" Will asked him. "Why?"

"He's my brother," said Cyprian.

The perfect novitiate. He stood there in his immaculate livery, and she thought of all his thousands of hours of practice, forming himself into a faultless candidate. He was made to drink from the Cup and become a Steward. He had never disobeyed a rule in his life.

Now here he was, in the cells under the Hall, with two descendants of the old world, siding with them against the Stewards.

"You trust me, just like that?"

"I don't *trust you*, Lion." Cyprian lifted his chin again, in that arrogant way he had. "If you're lying, I suppose you'll kill me. But for even the smallest chance that you're telling the truth, I'll take that risk."

"Then open the door," said Violet.

He stepped forward, put the key into the lock, and turned it. He was brave; it was infuriating, like his spotless tunic and his perfect posture. He stood without flinching as the barred door opened, and just gazed back at her as she came to stand in front of him in the passageway. She was ridiculously tempted to make a loud sound, or jerk toward him, to see if she could make him jump.

She turned her back to him instead, deliberately displaying the manacles. Cyprian shook his head. "No. Those stay on until we get outside the Hall."

"Why, you little—"

"*Violet*," said Will, bringing her up short.

"I'm willing to risk my own life to do this. Not the lives of everyone in the Hall," said Cyprian. His chin lifted again.

"The nobility of the Stewards," she said scathingly.

"You said James would be unguarded at dawn," said Cyprian, gesturing for her to keep ahead of him.

"That's right." Violet scowled.

"Then we don't have much time," said Cyprian. Will's cell door swung open. "Let's go."

CHAPTER TWENTY

WILL WATCHED IN amazement as Cyprian's calmly imperious words got them past the guards ("My father has sent for the prisoners") and out of the main building ("My father is waiting for me"). He had horses ready for them, waiting in the east courtyard. No one questioned why he needed the horses. No one questioned him riding out of the gate either. Not even with two mounted companions on lead ropes behind him, wearing Steward cloaks (procured by Cyprian) to hide their manacles.

True to his word, Cyprian unlocked their manacles once they were out on the marsh. The second they were off his wrists, Will felt better. His legs felt steadier. His head felt clearer. Cyprian bundled the manacles up in a cloth knapsack, and once they were covered, even the residual feeling they gave Will disappeared.

Rubbing his wrists, he looked over and saw that Cyprian had driven his horse two paces back and was watching them with the tight-jawed calm of someone facing down fear.

He really thinks we might kill him.

Cyprian had released two dangerous prisoners on only the slimmest chance that they would help him. He was probably expecting Violet to slit his throat as soon as she was out of her manacles.

And he had freed her anyway. For a chance that she would help his brother.

Violet broke the silence, challenging Cyprian directly. "What's the matter? Scared you'll miss morning practice?"

It wasn't what he was scared of, and they all knew it.

"You *have* been out of the Hall before?" said Violet.

"Of course I've been out of the Hall. I've done eleven full patrols on the marshes." Cyprian's chin lifted. His hands were tight on his reins.

"Oh, *eleven*," said Violet.

"Have you been to London before?" said Will.

"Twice," said Cyprian. "Just not—" He broke off.

"Just not what?"

"Alone," said Cyprian.

You're not alone, Will would have said to anyone else. But Cyprian had broken from the Stewards. And he was missing a lot more than morning practice. Once the Stewards realized he was gone, Cyprian would be branded a traitor who had betrayed the Hall to help a Lion.

In every way that mattered to him, he was alone.

So Will said, "We weren't lying. We're going to capture James and bring him back to the Hall."

Cyprian's wariness didn't relax. "Not even a Lion is strong enough to attack James head on."

"I know how to distract him," said Will.

That part was true. He knew he could lure James out. He knew what would turn James's head, what would hold his attention. It felt like innate knowledge. Like knowing the crate would break James's concentration on the docks. He'd never forget the moment James's eyes had met his—the sensation of coming home, as though they knew each other.

He told them his plan on the ride. Violet didn't like it, but there was no alternative, and she knew it. "Nothing else matters if we don't get Marcus back," Will said. He could see her remembering the Elder Steward's words. *Conjuring a shadow is the first step to returning the Dark King.*

They had this one chance. This one opportunity to capture James and learn the location of Marcus. Everything was at stake, not just Violet's reputation, or Cyprian's future with the Stewards.

Stripping back to her London clothes as they arrived, Violet blended in. Cyprian stood out, a storybook knight plonked down into the middle of London. His white tunic was the most pristine garment in the city. If it had been a light, Will would have told him to put it out.

"You look like a blancmange," said Violet.

"I don't know what that is," said Cyprian, lifting his chin again.

"It's like a trifle with none of the good bits," said Violet. "We could rub mud on him like we did with the horses."

"And with yourselves," said Cyprian, and it took Violet a moment, but her frown descended ferociously on her face.

"Let's see how clean you are after a dozen Stewards attack you on the marsh—!"

"Stop it, both of you," said Will. "We're here."

They had arrived with about half an hour before dawn. On the docks, the warehouses and the foreshore would already be bustling with activity. But in this part of London the streets were deserted, only one or two lights in the windows, lamps lit in the rooms of the earliest of risers.

"Are you sure you have to be the one to go in there?" said Violet.

"It has to be me. You know that."

She nodded reluctantly. Behind her, Cyprian stood with one hand on the hilt of his sword.

"The two of you get into position," said Will. "And don't kill each other until we have James."

A bell rang over the door into the silence, janglingly loud in a dark space crowded with strange shapes, and Will walked into the London shop alone.

Robert Drake's place of work was empty of people, though pale curving surfaces were everywhere. Robert was an ivory merchant, and Will was surrounded by the sepulchral shapes of the ivory. Elaborately carved tusks, ivory animals worked into caskets, clustered pale figurines.

He walked in slowly. There was a counter at the back of the shop, and behind it two huge bins of horns, thick and white and curving in all directions. A light was faintly visible from a back room, and Will glimpsed a pallid boy sitting at a dark wooden desk on a raised dais.

"Hello?" he called. "Hello there?"

"We're closed," came the reply from the back room of the shop.

Will tried again. "Your door was open. I thought perhaps you might—"

"I said we're closed. You can come back at eight, when we—"

The boy broke off.

"Could I persuade you to open early?" Will put his hand on his purse.

The boy was staring at him across the length of the shop, a pale smudge of a youth wide-eyed near the only lamp.

Will recognized him at once from Violet's description. The colorless features, the lank white hair under the cap. His pulse kicked up a notch. This was really happening. The boy was Devon, Robert Drake's clerk, and part of Simon's pseudo-court.

"Perhaps for a small fee?" Will touched his purse again. Filled mostly with rocks, it looked substantial.

"My apologies," said Devon, after a moment. "I forgot myself." He stood, lifting the lamp. Touching flame to candles, he lit the shop as he came forward, multiple sources of light that glowed on the surfaces of the ivory. "I am your servant." He didn't take his eyes off Will.

"No need for formalities," said Will.

"No?" Devon said. "Why— Why is it you're here?" Devon glanced at the purse again, then back at Will. "At this hour." It *was* early. And Will was a stranger. Devon's caution appeared to be warring with the potential to earn money. Will knew what he had to do. Show himself, get Devon talking, and then—

"I'm looking for something."

"Looking for something?"

"A gift."

His tension rose as Devon came out from behind the counter. It seemed that Devon had believed his pretext. But Will could still feel that he was inside the property of one of Simon's loyalists. It was like being inside Simon's home, the same dangerous feeling.

"Ivory is a splendid gift," Devon was saying. "Each piece is irreplaceable. You have to kill for it. Look." Devon gestured in the dim light to a Roman ivory diptych of men with dogs that looked like leopards. "This piece is an antique. The Romans hunted elephants throughout their empire. Now the elephants in Northern Africa are gone. For all we know, this was the last."

Will looked at the ivory in the flickering light and felt a twist of unease as he thought of those great creatures, now vanished. He looked back at Devon, who was continuing his tour through the shop.

"These days we hunt elephants south of the Sahara, where there are some remaining herds. More juvenile pieces make billiard balls, walking stick tops, hand mirrors, piano keys. The highest grade is reserved for ornamental sculpture and jewelry." Devon drew him through the pale shapes of the dead. "Perhaps one day a lady will wear the world's last elephant as a hairpin."

Will stopped in front of a wall-mounted specimen, and the hairs rose on the back of his neck. The ornate fixture held a horn both familiar and different. It was long, straight, and spiraled, tapering to a pointed tip—a shape he'd seen before.

But where the horn in the Hall of the Stewards had been a white spire, silver spume, helical fire—this one was yellowed in places, brown-lined where the curves of the spirals met, with the overall look of an old, dead tooth. καρτάζωνος, the plaque beneath it said in Ancient Greek. *Cartazon.*

"A unicorn horn?" he said.

"It's a fake," said Devon. "It comes from a narwhal, a type of whale they hunt in the northern seas. Others are crafted. . . . Artisans in the Levant have a method of boiling walrus tusks. If you steep a horn for six hours it becomes soft and pliant so that you can work it, straighten it as you like. They fetch a good price."

A *fake.* One dead thing masquerading as another, like rabbit skins stitched together to make a lion pelt. The horn in the Hall had been so different, this one felt like a mockery.

"You can touch it," said Devon.

Will looked at him. Devon was gazing back at him. It felt like some kind of test.

Lifting a hand, Will ran his fingertips along its length. It felt ordinary—a bull horn; a piece of old bone.

"Robert collects the fakes as curios," Devon said. "An expensive hob-by. People will pay a lot for the idea that something pure exists. Even if the trophy means they killed it."

"Have you ever thought one might be real?"

"The true *cornu monocerotis*?" Devon gave a thin smile. "The horn that neutralizes poison, cures convulsions, leads you to fresh water? That if you hold it in your hand will compel you to tell the truth?" Devon leaned back, a pale shape against the counter. "I've seen stacks of horns as high as buildings, entire herds slaughtered, carcasses littering beaches as far as the eye can see. It's never real."

The horn men seek and never find. Will's skin prickled, thinking of a world that was gone, but for a handful of relics buried deep in the Hall of the Stewards.

"You don't believe in unicorns?" said Will.

"I believe in commerce," said Devon. "Two hundred and fifty years ago, Queen Elizabeth was given a bejeweled horn at the princely cost of a castle. It wouldn't have been worth quite so much if she knew it was a fish tooth." The candlelight flickered, and the ivory that cluttered every surface seemed to take on a different hue. "Why? Do you believe in them?" The light played on Devon's face too. "A glade of newborn foals, each one with a little nub in the middle of its forehead?" There was something testing about the words.

Will said, "I'm not here to chase unicorns."

"No?" Devon's mild word had something underneath it.

"No. I believe I mentioned," said Will, "I'm here to buy a gift."

"For a lady?" said Devon. His words were casual, but Will felt a flare of recognition.

He knows, he thought, and the words made sense of Devon's testing manner and the way Devon carefully wasn't looking at him.

His pulse spiked. Now that Devon had recognized him, he had to get out. And he had to do it without giving the plan away.

"Yes, that's right." Will kept his own voice casual. "A lady."

"Cameos are popular." Devon moved to the desk and drew out a display tray. Five ivory cameo brooches were pinned to black velvet. "Or rings?"

His movements were slow and deliberate, like his breathing. Now that Will knew he had been recognized, he could see that Devon was afraid. Devon glanced at Will's hand holding the purse. His scarred hand.

"A necklace, perhaps," said Devon. "An ivory rose so fine that you'd believe a real flower adorned the hollow of her throat." *He's stalling.*

"I ought to come back with a lady's eye," said Will. "I'm spoiled for choice."

"Robert will be here soon," said Devon. "You could wait for him."

"I'm afraid I've taken up too much of your time already," said Will.

"It's no trouble," said Devon.

"I'll return at a more reasonable hour. A token." Will scattered what little of the contents of his purse comprised coins on the counter and walked out of the shop.

I've done it. He tried to walk calmly, letting anyone who was watching see him, exposed on the street. *Devon knows who I am.* He forced down the echo of that old voice, the moment when the world had changed and nothing had ever been safe again. *Run!*

Because there was only one thing that would lure James out.

Me.

He knew what he had to do next, and he had made it to his appointed spot, hoping the others were in position, when he saw Cyprian.

"Cyprian. You're not supposed to be here."

The back streets were deserted, tall houses rising on either side creating dark, empty canyons, perfect for an ambush.

Cyprian stepped forward with the earnestness of a bodyguard. "If you are what Justice says you are, you can't be alone."

This wasn't part of the plan that Will had shouted as they galloped, the wind on the marshes whipping the words from his mouth. "You have to get into position. Devon's going to tell James who I am."

"If you really are Blood of the Lady," said Cyprian, "I can't be the one who lets you fall into Simon's hands."

The words were as unexpected as everything else about Cyprian's presence here. The perfect novitiate breaking all the rules. He had seen Cyprian's discomfort at tricking the other Stewards to free them. Cyprian had an extraordinary sense of his own duty. But if they didn't get Marcus back, none of that was going to matter. "Cyprian—"

"Justice was right about one thing," said Cyprian, shaking his head. "Marcus did always believe in the Lady. He was sure you had survived. He thought that he would be the one to find you. He told me that he'd—"

Cyprian broke off, blinked, and then crumpled. There was no warning, no sound or change; he simply hit the ground in an unnatural collapse.

"Cyprian!" said Will, racing to his prone body. On one knee, he felt desperately for an injury, a dart or a bullet, finding nothing. Cyprian didn't respond, just lay heavy and motionless, eyes open as one frozen. Was he alive? Dead? He didn't seem to be breathing—

Will wheeled around to the dark, empty street, looking for an attacker, to see nothing, to hear only his own panting breaths in a silence that stretched out, just long enough for him to feel how completely he was alone.

And then, footsteps.

The leisurely sound of shiny boot heels on cobblestones. *Step, step, step.* James came strolling out of the dark as Will's pulse skyrocketed. James was dressed for an evening out, in exquisite tailoring. Everything faded, this world insignificant; James the only real thing in it. *You, you, you.*

James's extraordinary beauty pressed in like a knife; it hurt.

"No, don't get up," said James pleasantly, and before Will even thought to rise, an invisible force slammed him forward so that he sprawled onto his hands and knees.

It was like pressure. Like James's hands on him, if James had a thousand hands. It was hard to breathe. It was hard to do anything but stay on all fours, unable to move a muscle. He had seen James stop a crate in midair with his power; he knew James could do this. He hadn't realized it would feel personal, like James's hands all over him.

"The boy savior," said James conversationally.

"Simon's Prize," said Will.

That got James's attention. Will's own heart was pounding. The scent of night flowers in a garden . . . Everything felt so familiar. Having James close to him was making him dizzy. He was aware of James strolling closer when James's long legs came into view.

"Everyone thought you died at Bowhill," said James. "You were supposed to die there. Instead you survived and escaped Simon's ship. How exactly did you do that?"

"With pleasure," said Will.

James said, "Pretty necklace."

Will's breath shallowed. The collar of his shirt began untying itself, invisible hands pulling it open, exposing his neck, then his collarbone, then baring his chest. Will's pulse spiked with danger as the medallion swung free from his shirt.

It was part of the old world just like James was. For a heart-stopping moment Will wondered if James recognized it, not from this world but from that one. *James isn't merely a descendant,* the Elder Steward had said. *He is the Dark King's general, reborn into our time.*

It hit him fully then. James was a Reborn. Not a reflection in a mirror, nor a fake mounted on a wall. He was a living piece of the old world, somehow strolling around in this one.

No wonder London seemed to fade around him. No wonder being near him felt like reaching across time. *I will find you. I will always find you. Try to run.*

And they had thought they could capture him? The audacity of it struck him. Three of them against James—his plan felt foolish, juvenile. This wasn't hunting for rabbits with slingshots. This was bringing down big game. *The Betrayer.* Even the greatest Stewards feared him. Will remembered the squadron James had decimated, the bodies wrapped in gray cloth that he had torn apart without even touching them.

"Did you get it from your mother?" said James, and the fingers on Will's neck slid to his chin, tilting it up. They weren't James's real fingers. James wasn't close enough to touch him.

His eyes traveled up James's boots to his satisfied expression. Behind James, Will could see Cyprian's sword, lying in its sheath near his sprawled body.

"Don't touch it," said Will as the medallion started to slide from his neck.

"Or you'll do what?"

On Simon's ship, he had called a sword to himself—it had jumped to his hand. Now—he couldn't reach the sword; he couldn't move his arms or legs, no matter how much he strained against James's invisible hold on his body.

"You can't use your power, can you?" James said.

All those lessons, hours with the Elder Steward, trying to concentrate. He was supposed to be the one with the same powers as James. He was supposed to be the one who could stop him.

"You're weak," said James.

Will focused everything on the sword. *Reach beneath the surface. Look for a place deep inside.* The Elder Steward had taken him in believing that he could do this. Believing that he would be the one to help them. And he wanted her to be right . . . to prove her right.

"Like your mother."

And this time, when he hit that closed door, he threw everything he had against it, even though there was a part of him that was afraid of what was on the other side—

It hurt; a sick, nauseating pain, like pushing on a broken bone, but he forced himself through it, dots of black and red swimming in front of his eyes. And for a moment he saw—

—sparks of light on a dark field: torches, amid the massing dark of an army, and at its head a figure that at first he could not make out, but he somehow knew. It was turning toward him as the Lady had turned toward him, but he didn't want to see, didn't want to meet those eyes burning with black flame. No—

He gasped, panting, coming back to himself in a rush to a throat full of blood, as though something had ruptured. In the next second, James's fingers gripped his chin—James's real fingers, lifting his head up. James's eyes were blue, not black; he was looking down at Will with pleased satisfaction. Will felt James's fingers slip in the blood flowing sluggishly down his face, and he had the absurd thought that he was going to mess up James's jeweled rings.

"You're supposed to be the fighter?" said James. "You're no match for the Dark King."

Will let out a breath of laughter, dizzy with echoes of the past.

"Something's funny?" James's voice was dangerously mild. Will looked right at him, in the moment before the swing.

"I'm not the fighter," said Will. "I'm the bait."

It was James's turn to topple, Violet standing over him with the weighted knapsack she'd swung at his head.

"I'm the fighter," she said as James hit the ground, going utterly still.

It worked. The ruse worked! The invisible pressure on Will collapsed. Beside him, Cyprian drew in a shuddering breath—*alive*, thought Will with a rush of relief. Cyprian was alive. But there was no time to cheer. Will was pushing himself up desperately, seeing James already starting to stir on the muddy ground.

"Get the manacles on him!" said Will. Violet quickly shoved down the sides of the knapsack and pulled out the two heavy sets of Steward manacles that had just impacted with James's temple. They were the same manacles that she and Will had been forced to wear by the Stewards. As soon as they were out of the knapsack, Will could feel them, like an unpleasant taste in his mouth. But they didn't seem to take full effect until they enclosed someone.

Violet snapped Will's set of manacles around James's wrists. After a second, she snapped her own set of manacles on him as well.

"Just in case," Violet said, a bit defensively. Will let out a breath. It was part laughter, part hazy relief. On James's sprawled, boyish body, the manacles looked oversized, big and heavy. James might not even be able to stand up while wearing two sets of them.

"Do we have him?" Cyprian was blinking his way back to himself. One hand to his temple, he had forced himself to stand up, though he still looked disoriented and unsteady.

"We have him," said Will.

His plan had worked. James had taken the bait. James had followed him out after Devon had recognized him, thinking him unguarded. James had attacked him. And he had held James's attention while Violet had gotten into position.

But as he looked down at James, Will couldn't help feeling that what they had captured was a dangerous creature they didn't understand and had no idea how to contain. He drew in a shaky breath.

"Now we take him back to the Hall."

CHAPTER TWENTY-ONE

THEY PUT JAMES on a horse with Violet.

"You're the strongest," Will had said to her. But it was more than that. "You ought to be the one who hands him over to the Stewards."

Violet had nodded; Will had known she understood. She was the one who had risked her life to learn James's whereabouts from her family. She was risking more now, going back to the Stewards after they had thrown her in chains. The Stewards should have no doubt who to credit for James's capture.

Violet dragged James up without much effort, just as he started to come around. Will got to watch the entirely satisfying moment when James reached for his powers and found them blocked by the manacles.

"What is that?" said James, blinking at odd intervals and unsteady on his feet.

"The power of the old world," said Will as James shot him a killing look. "I suppose neither of us are a match for it." In fact, Will was relieved. There had been a chance that James might have been simply too powerful to contain. This felt precarious and exhilarating: for the moment, they had him.

Pushed forward toward the horse, James appeared to notice the identity of the Steward he'd almost killed. He let out a breath of contemptuous
familiarity.

"Cyprian. You must be loving this."

"You two know each other?" Violet's hands tightened on James's body.

"You could say that." James's eyes on Cyprian were mocking. "Your
brother talks about you all the time. He calls your name, begs to see you,
cries out for—"

"*Shut up.*"

James's head snapped to one side as Cyprian backhanded him across
the face. It was a shock, coming from the controlled teacher's pet. Cyprian's breathing was slightly disrupted.

James paused to run his tongue over his teeth. "That's the Stewards I
know," said James.

"Gag him," said Will, sensing the emotions beneath Cyprian's ordered exterior. "He's provoking you on purpose, and it's working."

He kept his eyes on Cyprian, but his awareness of James was a bright
and dangerous thing. He knew what James's power felt like, sliding over
his skin. He half imagined he could still feel it, even as James mounted, a
dangerous blue-eyed boy sharing Violet's horse. And from the look that
James gave him, eyes glittering over the cloth gag, James knew it too.

They galloped into the courtyard, four cloaked figures that no one
questioned, thanks to Cyprian, the wards parting for him. The courtyard
was quiet, the only Stewards visible those guarding the gate and walls.
When Violet dismounted and pushed her cloak hood back to reveal her
face, it took a moment for the attention of the Stewards to snag on her. A
head turned, and then another—

As Violet dragged James out of the saddle and pulled his hood away to reveal his blond head, the Stewards guarding the walls erupted. "*It's the Reborn!*" Stewards were drawing their swords; others were lifting crossbows to aim right at them. "*The Reborn's inside the walls!*" There was a fear in their shouts that hadn't been there even when they had learned that Violet was a Lion.

"We have James St. Clair!" Will called in a loud voice. "Call the High Janissary!"

James's head jerked up at that, and he turned to the Hall's entry with strange tension.

But it was Justice who came, at the head of a phalanx of Stewards, descending the steps to the courtyard. Cyprian made to move forward, but Will held him back.

Justice stopped at the sight: Violet standing in the center of the courtyard, holding a gagged and chained James by the shoulder. The other Stewards went quiet as Violet pushed James forward.

For a long moment, she and Justice just stared at each other.

"You needed him," said Violet, her young voice holding steady, "so I got him."

Justice didn't speak as something silent passed between them. Violet stood there straight-backed, and after a long moment Justice gave a single, slow nod of acknowledgment.

His words were like a signal as he turned to the Stewards behind him.

"You heard them. Fetch the High Janissary. James St. Clair is our prisoner."

He suited the Hall.

That was the eeriest part of James's presence in this ancient place. He looked like he belonged here. Standing in rows in their silver and white, the Stewards with their otherworldly appearance had always looked like the Hall's custodians. James looked like its young prince, returned at long last to his rightful throne.

It wasn't always the Hall of the Stewards, remembered Will. *It was once the Hall of Kings.*

James was tied to a chair, his legs lashed to the chair legs, his arms manacled behind the chair back. Will stood beside him, along with Justice, Violet, and Cyprian. In front of James, every Steward in the Hall was lined up in ordered rows. Ignoring all this, James had adopted a deliberately casual posture, an aristocrat sprawled and at ease, perhaps even faintly bored, looking for others to entertain him.

Will was acutely aware that despite the chains and the guards, the only thing truly restraining James were the manacles. It was frightening: the manacles were relics, no one really knew how they worked, and if they were broken, they couldn't be remade. Without the manacles, there might be no way to contain those with the old powers at all. A Reborn like James could rule this world like a god, crushing mortals like glass beneath the exquisitely turned heel of his boot.

The doors opened with a sudden booming. The High Janissary was silhouetted in the entry, flanked by four attendants in ceremonial robes. As the Hall went silent, he strode down the aisle in a processional, stopping in front of James to regard him with a heavy gaze.

James relaxed back deliberately into the chair, returned the High Janissary's gaze, and said:

"Hello, Father." Before Will could react to the words, James continued, in a conversational voice, "I met the boy you brought in to kill me."

Will turned hot, then cold. He looked around to the other Stewards, expecting to see his own disbelief on their faces. *Father?* No one looked surprised. But it was Cyprian's grim expression that made him believe.

You two know each other? Violet had asked him. *You could say that,* James had replied.

"What does he mean?" said Will. "He's your *son?*"

Distantly he remembered the Elder Steward saying, *He adopted Cyprian and Marcus after his first son died six years ago.*

It wasn't—it couldn't be—James, could it? Lounging in his chains, James's eyes glinted with goading provocation.

"I grew up wearing a little frock and reciting my vows like a good little Steward. They didn't tell you?" James leaned back, the corners of his lips curving.

The High Janissary was looking down at him without expression. Like the priest of an ascetic religion, his blue robes hung in folds, his thick chain of office gleaming around his neck. He passed his eyes over James coldly.

"That thing is not my son."

The words dropped like a cleaver. If there had ever been any connection between James and the High Janissary, it was severed.

Will swung around to look at the others. He saw the High Janissary's hardened expression on all the nearby faces. The only person mirroring his own shock was Violet.

So they knew about him, thought Will. *They all knew about him.*

"The Dark King's general born into the enemy Hall," said James to Will. "What better way to learn their secrets and their plans?"

He tried to imagine James as a Steward, rising before dawn to dutifully put on the gray tunic, perform menial chores, practice diligently with the sword. . . . It simply didn't connect with the gleaming scorpion in front of him.

Underneath that was his own unfolding horror at how a Reborn had come into the world: not magicked, but birthed, to an unsuspecting woman. He had to fight to keep his reaction from his face. A reaction, he thought, was what James wanted—and what he couldn't afford to give.

"You weren't the Dark King's general. You were his catamite," said the High Janissary. "You were in his bed. Just like you're in Simon's."

James's lips drew back from his teeth, not quite a smile. "If I were the Dark King's lover, Father, don't you think I'd stay faithful to him?"

"Bring the box forward." The High Janissary gestured to one of the waiting Stewards.

"Whatever you do to me, Simon will return to you tenfold."

A Steward carrying a cloth-covered rectangular box approached. As the cloth was removed, Will's stomach dropped. He recognized the long, lacquered wooden box underneath, dark wood, the length of a walking cane.

The High Janissary spoke with calm authority. "You're going to tell us where Marcus is. You're going to tell us Simon's plan. And then you're going to lead us to him."

"I'm really not."

"Yes. You will," said the High Janissary.

A second Steward stepped forward, a woman with curling dark hair. She flicked open two latches, lifting open the box lid.

Gasps and reverent murmurs rippled across the rows of gathered Stewards, as at a holy relic. Will saw it, was pierced by the sight of it, as breathtaking now as the first time he'd laid eyes on it.

Nestled on a bed of satin, its beauty was painful: the beauty of what was lost. It lay inside like a shaft of light—a long, whorled staff of pearlescent ivory spiraling up to a pointed tip. James turned white.

"The Horn of Truth," said the High Janissary.

Will remembered Devon's words. *The true* cornu monocerotis. *People will pay a lot for the idea that something pure exists. Even if the trophy means they killed it.*

"You know what that thing does?" said James.

Will said, half quoting Devon, "If you hold it in your hands, you'll be compelled to speak the truth."

James laughed when he heard that. "Hold it? Is that what they told you? You have to do more than hold it. You have to stab me with it."

It felt sickly correct the moment James said it. Will's heart was pounding. "Is that true?"

It was true. He could feel it in the thick silence that greeted him, and the sense that this was quickly slipping out of all control. James's eyes glittered.

"Are you going to do the honors, Father?" He tilted his head. "The chest? The thigh?"

No. Will took a step forward. "You're not going to stab your own son." He was standing between them. "It's not right."

"The savior speaks," said James behind him, the words curdling in his mouth.

Will ignored him. "I didn't bring him back here to be tortured. There must be another way."

"There is no other way," said the High Janissary. "James will not talk willingly, and Simon threatens us all. The horn was made to find the truth. If I am not to wield it, then it must be someone else."

"Let me," said Cyprian. "I'll do it, for my brother."

"No." It was Justice who spoke, the words slower. "Will's right. The Horn of Truth is not an instrument of revenge or cruelty. If this must be done, it should be a neutral party. Not someone who holds a grudge against him in their heart."

"No one in this Hall is neutral," Cyprian shot back. "Every Steward here has lost someone because of him. Have you forgotten Marcus? His life hangs in the balance."

"I'll do it," said Will.

He was already stepping forward. He didn't know if he was doing it to protect James, or to protect the Stewards. Take the Horn of Truth and spear James with it: he couldn't shake the feeling that if this was going to happen, it must be him.

James gave a soft, mocking laugh. "The boy hero," he said. On the dais, Violet was frowning, her eyes very dark and her hands fists. The High Janissary gestured to the horn.

Will's heart was pounding. He had never stabbed anyone before. He had never really even hit anyone, unless you counted his failed attempts to escape Simon's men on the ship. He approached the lacquered box where the horn lay and looked down at it. Longer than a man's arm, it would be like holding a javelin. Against the black, cushioned velvet inside the box it glowed white, a bright spear to pierce the dark. The Steward who held the box stood impassive.

He could feel everyone's eyes on him as he reached in. *Cartazon. The horn all seek and never find.* He closed his two hands around it. Like a spark, it made him breathless, the thrum of it, the bright pulse moving through him as he took it up. A hero's weapon, an instrument of purity like a righteous sword.

And then he looked at James.

There was something achingly similar about horn and boy. The impossible beauty, of course; the sense of a lost world to which they both belonged. And the desecration of that beauty: the sawn, stumped end of the horn; and James, with his face like a sigh, chained up and wearing modern clothes.

Easy to see why the Dark King had wanted him. No one could look at him and not want to possess him. Even in chains, James seemed to command the room.

Was he really going to do this? Hold James down and spear him with a horn?

"Don't puncture anything important," Will heard James say as he came forward, his voice mocking.

James knew Simon. James knew Simon's plans. James was the key to all of this, and this was their chance to learn what he kept secret. *Stab him with the horn, and he'll be forced to tell the truth.*

Subtly goading, James spread his legs and leaned back in his chair, challenging Will with his gaze. Will lifted the horn in the fist of his right hand. He aimed the tip over James's left shoulder. It pressed slightly into the fabric of his jacket. Under that, he could feel the warmth of James's waiting body. He put his left hand on James's shoulder, bracing it.

Then he lifted the horn up and drove it in hard.

James made a sound, completely against his will, and their eyes met. The horn was inside his shoulder. It pinned him in place; it had not passed completely through.

"Does it hurt?" said Will.

"Yes," said James through gritted teeth, and the furious look in his eyes was mixed with something else. Panic. Will realized with his heart thundering that James had just been compelled to speak the truth.

"Where's Marcus?" said the High Janissary.

"He's—" said James, obviously resisting. "He's— He's in—"

"Push it in another inch," said the High Janissary.

Deeper. Will pushed it in, twisting it like a corkscrew. This time the sound that came out of James was raw. There was a change in James too, a compulsion under his skin that he was fighting, hard. Will could almost feel it, the bright horn that couldn't abide falsehood, pushing everything else out of the way. It spread from the bloody point outward, utterly relentless as Will held the shaft steady.

"Where's Marcus?" said the High Janissary.

It was forced out. "Simon has him. You knew that."

"Where?"

"At Ruthern." And then: "Simon will move him as soon as he knows I'm captured. It won't help you."

"We'll judge that. How do we get inside?"

The fight was taking its toll. James's hair was damp with sweat. Will could feel the struggle up close as James fought with everything he had to keep the words inside. Keeping the horn in him required hard, continuous pressure.

"It would take a full-frontal assault. You're not strong enough to do it. It's guarded by all three Remnants and a contingent of Simon's men. You'll die on the walls. Although you'll have a better chance now that—" James gritted his teeth and tried to say nothing.

"You could try lower," said Cyprian. "Dig around and see if there's a heart in there somewhere."

Another inch. James said, "—now that I'm not guarding him."

"What is Simon planning?"

"To kill you," said James, the words seeming to bring him vicious pleasure. "To kill all of you, and to stand over a pile of your ashes as the Dark King returns and takes his throne."

It was chilling; it felt real when James said it. Will thought of the Shadow Stone in the vault and the words on the wall, carved in the last moments of terror and confusion. *He is coming.*

"Tell us how to stop him," said the High Janissary.

"You can't." After he said it, James closed his eyes and laughed breathlessly, as if the truth of these words had surprised even him. "Simon's going to raise the Dark King, and there's no one alive who can stop him."

The High Janissary took a step back; a murmur broke out in the Stewards behind him, tense looks, fear, a roil of unease, because James couldn't
lie—could he? James looked on with victorious satisfaction.

You did this, Will almost said, looking out at the faces of the Stewards,
then back at James's pleased expression. Talking around his subject, revealing almost nothing . . . James was playing with these Stewards, and
they were letting him.

He put his free hand on James's throat and forced his head back. He
ignored the shocked sounds from the Stewards, the way Violet made to
move toward him. He looked down into James's eyes.

"You went to Robert Drake to get something. What was it?" His
right hand was still hard on the horn.

"Nothing." This close, Will could see the sweat tendrils in James's
hair, feel the tremor in his body, even as James stared back at him defiantly. Will pushed the horn in harder. "I— Some information." Gritted out.

"Information about what?"

James was panting. Hand around his throat, Will felt him swallow,
felt the throb of the arterial vein in his neck, like the blood pulsing up
around the horn. "An object. An artifact. I—" He was fighting harder
than he ever had. "*No.*"

"What artifact? Something Simon needs?"

"Needs it. Wants it." The horn was slippery with blood. "Stop it, I
won't—"

"Why does he want it?"

"It will make him powerful—make him the most powerful man
alive—the moment he has it he—he'll—"

He was evading still, trying to talk around the truth. Will ground
down with the horn and focused in on the only question that meant anything. "What did Robert Drake tell you?"

"He told me—Gauthier had come back to England—that he was at Buckhurst Hill—that he had it with him, the c-c—*no, I'd rather die than tell you—*"

"You won't die." High Janissary Jannick's voice cut into the exchange. "You'll simply tell us. That's how the horn works."

High Janissary Jannick had stepped forward to reassert control. His words seemed to remind James that he was there.

"*You*," said James, looking up at his father venomously through his sweat-tendriled hair. "You want me to tell the truth?" said James. "I will. I'll tell it to all the Stewards in the Hall."

"Then do so," said Jannick sternly.

James looked back at him with too-bright eyes, and Will felt the tipping spill of danger, too late to stop it.

"I'll tell you why my father's so desperate to get Marcus back," said James.

Jannick's entire expression changed. "Pull it out."

The order was sharp and sudden, but Will's hand hesitated on the horn.

"I'll tell you why there are no old Stewards," said James, "why their lives are short, where they get their strength—"

"I said pull it out!" Jannick took a stride toward James as though to yank the horn out himself.

"No." Cyprian stopped him. "Will, don't." He was holding his father back by the arm. "It's about Marcus."

"Will Kempen," said High Janissary Jannick, "you will pull out that horn."

Will's hand, slippery with blood, slid on the shaft, but he didn't pull it out. His heart was pounding. James's goading eyes fixed on his father.

"The Cup of the Stewards." James spoke in a clear voice, letting the whole Hall hear. "Simon first found mention of it in a dig in the forests of Calabria. *Calice del Re,* the locals called it. The Stewards drink from it when they take their oath, but it never belonged to them. . . . It was a gift that was given to their king."

The Cup of the Stewards, Justice had told them. *We drink from it when we take our whites.* Will's skin crawled as James spoke the words of a familiar story:

"Four kings of the old world, offered great power in exchange for a price. And to seal the bargain? Drink. Drink from the Cup. Three drank and one refused. Those who drank gained extraordinary physical abilities, for a time. But when their time was done—"

"They transformed," whispered Will. And went cold.

In his mind he saw four kings darkly transparent, and a stone so black all light seemed to disappear into it.

The Shadow Kings.

"No one asked what happened to the Cup," said James. "Just like no one asks where the Stewards get their strength. Why they watch in pairs, for any sign. Why they train to always keep control. Why their lives are short. It's because of their oath. The oath they swear when they drink from the Cup." James's eyes were fever bright as he delivered the words. "To kill themselves before they start to turn."

Will looked out in horror at all the familiar faces—Leda—Farah—Carver—and even—his skin crawled—Justice.

Every Steward. Every single Steward had drunk from the Cup.

"Tell us you're not," he heard a novitiate demand. *"Tell us you're not shadows."* Janissaries and novitiates were staring at Stewards as if all they could see now were potential shadows, surrounding them, outnumbering them. Too late, Will yanked the horn out, and James collapsed forward, laughing breathlessly.

"Is it true?" said Cyprian, and James's laugh turned strange.

"Is it *true*?" said James, his shirt and jacket soaked with blood, still panting in pain from the horn. Truth was the point, even if its splinter had been wrenched from him now. He looked back at his father. "You don't tell the novitiates before they drink? Not even your precious little adopted son?"

Holding the white shaft that looked like it had been dipped in red paint, Will's mind was already traveling from one truth to another, far darker. *Simon seeks to conjure a shadow of his own*, the Elder Steward had said. He saw the yawning pit of his own realization begin to open in Cyprian's eyes.

"You said Simon had learned how to conjure a shadow. What did you mean?" Cyprian pushed his father out of the way to stand in front of James. "*What did you mean?*"

James didn't answer; he just gazed back at Cyprian and slowly smiled.

"He meant Marcus," said Will, knowing it in his bones. "It's why they're so desperate to get him back. Simon doesn't need the Cup to make shadows. All he needs—" Simon's plan was terrible in its simplicity. "All he needs is a Steward."

He looked up at Violet, their eyes meeting. Because there was another truth too. Simon wouldn't take a prisoner that he'd need to keep alive for years. No. Simon would have chosen someone who was half shadow already. Wherever Marcus was, he would not have long before the shadow inside him took over.

Will said, "Capture a Steward without much time, keep him alive, and wait for him to turn."

And watched the Hall around him erupt into chaos.

Torch aloft, Will descended the stairs to the underground cells, the flame he held sending shadows flickering out ahead of him.

He wasn't two steps down before the thick, oppressive feel of the cells stifled him, and he had to force himself not to shake his head to clear it, or rub at his temple. He already knew that didn't work.

Upstairs, a tumult of arguments and shouting. The novitiates and the janissaries were turning on the Stewards, with the High Janissary desperately trying to keep order. Here in the shiny obsidian depths of the cells, those seemed like the concerns of a different world.

He guessed at which cell they had tossed James into after that little performance: the same cell where they'd held Will, the most powerful cell in the Hall.

And he was right. But where Will had been left free to move around, James was chained to the wall.

Will opened the cell with the key that he had taken from Cyprian and stepped inside.

They had stripped James of his jacket—they must have cut it off—the manacles were still on his wrists. His torn white shirt had a bloom of blood that streaked down from his left shoulder. And he was stretched, his arms restrained above his head. Despite these deprivations, James was waiting for him in the kind of indolent pose that was utterly provocative.

"I wondered when my father was going to send you down here," James said.

"Everyone's talking about you upstairs." Will closed the bars behind him, letting the lock click. "You're the center of attention. But I suppose you're used to that."

"I'm not Simon's lover," said James.

"I didn't ask." Will flushed. "And there's no way to know if you're telling the truth now anyway."

"You could stick it in again."

Will stopped. He recalled, rather forcefully, that James had thrown the Stewards into chaos, just by talking. James might look like an angel fallen to earth, but he was Simon's creature, and he had chosen this approach because he thought it would work on Will, specifically.

"You don't carry Simon's brand." He could see the unbranded skin now that James was stripped of his jacket. "Why not?"

"Maybe it's just not on my wrist." James leaned the back of his head against the wall and gazed at Will lazily.

"Why not?" Will repeated calmly.

James gave him a long look, amusement at the edges of his lips.

"Unlace my shirt."

It was, undoubtedly, a challenge. Will dropped his torch into the wall sconce and came forward, slowly, James's eyes on his. He'd been this close to James upstairs; he'd stabbed him. That curled between them. James's breath shallowed slightly, though the languid pose didn't change, nor did the way James regarded him. *Unlace my shirt.*

It might be a ploy. Will knew that. He lifted his hands to James's neck and began to untie the shirt, an oddly intimate thing to do, like untying another boy's cravat.

The fine white shirt opened, and Will pushed it back farther, exposing James's shoulders and chest. He wasn't sure what he was expecting, but he couldn't hold back the sound of shock at what he saw.

"He tried. It wouldn't take," said James. Will stared, unable to stop. "It's one of the benefits of being the Betrayer. I heal quickly."

For where there should have been an open, bloody stab wound, there was only the smooth, unmarred skin of James's chest.

Will couldn't help touching it, spreading his palm over the place where the stab wound had been only an hour before. The wound had healed—had vanished—it was utterly gone. There was no mark, no scar—James had nothing to show for the violence that had been done to him. Anger stirred, moving under the surface.

"How many times," he heard himself say.

"What?"

"How many times did he try to brand you?"

He thought he saw a flicker of surprise at the question. James's voice dripped with amusement at Will's presumed naiveté. "I didn't count."

"You said it hurt."

Another flicker. "Good memory."

"You're more powerful than Simon. Why let him?"

"Are you jealous?" said James. "He liked the idea of his name on me."

"It's not his name," said Will.

He felt the exact moment when he got James's full attention. It was like a snap, James suddenly present. Will thought, *There you are.* Will hadn't lifted his hand, and James's pulse was a slow throb under his warm skin.

"Do the Stewards realize you're clever?" James's voice was intimate, new, and subtly approving, like he'd learned a secret. Will stayed where he was for a long moment, before stepping back to simply regard James from the opposite wall of the cell.

"Does Simon realize that you are?" said Will steadily.

Half-stripped, James was splayed out, open shirt revealing his unmarked chest and abdomen. The lack of any stab wound was still unsettling. Will wondered how much James's body could heal and how many times James had put it to the test. He wondered, with a curl of unease, whether the ability to heal was innate to James, or whether it was a gift bestowed on him by the Dark King, to keep his prize intact.

"He knows what I can do," said James. "Or did you think he only wanted me for my pretty face?"

"I think he wants you because you were the jewel in another man's crown." The answer wound out of Will in the flickering light from the torch. "I think he has no idea of what you really are, or who he's trying to summon. If he did, he'd never dare plunder the grave of a king."

He had taken James aback. Like the torchlight, the surprise darkened James's eyes, turning them from translucent blue to black.

"What are you really doing down here?" James said.

Simon's Prize. James was the Betrayer, the closest thing in this world to the Dark King. He was valuable to Simon: part of his collection of old-world treasure, like the armor pieces he'd unearthed, or the deadly Corrupted Blade. Like each of those things, James was a tool, a weapon, and a danger in his own right. And he was here, alone and accessible. Will had only one question that burned inside him.

"I want to know the name of the man who killed my mother."

He'd surprised James again; that strange flickering look was back in his eyes.

"What makes you think I'd tell you?"

Will stayed where he was, the cool obsidian wall at his back; it was stifling, an oppressive magic under its shiny surface. James felt it; they both felt it.

"I keep my word. I'm loyal to my friends. I don't forget when people help me."

"Didn't my father warn you not to bargain with the Betrayer?" James's eyes had gone very dark.

The Betrayer. It struck him afresh that James was a part of the old world, like the obsidian walls, but James was new as well, not only of that world but also now of this one.

"I think what people were is less important than what they are. And what people are is less important than what they could be."

James let out a strange breath, and Will saw that he had not only

James's surprise, but underneath it, something else. "You're not what I expected."

"Aren't I?"

"No. I don't know what I'd thought the Blood of the Lady would be like. A golden hero, full of righteousness like Cyprian. Or a hapless boy unready for the fight. But you're altogether more—"

"More what?"

"Effective," said James.

"Tell me who killed my mother," said Will.

James gazed back at him. In the Hall above, the Stewards were in disarray. They were arguing over James's words—over whether to attack, how to fight—but also over their very nature. The Stewards of the Cup were the elite inner circle, but with the dark price of their powers exposed, the novitiates and janissaries were in revolt. Yet down here, in this buried cell, priorities felt very different.

Just as Will began to doubt that he would speak, James said: "The one who struck the blow was Daniel Chadwick. But the one who gave the order was Simon's father. Edmund, the Earl."

Will felt his pulse race at hearing it, but there was one part that didn't make any sense. "Simon's father? Not Simon himself? But Simon's the one trying to return the Dark King."

"Fathers hold a lot of sway over their sons," James said, his voice faintly mocking. Upstairs, of course, the High Janissary was deciding James's fate.

"Now you answer a question," said James, as though they were in casual conversation.

"Go ahead."

"Did you like holding the horn?"

He had returned to the warm, dangerous tone from earlier. It conjured up the moment when they'd been locked together upstairs, as if violence was a temptation. Will almost felt the horn in his hand again, and the slow, steady thrum of James's blood.

Will said, "I think the Stewards asked you the wrong questions."

"What would you have asked?"

The provocative words were certainly a ploy. It suited James to keep him here, Will thought. And James was good at holding attention. Was it a natural skill or a learned one? Something from his other life or from this one? James was like the locked door to a world of secrets, unattainable and alluring.

"Do you remember him?" Will said.

He felt the shift—as if the past were here with them—an aching enmity—a war almost lost—James in princely red, with rubies around his throat. And a dark presence that he'd summoned without even speaking its name, growing, gathering its forces, becoming ever stronger—

"No one else has ever asked me that." James's voice was a little shaken. *You feel it too*, Will almost said. Instead of answering Will's question, James said, "Do you remember her? The Lady?"

"No," said Will, feeling unsteady. He made himself say, "But I'm a descendant. You're a Reborn. You were there."

They were staring at one another. The cell was quiet, heavy stone silencing any sound from upstairs, so that you could almost imagine that you heard the flaming of the torch in its sconce.

"I don't remember that life," James said. "I don't remember who I was, or what I've done. The names, the faces . . . I only know them from Steward stories and Simon's excavations. But there's one thing I do know so well that it's part of me. Him. The fact of him. The feel of him. It's deeper than memory, deeper than self, carved into my bones. And I can tell you this.

"Simon isn't a tenth of him. Simon's plans, his power, his ambitions are nothing. . . . Simon can't comprehend him, as the warmth of a single day can't comprehend a night that lasts for ten thousand years."

Will felt the dark and cold of the shadows in the obsidian cell close in around him. "You think he's coming for you."

James leaned his head back against the wall and smiled. "He's coming for all of us."

CHAPTER TWENTY-TWO

"YOU ARE NOT in danger!" Jannick was trying to make himself heard over the din in the Hall. "Your companions are not your enemy! No Steward has turned in all the thousands of years of the Hall!"

On the dais next to him, Violet looked out at the chaos, her stomach twisting. *Shadows. The Stewards are shadows.* Jannick was trying to hold the Order together, but there was a jagged rent between the Stewards, who had all drunk from the Cup, and the novitiates and janissaries who hadn't, and who were frightened, shocked, and angry.

"Not in danger?" she heard Beatrix call. "The Dark King's shadows are inside our Hall!"

"How many?" It was Sarah, one of the janissaries who had shown Violet to her rooms on her first night in the Hall. "How many of you are there?"

Beatrix said, "Every single Steward is a shadow—or will be!"

"You're right." A familiar voice from the doorway cut through the ruckus. The Hall fell silent, so that the only sound was the rhythmic clink of a staff against stone as the Elder Steward made her way to the front of the Hall. "Those who have drunk from the Cup will all become shadows. Including me."

Violet stepped back with the others to let the Elder Steward pass. There was something different about the way the hushed Stewards looked at her, a new, fearful awe. Her age . . . the only Steward with white hair, the only Steward with rheumy eyes and wrinkled skin. With a shiver, Violet understood that the Elder Steward's age was a sign of her power: she had held her shadow back longer than any other Steward.

"Now you know what the Stewards face," she said. "We fight on every front, without *and* within. We cannot ever abandon our duty. We cannot ever relax our guard. For what stands between us and the Dark is only our training, and the vow that we have taken to die before we turn."

It was Justice who Violet looked at. His gifts would have marked him as a candidate for the Cup early. He would have spent his youth training for it. A childhood of ascetic self-denial: no child's mischief, no teen's rebellion, no flush of adulthood and first lover. He had sublimated all his body's desires into mastery and control, without knowing what he was training for. *The Cup will make you strong. The Cup will give you power.* That's what the novitiates were told.

When did they learn the cost of that power?

No one could agree to drink if they really knew the price, she thought—or would have thought, except that she could see the faces of the novitiates. Beatrix had straightened her shoulders. Emery had lifted his chin. They knew the price now. And they were deciding right before her eyes that they would drink. Just as Carver had drunk.

They had already been ready to give up their lives for the cause. The Cup was just one more step.

Was this how it happened? They trained for it, they learned the price, and then they drank? And then they watched in pairs for any sign, ready to kill their shieldmate, while their shieldmate watched, ready to kill them?

And if their training slipped even for one second—?

Violet drew in an unsteady breath. "What happens when you turn?"

The Elder Steward's eyes were grave. "Bound to the Dark King, a shadow has no will of its own, but only follows the orders of its master. Barely resembling the man or woman it once was, it is an incorporeal horror that can pass through any door or gate or wall. And it cannot be fought. No mortal can touch its shadowy form. It kills and maims and rends, and all the while stays invulnerable."

"And that's what will happen to Marcus?" said Violet.

The Elder Steward nodded. "If Marcus turns, it is unlikely that any-one here can stop him."

Violet felt cold, remembering the Shadow Stone deep in the vault, its darkness so strong she hadn't even been able to go near it. *An ancient terror, one of Sarcean's greatest weapons, they led his army of shadows on their nightmare steeds.* She could feel how much those Shadow Kings wanted to be free to command their armies once again, a legion of shadows that the world had thought had been put to rest.

"But the wards. The wards on the Hall are magic," said Violet. "They've kept out shadow armies before. In the old world. The Undying Star, that's what this place was called. He can't get inside the Hall."

"The wards open for any of Steward blood," said the Elder Steward, the truth of it in her eyes. "That will include Marcus."

Inside the Hall. She saw Emery look at Beatrix with real fear, and even full Stewards blanch at the idea of facing an enemy that they couldn't keep out and couldn't fight.

The Elder Steward raised her voice to be heard over the murmurs.

"That is Simon's path to power. He learned of the Cup in one of his ex-cavations. And he learned he could be master of shadows. He is the Dark King's descendant. His bloodline is strong enough to make shadows obey him. And if he takes command of a shadow, he will use it to annihilate anything that stands in his way. He will breach our walls, take the Shad-ow Stone, and release the Shadow Kings. And they will clear a path for their true lord and master, the Dark King, who seeks to return dark magic to the world and rule with it forever from his pale throne. That is why we must put our differences aside and focus with one mind on Marcus." There were nods in the hall, agreement forming at her words.

Cyprian pushed forward to speak. "How close is he?" The Elder Steward was silent, but Cyprian was already shaking his head and an-swering for himself. "He's strong. He'll survive. He won't turn."

"Cyprian—" Justice began.

He was the wrong person to speak. Cyprian rounded on him. "You were supposed to be his shieldmate. How could you have let Simon's men near him?" The perfect novitiate faced down the perfect Steward. "How close are *you*?"

Justice looked like he'd been slapped; Cyprian's words had shocked him breathless. *They don't talk about this openly,* Violet realized. Stewards nev-er spoke of their shadow selves, perhaps not even to their shieldmates in forbidden whispers late at night. *Am I showing any signs? Do you think I'm changing?* These were private matters, painfully exposed.

"Or were you just going to kill him to stop it? It's all lies, isn't it? The strength of Stewards, their great destined power . . . It's lies to hide what you all have to do. If you cared about my brother at all, you'd never have let him drink from that cup," Cyprian said.

Violet was stepping between them, taking Cyprian by the shoulder to hold him back. "Cyprian—" But Justice's voice cut across hers.

"Marcus chose."

Justice didn't try to lie or avoid it. He met Cyprian head on.

"The heroes are dead. The old powers are gone. There's only us. A handful of us." Behind him, the vast hall with its cracked stone and faded colors seemed to prove his words, ancient and all but empty. "We're all that's left, and we're not enough. What would you do, if there was no one else to hold back the dark? Would you drink from a cup that tarnished you, in order to be able to fight?"

"It's the Dark King's bargain." Cyprian's hands were fists. "He's inside this Hall. He's inside you. You've all corrupted yourselves."

"We pay a terrible price," said Justice. "We do it because we must. It's the only way we can fight."

"You could have fought without it. Any of you could." Cyprian's jaw was set. "Maybe you wouldn't have been as strong. But you would have stayed Stewards." He looked around at the Stewards bitterly. "That's my choice. I'll never drink from the Cup."

Violet found her way to the training yard.

Inside the great hall, Jannick had begun talking of preparations for an attack, while the Elder Steward moved between small knots of novitiates and janissaries like an almoner, offering comfort and wisdom. Violet had looked around for Will, but he had vanished.

The training yard was now empty of Stewards, as if to say, *The time for training is over. The time for battle has come.*

Wanting desperately to achieve the faultless excellence of a Steward, she had spent hours here, practicing until her limbs trembled, her breathing ached, and the sweat dripped from her skin.

But the Steward drive for perfection now looked different. The unwavering rows of sword tips, the absolute control that they strove for was no mere desire to achieve an ideal, but a terrifying necessity. Their self-denial, their turning away from the flesh, their strictly regimented lives, all of it was to hold their shadows back.

Justice stood by one of the columns, looking out at the space where he'd spent so long in training. His handsome face was drawn and silent; he didn't greet her as she came to stand beside him. Following his gaze, Violet looked out at the empty yard, knowing now that she didn't see the same things that he did in the Stewards and their practice, and never had.

Everything was different now, of course. In London she had been a naive, unthinking girl when her identity had shattered her world open. *Lion.* This felt like a similar breaking open, the Stewards forced to face what they were for the first time. She said quietly, "Are you all right?"

Justice gave a small, wry smile. "You show me the kind of compassion that I did not show to you."

She thought of all the ways that was true. He had lied to her, while refusing to forgive her lies. He had called her a creature of darkness, while he carried darkness within himself.

But in his world there were no shades of gray. She saw that now. Once you drank from the Cup, you were going to turn. There were no second chances, and the only way out was death.

"You took me in," said Violet. "You trained me." His words to her on her first day in the Hall came back to her. "You said everyone should have someone on their side. Someone to look out for them."

Justice didn't answer for a long moment, his eyes on the training yard. Empty now, the wide, silent yard seemed to suggest generations of Stewards who had trained, and drunk from the Cup, and died before their time. "We stopped at a roadside inn," Justice said eventually. "We were returning from a mission in Southampton. We should have come straight back, but he looked so happy, I suggested that we stop. . . . A stolen night out together, no curfew, no duties. It's against Steward training, but I wanted to give him one night to just be himself. I only left him alone for a moment."

He was talking about Marcus. Violet drew in a painful breath, imagining their last moments together. "You two were close?"

"We were like brothers. The shieldmate bond is . . . We did everything together." Justice said it holding his body very still. "To fall into darkness . . . it was his greatest fear. And I left him alone with that."

In his voice she could hear what he had not allowed himself to show in front of Cyprian. Guilt, greater than that of a man who had simply left a friend alone to be captured. She understood, her chest hollowing.

"He's turning, isn't he?"

Justice gave her the slightest nod, the barest acknowledgment. "I saw the first signs in Southampton," he said. "I thought we had more time."

It made everything very real suddenly. The darkness gathering on the horizon. The threat of shadows, Simon's malevolence dragging the past into the present. And Marcus. His final days spent in terror of what he was about to become.

"How long?"

Justice's eyes were dark. "They say that when the three kings drank, they lived a full life of power, and only became shadows after they died natural deaths. But the Blood of Stewards is not as strong as the Blood of Kings. We can only resist the Cup for so long. If an ordinary human were to drink, they would turn to shadow instantly. Even those with weaker Steward blood would turn too fast—a day, a week. That's why only the strongest of us drink. The stronger your blood, the longer you last. But of course, you can't know for sure."

It was the closest he'd come to admitting the weight of the burden he carried. *We do it because we must*, he had said. The Elder Steward had said that the only thing that lay between this world and the Dark was Steward training.

He said, "You can ask it."

She drew in a difficult breath. "Are you turning too?"

"We're all turning," said Justice. "It starts the moment you drink, and continues until the shadow has you." He spoke with scrupulous honesty. "But I've shown no symptoms yet."

It was enough, she thought. It had to be. For both of them.

"Maybe fighting is knowing there's darkness in you, and still choosing to do what's right," she said. She wanted to believe it. But it wasn't as simple as that. The shadow would take Justice over eventually, no matter what he chose. She didn't want to think about what she would do when that day came. Justice had always seemed so strong, such a steadfast guiding light. She couldn't imagine facing the dark without him.

"If you mean that darkness is a test, you're right. How we face it. How we fight it," Justice said. "How we keep to the light."

She nodded, and made to push away and leave, when his voice called her back. "Violet."

She turned.

"I was wrong to doubt you," said Justice. "You've never faltered, even when the Stewards cast you out. I know that I've betrayed your trust." Justice's brown eyes were serious. "But I'd be honored to fight beside you, Steward and Lion."

She swallowed the emotion in her throat. "Don't Stewards fight with a shieldmate? What happens with Marcus gone?"

"While Marcus is missing, I can't form a new shield bond." The words were an admission. "I don't have anyone to watch for me."

She thought about what it meant to fight—as a Lion or a Steward, or any person trying to find a path through the dark. "Maybe we can watch for each other."

"A full-frontal attack."

Leda spoke as captain to the small group of twelve that had returned to the great hall. Violet stood at the foot of the dais steps. The High Janissary and the Elder Steward stood beside her, and with them were Justice, Farah, and a handful of Stewards and janissaries who manned the armories and led the patrols. Will had returned quietly, slipping into place beside Violet.

Violet found herself looking up at the four empty thrones, an eerie symbol of what they were fighting against. The four kings had ruled over the ancient world before the Dark King had turned them into shadows. Now Simon threatened to make a shadow that could destroy the new world. If they couldn't rescue Marcus . . .

"The grounds of Simon's estate at Ruthern will be dangerous," said Leda. "We've made assaults on Simon's strongholds in the past. Justice lost eleven Stewards fighting to free Will from Simon's ship. But it wasn't the sailors and cutthroats who killed Stewards, it was—" She broke off.

"Simon's Lion," Violet finished for her. *Tom.* Her mouth went dry. Tom would be there. Tom would fight—would kill Stewards like he had on the ship—or be killed. An almost overpowering desire to warn him seized her, and she had to force herself to speak. "I'll distract him," she made herself say. "He won't attack me."

"It's true, we have a Lion of our own," said the High Janissary speculatively.

"I'll stop him from killing Stewards," said Violet. She didn't know how; she only knew that she had to. She saw a few of the others exchange glances, nervous, skeptical.

Will knocked his knee against hers, an oddly reassuring gesture. Her eyes flew to his and he gave her a small nod. *You can do it.* The others didn't seem to notice—neither his quiet reassurance nor her own spike of nerves. She drew in a breath and nodded back at him.

"Simon's deadliest fighter isn't the Lion, it's the Betrayer," said Leda. "James may be our prisoner, but that doesn't mean this will be a fight without magic."

She felt Will's shoulders stiffen.

He still hadn't learned to unlock his own magic, she knew. Even against James he had tried and failed to use it. He never talked about it, but she had seen him devote hours and hours to practice, poring over ancient books, searching for new methods, losing himself in chants and meditations, all to no avail.

We have a magic user of our own as well. She could almost hear the unspoken words. They hung in the silence, but no one said them aloud because they knew that Will had shown no sign of his power.

It was Will who confronted the topic head on.

"I know I can't use magic," said Will. "But I want to help you fight."

Justice shook his head. "You're too important to risk. If the plan goes wrong—we can't lose you to Simon. Your role will come later. We need you safe in the Hall."

Will flushed but said nothing.

"What can we expect at Ruthern?" said Jannick.

Violet looked back at Leda, who addressed them all in her captain's cloak. The Stewards were strong, an unnatural strength granted to them by the Cup, but they had no easy way to fight against magic.

"First, the branded men," said Leda. "We do not yet know the extent of the power the brand grants them. There are rumors that a branded man can become Simon's eyes, that Simon can feel what they feel, see what they see."

"—but *Tom* has a brand," said Violet, and then wanted to bite out her own tongue as the Stewards all turned to look at her. Did Simon look out of Tom's eyes, inhabit his body? She instinctively clasped her own wrist, remembering her own desire for a brand, not that long ago. The thought that Tom had given his body over to be inhabited by Simon made her skin crawl.

"It's said to be how the Dark King commanded the battlefield," said Leda. "His minions bore his brand and that gave him mastery."

It was somehow even more frightening than turning people into shadows, the idea that once they were branded, his armies belonged to him fully, that he could inhabit their bodies, individually or many at once. She imagined looking into the eyes of hundreds of soldiers, and they were all the Dark King—

"Second are the Remnants," said Leda. "The men with pale faces that we drove back on the marsh. Each wears a piece of armor once worn by a member of the Dark King's inner guard. Or—should I say that the armor wears them. We believe it changes them. Their fighting style . . . it is eerily similar to ours, as if the armor knows the ancient skill of its old wearer. We have never faced them in open battle, but on the marsh it took twelve ward stones to drive them back."

The three blank-eyed men in strange pieces of black armor galloping across the marsh, their hounds streaming out ahead of them. Violet's stomach churned at the idea of fighting not the men but the ancient armor itself, still animated on its quest to protect the Dark King.

"They can be fought, but not easily," said Justice. "It takes spears, or long-range weapons. You cannot get close. A single touch is deadly. That may be how Simon knew where to dig for the buried armor: anything it touches withers, never to regrow. Above the ground where it was buried no tree took root nor bird would fly." His eyes were serious as he spoke the warning: "As you approach the estate and its parklands, beware the dead grass."

Beware the dead grass. Violet shivered and kept that in mind.

And then there was a silence. Violet looked around at the gathered Stewards, all of whom had gone quiet, almost as if there was something they did not want to face.

"And the last—" Leda broke off.

"The last?" said Violet.

Leda didn't answer, as if she found the subject too disturbing. Violet saw Jannick and Justice exchange looks. The silence stretched out. In the end, it was the Elder Steward who spoke.

"The last is Simon himself," said the Elder Steward.

"Simon!" said Will.

Violet knew Simon as a distant figure, the man her family had worked for over many years. There had always been rumors about him, communicated in hints and sidelong looks. That his rivals met misfortune, that it was dangerous to take him on. When she'd imagined fighting him, she'd imagined fighting the forces of his trade empire, not the man himself.

"Do not forget who he is. Simon is the Dark King's descendant, the heir to his throne," said the Elder Steward. "Simon may have no magic of his own, but his blood allows him to use the Dark King's objects and weapons, just as we use objects of the Light."

"His weapons?" said Violet.

"The sword you saw on the ship," said the Elder Steward. "Ekthalion, the Black Flame."

The moment she said it, it felt inevitable. That sickening, terrible black fire from the ship, sailors on their knees vomiting up black blood. But—

"How can he use it? He'd die. Everyone would die." Violet could almost taste the river water in her throat. She had never wanted to see that thing again.

"There are a lot of legends about the sword," said the Elder Steward. "It is called the Corrupted Blade, but it was once the Sword of the Champion, forged to kill the Dark King. *The Sword of the Champion bestows the power of the Champion.* . . . Those words are cast into its length. But it was utterly defiled, corrupted by a single drop of the Dark King's blood. Now it shares the destructive instincts of its master."

Violet remembered the way it had torn through the hull of the ship and the feeling she had had that it was trying to get out. The men closest to it had seemed to rot from the inside out.

"Its sheath was forged to hold its power back," said the Elder Steward. "But when it is drawn . . . That single drop of the Dark King's blood is more destructive than anything in our world. And you're right. Once it is fully unleashed, everyone and everything around it dies . . . except Simon himself, who cannot be harmed by the Dark King's blood, because that selfsame blood runs in his veins."

The Sword of the Champion bestows the power of the Champion. Those words stuck in Violet's mind.

"If it was once the Sword of the Champion—" said Violet.

"No. Do not attempt to take up the Blade yourself. Many have tried, chasing the old tale, believing they could cleanse the Blade and restore the sword to its glory. All are dead. If Simon has Ekthalion, our only chance is to prevent him from pulling it from its sheath."

"He won't risk drawing the Blade if there's a chance it will kill Marcus," said Will.

Violet blinked, startled by the insight. Will had been quiet throughout the discussion. It was very like him, she realized. Every now and again, he came out with that kind of unexpected observation, as though his mind worked differently from other people's, leaping several steps ahead.

"We can use that against him during the fight," said Will.

"He's right," said Leda slowly, as if this sort of artful tactic would not have occurred to her straightforward Steward mind.

"How many Stewards will we need for the attack?" asked Jannick.

"All of them," said Leda. "From the newest to the oldest, every Steward must fight."

"As well as those of us who aren't yet Stewards," said Cyprian, entering the great hall. He came down the center aisle through the forest of columns. "I'm coming too."

"This battle is no place for a novitiate," Jannick said.

"I might not have drunk from the Cup," said Cyprian, lifting his chin, "but I know how to fight. I'm more than just a novitiate. I'm the best trainee in the Hall. Better than some full Stewards." That was true, no matter how much Violet had always wanted it to be misplaced arrogance. She could almost feel the hot jealousy that flooded her any time she'd watched him fight: that perfect technique, that effortless mastery of form, even if he didn't have a Steward's strength. "If we lose this battle, we lose everything. Everyone who can should fight."

Jannick's eyes were on Cyprian's as he gave a slow nod. "Very well. We will call up the novitiates. Leda, I leave that task to you."

If he's willing to take novitiates, he's desperate. Cyprian might be the greatest fighter in a generation, but Emery or Beatrix would be slaughtered by someone like Tom. Her stomach turned over at the thought. *If Tom's there, I'll find him. I'll find him and stop him.*

"Marcus is our priority," said Leda. "If we can't reach him, we've failed. We will engage while a smaller group penetrates the estate and aims for Marcus. If we do get to him—"

"I know what to do," said Justice steadily. "I made him a promise, and I intend to keep it."

"You mean kill him," said Cyprian.

"If I can," said Justice. "Even if he hasn't turned, the shadow in him will fight."

Cold fingers of horror splayed across Violet's spine. She didn't know how it would play out. But she had a sudden terrible glimpse of a creature, half shadow, fighting, grasping, and clawing, wearing Marcus's face—

Cyprian had gone white. "I understand. If it comes to . . . I won't get in your way."

"If he's turning, how will we—" Violet swallowed. "What are the signs?"

There was another silence, this one almost painful. She had stumbled across one of those Steward taboos. Jannick forced the words out, though they were bitten off, unwilling.

"A tremor in the hand. Heightened emotion in the voice. Loss of control. In the later stages, you can glimpse the shadow. Behind the eyes. Under the skin. The Steward starts to become insubstantial."

A line of unwavering Steward swords, all in a row. Voices chanting in perfect harmony. Forms practiced over and over. Every Steward exercise was like a test, taken day in, day out, to prove they were still themselves.

And if they failed—

"Marcus was never afraid to die," said Justice, as if reading her thoughts. "It's the half life he feared. It's the same for all of us. I'm not afraid to die fighting. I made that choice when I drank from the Cup. I've already given my life to the fight."

Jannick nodded for them to begin their preparations, and several of the Stewards stood up from the table.

"The light will shine for you in the Hall," said the Elder Steward.

"The janissaries will tend to the fire, the Final Flame that has never gone out. For there will always be a light in the darkness, while a Steward lives to defend it."

Will stopped her in the hallway, a hand on her wrist, tugging her aside.

"What is it?" she said as he guided her to a quiet alcove where Cyprian was waiting. Will's voice was hushed as he spoke to both of them under the curved gray stone.

"This is a suicide mission. They're preparing to go in there and die. And they don't even know if they can get to Marcus."

Cyprian immediately stiffened. "They don't have another choice."

"What if they did?" said Will.

The shadowy light in the alcove emphasized a quality he had of nighttime beauty, his pale skin and dark hair made for the evening. Will hadn't spoken while the others had clashed heatedly in the Hall. Now he was talking in a quiet voice, in a space hidden from the Stewards.

"What do you mean?" She felt her heartbeat speed up.

"What if there was another way to get inside Simon's estate?" said Will. "Not an attack, with Stewards trying to fight against magic. The three of us slip in secretly. I could maneuver us past any guards. Violet could break any locks or chains. And Cyprian—Marcus is your brother. If he's still himself, he'll trust you enough to come with us."

Violet felt the possibility stir in her, a way to avoid the bloodshed, the carnage of a full-frontal attack.

"And if he's turning?" Cyprian didn't flinch as he said it, his handsome face steady. "You heard them. If he's turning, I'm not strong enough to fight him."

"You and Violet are, together," said Will. "And you can help him hold on. He'll fight the shadow inside him harder for you. You're his brother."

Violet was shaking her head. "There's no secret way in. James said that getting to Marcus would take a full-frontal assault. He can't lie under compulsion. Can he?"

"He can't lie," said Will. "But he doesn't know everything."

His face in the dim light was full of delicate planes, all cheekbones and dark eyes. He was still too thin, though he no longer looked underfed, and he was animated by the bright spark of a new idea.

"I know someone who can get us inside," said Will.

CHAPTER TWENTY-THREE

KATHERINE STEPPED OUT into the garden at dusk. She had told Mrs. Dupont that she enjoyed the brisk air, and she told herself that as well. It was proper, she thought, for a young lady to take a constitutional. There was nothing remarkable about it. She drew her shawl around her shoulders against the chill. And so she had found herself out here each night, waiting until the light faded.

The garden was comprised of three paths, which only a few weeks before had been quite yellow with fallen elm leaves. The bordering flowers in early winter were quiet shrubs of dark green. Ivy covered the cast-iron fencing, and garden benches nestled under trees that had a bare, wintry look to them, one or two sharp frosts having stripped them of the last of their leaves.

She took the eastern path, feeling the cold air chill her cheeks, and she stayed outside until night fell, until it was dark and she had to go back. She told herself that she didn't feel foolish, because she had no expectations.

And then she saw the jacket, folded and resting under one of the bare trees, and felt her heart begin racing.

He was here.

She could feel it, like a change in the air. It had been three days since he had dressed in the stables, then disappeared out into the night. Three long days, marked by her aunt's sharp comments. *Katherine! Stop mooning about at that window and return to your needlework!*

It was a thrill that turned her days and nights of waiting into a single, pleasurable build to this moment.

"You came," she said to the garden.

"I made a promise." His voice was closer than she had expected—the warm tone of it—behind her—

"It's dangerous," she said. "The servants—"

"I'm not afraid of them," Will said, and she turned to look at him.

He was standing under the night-green branches of a tree. His dark hair was a tumble over his forehead. His eyes, always intense, were fixed on her, as hers were on him.

"You should be." The shock of seeing him again felt physical and came with a cascade of remembered moments: her fingers on his bare skin as she tied his neckcloth. The moment when she'd seen him in her fiancé's clothes. "Mrs. Dupont likes to come out and check on me."

"I know the risks," said Will.

He wasn't wearing Lord Crenshaw's clothes now. He was dressed in strangely old-fashioned garments, a thigh-length tunic with a star emblem that nevertheless seemed to suit him, as though he'd just stepped out of an ancient court.

"I came to ask for your help."

His voice was serious. He sounded like he was in need, even in danger, like he wouldn't have come to her if he had any other choice.

"My help?"

She thought he looked like Lancelot in those clothes. She liked the idea of herself as Guinevere, the two of them acting out the myth, meeting in a garden where no one else could see or hear. She even liked the idea that he needed her help for some urgent business.

"You asked me before who I was. The truth is, I know Simon."

"You . . ." The words weren't what she expected. She remembered him asking about Simon in the carriage. She felt the quality of the air change.

"You should call him Lord Crenshaw," she said. "He's far above you in station."

"I know what he is."

"Then you know you shouldn't be here."

But he was; he'd come. As she'd known he would, giving him Lord Crenshaw's jacket because it was something to return.

"Katherine." Will said her name in a way that made her shiver; it was so intimate, saying her given name like that. She wanted him to say it again. "Simon isn't a good man."

She told herself it was part of the flirtation, and a part of her even liked it, the idea that he would take her away from her engagement, freedom waiting on the other side.

"I suppose Lord Crenshaw, one of the foremost gentlemen in London, is a bad person," she said, "while you, climbing garden walls, are the good one."

"People aren't what they seem," said Will.

"I do know him *quite well*," said Katherine.

"You don't know him at all," said Will.

"I know he's generous and charming. I know he's handsome and attentive. I even know that he's in London right now. On important business. He told me—"

Will said, "He killed my mother."

Everything seemed to stop. She felt the chill of cold night air as it touched the shadowed places in the garden. Around her, dark green shapes were moving, rustling softly in the breeze. ". . . What?"

"We lived at Bowhill, in the Peak District," said Will. "I was collecting wood when I heard her scream. She tried to fight, but she—there was so much blood, soaked into the earth. By the time I got to her it was too late. I came to London to find out who had done it. Who had sent those men to kill her. It was Simon."

His gaze had always been intense, but his face was pale and serious, and he wasn't saying it as if he was joking; he was saying it as if it was true. As if Lord Crenshaw had given the order to kill someone.

"You're lying." She stepped back instinctively. "You're trying to besmirch a good man's name. It's not becoming." She had thought Will was a gentleman, but he wasn't. A gentleman wouldn't say these things.

"I'm not lying to you, Katherine. It's why I came. Simon's holding a man hostage at Ruthern. And terrible things could happen if that man's not rescued. You're the only person who could get us onto the estate to help him—"

"Then you've been lied to," she said. "Because Lord Crenshaw would never do that."

But she was filled with the vision of it, of Lord Crenshaw giving orders, and sending out men to hunt down women.

"There are things happening," said Will. "Things bigger than both of us. Things that if I told you, you wouldn't believe—"

"I don't believe it." She was breathing quickly. "Lord Crenshaw is a good man, and we're going to be married at St. George's Hanover Square, and after that we'll live at Ruthern; it's all been planned out."

He was looking at her as though she stood on the other side of a chasm. "Katherine—"

"You hate him." As the ground seemed to shift under her feet, she remembered Lord Crenshaw's lawyer saying, *The boy.* "You came for him. You never came for me." She flushed, the painful truth behind her re-alization just slipping out. *The boy. Lord Crenshaw's enemy. The boy who sank the ship.*

It's you. She felt those words deep within her. Mrs. Dupont had aban-doned her that day because of a boy. *It's you.*

She had feelings for an enemy. Self-knowledge made her shiver. Because she knew now that she didn't want Lord Crenshaw. She wanted this, danger and mystery, and something on the very edge of her understanding—

"I came for you." Will's dark eyes were a tumult. "I came for you. Maybe at first I thought—but the moment I saw you, it was like nothing else mattered." Will said it as if he was trying to hold the words back and couldn't. "I know you feel it too."

It was true: as if her life had been a dream, and he was the only real thing in it. It was a vital quality he had. Even here in the garden, he made everything fade around him, a dim nighttime haze and the dark, far-off impression of trees.

They were going to kiss. She could feel it as something inevitable, a pull that was irresistible. She'd been kissed once, on the back of her gloved hand the day of her engagement to Simon. She hadn't felt like this then. She moved in toward Will; she was the one who moved. His eyes were very dark. "Katherine—" He looked like he wanted to turn her away, but there was no way to stop it.

A kiss; around her light started to shine as if his touch was conjuring it, racing from him into her veins, a radiance that she could see and touch and feel, and as the feeling reached its climax, the light exploded outward and the dead winter tree above them burst into bloom—

Will jerked back, his eyes wide, and she was staring at him across a spray of white flowers out of season, still half aglow; like fires on distant ramparts; like stars in the dark.

It was magic, impossible, the tree above them glowing with light that only made him look more strange, a fey creature. *He did this. I felt it. He—*

"What's happening?" She was staring at the tree above them, its branches spilling over with new blossoms, a riot of white flowers impossible in the early winter. How could it be? How could there be light—and flowers—? "What is that?"

"It's a hawthorn tree," said Will, in a strange, raw voice. He was staring at the tree, his shock transforming into something else as he looked back at her. She realized that he was afraid. Of what he'd revealed, of what she'd seen him do. *He lit the tree and made it flower.* Above them the hawthorn tree was bright with blossoms, each one still flickering with light. She saw the light play on his face, on his clothing.

"How did you do it?" she said, staring at him across the white flowers. He wasn't answering her. The strangeness of it started to become frightening. There was nothing in the natural world to explain it. There was nothing to explain *him*, a boy she hardly knew. And then: "What are you?" Her heart was pounding.

"Katherine, listen to me. You can't tell anyone. You can't tell anyone about this." There was real fear on his face. He took a step forward, and she stepped back instinctively.

"What are you?"

The flowers were temporary. The petals had already begun falling around them. She could still see the last fading glow of the light. It was beautiful and frightening—like him, standing in his strange, ancient clothes against the falling petals like the swirl of ash or snow—

—like a figure from another world—

"Katherine?" It was a voice calling from the house. "Katherine!"

"That's Mrs. Dupont," said Katherine.

"Come with me," said Will. "I was wrong to . . . I'll tell you every-thing you want to know if you just come with me."

"I'm not going to do that!"

"Katherine?" Mrs. Dupont's voice was closer. "Katherine! Where are you? What was that light?"

"You can't stay here," said Will urgently. "If Simon learns what happened—if he thinks you're connected to me—"

"I'm not going with you," said Katherine. "This is my home, Lord Crenshaw is my fiancé, and you—you're—" She could hear Mrs. Du-pont's footsteps on the path. They both turned toward the sound. They only had a moment before Mrs. Dupont turned the corner and found them together. "You're *unnatural*—"

Instead of leaving, Will drew in a shaky breath. "If you won't come, listen. At the first sign that something is wrong, run. Don't stay as the warnings pile up, telling yourself that Simon is a good man. Protect your-self. And if you ever need a safe place, look for me at the gate on the Abbey Marsh, past the River Lea."

For a moment she stared at him, the unusually earnest look in his eyes, coupled with the striking features and strange clothes that gave him an otherworldly look. She felt like she was seeing him for the first time. Her thoughts were broken by a voice.

"Katherine?" said Mrs. Dupont, appearing at the end of the path.

Katherine jerked to face her, heart jolting at the idea of Mrs. Dupont catching her with Will. But Mrs. Dupont didn't seem to react, and when Katherine looked back, Will had gone, like the light that had vanished, and she was alone with her lady's maid in the dark.

"Are you all right?" was all Mrs. Dupont said. "I thought I saw—"

"I saw it too," said Katherine, glad for her shawl to hide that her hands were shaking. "A strange flash of light. I thought a streetlamp had exploded."

Mrs. Dupont instantly turned in the direction of the street. "Go inside. I'll check for any sign of fire. Mr. Johns!" She called for the groom.

Katherine nodded. *Whatever that light was, it doesn't have anything to do with me,* she thought, walking past Mrs. Dupont over a cold ground pale with dead petals toward the house.

CHAPTER TWENTY-FOUR

THERE WAS A difference between guessing and knowing, between believing and seeing.

After weeks in a small room with a dark, dead stone tree, to look up and see a hawthorn tree breaking into flower—

What are you? she'd said, staring at him in horror. *What are you? What are you? What are you?*

He couldn't think about that. He couldn't think about the light or what it meant, the way it had felt suffusing his skin, spilling out around them both, all of it tangled up with his feelings about her, the beautiful glow of the trees, the fall of white petals, the soft muslin of her skirts, the flutter of her breath as her lips parted against his—

The brilliant burst of it reflecting on her frightened face, looking not at the tree but at him.

The worst thing that could have happened.

An explosion of power, and the trumpeting of identity . . . He should never have gone to her. He should never have talked to her the way he had, so openly, about Simon. About his mother. And now she was in danger, more danger than before. If Simon knew what had happened—if he found out—heard—

Violet and Cyprian were waiting for him at the rendezvous point with the horses. They both turned toward him as he approached.

"Well?" Violet's voice was expectant.

They were waiting for him to tell them his plan, the chance he had promised them to get into Ruthern. A way to rescue Marcus that avoided a slaughter.

"I couldn't get it done." He kept his voice steady. "I'm sorry. I thought I had another way for us to get into Ruthern. I don't."

They were in a dirt laneway on the edge of the city, and it was late enough that there was no sound beyond the distant bells and calls from the river. Violet was holding the horses, Valdithar a shadowy shape, the two Steward horses pale glimmers in the dark.

"Then it's the attack." Cyprian's voice was matter-of-fact, as though he'd known from the start that Marcus's rescue would cost them. "We ride on Ruthern with the Stewards." He moved toward his horse. Before he could, Violet stepped forward.

"It was Miss Kent, wasn't it?" said Violet. "That's who you were going to see. You thought she could get us into Ruthern."

He didn't answer.

"Will. What happened?"

Katherine's frightened eyes staring at him, a bright glow all around them as petals swirled and fell like snow. *What are you?*

Don't think about that.

"Will?"

"There was a light."

"A light?"

"Like the one I've been trying to conjure with the Elder Steward. It scared her off." He turned and took up his horse's reins, placing one hand on the saddle.

Violet's voice beside him was confused. "But—I thought you couldn't conjure the light—"

"I couldn't."

There was a scooped-out feeling in his chest, like he had felt when he had failed to light the Tree Stone, worse now that he had seen it shine.

"What made you call it now?"

He couldn't answer that. But the silence gave him away, and it was as if Violet guessed everything that had happened in the garden just from the way he wouldn't look at her face.

"Will. She's *Simon's fiancée.*"

"I know that. I know. I know that I shouldn't have—"

He shouldn't have. It had left her in more danger than before. He wanted to go back to her, he wanted to bring her to safety, and he couldn't. She wouldn't go with him no matter how much he pleaded with her.

He expected Violet to be furious with him for his foolishness and his failure. For kissing Katherine Kent under a tree in a garden. *It's not what you think,* he wanted to say. Except that he was remembering the way he'd felt when he'd met Katherine, how drawn he had been to her, and somewhere deeply buried there was an awful awareness of what had happened. What he had let happen.

But when he looked up, Violet wasn't angry; she was looking at him with a dawning expression of awe and excitement.

"Will, don't you understand what this means?"

He found himself caught without words, staring back at her, unable to understand the excitement in her voice.

"You can use your powers," said Violet. "You can use your powers when we fight Simon."

"No," he said, because she had misunderstood everything. "I can't. It's not like that. It's—"

"You can," said Violet. "Don't you get it? The Stewards—they think everything is about control. The meditations, the candle—but it was never about that—"

It was about a door. A door inside that wouldn't open.

Violet had taken another step toward him.

"On the ship, you thought everybody was going to die. And with Katherine you—"

"Violet—" said Will warningly.

"—kissed her. That's what happened, isn't it?"

He couldn't bear to tell it as it was; he just stared back at her and felt the truth slice at him. He had kissed her. Let her kiss him. A single perfect moment, and then a spill of radiant light.

What are you? What are you? What are you?

"You *what*?" said Cyprian.

Violet frowned. "Matters of the flesh. You wouldn't understand."

"I know what a kiss is," said Cyprian, but he'd flushed slightly.

"It's emotion, isn't it? Strong emotion," said Violet. "That's what brings your power out."

Passion and death; the garden and the ship. She was looking at him like she wanted to hear him say it. Will stared back at her, needing to deny all of it. He felt his own flush of hot shame. The words didn't come.

"Carnal feelings drive his power?" said Cyprian, that slight flush still on his cheeks.

"Not just *carnal* feelings," said Violet. "Any feelings. That's it, isn't it."

Was that true? Was that what had unlocked it, light streaming around them, as petals drifted like sparks? Had strong feelings caused the burst of light?

Violet swung up into her saddle and looked down at him with urgency.

"We have to tell the Elder Steward," said Violet. "This gives us a
chance. You were born for this battle, and now we know how to use your
power."

"The Lady, a Lion, and the Stewards," said Cyprian, nodding. "Now
it's a real fight."

They made good time, a hard canter over the marshes. Valdithar shook his
neck, eager to run; beside him flowed the two graceful Steward horses.
Cyprian knew the paths that avoided the treacherous, boggy water, and
they raced through the cold night air together.

Soon the broken arch came into view.

Will found himself leaning forward in the saddle, wanting the fight
that was coming. Not only to help Marcus, but to deal Simon a blow from
which he would never recover.

Cyprian also seemed reenergized, his long hair streaming out behind
him as they rode. He was clearly eager to see his brother. With Will able
to manifest his power, Simon was a less formidable figure, he said.

"Simon's not at Ruthern," said Will, remembering what Katherine
had told him. "He's in London." On business, she had said. "That gives us
a window to attack. We'll still be facing his minions, but Simon won't be
there to use the Corrupted Blade."

That was an advantage, and Cyprian seized on it. "Without a leader,
his men will be easier to fight."

They slowed their horses to a walk as they approached the gate. Will
saw a figure in a red tunic; it was Leda, standing with her back leaned
against the arch.

"Leda! We're back with news!" called Cyprian.

There was a silence as the sky beetled overhead and a birdcall echoed over the marsh.

"I'll stable the horses," Cyprian said. "You go straight to the Elder Steward and tell her what you've learned." And then he called to Leda, "We're coming through the gate."

The silence went on, continuing a second too long, past the time that Leda would have hailed them. She was standing still at her post, the wind fluttering aimlessly in her hair.

"Cyprian," said Will.

He could see her: the hand that did not wave, the vast silence of the surrounding marshes in which there was no movement at all but the insects and the birds. Valdithar tossed his head and the chink of his bridle was too loud. Will was staring at Leda's tunic.

His skin prickled. "Look at her clothes."

Cyprian turned with a quizzical expression that changed as he looked at Leda. It was like a picture coming into focus, the way she was leaning, the oddly angled line of her neck, her open mouth, and her tunic, wet and red.

Will's whole body came alive with danger.

Cyprian was swinging down off his horse, running toward her through the mud. Will saw a marsh insect crawl across the corner of Leda's right eye, barely disturbed when Cyprian took hold of her shoulders. "Leda?" Cyprian's face was full of disbelief. His hands, which had grasped her clothes, came away red. "Leda?"

No. Will looked at the marsh around them, his blood thundering in his veins. There was no sign of an attacker, just the empty landscape of water and grass.

Leda's lifeless body had been here long enough to attract insects, with no Steward coming to her aid, and no sign of a struggle or a fight. And her attackers weren't here. With a terrible feeling of foreboding, Will lifted his eyes to the gate.

"We need to tell the others," Cyprian was saying. "We need to warn them, so that they can send out a patrol—"

"Cyprian—!" said Will, but he was too late, Cyprian was running through the gate and into the courtyard. "Stop him," he said to Violet, but the sickly blank look on her face said that she didn't understand. "*Stop him.*"

She seemed to snap out of it, and even if she didn't understand, they were both dropping down off their horses and racing after Cyprian, in time to pass through the gate with him.

They stopped where Cyprian had stopped, three steps into the courtyard, and even Will's fears had been nothing like this.

It was a massacre.

A battlefield where no one fought. All the Stewards were just shapes, piles of lifeless nothing, as if the emptiness of the marshes had penetrated the walls. Nothing moved except the banner with its single star, lifting and dropping in the wind.

His eye was repelled; his gorge rose. The closest body was two steps away; torn open, it was not recognizable, just another horrifying shape spread out across the stone.

You're safe here, the Elder Steward had said. *No one can challenge us inside these walls.*

"No," said Cyprian, and Will's mind snapped back to the present. He saw Cyprian's contorted face, and beyond that, the walls rising overhead, the windows that faced them, a hundred arrow slits and crenels trained on them.

"Hold him back," said Will quickly, because they weren't safe. Nowhere was safe, and the attackers might be anywhere in the Hall. "Violet, hold him back before he—"

Violet grabbed Cyprian by the tunic, right before he started to run toward the Hall.

"Let me go. I have to—have to help them. Let me *go*—" Cyprian was struggling desperately against her, but she was stronger than he was, crowding him until his back hit the wall, then pressing him into a small, shaded space between jutting blocks of stone, and holding him there.

Will followed, ignoring the voice in his head screaming at him not to turn his exposed back to the courtyard. The voice from nine months of hiding. The voice that said, *Run*.

"Listen to me. Listen." Will kept his own voice low, trying somehow to get through to Cyprian, who was glaring at him furiously, panting. "We don't know who did this. They might still be here. We're in danger. We can't just rush in."

"My home has been attacked." Cyprian spat the words out. "Why should I care about danger?"

"Because you might be the only Steward left," said Will, and he saw Cyprian go white.

And then he saw him take it in: the silence of everything; the palpable, pressing, silence; the walls unmanned; the doors at the top of the steps open. Above their heads, a banner was flying like a horror over the dead that no Steward had come to claim.

Like a brace of butchered rabbits that a hunter had tossed to the ground, three Stewards lay in contorted shapes a step to their left. Cyprian started to crack right in front of him.

"They're not dead. No one can get inside the Hall. No one can—"

Will took him by the shoulders. "Steward, hold to your training!" Cyprian's eyes, meeting his, were blank, as if Cyprian himself was barely there.

Months with the Elder Steward doing meditations had never helped him. But now Will spoke her words to someone else. "Breathe, center your mind." And then, "Again."

Cyprian took one breath, then another. He had always been the perfect novitiate, more dedicated and more disciplined than anyone else. Now he called on that Steward training, and Will watched him physically reassert control over himself.

"Now look at me," said Will, and Cyprian's eyes opened, circles of green. They were still a little blank around the edges—but he was Cyprian again.

"If there are survivors, we'll find them," said Will. "But to do that, we need to keep ourselves alive. Can you do that?" Cyprian nodded.

"I will not fail my Order," Cyprian said, the words raw but steady. "My training will hold."

Slowly, Will released his grip. Then he turned and looked.

The last time a slaughter had taken his home from him, he'd been the one stupid with emotion, stumbling through it, making mistakes that had gotten others killed. Now he knew: Don't grieve. Move. One foot after another, that's how you survive.

Beside him, he heard Violet say, "It's like an army came through here."

"Leda was one of the strongest Stewards in the Hall." Cyprian's voice was strained but steady, still threaded through with disbelief. Underneath both their words lay the same terrible question:

What could kill this many Stewards?

Will's eyes were on the bodies, their eyes staring open and turned toward the gate.

"They didn't sound the alarm," said Will. "They didn't even have time to draw their swords."

It had been the same outside. Leda had died at the gate and given no alert to the people inside the walls. Whatever had happened here had taken a hall full of Stewards by surprise.

"These attackers were fast, and strong," Will said, his eyes lifting grimly to open doors, like a dark, yawning cave. "They came in from the gate then moved inside. That's where we're going. Stay behind me, stay quiet, and stay out of sight."

Inside, the bodies took on an anonymized sameness, though certain images stuck. A Steward impaled on a wall sconce. A severed hand near a shard of pottery. A smear of blood across a white column.

Will led, as though by seeing everything first, he could somehow protect the others from it. Cyprian followed, his expression determinedly blank as he stepped over the bodies of those he knew. Violet brought up the rear.

Around them, the hallways were silent. No voices. No chants. No bells. That was the eeriest part, along with the lack of light. Here and there, torches still flamed, but many had been knocked over or had burned out, so that the corridors were dark with only flickering patches of light. Once, they saw a torch overturned onto a floor covering, a fire burning across the ground and partway up the wall. Violet moved quickly to put it out.

Deeper inside, they saw the first signs of real fighting. Here the Stewards had died with swords, standing in basic formations, all facing a single direction. No one had tried to break or run. They had held their ground and fought. They were brave, and strong, and they had trained to fight every day of their lives. But it had made no difference.

"This way," Will said, at a corner. He didn't need to ask where to go. He was following the path of the dead, trying not to think that he was being led toward some dark heart at the center of the Hall, or about what he might find there.

It brought him to the doors of the great hall.

Violet was already striding forward to try to push them open, her palms flat against the carved metal. They didn't budge, despite her formidable strength. "They're barricaded from the inside."

"That means someone's in there," said Cyprian.

Will took a step forward to stop Cyprian doing something foolish, but it was Violet who turned back to the door and started pounding on it with her fist. "Hey! Hey in there!"

"*Violet!*" Will grabbed her wrists, but not before the pounding on the brass doors created a vast booming sound that echoed through the halls.

The three of them froze as the sound faded into silence, waiting as if some terrible creature might now be following the noise to where they were. Will could hear his own heartbeat in the silence.

But there was no answering sound from the hallways, no attackers bursting out toward them . . . and as thick silence settled back around them, they each looked back at the doors.

Because there had been no sound from inside the great hall either.

"I'll try again," said Violet, and then, at the alarmed looks of both boys, "Quieter."

This time she set her shoulder against the doors and threw her whole weight behind it, but even her strength couldn't budge them. She broke away, panting.

"Maybe one of the windows," said Will.

They weren't exactly windows, more like high thin slits, but Violet looked up and nodded, fixing her eyes on one of them. "I'll need a lift."

Cyprian braced himself against the wall, making his back into a step. Violet ran three steps, then sprang up from Cyprian's back to grab a jutting corbel, where she hung briefly before pulling herself up farther. She leaped from the corbel to the window. Gripping its slim edges, Violet swung herself inside, then dropped. They heard the sound of her feet hitting the stone on the other side.

And then a stretch of silence so long that Will's stomach turned over.

"Violet?" he called quietly, right into the seam of the doors.

Nothing.

"Violet?"

Are you all right? Are you there? She couldn't be gone. She was strong. But the Stewards had been strong too.

Heart pounding, he opened his mouth to call again, when he heard her subdued answering voice. "I'm here! I'm opening the doors."

The doors didn't open right away. Instead, Will heard the heavy scraping sounds of wood pulled across stone. This went on for long minutes. Finally, the immense metal latch beams of the doors were lifted, and there was Violet, pulling the doors open from the inside.

He saw at once what had taken her so long.

The Stewards had pushed every piece of furniture in the great hall up against the doors to barricade them shut. The chairs, the candle stands, the tapestries, the statues cut from their pedestals, even the long table that had always looked immovable. Only the four empty thrones were intact, too immense to be hacked out of the stone.

One by one, Violet had dragged the pieces of furniture away, so that they lay in a circle of useless detritus around her. She was panting with effort, her hair wet with sweat, her eyes hollow. And she was shaking, not with exertion, but from the pressing horror of the room. Will saw the spot where she had vomited, by an overturned chair.

Beside him, Cyprian pressed his forearm to his mouth and nose. The room smelled of fresh meat, like a butcher's shop, a thick smell of blood and exposed fat.

Will walked forward into it. He could feel the stickiness of the stone under his feet. He looked and his breath clogged in his throat.

The last of the Stewards had made their stand here, in the long dark of the great hall, with its ghostly white columns.

And behind them, the novitiates and janissaries who they had tried to protect. Carver lying two steps in front of Emery, who would have seen him fall seconds before he fell himself. Beatrix near the front, having pushed her way forward to fight alongside Stewards ten years her senior. He had seen them all this morning, preparing for the attack on Ruthern.

"Simon," Will heard himself say, and then: "Katherine said he was in London on business."

"These are the greatest fighters of the Stewards," said Violet. "Not even an army of Simon's could defeat them in their own Hall."

"It wasn't an army," said Will. "It was something that could pass through the doors."

He had known it the moment he had seen Leda, the understanding breaking into their naive, jubilant return to the Hall.

"No," said Cyprian.

"The doors were barred," said Will. "There are no enemy dead. It's only Stewards. It's only Stewards here and in the halls."

"No," said Cyprian, as if Will hadn't spoken. "It was an attack. We keep going. If there are survivors, we find them. That's what you said."

They stared at each other, Cyprian's handsome face set in stubborn lines, Will feeling full of awful knowledge.

"There might be rooms that were overlooked," Violet volunteered quickly. "Or places in the citadel to hide."

Places in the vast, empty citadel, full of crumbled stairs and unvisited chambers built by people who had lived and died and fallen to dust. Will knew where they had to go, into the heart of the gloom.

"The Tree Chamber," he said. "The Elder Steward once told me that it was the final retreat in ancient times, when the forces of the Dark attacked the Hall."

"Then we go," Violet said.

Will took up a guttering torch from one of the wall sconces. He knew it was dangerous to draw attention, but it was that or grope blindly in the dark. Once they left the great hall, there were fewer bodies, but the feeling that they were approaching something terrible was stronger. The flames from the torch were too loud, a sound like flapping linen.

He had come this way every day, to train with the Elder Steward. But the macabre, flickering dark turned the corridors unfamiliar. He moved forward slowly, staying as quiet as he knew how. He looked at the few bodies they passed for the gruesome purpose of seeing how fresh they were. The closer they got, the fresher the kills.

He had thought he was prepared for anything, but when he reached the room leading to the Tree Chamber, he stopped, his stomach turning.

It was not like the scenes they'd seen elsewhere in the Hall, where Stewards had been killed so quickly they'd barely drawn their swords.

This was the last stand of a champion.

The room had been destroyed, a devastation that Will could not take in all at once. Rubble, cracked walls, smashed flooring: a force so terrible it could raze parts of the citadel had fought here against a single opponent determined to hold it back.

Justice had been the greatest fighter in the Hall, and his attacker had torn the room apart, shredding tapestries, splintering furniture, even shattering stone in an attempt to get at him. From the sheer extent of the destruction, Justice had lasted against his attacker for some time.

His eyes were sightless, fixed on some distant nightmare. His hand was still on his sword. Will remembered the moment he had woken up to Justice's reassuring presence in the White Hart. Justice had always seemed to know what was right. A lodestar. Someone who would guide you through the night.

Violet was on her knees beside him. She was saying his name as if she could speak with him. She was pressing her hands to his body as if to stanch blood that had stopped flowing, or find some warmth where there was only cold.

Will found himself looking up inexorably at the doors to the Tree Chamber.

Justice would have known better than anyone that he couldn't win, and he had fought anyway. Delaying the enemy. Delaying him as long as he could.

Will didn't need Violet's strength to force the doors. They were already open.

He walked inside alone.

The Tree Stone was dark. Its dead, brittle branches a testament to Will's failures. No glowing light here, no sweet smell of hawthorn or soft fall of white flowers. Just a dead thing that had once been alive. Will had to lift the torch to light up the room, a bitter irony.

But the enemy they sought was here, its pitch-black form revealed for all to see. It was dead, like the Tree. But it had not left behind a body, just an imprint, burned into the wall.

Looking at it was like looking into the blackest pit from which no light could escape. Darkly unnatural, it loomed over the chamber, taller than any man, monstrous and distorted. It was all that was left of the creature that had destroyed the Hall.

Marcus.

Behind him, he heard Cyprian make an awful sound. Will stumbled slightly as Cyprian pushed past him. Cyprian stared up at the burned outline, and then he put his hands on it, as if by touching it, he could somehow touch his brother. His fingers curled and he slid downward, kneeling, his head dropped in utter despair. For a single disturbing moment, he and his brother seemed like one: a Steward and his shadow cast upon the wall.

Will turned back to the door. And a second wave of horror passed over him, as, lifting the torch, he saw the words carved above the doors, centuries ago, by those who had waited scared in the dark.

He is coming.

"The Elder Steward fought it off," said a voice, and Will whirled.

A figure was stepping out of the shadows. Heart slamming in his chest, he recognized Grace, janissary to the Elder Steward, her face streaked with tear lines, and her clothes torn and stained. Behind her, a second janissary—Sarah, her expression haggard.

"Now she is dying," said Grace. "If you wish to see her, come. There isn't much time left."

CHAPTER TWENTY-FIVE

THE ROOM WAS small, with a pallet laid out on raised stone. Someone had lit a single brazier to warm the space, and brought it close to the place where she lay under a thin blanket. Her face was sunken, her skin almost transparent. Will hadn't known what to expect, but there was no blood, no sign of injury, just her white hair on the pallet and the slow rise and fall of her chest.

He was not sure he was wanted. From the doorway, he watched as Grace and Sarah moved around her with the surety of attendants. Cyprian fit the moment, an austere figure in a silver tunic. A novitiate and two janissaries: the three of them belonged here. Will felt like an interloper, even as his chest clenched at the sight of the Elder Steward. Violet hesitated beside him, the two of them outsiders in a private moment of Steward grief.

"The end is close," Grace said quietly. "The fight took all she had."

He could see the difficulty that she had in breathing. The act seemed to be a pure effort of will. At Grace's words she stirred and said, "Will?" Her voice was no louder than the rustle of dried paper.

"I'm here," said Will, and in two strides knelt at her side.

Up close, the lines of pain were etched into her face, as though some part of her was still locked in battle.

"He came so fast . . . our preparations were all for nothing. Our own desire for strength has destroyed us . . . unleashing the shadow that could not be fought."

"You fought him," said Will.

"I fought him," said the Elder Steward. "I fought him when no one else could. You know why."

He did know. He had known since he had learned of the shadows, a kaleidoscope of moments, all running together into the truth. The tremor in her hand. The way the candle holder had seemed to fall right through it. Her frequent absences from gatherings in the Hall, and the excuses Jannick had made.

"You're turning," said Will.

He only half heard the shocked reaction of the others behind him. He looked into the Elder Steward's rheumy eyes and saw her painful acknowledgment. No human could defeat a shadow. But perhaps two shadows could grapple with one another.

He felt no fear of her, but maybe he should. Her skin was so diaphanously fine he could almost see through it; and every now and again, something seemed to flicker underneath, like the glimpse of a creature moving underwater.

"His power was great," said the Elder Steward, "but the shadow inside me is greater. If I were to turn, I would be strong enough to rule this world. Yet I would be but a slave to the Dark King's will. Even now I can feel my own will diminish. . . . I could not complete the morning chant, or hold the sword point steady. But I have enough willpower left to remain myself long enough to speak with you."

The reign of her will was there in each breath, in and out, each measured word taking one more piece of her strength. She was the oldest Steward and had fought her shadow the longest. Her great strength showed now, as she held herself together for him, for them.

"It is coming, Will. The events that I have spent my life preparing for are here, but I will not see them come to pass. That will fall to you." Another labored breath, her eyes dark. "I thought we could be the star at your back. But in the end it will be as it was. The Dark King and the Lady." Her white hair was fine against the pillow, and when he took her hand in his own it felt even less substantial.

"I don't know what I'm supposed to do," he said—whispered. It felt like telling her his deepest secret. Her trust in him, so near to the end, hurt. He could see her weakening, each breath more painful than the last.

"You must stop Simon from calling him forth. For he is very close now. The Shadow Stone has been taken. Simon need only free the Shadow Kings and he has all he needs to raise the Dark King, and end the line of the Lady."

The Shadow Stone. He remembered it, the dark force of it, far more frightening than Marcus's shadow on the wall.

"You told me once that I would have to fight him." He remembered her words at the Tree Stone. *The Stewards are here to stop Simon. At all costs, we will fight to prevent the Dark King's return. But if we fail, you must be ready.*

"I told you that there was more than one way to fight. The power to stop the Dark lies within you, Will. If I didn't believe that, I would not have brought you into this Hall. I hope you will remember that, when you make your choice. I hope you remember me." Her hand briefly squeezed his.

"Violet," she said. Will saw Violet lift her head, startled. Will beckoned her forward, stepping back to let her take his place at the Elder Steward's side. He released a shaky breath as he did so, even as the Elder

Steward turned her eyes to Violet.

"You are the strongest fighter the Light has left. You have it in you to become a true Lion, as the Lions of old . . . for you have Lion blood on both sides, from your father and your mother."

"My mother?" Violet's hollowed eyes were dark.

"Did you think your power came only from your father? You fear your Lion fate, yet the time will come when you must take up the Shield of Rassalon. Do not be afraid. In your blood run the brave lions of England and the bright lions of India. You are stronger than your brother."

Violet nodded, looking pale. Then, as she stepped back, the Elder Steward said the final name.

"Cyprian."

And it was Cyprian's turn to come forward, and he did, kneeling and bowing his head. He was the picture of the novitiate obedient before his elder. The light from the brazier seemed oddly bright.

"You are the last of the Stewards. The only one left to remember. Your road will be hard, and your trials will be great. I wish I could give you comfort. . . . Instead I must ask one more thing of you."

He lifted his head where he had bowed it and looked up at her with dark eyes. "Anything, Elder Steward."

"I have no shieldmate," she said. "My vow was to your father, and he is dead. I ask you to take his place." Will saw Cyprian's face go white as he realized what she was asking. "Do what he cannot. Let me go into the night in peace and rest. For I am all but shadow now."

It was Grace who stepped forward with the knife.

It was plain-handled, with a straight blade. Cyprian stood and took it from her. He had never shirked his duty.

The Elder Steward looked up at him one last time.

They seemed to share something in that moment: past and future;

Steward and novitiate; part of a tradition that was passing from the world.

Cheeks wet with tears, Cyprian lifted the knife and brought it down, and that was the end; she was still, and the light in her eyes had gone out.

It was Cyprian who said, "We burn the bodies and refortify the gates." He said it with the same strapped-down resolution that he'd had when he lifted the knife.

They were huddled in the Elder Steward's small rooms. The immense citadel with its gruesome contents loomed around them, a reality no one wanted to face. The candle at the center of the oak table was flickering. A silence opened up full of the terrors of the darkened Hall.

Cyprian had not spoken since he killed the Elder Steward. He had blood on his white tunic, though whether it was the Elder Steward's or from brushing against what remained in the halls was uncertain. Earlier, he had gone grimly to check the vaults.

The Elder Steward lay in a room through a door to the left. Grace and Sarah had covered her in a shroud, folding the sides of a white linen sheet over her, preparing her to go to her rest.

"We can't burn them." Sarah said it in a dull voice. "There are too many bodies." Her hands were covered in white and red semicircles where her nails had pressed into her skin.

"We ought to at least count them," said Violet. "If we count the dead . . . maybe someone survived, maybe they were outside the Hall when the attack happened. . . ."

"That was you," said Sarah, and her words shut everyone up again.

Will looked at each of their faces. Horrific practicalities awaited them. Burn the bodies . . . how would they even gather them? Many of them were people they knew.

Yet what was the alternative? Close up the Hall like a tomb and leave it to the rotting dead? Let the walls fall to silence and ruin, let the marsh creep in, let the passage of time take this last piece of the ancient world?

No one wanted to be the one to give up on the Hall, to end centuries of tradition, to admit that the Stewards' long watch was at its end.

Alongside practicality was fear. Will thought of the creature that had seemed to flicker under the Elder Steward's skin, and he understood why the Stewards burned their dead. He drew in a breath.

"Cyprian's right," said Will. "It's almost dawn. If we work hard, we can be done by nightfall. One day's work." They deserved that much. "We use that time to decide what to do."

If Simon has the Shadow Stone, there isn't anything we can do. He didn't give voice to the cold reality that faced them. *If a single shadow could do all this, then what chance do we have against the Shadow Kings?* Looking at the devastation of the Hall, it was hard to believe that Simon now held a greater force in his hands. But Marcus was as nothing to the terrible power of the Shadow Kings.

With sudden fierceness he missed the Elder Steward. She had always been there to guide him. She would know what to do. He missed her wisdom and her strength, her kindness, her caring. He missed her trust in him when he didn't trust himself, and hadn't since the night his mother had died. *Promise.*

"The vault is empty," said Cyprian. "It was cleaned out. Simon's men . . . following after Marcus." His voice was thick with the desecration of outsiders ransacking the Hall. Simon's men . . . *Branded men*, thought Will. Marcus must have let them through the wards. The thought that they couldn't return was no comfort. The violation had been done. "The Shadow Stone. The Horn of Truth . . . sacred relics of the Order, kept from harm for centuries. All of it's gone."

"Not all of it," said Grace.

There was a pause.

Will could see Grace and Sarah communicating something wordless-ly. After a moment, Sarah nodded, once, though her hands were taut in her lap.

"We did manage to save one thing," said Grace, and she drew a shape-less bundle from her tunic, a lumpen object wrapped in soft white cloth.

A single artifact rescued from the wreckage. Will's pulse sped up. Was it something they could use? A weapon that could help them fight? Grace began to unwrap the bundle, and as she drew back each corner of the cloth, Will felt all the breath leave him.

Gleaming like a dark jewel, it was the Cup of the Stewards.

It rose from a flared stem to a curved drinking cup the shape of an upturned bell. The color of polished onyx, it was ornately carved with four crowns. The inscription curling around the base like coiling flame read *Callax Reigor.* The Cup of Kings.

Drink, it seemed to say, offering the bargain that had enticed the Stewards. *Drink and I'll give you power.*

There was a sudden scraping sound as Cyprian pushed his chair back from the table. He was standing in front of Grace, towering over her. Reacting directly to the Cup's call, Cyprian's face twisted.

In the next second, he slapped it out of Grace's hands, and it hit the floor with a heavy clang, rolling over the stones into the corner, where it rocked for a moment before it lay still.

Will couldn't help his eyes following it. It was the same for the oth-ers, all of them staring at it, unable to look away.

Cyprian stalked to the doorway without a backward look.

Will followed him out.

He half expected to have to chase him; but then again, there was nowhere to go. Cyprian had stopped in a small courtyard with an empty fountain and a distant view of the wall. Will saw the tense line of his back where he stood on the far side of the fountain, the stained white of his tunic, the long fall of his hair.

"I'm sorry."

"You didn't do this," said Cyprian. "You don't carry the blame."

The words were a knife in Will's gut. He tried to think of what he could say. What he had wanted to hear at Bowhill, stumbling through the mud, trying to survive.

He said, "You're not alone."

But it wasn't true, not really. Cyprian was alone, in his grief, in his pain. The last of his kind, he carried a history inside him that was shared with no one else.

That was what Simon had done. He had whittled them down until each of them was alone. He had carved them away from connection and from family. *I don't want to kill anyone*, Will had said. But the people he cared about always died. Simon kept killing.

And he could stop it. He was the one who could stop it.

If he didn't, Simon would take, and take, and take, until there was nothing in the world that wasn't his to command, or dead.

He took a step forward. He wanted to tell Cyprian that he would fight for him, fight for this Hall where for a moment he had felt safe.

"You're not alone, Cyprian."

A tremor in Cyprian's flesh, that he immediately stilled. Steward training, thought Will. Hold the blade tip steady though your arms were aching.

"I should have been with them," said Cyprian. "I should have—"

Died with them. Will could almost hear the ringing words.

"I shouldn't be the last," he said. "Not me."

His body was steady, but his voice was raw, like he didn't know what to do. He had spent his life striving to achieve Steward perfection: to follow the rules, to excel in his training, to be immaculate in his discipline, and now all of that was gone. What was a Steward without rules, without traditions, without his Order?

"You heard the Elder Steward," said Will. "It's never truly dark while there's a star."

Cyprian turned to face Will, and with his long hair and old-fashioned clothes he suited this place so well, like one of its ancient and beautiful fittings. His eyes were wide, Will's words seeming to strike something deep within him. Then his expression shuttered.

"Look up," he said bitterly. Will followed his gaze to the battlements. He tried to understand, but saw only the empty jut of the outer wall.

"Let him go," said Grace, arriving behind him, just as Cyprian turned and stalked away. "He was born in the Hall. It was his whole world." Her eyes were on the walls too.

"What did he mean, look up?" Will said.

"The Final Flame," said Grace. "It burned since the founding of the Hall, a symbol of hope for the Stewards." Grace gave a strange, sad smile. Will remembered looking out of his window at the Flame on his first night in the Hall, its warm light a reassurance, a sign of safety. With an awful, dizzy feeling, he looked back up at the battlements and saw no light, only abandoned crenels and empty sky.

Grace said, "And now it has gone out."

To clear the bodies, they had to split into two groups: Will went with Grace to the courtyard, while Violet took the corridors and inner rooms, including the great hall. Cyprian and Sarah went with her. Violet was strong enough physically to move bodies by herself, but Will had seen the hollowed-out look in her eyes. No one should have to enter inner rooms for the first time alone.

He forced his mind to the grim reality ahead of him. Collect the bodies and bring them to a place beyond the wall. They ought to start in the main courtyard, which had been crowded, then move to the outbuildings and stables. The funeral pyre should be lit away from the main buildings. The smell from the fire would be terrible.

He had never spent much time with Grace, but she was a hard worker. It took two of them to lift the bodies. They used a wheelbarrow. It was thirteen trips to clear the main courtyard.

Grace took an arm of the wheelbarrow alongside him and pushed. Her lean face and spare body looked as if its lines had been carved. She was reacting very differently from Sarah, who'd taken on a nervy, flightish quality, like a spooked horse. It was Grace who had found them on the Elder Steward's orders. When the Elder Steward had asked to die, it was Grace who had brought the knife.

And when they stopped to take a brief rest, it was Grace who spoke.

"I know she was like a mother to you."

"Don't," said Will.

"She took me in when I was an orphan too."

"I said don't."

His harsh voice ran over hers. Her words felt like a knife, pushing into him. He tried to shut them out. To focus on the wheelbarrow, the task. One foot after another. That was how you survived.

"All right," said Grace.

They had reached the stables. Walking this way was so familiar to him that for a moment he forgot why he was here. *Farah*, he thought, as though at any instant she was going to come crunching down the path, teasing him for spoiling his horse.

Will had worked in the stables long enough to know all the Steward horses, ethereal creatures that ran like bright foam on a wave. Justice's horse was a silver mare with a high tail. Will had fed her an apple once, when Valdithar wasn't looking. It had felt illicit. She had whuffled it up and raced off to join the others, while they kicked up their heels and ran for the joy of it, wheeling this way and that, graceful as the flitting turns of a school of fish.

It took him a moment to understand what he was seeing.

Silver and pearl, with soft velvet muzzles and slender legs, they lay across the muddy field like clumps of snow lingering after a melt. Their tails, like long, silky banners, flowed out across the earth. They would not gallop now with the wind at their back, tails high and manes flying. They were still, strewn like silver coins discarded by an uncaring hand.

"She fought to save them," said Grace, and Will saw Farah, her face upturned, her sword knocked from her hand. Dead, of course. She hadn't saved them. He supposed she had fought as hard as she could. He supposed everyone had.

Exhausted, Will looked at the twelve giant pyres and the shapes that lay on them. They had dragged together all the stocks of fuel and kindling that they could find—from woodpiles to torn hangings to clothes to splintered furniture—raiding the armory for tar and pitch and the kitchens for oil. The pyres were immense. It had taken almost as long to build them as it had to collect the bodies.

They had worked past nightfall. The eerie marshland in the space beyond the walls but within the wards was dark. The torches that they held were the only light.

It was enough to see the dirt and fatigue on everyone's faces, the orange light dancing in their eyes.

Will didn't know the Steward funeral traditions, but he imagined it was a ceremony, a phalanx of Stewards in white bearing the body to its flame, the High Janissary speaking the ritual phrases while the Hall looked on in regimented formation.

Instead, the five of them stood, a huddle of faces in the cold. There was no one to say the words. Cyprian took a long, shaky breath, and stepped forward.

Will tried to imagine what he would say. *You took me in, and you died for it. All those years of fighting. . . . You did it because there was no one else. You kept the light burning as long as you could.*

So much lost: lives ended, and with them, knowledge that would pass from the world forever.

"Go into the night as light, not shadow," said Cyprian. Above him the sky was high and cold, with a scattering of distant stars. "Never again fear the dark."

Cyprian reached out and struck his torch to the pyre.

Fire raced through the thatched kindling, searingly fast, curling the twigs and the fabric of shrouds. Beside him, Will saw Violet stepping forward to Justice's pyre, where he lay like a knight carved on a tombstone, his sword placed atop his wrapped body. Before Will lost his nerve, he went forward to the thatched pile in front of him.

The heat was immense, each of the pyres burning, huge flames to the sky. It scalded his own cheeks, his throat choked with the thick smoke, his eyes burning.

He was looking at the Elder Steward's face as he lit the straw, and he made himself keep looking at it as he stepped back, at eyes reflecting flame, and then a face of flame, crinkling and then turning to blackened ash.

For hundreds of years, the Stewards had kept their watch. They had been the last of those who remembered, bearing the star across centuries of careful tradition.

Now their star was flame; their strength was flame; their fate was flame; and all that they remembered would flicker and grow cold.

We're all that's left. Will looked at the others: Sarah, her face streaked with tears and soot; Grace beside her, holding her hand; Violet, whose eyes had looked lacerated since she had found Justice; Cyprian, who had lost everything. None of them had the training to lead a fight against the Dark King. *We're all that's left. And we're not enough.*

The fight they faced seemed immense. Not just Simon but all he could do, his power to take what was good in the world and turn it into ash and destruction. Now he had the Shadow Stone and the power of the Shadow Kings, and no Stewards to fight against him.

The Shadow Kings would be nothing like Marcus, a new-made shadow of weakened Steward blood. The Shadow Kings were far older and more powerful, the commanders of great shadow armies, and Will remembered how they had felt in that Stone. They had wanted to get out.

Was this how it had been in those ancient days? The lights in the world going out, one by one, as the Dark King's forces marched toward victory?

The fire roared, dwarfing them as they stared up at its flames, and he'd never felt so small and alone against a fight that seemed vast and unending.

It was Cyprian who broke the moment, scrubbing an arm across his face and picking up one of the unlit torches. He stuck it into the closest pyre, letting the flames engulf its tip. When he drew his arm back, the funereal fire had transferred from the pyre to the torch. He took the flame and held it aloft as he set out determinedly for the wall.

Will exchanged a quick look with Violet and then followed him, with the others behind.

The wind was sharper and colder up on the wall, where Cyprian walked along empty battlements under a circle of orange light. He stopped at a huge iron receptacle six feet across, the inside blackened and charred. Will could smell the charcoal and ash of its extinguished fire, acidic, earthy, and cold, the remnants of a perpetual blaze.

It didn't need wood to burn; Will knew that from the Elder Steward's stories, but also from some instinct deep inside himself.

Two Stewards had used to guard it, standing on either side of the iron dish, like sentries at their post, a vigil kept for centuries. For this had been the ancient beacon that the Stewards called the Final Flame.

Cyprian stood over it, holding up his torch. He was lit up in flame light, Will and the others gathered around him. In the reflected light, Cyprian's breathing was shallow, but his voice was clear as he made his pledge.

"I am the last of the Stewards," he said. "And this flame is my promise: while there is a single star, there is still light."

And he threw his torch into the bowl of the beacon, and it came alight, leaping into flame that grew, brighter and brighter. Will imagined it visible across the marshes, a light that could be seen for miles, a message to Simon, and to the Stewards, past and future, guiding them home.

It was only much later that they thought to check the cells under the Hall, but James was gone.

CHAPTER TWENTY-SIX

TO FALL INTO *darkness . . . it was his greatest fear. And I left him alone with that.*

Violet pushed out onto the battlements, Justice's words ringing in her ears. She had wanted to get out, to be alone on the cold, high wall, but she found herself drawn to the Flame, its immense heat and its light. A burst of sparks lit up the empty-toothed crenels, and she found a place at one of them, looking out at the black marshes with its heat to her back. One thought had driven her out here, to stand on the edge of the wall, her breathing fast, her hands fists.

I should have been here.

She was strong. She was fast. There must have been something she could have done, something to help, something—

The others were in the gatekeep, the four of them in one room on makeshift pallets, sleeping as best they could. They had agreed they ought to be near the gate in case of a further attack, but the truth was that no one wanted to spend the night in the empty Hall. Even in the gatekeep, she hadn't been able to close her eyes, lying wide awake before pushing herself up to stalk out into the night.

Justice had saved her life. It was the first thing he had ever done for her, taking a bullet for her before they even knew each other.

Maybe we can watch for each other.

The last words she'd said to him. Then she'd left him to face his greatest fear alone.

She felt his absence like a gaping hole. Justice had been a rock, holding everyone steady. If he'd been here, he would have known what to do. She had looked up to him like—

A brother. She could feel the irony of that, like a painful band around the heart. Her brother was a Lion, who bore Simon's brand and had killed his share of Stewards.

A Lion should have been here. A Lion should have been fighting for the Light. *You have Lion blood on both sides,* the Elder Steward had said. What good was a Lion if she couldn't fight?

The crunch of a footstep behind her made her turn, heart pounding. But it was only Grace, a blanket wrapped like a shawl around her shoulders to shield her against the cold. She came to stand beside Violet, leaning her forearms on the battlements, her pendant hanging away from her chest.

"Couldn't sleep?" said Grace.

It wasn't a question. Violet could see Grace's profile in the light from the Flame, her high, smooth brow, and her long, elegant neck. There were creases under Grace's eyes, but they had been there since the morning. Grace's voice was dulled with more than exhaustion.

"You saw it, didn't you?" Violet asked her.

It. There was no need to explain what she meant. It hung over all of them. Grace said nothing for a long while, but Violet had seen Grace and Sarah both avoid the dark and shadow in the gatekeep in favor of the light.

"You can ask me," said Grace after a long moment.

"Ask you?" said Violet.

"What it was like."

Violet shivered. Grace had seen something no person had seen in centuries, and when Grace turned to look at her briefly, it was there in her eyes. Grace was the one who spoke.

"You want to know if there's a way to fight it. If it could be tricked. If it could be trapped. If it had any weaknesses."

"And did it?"

"No," said Grace.

Violet stared at her, feeling the oncoming terror of it, an implacable enemy that could not be fought. She didn't think Grace was going to say more, but then:

"It was cold, like the air was frozen," said Grace. "We saw a dark stain spreading on the door, black, like a hole. But it didn't crawl through the hole, it *was* the hole. The Elder Steward stepped out in front of us, telling us both to stay back."

A muscle moved in Grace's jaw, though she kept her eyes on the sky beyond the battlements, her voice steady.

"They grappled hand to hand like two dark whirlwinds. I'd never seen her fight before, nor seen this side of her come out. For a moment, it was as if two shadows fought. She forced it to the wall as it thrashed and shrieked. She held it there until it gave a final scream, and vanished, leaving only its burned imprint on the wall. And then she fell."

Violet felt her mouth dry, her hands curled into fists again. *I should have been here. I would have fought.*

"I thought in their darkest hour the king was supposed to appear. Isn't that what Stewards believe?" said Violet bitterly. "That they'll call for the King, and the King will answer?"

Grace was looking back at her strangely, as if the words sparked something internal. But: "I asked the Elder Steward that," was all Grace said. "Sarah was with me. She cried and begged. The Elder Steward said it was not yet time to raise the call."

"Why not?"

The flame light on the empty battlements leaped and fell, high and red. But beyond it the night stretched out, endless shadow that covered all the land.

"Because this is not our darkest hour," said Grace. "That is still to come."

A huge, wordless emotion swelled in Violet, its edges painful. She heard the Elder Steward in those words, and generations of Stewards, dutiful in their service. All these people were dead, and for what? For Simon's own power and greed?

She wanted to shout, to scream, her anger growing until it overwhelmed almost every sense, feeling powerless in the face of the enemy but needing, above anything, to fight.

She pushed herself away from the wall.

It was a two-hour ride to London, but she knew where to find Devon, the warren of streets and alleyways where he did his backroom dealings, chasing down leads on objects in collections for Simon, part of the net Simon used to drag artifacts to himself from across the world.

Violet was waiting when the door opened, and Devon came down the shallow stone steps into the alley, pulling his cap down low over his stupid flop of hair with a characteristic dip of his head. He didn't see her until he was two steps into the alley, and by that time, the door had closed behind him.

"Where is it?" said Violet.

The alley was a crack between buildings, and it had started to rain. She was only half aware that she was wet. The closest gas lamp was on Turnmill Street, but she could see the night gleam of the wet cobbles, the darker shapes of the rotting boxes on her right, and she could see him, could see the pale fringe of hair that hung down like a valance under his cap. Devon took a single step backward. His heel slid on the muddy slush of a cobblestone.

She said, "Where is the Shadow Stone?"

"Why don't you ask your friends the Stewards?"

She hit him.

He went sprawling onto all fours in the wet mud, his white hair tangled in his eyes under the cap, which had survived the brief journey. Ridiculously, he clutched it to his head with a lifted hand. Then he raised his chin, blood blossoming on his lips, and looked right at her.

"Oh, that's right." His teeth were red when he smiled, sickly. "What was your story again? They kidnapped you? Then you'll be glad they're dead, won't you? All that Steward self-righteousness rotting in the ground—"

Violet's vision blurred, and she was grabbing him by the shirt collar, dragging him up, and hitting him again, knuckles against flesh. The impact was a reverberation, sickly satisfying. It snapped his head to one side, knocked the cap from his head, and finally—finally—he was struggling against her, bareheaded as she'd never seen him, his eyes huge and dark as he scrabbled on the muddy cobblestones. Her fists were in his shirtfront; she had followed him down into the mud. Her body was above his, pinning him down with her weight.

"Shut up. They were good. They were good and you killed them—"

"I knew you were one of them," Devon sneered up at her. "Your brother didn't believe it, even after you ran out on him. He kept saying you were loyal—"

"You did this," said Violet. "You and my father, you dragged Tom into it. Got your hooks into him. He'd never be a part of it if he knew—"

Devon's cap was gone, but under it he was still wearing a dirty bandana, and she snatched at it, furious at him, instinct acting to deprive him of possessions, of composure, of dignity. And suddenly he was *really* fighting her, grabbing desperately at the bandana, trying to hold on to it and looking for the first time truly afraid.

"Stop it, let go of me, let go—"

She ripped the bandana away from him, threw it to the side, and Devon let out a terrible cry, as if the sound had been ripped from him too.

Devon was staring up at her, horror in his wide eyes, his forehead totally exposed.

There was a deformation right in the center, a lumpy thing that had been hidden by the bandana. For a moment, she didn't understand what she was looking at.

She stared at it—at the wrongness of it, a grotesque artifact under the wet hair; it protruded half an inch. A ruined pearlescent stump, growing from the middle of Devon's forehead.

The alleyway seemed to fade from view, and her hands opened, releasing him.

She remembered lifting it from its lacquered black box: a long, straight wand of ivory, spiraled from end to tip. She remembered holding it in her hands, the reverence of it, the way it changed the beat of her heart and shallowed her breath. *Long gone. Long gone now, the last of them bright.* She recalled the tactile, physical sensation of it, the wide base rougher at one edge, as though it had been partway sawn and then snapped off. She had touched that jagged wick with her thumb, like testing the sharpness of a blade.

The horn all seek but never find.

She was staring at its mutilated fit now, sawn like bone, an amputat-
ed limb. "You—you're—"

She felt sick. She was going to be sick.

Devon was trying to get up, get away from her, but he couldn't; he
was too hurt, something wrong with his ankle and shoulder, lank white
hair plastered to his head more steel than silver in the rain, blood sliding
slowly down his face.

"Why didn't you tell us? Why didn't you tell us—" Her words
scraped out. "That you—were—"

"Why?" Devon's voice was thick with blood. "So you could put the
rest of me in your collection?"

"We wouldn't," said Violet, "we wouldn't have."

His cap was tight in his muddy fist; he'd clutched for it as if it could
help him, or keep her back. Half rising, as if he had been shot, he pushed
away from her, stumbling slightly. She let him go, still kneeling herself,
wet seeping through the knees of her trousers.

She had asked Justice about the horn, and he had told her, humans
used boar spears, they tied them down, chased them with dogs, hobbles
and ropes and horseflesh, screaming.

The alley was filthy. The rain had spilled over the contents of the gut-
ters to cover the pathway, filling its hollows, a compost of mud and clay.
Devon was smeared with it, his chest rising and falling under his torn
shirt. She looked at him and saw a tapestry on a wall, its colors faded, the
white curve of neck and mane still visible against the dimmed red.

Long gone now. They say this one was the last.

"Then give it back," he said.

He'd pushed himself to the steps of the building he'd exited, but no
farther. He said it in a voice too steady for coax or plea. He said it like
he meant to prove a point. She remembered that he'd lied to Will. She

remembered what Simon had done to the Stewards.

Simon has it, she didn't say. Did it matter? If she had the horn, would she give it back to him? She realized that Devon's steady tone exposed the truth, and she answered in the same level voice.

"I can't give you the horn," she said.

By then, Devon, with a kind of brutal persistence, had pushed himself upright. She had risen too. She was the one holding back now, like she had when she had first looked inside the black lacquered box and seen what was inside. She hated that Devon realized it.

"Then what? You drag me back to the Hall with a chain around my neck?" It was so reminiscent of what had happened to her when the Stewards had found out she was a Lion that it stuck in her throat.

"If I let you go," said Violet, "will you go back to Simon?"

"Yes."

Her hands were fists. "How could you? How could you serve him, when you're—"

"How could I?" Devon laughed with a mouth full of blood. "It's the Lions that fought for him. A field full of Lions. Now you fight for an Order who digs through our bones and puts them under glass. Who else have the Stewards put in their collection?"

"They're not like that. You twist everything."

"You're like me," said Devon. "We're the same. You're more like me than you are like them. It's in your blood."

"I'm nothing like you. I will *never* fight for the Dark King."

He laughed again, the sound a breath that was helpless and unconstrained, weight given up to the wall behind him, his eyes glittering beneath his white lashes. "You will," he said. "You'll betray every person you love to serve him. You're a Lion."

She was going to hit him again. "Do it," he said. His body was a taunt. "Do it. If you let me walk away, I'll go back to Simon, and he'll kill you. He'll kill all of you like he killed the Stewards."

She didn't hit him. She felt the anger crest and transform into something hard and implacable.

"Crawl back to him, then. Crawl back to Simon and tell him, the Lion and the Lady stand against him, and as long as we draw breath, he will never conquer the Light."

He didn't crawl back to Simon. He went home, to Mayfair.

It took time, his hands shaking, to rake his fingers through his hair, drawing it down over his forehead. The bandana was a useless strip of muddy wet. Devon refused to wring it out, scrape the muck off, as he did with the cap. He replaced the cap with slow, careful movements, one shoulder against the wall. He shoved the bandana into his pocket, the end trailing.

The journey from the alley to the house near Bond Street was one of dogged determination. He entered the house through the side door and went to his room without attracting attention, as he often did when he came and went on some errand. In his room, he dragged off his jacket, a crumpled puddle on the carpet. He sat on the edge of the bed.

He knew he should wash his face; he should bathe and clean the mud from his skin, peel off the rest of these clothes. He did none of those things. His shirt hung open, bloodied and torn.

There was a shape in the doorway.

"Hello, Robert," he said. His voice sounded blurred, as if he were drunk. He added, in the same blurred voice, "I didn't think you were home."

He said it without thinking. In the next moment he felt a sudden flickering sense that it might not be Robert after all. He looked up, feeling a startled spatter of heartbeats, as if rolling around in the mud with lions could conjure up a figure impossible and long dead.

It was Robert. It was ordinary, human Robert. The look on Robert's face wouldn't have been there on the other.

Devon wondered what Robert saw. The bones in his face were intact. His lips felt bloated and shapeless; his eye was swelling closed. He still wore the cap. His clothes were wrecked, even those that were still on his body and not on the floor. He would have liked to have said, *It was six men.*

"Who?" said Robert.

"It doesn't matter. I am going to take care of it." Speaking required care with fluffed lips.

"I know you're involved in something. Whatever it is—"

"It's not your concern."

Robert sat down on the bed beside him.

After a moment: "You don't need to tell me. I don't ask that of you."

Robert's presence made him feel stupidly grateful, which in turn provoked a violent surge of anger. A human to hurt you, a human to help you. It was stifling, the world clogged by them. If Robert tried to comfort him, he would push himself up and over to the other side of the room. If Robert tried to touch him, he would bolt.

Robert just sat beside him, long enough that the anger faded, until he was aware of Robert simply as a confusing presence. It upset the unspoken terms of their association, which for ten years had run along the professional lines, an ivory merchant and his clerk. Yet he was aware—confusingly—that if he had come upon Robert alone and in a similar state, he would have done the same. He pushed the words out.

"I'm fine. I heal quickly."

"I know that." And then: "I have something for you."

Robert had been carrying something. Cloth-wrapped, it was the length of a man's arm. An umbrella in a box. It would have been useful earlier, when it was raining.

Robert undid the string and drew the cloth aside. Devon felt the room tilting under him as he saw the shine of black lacquer, a polished box, with two filigree clasps, like the case for a musician's instrument.

His eyes flew to Robert's face, only to find Robert was looking back at him, a calm look that demanded nothing. There was no surprise in Robert's eyes, nor any anticipation of surprise. The truth was expanding between them, and Devon felt, for the second time that evening, the feeling of being looked at and *seen*. Violet's horrified scramble backward was nothing to the calm knowledge in Robert's eyes.

"'I have hunted the unicorn mostly in libraries,'" Robert quoted softly.

He thought, ten years of working together, ten years in which Robert had aged and he had stayed as he was, a fifteen-year-old boy with a cap pushed down low over his forehead. He couldn't make his hands move over the lacquered box.

"How did you get this?"

"Simon Creen is not the only one who can steal objects from other men."

He forced himself to look down. His fingers moved as though they belonged to someone else. He watched them unfix the clasps and push open the box.

It was strange, considering how everything else had changed, that it was so perfectly as it had been, white and looped and long and straight and beautiful. There was nothing like it left. There was nothing of the toss of his head and the way it had felt to run, hooves on snow.

"I'm sorry this was done to you."

He looked down at the horn, and he heard himself say, "It was a long time ago."

"I wondered," said Robert, "if it could be restored."

"You mean reattached?" he said. "No."

Devon looked up at Robert.

"No," he said again, and he felt that bewildered sensation. "But I am glad to have it all the same."

The lamps in the room weren't overbright, but it was enough to see everything. It felt intimate, with Robert's serious eyes on him. Like being helpless to the truth. Devon found himself lifting his hand and pulling the cap from his head. It dropped from his fingers onto the carpeted floor, so that there was nothing hidden between them. His heartbeat was intrusive in his chest. Being exposed felt like being found out and waiting for the blow to fall.

Robert said, "Are there others?"

"No," he said. "I am the last."

"So you're alone."

Devon stared at him. The fingers of one hand had curled around the horn, and he was holding it so tightly in that hand that his knuckles were white.

Robert said, "Whatever you're caught up in, if there's something you need, I can help you."

Devon closed his eyes, then opened them. He said, "You don't want to do that."

The walls of the room felt too close, and his face throbbed. Robert had known, probably for a long time. He might have wrapped his forehead in cloth, but in ten years, he would have pushed his hand across his brow, or tilted his cap at the wrong angle, or rested his head on the back of an armchair for a nap. The lump beneath the cloth would have shown, under the white hair, under the line of the cap.

Robert was an expert in the ivory that made its way across the continent in ceaseless trade, in bins of horns and tusks, in cameos, in spinet keys, in carved frames, in billiard balls, and the handles of women's parasols. And Robert was a hunter; and sometimes you rode down your prey, and sometimes you offered your prey an unlooked-for kindness, and, wounded and exhausted, it bowed its head for the silken rope.

"I've worked with ivory my whole life," said Robert quietly. "I know when something different comes along."

His breathing felt strange. He wondered if Robert had picked up the horn, had handled it, at the same time that he knew with perfect surety that Robert was too much of a gentleman to have opened the box.

He knew, in the same way that he knew that Robert did his best work in the morning, that the mark on Robert's cheek was the imprint of the eyeglass he used to inspect ivory, that he liked to take a brandy to his study after dinner while he went over the inventory, and that he was stubborn and considerate, and human, in the end.

He felt himself moving. His grip on the horn changed. It felt wrong to wrap his fingers around its middle, a way that he would never let anyone else touch him, the way they had held him down in the moment before they brought out the saw.

His grip on the horn changed; then he drove it into Robert's unprotected body.

The tip was sharp and could puncture armor. Cloth shirt and waistcoat were nothing. It went in, pushing Robert backward, in and angling up, the point seeking for what it could find, easily.

Heart.

There were a few awful moments of struggle, the last spasming kicks of a drowning man fighting for air. Robert's eyes were wide and shocked. Robert's hands were over his, clutching at them. He felt the warm pulsing wet between his fingers. A second later, he put his hand over Robert's mouth to stifle the words: *"Devon, please, Devon, I care about y—"* He didn't want to hear what came out when Robert could only tell the truth.

And then everything went still.

He was on all fours on the bed above Robert's still body, panting. The covers were disarrayed, a red plume spreading slowly into the bed. With a yank, he pulled the horn out and pushed backward. His legs felt unsteady, so that his step back was uneven, before he stilled himself. In the silent room, he answered the question that Robert hadn't asked.

"You thought you knew what a unicorn was," he said, his breathing still shallow. "But you were wrong."

CHAPTER TWENTY-SEVEN

WILL WOKE WITH a jerk to the sound of hoofbeats. Grace and Sarah were still sleeping, soundless shapes under blankets in the small room in the gatekeep tower. A light sleeper, he rose quietly and looked out from the gatekeep window. Cyprian was on watch on the high walls, having just opened the gate. In the courtyard below, Will saw Violet returning from an excursion that had had her out half the night. He went down to greet her.

It was the early hours of the morning, and the light was still gray and blue. Will had dozed and woken throughout the night, snatching rest where he could. Most of his alertness had centered on Cyprian, silent and closed off since he had lit the Flame. But it was Violet who had pushed out of the gatekeep in the dark and ridden out of the Hall.

He approached her in the gray light as she dismounted. She looked like she'd had no sleep, her face drawn and her knuckles bruised, her tunic covered in blood.

"Did you kill anyone?"

He asked it steadily, holding her gaze as she turned to him with dark, hollowed eyes. She didn't deny it at first, just drew a breath and looked away to one side.

"I didn't kill him. I wanted to."

"Him?" She didn't answer. He watched her loop her horse's reins through an iron ring in the courtyard holding area, then stop, resting her hand on its white neck as if drawing from its strength. "Who?"

Another silence.

Then: "After we found the horn, I asked Justice about unicorns. He told me they survived the war, but were hunted by humans until there was only one left. He said humans found the last unicorn, chased it down with dogs, hobbled it, and cut off its horn and tail. The Horn of Truth . . . it came from that unicorn."

Will nodded, slowly, as Violet drew in a breath.

"He's not dead. He's alive," Violet said, looking up at him. "It's Devon."

"*Devon?* But he's—"

A boy, he wanted to say. *He's a human boy.* Will felt the strangest sensation pass over him, remembering Devon looking up from the dark wooden desk at the back of the shop, between bins of horns. White hair and too-pale eyes, and the subtly mocking way he had talked about ivory.

"I found him near Bond Street. I wanted . . . I hit him. It felt good. But when his cap came off, I saw—"

The horn.

As Violet's fingers lifted to the center of her forehead, Will remembered Devon's low-slung cap. *Is it really true?* he wanted to ask. But he could see the sick certainty in her eyes.

The stifling sense of that shop crowded with ivory came back to him. The shop that was a graveyard of dead animals, tended by a ghost. Devon, pale as a relic, watching over bones.

How could it be? How could a boy be a unicorn? He'd seen unicorns in his vision, white horses with spears of light on their foreheads charging into battle. Had one of them transformed?

His skin crawled as he remembered the moment in London when Devon had recognized him. *Devon knows who I am,* he'd thought, not understanding how deep that recognition might run.

And the thought that followed: If Devon was really a unicorn, what else might he know? The Stewards had legends passed down over generations, as writings faded and books crumbled to dust. But this was knowledge carried across time by a single boy.

"That's how Simon knows where to dig."

"What?" said Violet.

Will was staring at her. "Simon has digs across the globe. He spends his time unearthing artifacts . . . the Corrupted Blade . . . the armor pieces of the Remnants . . . He knows just where to go and what to do. It's Devon."

"I don't understand."

"He was there." Will felt dizzy at the thought of it, darkly impossible. "Devon *was there*, he lived through the war, he was alive when the Dark King fell."

Someone for whom the stories were more than just stories . . . someone who lived them, breathed them . . . it made the old world suddenly seem frighteningly real. And close. As if he could reach out his hand and touch it, as alive as memory.

"It's how Simon knew the secret of the Cup. It's how he knew how to make a shadow. How he knew about the Shadow Stone," said Will. "Devon told him."

Violet's shocked face made it clear this thought was new to her. "That would make Devon as old as this Hall."

His thoughts were already moving ahead, the strangeness of a unicorn fighting for the Dark. "Why is he working for Simon?" That was the part of it that didn't make sense. "All the images that we've seen of unicorns, they were fighting for the Light."

"People change sides." Violet said it with an odd defensiveness. Will searched her face.

"What did he say to you?"

"Nothing." She cut him off; he would get no more from her. "Come on. We need to wake the others."

A single table and some stools were the only furnishings in the gatekeep. At Will's call, the five of them had gathered in the lower room, down the short stairs from where they had slept on pallets on the floor. The gatekeep's stone walls were solid and enclosing, and its mantel held a newly lit fire. With the door closed, you could almost believe that the Hall outside was intact. Almost.

He could see the haggard faces of the others, the shadowed tension in their eyes, the haunted look each of them wore. They had each ventured out into the emptiness of the citadel, Grace and Cyprian to scavenge the supplies they would need for breakfast, while Will and Violet saw to Valdithar and the two remaining Steward horses. Its vast silence had left its imprint on all of them. Only Sarah hadn't left the gatekeep, spending much of her time curled up on her sleeping pallet upstairs, her back against the wall.

"The Stewards are gone," said Will. "We're all that's left." Cyprian's shoulders stiffened at that, but he stayed silent. "The Elder Steward told us that Simon was close to returning the Dark King. It's up to us to stop him."

Silence greeted his words.

"He has the Shadow Stone," said Sarah. It was her way of saying, *We can't stop him.* He could hear the dull defeat in her voice. He shook his head.

"The Elder Steward said the Shadow Kings were the first step to returning the Dark King," said Will. "We don't know why or how. But we know Simon hasn't released them from the Stone yet."

"How do we know that?"

"Because they would have destroyed everything," said Will.

No army on earth could stop them. Will saw the vision that had overwhelmed him when his fingers had grazed the Shadow Stone: the Shadow Kings on their shadow steeds, a torrent of darkness that nothing could hold back. But now he saw it happening in London, the Shadow Kings sweeping over the city, killing everyone they found, forcing the others to their will, until there was no resistance, only those who served the Dark, and those who were dead.

"We're safe here for the moment," said Cyprian. "The wards opened for Marcus because he was a Steward." He flushed slightly when he said his brother's name, but he didn't falter. "They'll hold against Simon. But if he does release the Shadow Kings—"

"If he releases the Shadow Kings, we fight," said Violet.

Something bitter rippled across Sarah's face. "You think the Stewards didn't try to fight? Leda and the guard didn't even have time to draw their swords. One shadow . . . One shadow killed our greatest fighters . . . even Justice . . . killed by his own shieldmate. It had no pity, no humanity, just the ravening desire to kill." Sarah looked out at all of them. "If Simon releases the Shadow Kings, all we can do is hope that they can't get through the wards."

The thought of being holed up here, while dark winds raged outside, made a terrible claustrophobia claw in Will's throat.

"We still have time," said Will. "He hasn't released the Shadow

Kings. We still have a chance to stop him."

"He'll release them," said Sarah. "At any moment—"

"No," said Will, knowing it right down to his bones. "He's waiting for something."

"For what?"

It was why he had gathered them all here. He had seen the defeat they each felt. The thought that if the Stewards couldn't beat Simon, what good would the five of them do? But from the moment Will had seen the destruction Simon had wrought on the Hall, he had felt a new resolve hardening inside him.

"James said that Simon was searching for something. An artifact. Do you remember? We questioned James with the horn, and he said there was an artifact that would make Simon the most powerful man alive."

James had fought the Horn of Truth desperately to try to keep that secret. He had fought harder than he had to hide the location of Marcus. Will remembered his panting breath and the furious look in his blue eyes.

"When we captured him, he had just learned where to find it. A man named Gauthier who had come back to England and was staying at Buckhurst Hill. James didn't want us to know about it. If it's that important—"

"Maybe it's what Simon needs to release the Shadow Kings," said Cyprian.

"Or a weapon we can use against him," said Violet.

There was a silence. Cyprian scrubbed at his face.

"It's all we have," said Cyprian.

"Do you know the place?" said Will. Expecting a response, he found himself instead looking into the blank faces of a novitiate and two janis-saries who knew everything about morning chants and ancient swords and nothing about the basic geography of London.

It was Violet who answered. "Buckhurst Hill. It's north of here, a scattering of houses near the stagecoach route to Norwich. The three of us should make good time on horseback."

The three of them—that meant Will, Violet, and Cyprian. A stab of pain at that: there were only three horses left. The two janissary girls nodded.

"And if Simon's men are there?" Sarah demanded.

Everyone was afraid; Will could see that in their faces. That a ride into the countryside was all that stood between them and the release of the Shadow Kings seemed a tenuous hope. But he lifted his chin and returned their gazes.

"Then we fight."

It was an old farmhouse on the outskirts of Buckhurst Hill. The first two farmsteads they searched had been empty. This one looked empty too, tiles missing from the roof, a deteriorating fence, and overground fields without farm animals. Until Will saw a glossy black horse tied up outside. Every nerve in him came screaming to life.

"They're already here," said Violet in a tense voice.

Will said, "It's only one horse."

His heart was pounding. They tied their own horses to the trunk of a birch out of sight and crept forward cautiously.

The farmhouse was a large building of gray stone, the approach a deserted tangle of brambles and high grass. The faded farm sign said *Paquet*, and the nearest glass windowpane was broken, like a jagged black tooth. The door swung open soundlessly.

The cracked basin of the abandoned kitchen inside was covered in leaves and dirt, as if a season's detritus had blown in from outside. There were no signs of food or supplies. But in one corner, there was a pitiful bundle of twigs, gathered recently enough that they had not been scattered by the wind. Will pointed to it, and Violet and Cyprian silently drew their swords.

The place was too quiet. As they lifted the catch to the hallway, a wood pigeon flew up and out of a hole in the ceiling, and they all froze for long moments. Through the first door on the left, Will saw a small, bare room with a half-missing glass window. Empty. Through the second he saw a stained pallet, spilling straw—

—a dead girl lay on the pallet, her eyes staring upward. Someone had thrown a wrinkled coverlet over her body. Cyprian went still at the sight of her, newly dead, the coverlet recent. There were footsteps in the dust.

Will barely had time to react before a sound at the end of the hall jerked his attention forward.

Whoever was here was through that door.

He thought of the horse outside. The high black gloss of its coat. He turned to the others—Cyprian's pinched face, Violet's hands tight on her sword—and they moved forward slowly, quietly, toward the sound, until they reached the end of the hall.

He saw everything all at once. The half-open doorway. A decrepit room with litter scattered over the floor, and rotted boarding showing through the broken plaster walls. An old man in a chair, with filmy blind eyes. Will's hand shot out to keep the others back.

Don't move. Don't make a sound.

Through the doorway, strolling in elegantly over the trash, was James.

He had clearly spent the night in good lodgings. Perhaps he had returned to Simon after escaping the Hall, or perhaps he had taken rooms nearby. His torn, bloodstained shirt had been replaced by fresh linen and an elegant riding jacket along with the kind of shiny boots that a rider might tap their whip against.

James wasn't making any effort to be quiet. He toured the room, his eyes passing over all the signs of decay before returning to the old man. Sunken in his chair with blankets over his lap, he had a gray, shriveled look, like he was part of the decaying house. His head had lifted jerkily toward James at the first sound, seeming confused that someone was with him. "Sophie?"

"It's not Sophie," said James, with a thin smile the man couldn't see. "Sophie's dead."

The girl on the pallet. Had she been a servant? She had worn the clothing of a girl used to hard work on a farm. The old man stared at James blindly.

"Who are you?" he said, clutching the blanket in his lap to himself. "What are you doing in my house?"

He looked frightened. He didn't seem to know what was happening. He didn't even seem to have a firm grasp of where James was standing, his eyes staring past him.

"You know, I thought I'd recognize you," James remarked, as if the old man hadn't spoken. "But I don't. You're just a blind, pathetic old man."

The old man kept turning his head to follow the sounds of James as he moved around the room, as if trying to locate him. "If you're here to rob me, you're too late. I don't have anything."

"That's not quite true, is it, Gauthier," said James, and there was a moment when the old man's face changed, in terrible new recognition.

"Who are you?" said Gauthier. "How do you know my name?"

He was breathing shallowly. James ignored him and continued to stroll the room, lifting a scattering of papers, pulling a rotted piece of wood from the wall. His boot heel crunched on a broken shard of porce-lain.

"Where is it?" said James, and Will felt his heart rate spike. They were closing in on why they had come.

Gauthier's hands tightened on the blankets. "I don't know what you're talking about."

Will looked over at Violet and Cyprian, who realized it too. They were speaking of the object that they had come here to find. The object Simon wanted, that he'd sent James here to get.

"Where is it?" James repeated. He had stopped at the old mantelpiece, resting a shoulder against it as he coolly looked back at Gauthier, whose hands quivered.

"It was stolen. Years ago. I was glad to see it go. I wish I'd thrown it away myself."

This time a silence stretched out after the answer, stretched to a breaking point as the quiver increased.

"Where is it?" said James, in the same voice, but it felt different.

"Do you think I'd keep that wretched thing! With its accursed lure bringing the wolves to my door!"

Will saw it before James, the way that Gauthier's hands were gripped to the blanket, and the strange lumpen shape underneath. *He has it.* Whatever it was, this prize—he had kept it, holding it close to himself, clutched to his body as his house rotted around him and his people died.

"I know you've kept it," said James. "Everyone keeps it. Everyone wants what it can do."

Then Gauthier said, as if learning a great truth, *"The Betrayer!"*

James looked like he'd been slapped. "Why do you know that name?"

"It knows you." Gauthier started laughing, a terrible sound on the edge of madness. "Have you come to get it for your master?" James's face turned white. "Do you want it? Do you want it the way it wants you?"

"I knew you'd keep it with you!" James spat the words out venomously. "You knew Simon was coming for it. . . . You could have gotten rid of it. You could have destroyed it. Why didn't you?"

"You don't know your master if you think it can be destroyed." Gauthier's voice took on a dreamlike quality. "It's the last thing my eyes remember. The look of it. The ruby and the gold. It's perfect. It can't be broken. It can't be melted down. It's waiting. For you." Those sightless eyes turned to James, and Gauthier's face split in a smile. "You don't want it to be destroyed. You want it. You want it on you."

James snapped at those words, his invisible power slamming Gauthier and his chair violently backward with a crackle of air. Sprawled on the ground, Gauthier began laughing again. "There you are—you want me to put it on you—?"

It was their only possible chance—James's eyes, his whole attention was on Gauthier furiously. *Now,* Will signaled to Violet and Cyprian. And in the single moment that James was vulnerable, the three of them attacked.

It had worked before. In London they had used Will as bait, while Violet attacked James from behind. And before that, Will had disrupted James's power on the docks by crashing a crate down on top of him, the very first time they'd seen each other.

Now James's head whipped around so fast that he glimpsed Violet's explosive movements at the first sound—throwing out his hand. As if a great invisible force gripped her, she was thrown violently upward, hitting the ceiling with a cry of pain, then slamming back down again in a burst of fine plaster.

Hand still outstretched toward Violet, a single glittering look sent Cyprian flying backward across the room to hit the wall with a sick smash, blood coming from his nose and mouth. Pinned like a butterfly, Cyprian stuck there, halfway up the wall and unable to move.

And then those blue eyes were on Will.

Will had barely had time to pull the manacles out of his pack before he was yanked down to his knees and held there, his head forced to the ground and subjected to a crushing pressure, as if it were being stepped on by a shiny boot. He made a furious sound, unable to do anything but hold in place.

James barely looked ruffled. Dispatching the three of them had taken a scant few seconds. Will could taste the static in the air, the power around James crackling like the vengeance of a young god, even as he made it look effortless. He might just as easily have brushed a speck of dust from his sleeve, except for the killing look in his eyes.

The Dark King's most ruthless lieutenant. James strolled forward like a destroyer of worlds, and Will saw how utterly they had underestimated his power. In the old world he had ridden at the front of dark armies. In this one he had decimated a squadron of Stewards, lifting them out of the saddles and snapping their necks with his mind.

Now his attention fixed on Will.

Behind James, on the ground, Gauthier was trying to get away. Dragging himself from the chair with his arms made the thin blanket on his lap slip. Gauthier let out a cry as something spilled from the blanket to the floor and rolled, and for a moment, Will saw a curving flash of rubies and gold.

James turned helplessly toward it—and as he saw it, his eyes dilated, growing huge with pupil, and his whole body swayed toward the object.

Feeling the hold on him loosen, Will lifted his head. At the same moment, Cyprian slid down the wall with a thud, and Violet pushed herself up onto all fours.

James blinked, shaking his head as if to clear it. He tried to reassert control. Violet was thrown back again, though this time James looked unsteady. Breathing shallowly, James gestured and the room's huge, rotting oak table slammed into Cyprian, crushing him against the opposite wall.

Or it was meant to.

Cyprian had never drunk from the Cup, and he didn't have Violet's strength, but he had always been the best of the novitiates. Even injured, he had a perfectly trained grace and an astonishing athleticism. He vaulted the table the way a Steward might have, landing and rolling to hit James low, knocking his legs out from under him. Cyprian started choking a second later, but James still looked half-dazed. He had barely begun to constrict Cyprian's throat with his power before Violet was on him, delivering a blow that allowed Will to snap a manacle closed on his wrist.

The static air of magic in the room went out. Cyprian drew in a shuddering breath. On the ground underneath the restraining hands of Will and Violet, James was panting, his eyes hugely dilated, black with pupil.

They had him. They *had* him. Victory surged in Will's blood. James was satisfyingly roughed up, his jacket off, his shirt torn, and his hair falling from its part into his face, blood on his lip from Violet's punch. Violet and Cyprian both were bloodied, but the manacles were on James's wrists now and Violet was holding him down.

The room was a wreck. The table had splintered, the floor was rained with burst plaster, and Gauthier's chair was overturned. Gauthier was sprawled on the ground, and his fingers groped frantically in the grime, wormlike, for the curved circle of ruby and gold that had rolled away from him to lie a few steps out of his reach.

Will rose. Gauthier made a desperate sound at his footsteps.

"We're not your enemy," Will said. "We're here to help you."

"You're not here to help me. You're here for *it*."

It. Will could see it. A thick circle of rubies, set in gold. Too large for a bracelet. Too small for a crown.

"For the *Collar*," said Gauthier.

Collar. That was the word for it, Will thought. It was made to close around a throat. Gauthier let out a low moan, as if he somehow knew Will was bending down to pick it up. Will looked up and saw the grasping way Gauthier was reaching out for it. At the last moment, he snatched up the blanket and used it to bundle the Collar up rather than holding it in his bare hands.

"No—" said James, struggling against Violet as Will turned back to him.

It was heavy. A choker. The gold of its rim was high enough to force a chin up. Set with rubies, it gleamed redly, like blood welling from a gash. Like the manacles, it opened on a hinge. Two semicircles of rubies and gold that swung open and would close with a snap on the right throat.

"Don't worry. I told you. We're not going to let James take it," said Will.

The old man began to laugh. "You don't know what it does!"

Will looked over at him. "Simon wants it. It will make him powerful—"

Gauthier laughed his mad laugh. "Aye. That's true enough. It would make Simon the most powerful man alive."

Will couldn't help looking back at it, the deep red glint of the rubies and the gleaming curve of the gold. He felt the same pull from it that he had felt from the Cup. No, it was stronger, like a whisper in his ear, over his skin, in his blood. *Take me. Use me. Do it.*

"What does it do?" His fingers reached out to skim the edge of it, a desire to touch it, to feel it warm under his hands.

"It controls the Betrayer."

"What?" said Will. His fingers jerked back from it. He was staring at Gauthier.

"You put that around his neck and he'll obey you utterly." The words started a strange rushing in Will's head. "The Betrayer! The only Reborn in the human world! He's just a boy now, but when he's fully grown? To command all that power?"

James was on his knees with his hands manacled behind his back. His split lip had already begun to heal, its only trace a smudge of red. Violet had a fist in his hair, holding his head up. Cyprian had a sword to his throat.

"*He's lying*," James ground out, but Will knew he wasn't, could feel it. There was fear somewhere deep in James's eyes. Will remembered the way James's pupils had dilated when the Collar had been exposed. The way his whole body had swayed toward it. It was made for him; designed for his throat; red as his blood; gold as his hair; a perfect fit. And it wanted him. Ached for him.

A study in sadistic opulence, its bejeweled circlet turned even the idea of James into a possession. *Simon's Prize.* Will shivered as he saw that the Collar had a gold link set at the back.

"It pleased the Dark King to take the Light's greatest fighter and turn him into a lapdog," said Gauthier. "His people never knew he was ensorcelled, only that he'd become the Dark's lieutenant. They called him *Anharion*, the Betrayer. He kissed the Dark King's lips, rode at the Dark King's side, and slaughtered his own kind. They thought he did it of his own free will."

"You mean he didn't choose to serve the Dark King?" Will's heart was pounding strangely. "He was forced to do it? Under some kind of spell?"

Will's eyes swung to James in shock, and for a moment James was utterly exposed by the truth, his blue eyes wide and vulnerable, and in that single look Will could glimpse the pure youth he might have been, before the Dark King had warped and twisted him.

"That is the power of the Collar! It takes the will of the Betrayer and replaces it with your own. Put it on him and you can make him yours . . . you can make him do anything. That's how Sarcean kept him as a plaything in his bed at night, and by day sent him out to kill his own people."

"Please," said James. "Don't give it to my father."

The words seemed forced out of his throat. He looked stripped down to the bone, like a man taken apart, with nothing left. He was soaked with sweat, his damp hair falling into his face, his shirt wet.

"Your father's dead," said Will.

There was a flash of incomprehension on James's face. "What?"

"You didn't know?" Cyprian said bitterly. It was as if the spell of Gauthier's words was broken, the smaller hurts of their own history intruding. "Did you think he escaped when the shadow came?"

"The shadow?" said James, and then, eyes widening, "Marcus *turned*?"

Hearing James say his brother's name was too much for Cyprian, and he discarded his sword and dragged James to his feet.

"*Betrayer*," said Cyprian, holding a fistful of James's shirt. "You didn't need a Collar. You served Simon of your own free will. You know exactly what happened in the Hall. You were there." And then, revolted: "Did you hear them die? Did you watch? Did it make you happy to kill your own family?"

"I wasn't *there*," James returned. "Emery let me out."

Emery? Will thought of the shy, curly-haired novitiate who had been one of the first to be kind to him in the Hall. It seemed so unlikely, Will's mind couldn't make sense of it. But when he looked at James for any sign of subterfuge, he found none.

Cyprian's grip tightened. "Why would Emery *ever* do that?"

"Because he's been in love with me since we were eleven. Don't tell me you didn't know that."

After a long, violent silence, Cyprian's face twisted. He released James with a shove, sending him sprawling across the floor. Cyprian stalked off to the mantel and stood gathering himself, his back to them taut with tension, his arm braced on the wall.

"Well, he's dead," said Cyprian, after a long silence. "They're all dead. Because of you."

"Because of me?" James's voice taunted him. "Because of Marcus. He's the one who drank from the Cup."

Cyprian turned. Will saw the knife of James's smile and stepped hastily between them, remembering James in the Hall of the Stewards, inciting violence with just his words. He had to hold Cyprian bodily back. "Stop it. Stop. He wants this. He's baiting you. Stop."

Cyprian wrenched away, breathing hard. James was watching with a dangerously provocative expression, even sprawled as he was on his elbows, his hands manacled awkwardly behind him. Cyprian's shove had pushed James a couple of feet farther away from Will and the Collar, which perhaps had been the entire point.

Will turned to Gauthier. "You're saying this Collar has the power to control a person."

"Not any person," said Gauthier. "Only him."

"How do you know that?"

"Plenty of fools have tried to put it on others. Some who crave submission have tried to put it on themselves. It doesn't work. It was made for one person. To close around one throat."

Weighing the Collar in his hand, Will looked right at James, who was staring back at him, eyes wide, though his gaze couldn't help dropping to the Collar, his breathing shallow.

"But it does have power," said Gauthier. "Men want it. The control it promises. . . . The mastery. . . . The command. Like dragons hoarding jewels, all who touch the Collar crave to possess it. . . . Because they crave to possess *him*. And Simon . . . Simon wants it to secure his dominion. Simon has hunted me all these many years, seeking what is mine until there was no refuge and no rest."

Will thought about Gauthier, driven to this dead, empty farmhouse. He could see it in Gauthier's needy, grasping quality—the way he was almost hollowed out, as if his time with the Collar had sucked him dry of anything but the desire to take and to hold. The Collar was all he could think about, the one image burned in his mind.

Will turned his gaze to Violet.

"There's a room next to this one," he said to her. "Lock James in it."

"And then?" said Violet.

CHAPTER TWENTY-EIGHT

"WE USE IT," said Cyprian.

Will looked up as Violet returned from chaining James up in the kitchen, the door closing behind her with a soft click. Cyprian had righted Gauthier's chair and returned him to it, while Will put the Collar on the mantel. It was still wrapped in the blanket, but he could feel it, a heavy presence, drawing his mind and attention.

"We put the Collar around James's neck," said Cyprian, "and send him in to attack Simon."

"We can't just make James into our lackey," said Violet. "Can we?"

The question hung in the air.

"It's not forever," said Cyprian. "If he makes it out, we take the Collar off."

"You can't take it off," said Gauthier.

Everyone turned to him; Will felt his words sink down into him, a cold stone in a lake.

"What do you mean?" said Will, his skin prickling.

Gauthier was in his chair, his dirty, rumpled jacket wrapped around him, part of the decay and disrepair that surrounded them. He clasped knotted hands that were blotched in the dim light. His pearly, sightless eyes looked not quite at Will.

"There's no latch. There's no key. When you put it on, he's yours forever." Gauthier's whole body rocked in place slightly, as if eager. He spoke like a man quoting dark scripture. "Only his death will free him."

Yours forever. The idea that the Collar was permanent, that James couldn't take it off, made the prickling of Will's skin turn into a deep shivery sensation.

Only his death will free him, thought Will, but it hadn't. James was Reborn; he had died and risen again, and the Collar still wanted him.

Will looked down at the Collar, the shape of it under the blanket, the remembered gleam of its gold. The full scale of the choice they faced was before him. They could stop Simon, but the price—

The price was James. Forever.

"How do you know that?" said Will, looking back up at Gauthier. "How do you know what happens when James puts on the Collar?"

"My ancestor was his executioner," said Gauthier as the breath left Will in shock. "Rathorn killed the Betrayer and interred him in a tomb, but even then, the Collar didn't open. He had to saw off the Betrayer's head to get it."

"He used a saw on James's dead body?" said Violet, revolted. She had taken two steps back.

"The Dark King gave the order." Gauthier recited the words as if it was an old story told and retold many times. "Kill his servants, so that they would be reborn with him. Rathorn killed the Betrayer on the steps of the Dark Palace. He was supposed to inter the body in the Dark King's tomb. But he couldn't resist the Collar. He sawed through the Betrayer's neck and took it. . . . There was no one left to stop him."

The horror of those final days swept over Will. The Dark King defeated by the Lady. The forces of the Dark driven back. And the death . . .
a wave of death. How many servants had the Dark King ordered be
slaughtered? Will imagined the executioner in the halls of the Dark Palace, looting the bodies like a crow picking over carrion.

Would that be their future if the Dark King rose? Miles of ground
littered with the dead?

"Rathorn fled with the Collar, hid it, kept it safe. A family secret,
handed down over centuries. Now I'm the last, and Simon has tracked me
down. . . . He wants it . . . Wants it . . . He killed my son, you know. He
thought I had passed the Collar to him. I would have. I just needed a little
more time with it. I just needed—"

Gauthier's hands clutched instinctively. The Collar had hollowed
him out like a husk. Will thought of Rathorn, the long-ago executioner,
taking the object that would blight his family, withering his descendants
until all that was left was an old man in an empty house. He had thought
it a treasure, but it had been a curse. Had he ended up like Gauthier,
alone, half-mad, curled around the Collar in jealous protection?

But there was one thing about the story that didn't make sense.

"James was at his full power then. How did Rathorn capture him?"

Will looked at Gauthier, trying to see in him some echo of the past,
a champion who had been able to defeat the Dark King's greatest general.
Gauthier stared back at him blindly.

"Capture him? There was no capture. You don't understand. It was
the Dark King's will, so James knelt and bared his throat for the stroke."
Gauthier's voice was a dark promise. "I told you. Put it around his neck
and he'll do whatever you tell him."

The Betrayer. The Dark's lieutenant. The ultimate weapon: one they
could wield.

Will looked up at Violet and Cyprian, two faces set with grim purpose similar to his own.

Will said, "Give me the Collar."

James lifted his head when Will walked in.

Violet had chained James to the cast-iron range in the small bare
kitchen with its smashed glass window, out of earshot of the others. James
had adopted a posture Will recognized from his own time as quarry: back
to the wall, eyes on the door. At the far end of the house, they were alone.

When he saw the Collar in Will's hands, James's whole body squared
off toward it, and his face changed.

"What's it going to be?" said James. "Feed you a grape? Grovel at
your feet? Or will you just send me back to kill everyone I know?"

"Like you did to Marcus?" said Will.

He drew the blanket back from the Collar, exposing a ruby curve to
the air, while being careful to keep hold of it through the rough fabric and
not touch it with his bare hands.

"You can feel it, can't you," said Will.

The ugly look that James gave him was a yes.

"What does it feel like?" asked Will. "Does it hurt?"

"It doesn't *hurt*, it—" James bit off the words. The next look was even
uglier, and said everything.

Do you want it? Gauthier had said. *Do you want it the way it wants you?*

James was breathing shallowly, his cheeks flushed and his full attention now on the Collar.

"So you do want it," said Will.

"I don't *want it*," said James.

Will came forward, over the leaves and dirt that had blown into the
empty kitchen. "Gauthier said that his ancestor sawed through your dead

throat to get it. Is that true?"

"I don't know." James had said that before too. *I don't remember that life.* Now he said it as if he was angry, as if he wanted to remember but couldn't.

"But you knew the Collar. You knew what it was for. How?"

James was silent, his chest rising and falling rapidly.

"He had to saw through your throat because it doesn't come off. Did you know that?"

"That's the appeal, isn't it?" said James, with brittle defiance. "Simon's Prize is yours forever."

Will heard his own voice, curling with the feeling of the Collar. "Did you hate it when you followed orders? Did it keep you awake behind the compulsion? Or did it take over your whole mind, so that you believed you wanted to do everything?"

"God, you like this, don't you. You liked it with the horn too. Keeping me pinned. Drawing it out. Put it on me if you're going to. Or are you too much of a coward?"

Will said, "Turn around."

James turned, after a moment when his cheeks filled with color. Will saw the line of his back and the exposed nape of his neck. This close, it seemed James obeyed just as if the Collar were around his throat, though he stood like a stallion halfway through the breaking process, quivering and dripping with sweat. Will reached out and put his free hand on James's back, between his shoulder blades, and felt the shivery hot muscle through the shirt and silk of his waistcoat.

Will's hand slid down until he felt the manacles, where James's wrists were crossed just below the small of his back. James's throat was a pale, slender column beneath licks of gold hair. It looked naked. Vulnerable. Will felt in his teeth that this was the closest the Collar had come to the place where it belonged. Where it fit.

Put it on, and make him mine.

Breathing shallowly, he quickly unlocked James's manacles and let them drop heavily to the floor. Then he stepped back.

"What are you—" James swung around to stare at him. His eyes were wary, uncertain. James instinctively clasped his own wrists, as if he couldn't quite believe that he was free from the manacles. Then he lifted the fingers of his right hand, touching the bare skin of his own neck.

Will held out the Collar to him. It felt like holding out bread to a starving man who might snatch it and stab him for it anyway. James didn't. James's wariness was greater.

"Why would you give it back to me?" He was staring at Will with dark eyes.

"You came here alone."

"What does that have to do with—?"

"You came here alone because you don't want Simon to have it," Will said. "Simon doesn't know you're here." He watched the slight changes on James's face. "I'm right, aren't I."

"So what if you are?"

James looked primed for a trick. He hadn't taken the Collar, or even reached out for it, though his whole body was taut, as though at any moment he might snatch at it, or simply bolt.

"The Stewards found out what you were," said Will. "You fled. You were a child. You had nowhere to turn. I think you went to Simon because he was the only person who could protect you. He took you in, he raised you knowing what you would grow into. Maybe he told you that you'd be at his side in the new order, and maybe you believed him. But at some point you learned about the Collar."

James stared back at him. Will could feel the words had shocked him on some core level, touching some part of him unused to being seen.

"You learned he was looking for it. You learned he wanted you in it. The man you trusted wanted to enslave you. But you couldn't leave him. You needed to find it before he did, and staying close to him gave you the best access, the best information, the best chance of success. So you did his bidding. Simon's Prize. You let him keep you like a pet. And when you learned that Gauthier was in England, you came here alone."

There was a silence in the empty room, as James held himself very still, as if even the act of breathing would give something away. It seemed as if James wasn't going to speak. And then:

"It was his father," said James. "It was Simon's father who raised me, more than he did."

"How old were you when you joined him?"

"Eleven," said James.

"And when you learned about the Collar?"

"A year later."

Will lifted the Collar, proffering it again.

"I'm not a Steward," said Will. "I keep my promises. I'm loyal to my friends. I told you."

Enlarged pupils had turned James's eyes very dark. The wariness in James was now a long, searching look, seeking something beyond a trick or a trap.

"What's to stop me taking the Collar and killing you right now?" James said.

"Nothing."

"And Simon? I thought you couldn't stop him without me."

Will felt his lips curl, a brittle new feeling pushing inside him. "Don't underestimate me."

"I'm not going to help you fight him."

"I know that."

Still, James didn't take the Collar. He just looked at Will with that strange, searching look.

"I don't understand you."

"I know that too."

Slowly, James extended his hand. He didn't take the Collar right away; he hesitated before touching it, fingers hovering over it, and at the last second he avoided grasping it bare-handed. He took hold of it where Will held it, the wrapped section. His fingers brushing Will's felt cool. The moment Will released the Collar, it was as if a spell was broken. James wrapped the Collar swiftly back up in the blanket, tucking it under his arm, and seeing it disappear helped too. James made as if to leave.

And stopped, looking back at Will. Will could see another question forming on his lips.

But instead of asking it, James shook his head and left in silence by the rickety door, with only that single searching look back at him.

Violet was perched on the edge of the splintered table, but she leaped up at his arrival. Equally tense, Cyprian was standing next to Gauthier, sword in hand. Their body language was edgy with expectation, shot through with shame. Both of them looked with nervy tension at Will, and then past him to the hallway. When they didn't see James, the tension grew urgent. Cyprian stepped forward.

"Did you do it? Is it on him?" Cyprian flushed after he said it.

Violet had taken two steps down the empty hallway, looking for any sign of James. "Have you sent him after Simon already?"

"I let him go."

They both swung toward him, staring. A shocked moment of silence. Cyprian's tunic was a little bloodied from the injury he'd taken when he hit the wall, during James's capture. He changed color, patches of red appearing on his cheeks.

"You what?"

"I let him go."

The room was strewn over with the signs of their earlier fight. The furniture was smashed, the ceiling half smashed through, rubble scattering the floor and fine dust from the plaster drifting through the air in the dim streaks of light.

"And the Collar?"

Will said, "It was his. I gave it back to him."

Into the thunderous silence that followed, Gauthier gave a low, painful moan. "*Gone—it's gone—he gave it away—*"

Cyprian clenched his hand over the hilt of his sword. He had half moved toward the door before he stopped. He had no way to undo what Will had done: James was long gone, on horseback with a head start, and he was too powerful to subdue even if Cyprian did catch him. Will felt the battering emotions as Cyprian realized that it was too late, the decision made without him.

"We agreed. We agreed to use it to stop Simon."

"I never agreed to that," said Will. "I listened to Gauthier, and I made my decision."

"*James,*" said Cyprian, as though the name was dirt. "He used you. He fooled you into feeling sympathy for him, and you fell for it."

"It was the right thing to do," said Will.

"Did he hook you like he did Emery? You're in love with him too?"

"It was the right thing to do," Will said steadily.

"It wasn't the right thing to do!" said Cyprian. "He held my brother captive for months, keeping him alive until he turned. And then he set him loose to slaughter the Stewards. How do you think Marcus felt, knowing the shadow was in him, but not being able to stop it? James said Marcus begged, do you remember that? And now Simon has the Shadow Stone—"

Will said, "This isn't about Marcus—"

"No, it's about Simon," said Cyprian. "Simon is going to release the Shadow Kings, and they will rain down death and destruction on this world. Nothing can stop them. No power alive is strong enough."

"I know the stakes. I know what Simon can do."

"We had one chance to defeat him. We had it in our hands and you gave it up! You heard the Elder Steward. Once the Shadow Kings are free, Simon can raise the Dark King. And when the Dark King returns, he'll bring the dark past with him, returning magic and subjugating our world! We could have used that Collar to stop it."

"Used it the way the Stewards used the Cup?" said Will.

Cyprian went white, as if the flesh on his very bones marbled. He looked as if he'd been cut but was so drained of blood that the wound was bloodless. Silence rang; everything stopped, the only movement the drift of small motes of dust in the shabby room.

"It's not the same."

"Isn't it?" said Will. "Which part? Enslaving your enemy? Believing you can use a dark power without becoming what you fight?"

"It's not the same," Cyprian said again. "Using the Collar doesn't put anyone at risk—"

"It's the Dark King's will!" said Will. "He's everywhere, can't you feel it? His artifacts. His power. The Stewards are dead because they drank from his Cup. They never had a chance; the Dark King was inside the Hall the whole time, inside their bodies, inside their minds. Did you think that was an accident? A twist of fate? He planned it! Just like he planned this! He wants the Collar on James's neck. And you want to do his bidding." He didn't relent. "Just like the Stewards."

Cyprian's hands became fists. "The Stewards weren't doing his bidding. They were good people standing against the Dark. They held the line for centuries. They were fighting long before you came to the Hall. And when the shadow came, they gave their lives to stop it!"

"Look." Will grasped Cyprian by the arm and dragged him around to face the old man rocking in his chair. "Look at Gauthier. The Collar twisted his entire line until they were unable to do anything but keep it close and deliver it across the centuries to this house—to us—to James." Looking at the old man, Will could feel it, the stifling influence of the Dark King, spreading out over everything, so thick that it almost choked him. A thousand dark tendrils, reaching out from the black pit of the past, seeking hold. "The Stewards thought they were in control, but they weren't. *He* was. He wanted them to drink. That's how his objects work. You think you're using it, when it's the one using you."

"Then what can we do!" said Cyprian. But in the agonized look in his eyes Will could see that he knew already that this path was the right one. "Without the Cup, without the Collar . . . It's just the three of us. The three of us against the Dark. How can we fight when a single shadow killed every Steward in the Hall?"

"I don't know," said Will honestly. "But we're outside of his plans now, maybe for the first time. You're the last Steward left. And you're the first Steward beyond his reach. You're a Steward who hasn't drunk from the Cup."

Cyprian took in a shaky breath.

"You think James will go back to Simon?" said Violet, into the silence.

"I don't know that either," said Will. "But now he's free from the Dark King too."

"And Gauthier?" She looked at the shrunken old man, skin tight on his bones and still rocking a little on his chair.

Will knelt down in front of Gauthier, so that he could speak to him from his own height. "Mr. Gauthier. I'm afraid that James was telling the truth about Sophie . . . you're alone here. Is there someone we can fetch for you? Something we can do?"

"Do!" said Gauthier. "You can give it back to me, that's what you can do! I'm the one who's supposed to put it on him. I'm the one who's supposed to have him! Not you—!" Will stood quickly, his stomach roiling.

They brought in the bundle of kindling, six eggs that they found in the old outside coop, and a sheet full of apples from the overgrown tree, along with a fresh pail of water. Then they left the room in the farmhouse, where Gauthier's voice still echoed. "He's supposed to be mine! Obeying my orders with my Collar around his neck—!"

They rode back over the marsh toward the broken arch that now led to a silent, empty courtyard. Will didn't want to go back into the Hall. He could feel his own resistance, the arch ominous in his mind, like the gates of a graveyard at night. Around him the marsh stretched out cold and wet under the gray sky, their horses plowing through the mud.

"What are we going to tell Grace and Sarah?" said Cyprian, drawing up on his horse alongside him.

Cyprian had been quiet on the ride back, absorbing Will's words. He had spent a lifetime training to be a Steward, following their traditions and their code. A Steward's life was all he knew. Without the Order to guide him, he was lost—unwilling to drink from the Cup but without another framework for how to live. The idea that he might still be a Steward, but as Stewards were meant to have been, was a new thought. He asked about Grace and Sarah now without acrimony, a practical question that needed an answer.

But Cyprian was right. What to tell them? That they had come back empty-handed? That Will had given away their only weapon against Simon? That the Shadow Kings would be released and now there was no way to stop them?

The future seemed to stretch out with all his plans for Simon slipping away, and only the thought that he was not up to the fight that was coming.

"Will?" said a voice, and he was half aware of Violet behind him drawing her sword as two figures on horseback emerged from behind the gate.

Her beauty was like the golden sunlight of spring, even here on the cold gray marsh, though she and the pretty dappled gray mare she was riding looked utterly incongruous, the skirts of her blue riding habit soaked with mud that splattered and stained the legs and belly of her bedraggled horse.

Behind her was a young girl of about nine or ten, with thick eyebrows and a pasty face on a short pony. They looked very different, one beautiful and golden, one stout and plain, but the two girls turned to him as one.

"You said if I was in danger, that I should come," said Katherine.

CHAPTER TWENTY-NINE

KATHERINE COULDN'T STOP staring: at Will, at the strange clothes that he wore, at the mud and grime all over him, even at the black horse he rode. He dismounted and took a step toward her, his eyes wide and shocked. His friends looked like they'd come from a battlefield, their clothing bloodied and torn. His friends looked, she thought, like this ancient ruined gate, part of this bleak, empty, and terrifying place.

"You came," Will said.

He was here; she wasn't alone on the marsh. She wanted to go to him. She wanted him to take her into a warm parlor, with a fire where she could sit and warm herself, and servants to bring her tea, while he wrapped a shawl around her shoulders and held her hands. But nothing was happening the way she had thought.

The rain had made the ride over the marsh at night into a cold, bedraggled slop through mud, her heart dropping out every time her sweet-natured mare, Ladybird, stumbled, Elizabeth struggling gamely behind her on Nell the pony. It hadn't been long until they had both been sodden, shivering in their waterlogged skirts.

Her teeth were chattering. The boy and the girl standing behind Will were staring at her with unfriendly suspicion.

"What is she doing here?" the girl demanded, drawing her sword, a long, frightening weapon that looked too heavy for her slight body.

"Will?" Katherine said, not understanding what was happening, but scared of the two strangers and their drawn swords. She was so cold, her fingers numb in their wet gloves, her sodden skirts heavy. She didn't know what to do.

"It's all right," Will said to her, and then he looked at the others. "Stop it," he said. "Violet. Stop it. She isn't a threat."

"She's Simon's fiancée," said Violet.

"Simon!" said the boy on horseback next to her, and he was drawing his sword too, a clear warning.

Her heart jammed in her throat. Will stepped out in front of her, facing down the sharp steel.

"I told her to come," said Will. "She's not a threat. She's alone. She came here for help." And then he was coming toward her, putting his hand on Ladybird's neck, and he said quietly, "Didn't you, Katherine."

"I wasn't followed," she said, remembering the slow, creeping escape from the house with Elizabeth, avoiding cobblestones to muffle hoofbeats and praying the horses wouldn't whicker. "I wasn't—Lord Crenshaw doesn't know I'm here—I wasn't—"

"You did the right thing," said Will with a warning glance back at Violet and the boy. "First let's get you and your sister inside."

Katherine was wet and cold, but there was nothing here, no sign of civilization. The empty marsh seemed to stretch out in every direction. "Inside?"

"If Cyprian allows it," said Will. He turned to the boy. "You're the only one who can let them through the wards."

"I don't trust her," said Violet.

The boy—Cyprian—seemed to look her over, weighing the decision. Sitting straight-backed on his white horse, he looked like a paragon of some bygone era. She wished she weren't wet and shivering. She wished her teeth weren't chattering and her curls weren't sodden. She tried her best, despite all this, to look respectable.

"My father wouldn't have let her in," said Cyprian. "He thought of the Hall as a fortress that we had to protect." Looking at her, he seemed to remember words someone else had spoken. "But in the old world, the Hall wasn't only a fortress. It was also a sanctuary." He sheathed his sword and gave her a nod. "If you truly need our help, then you are welcome in our Hall."

Will rode alongside her. His huge black horse with its arched neck dwarfed Ladybird, but he reached down and took her gloved hand in his, holding it as her heart thundered in her chest. "Don't be afraid," he said.

But she was afraid; she was terrified.

Ahead of her, Cyprian and Violet rode through the broken arch, and simply disappeared. "Will?" She said his name as a cry for help. His hand squeezed hers. *I don't want to go.* He urged them both forward.

She felt a lurch, and the marsh was suddenly gone, and in its place there was the black outline of a bleak castle, its beacon the last ember in a dead fire. She shivered looking up at it. Where were the lights and the servants and the warmth of a welcome?

What had happened here? She remembered the light Will had conjured in the garden. Some part of her had thought Will would lead her to a place of light. A place of safety. But this place was dark and terrible. She looked at Will as he swung down from his horse in the courtyard. *This* was the world that he had come from?

"Is th-this—where you live?" she asked Will.

"It's where I've been staying," said Will.

"It's horrible," said Elizabeth. "Like it's dead."

"Elizabeth!" said Katherine.

"It's all right," said Will, looking around at the courtyard grimly. "She's right. It's not where I would have hoped to bring you. But it's where we'll be safe."

With the castle behind him, he looked different, changed from a handsome young gallant to a fey, unknowable young man. Her old life was falling away, as if it hadn't been real, as though the event that had brought her here had shattered an illusion, revealing a reality that was as dark as it was true.

"Come," said Will, holding out a hand to help her down from her horse.

Katherine sat in her drying skirts on a three-legged stool by the fire and tried not to think about why she had come.

Will hadn't taken her into the castle but into a smaller tower at the wall that he called the gatekeep. But the thought of the castle's black outline still hung over her, an ominous shape that made her shiver.

The room itself was nothing like a parlor. It was more like a barracks, cut out of stone that was darkened and cracked with age. Up the short stairs was a room filled with five makeshift sleeping pallets, as if Will and the others were all camping together in this bleak ruin. Two girls in blue tunics had come out of the gatekeep to greet them. Will had defended her presence to them, before leading her in to sit by the fire.

Elizabeth was inside too, her too-dark eyebrows heavy in her drawn face. She sat back from Katherine in her short child's dress, near the wall. She had been given a bowl of stew and was eating it hungrily. Katherine couldn't stomach the idea of food. If she thought about eating, all she could think of was the lovely dinner service at home, while here there were no carpets, no wallpaper, no staff, and no signs of civilization.

Elizabeth had been surprisingly matter-of-fact when Katherine had come to her, heart pounding, and told her they had to leave. Cautioned to bring nothing but essentials, Elizabeth had stopped only to get her coat and her day's schoolwork, and had returned grim-faced and ready. Katherine had considered taking some of her fine clothes and jewelry, but in the end she had put on a simple old blue riding habit. She had seen the groomsman saddle Ladybird a hundred times, but when she tried to do it herself, she had no idea where to start, and it felt like a long, panicked interval of struggling trial and error before they set out into the rain.

"Here," said Cyprian, proffering her a cup. From a wary distance, he had kept his eyes on her. As though the very fact of her was an intrusion. As though she was the oddity, not him. As though she might be dangerous— and with a curiosity at the exotic, as though he'd never seen a gentlewoman before. Now he handed her a strangely shaped glass filled with hot liquid.

It turned out there was tea here, but it was not good brown tea with milk in a porcelain cup. It was green, with bits of something that looked like grass floating in it.

"You are very kind, sir," she said.

"My people make this. The herbs that grow here have qualities that have been cultivated since the old world. It's restorative."

"Your people?" she said. "You mean Continentals?" And then flushed because this was somehow the wrong thing to say, but she didn't know why. She didn't know what to do.

"He means Stewards. Your fiancé killed them," said Violet.

She took the tea and just stared down at it, pale green with a few flecks and stalks swirling at the bottom.

"I see. Thank you," she said.

She sat down again. She was dully aware of them drawing off to one side and talking about her in low voices. *"We still don't know why she's here."* *"She came alone. Simon's not with her."* *"And if she's a Trojan horse? We can't trust her."*

She stared at the fire until the flames blurred together. She shouldn't be here. She should be at home, dressing for dinner. She wouldn't be here, if not for what had happened. The terrible, overwhelming thing that had driven her out of the house and into the mud and rain.

Will pulled up a second stool and sat beside her.

"You heard something, didn't you."

He spoke quietly, leaning toward her, his forearms resting on his knees. The words made her seize up. She couldn't say it. Didn't want to say it. Around her, she felt a thundering pressure. She held the cup so tight she was surprised it didn't break into pieces and cut into her.

"Simon came to visit you," said Will. "He was in London on business."

The whole room was so quiet, she felt like she could hear each flame in the fire. Will said it like he knew what she had heard, when he couldn't. He couldn't know. No one could. The pressure grew. She didn't want to say it, because that would make it real. That would make all of this real. This cold, empty castle. The mud soaking her dress. The words that had made her world fall apart.

"He would have been in a good mood. His business in London had gone well." Will said it grimly. "Maybe someone arrived to see him. Maybe an associate. Maybe a messenger. I had made you curious enough to eavesdrop. And you heard something."

The first time Lord Crenshaw had come to call on her, they had set out a porcelain tea set decorated with pink rosebuds, furled green leaves, and gold trim. He had been the perfect gentleman, asking her questions, showing his interest. The whole family had been so happy, their fortunes made. Her aunt and uncle had fussed over her, and she'd eaten her favorite treat that night, apricot ice cream.

She had clambered into bed, too excited to sleep, braiding her sister's hair and talking about the house that she would have, and the balls that she would attend, and the society that they would move in.

"He said it wasn't enough," Katherine said.

"What wasn't enough?"

He'd come to visit her many times since, each time the picture of courtesy and good manners, solicitous and charming, as he had been on his last visit, when he'd risen to speak with a messenger, and she had followed him out into the hallway.

"Blood," said Katherine.

Looking down at her cup, she felt the cold strangeness of this small, bare room. Her old life seemed to recede, the dresses, and the shoes, the little string of pearls that matched so well to sprig muslin, the thrill of her first time getting her hair done *à la mode*, lifted high up off her neck by her new lady's maid.

"He said he'd killed ladies before and one wasn't enough," she said. "It had to be all of them."

He killed my mother, Will had said to her, and she hadn't believed him. Until she'd heard the words that had turned her blood cold, and then the only thing she'd remembered Will saying to her was *Run*.

I need to kill all of them, Lord Crenshaw said in a conversational voice. *And I have. They're all dead. All but one.*

Will pulled his stool closer and spoke to her urgently.

"Was there anything else?"

Standing terrified behind the door, then having to find her way back to the morning room, watching him sit, and making small talk and smiling. All she could remember was pressing herself to the wall, shoving the side of her hand into her mouth to stifle the scream in her throat.

I was a fool seventeen years ago, acting on hints and rumors. I thought I only needed to kill one.

I was wrong.

I needed to kill all of them. And I have. They're all dead. All but one.

Now I have the Stone, and I can finally succeed where I had failed all these years.

Her blood will release them from their centuries of prison, and by their hand His enemies will be felled. And when all of them are dead, He will rise.

"He said he needed her blood to open a stone." She was only half aware of her words impacting the others, the looks they exchanged. "He'd release prisoners from the Stone to kill any resistance. He said when the ladies were dead, a king would rise."

Will's hands closed over hers, steadying them. "You did the right thing coming here." The startling touch grounded her back in the room suddenly. Her heart started beating in a different way when she realized Will had taken her ungloved hands in his and was simply holding them.

"He's mad, isn't he? His mind is . . . He's a madman." She looked up at Will, wanting nothing more than to be reassured that all of this could be put aside, like a bad dream.

"I told you that if you came with me I'd explain everything," said Will. "And I will."

Will didn't look away from her, but from the other side of the room she heard Cyprian say, "Will, you can't bring her into this—"

And Will's voice. "She's in it already."

"I don't understand," said Katherine, in a small voice.

Violet had taken a step forward. "At least have the sister leave the room."

That was the worst possible thing to say.

"I can listen to anything Katherine can!" Elizabeth had stood up on her short legs and was glaring at Violet.

"They came here together," said Will. "They're in this together."

"Tell me," said Katherine.

"You saw the tree light up in the garden," said Will. "You said it wasn't natural. You were right. It was magic. Like this Hall. There used to be magic in the world, a long time ago."

Magic. The strangest sensation passed over her as he spoke, the eerie sense of something lost, as though the dead, dark castle was a vestige of something vanished.

"What happened to it?" she said.

It felt important. As if what Will could tell her was more important than anything else. As if she had to know it.

"A long time ago," said Will, "there was a Dark King. He was powerful and merciless, and he liked to control people. He wanted to rule the world. He almost did. He was only stopped at great cost, after he caused destruction and death."

It felt true. With the flame light flickering in this cold ruin of a castle, it all felt true. A Dark King, rising up out of a past that seemed real as soon as Will spoke of it. But it was as if there was a piece missing, something right on the tip of her tongue—

"Stopped," she said. "By who?"

"A Lady," said Will, and suddenly she was caught in his gaze, unable to look away from him, magnetized. She remembered the flare of light in her garden. She felt like she was on the edge of understanding, even as something in Will's eyes now flashed painfully. "They loved each other. Maybe that's how she killed him. But even then, it wasn't finished. The Dark King swore to return."

"Return . . . from death?" said Katherine.

"The Lady couldn't return as he could, so she had a child, hoping that if the Dark King rose again, her descendant would take up the fight."

You. She felt the word, like a throb, as she looked into Will's eyes. *You, you, you.* And there was something about him, something that felt ancient and part of this, like he was the key, like he was terribly important, if only she could grasp the edge of it—

"Simon's killing the Lady's descendants," said Will. "He thinks it will return the Dark King."

A Dark King who was merciless. A Dark King who wanted to rule. A Dark King who could destroy the world. . . .

Katherine shivered in her wet clothes. Even by the fire, she couldn't seem to get warm.

"And will it?" said Katherine.

Will didn't answer right away. He glanced across at Violet, and the two seemed to share something before he looked back at her.

"He killed my aunt before I was born," said Will. "I think she was the first. When the Dark King didn't appear after he did that—"

"He had to kill all of them," said Violet. "Anyone who might have the blood."

"It's why he killed your mother. It's why he's chasing you," said Cyprian. "*'Killing one isn't enough. It has to be all of them.'*"

Lord Crenshaw's conversational voice saying, *I needed to kill all of them. And I have. They're all dead. All but one.*

She looked at Will, the flames from the fire lighting his face.

You. It made sense of his strangeness, the otherworldly quality that he had, the way he'd always seemed—sharper and brighter in her mind than other people, even as he'd seemed separate and apart.

Will was the one Lord Crenshaw was chasing. The one he needed to kill to succeed in his plans.

"The Shadow Kings can't be stopped," said Cyprian. "If he sends them after you—"

"He hasn't released them yet," said Will. "He needs the Blood of the Lady to release them from the Stone."

"Your blood," said Violet to Will, and Katherine felt her skin prickle.

"And once he has it?" said Cyprian.

Will said, "He'll release the Shadow Kings, slaughter his enemies, and end the Lady's line."

"And He will rise," said Cyprian, as cold ran down Katherine's spine.

She saw the look Will exchanged with Cyprian and Violet, right before the three of them left the gatekeep together. She waited just long enough after they had gone, then rose from the fireside stool, telling the two girls, Grace and Sarah, "I need some air."

And just as she had followed Lord Crenshaw, she slipped out after Will and his friends, wanting to know what they were saying when they thought she couldn't hear.

She saw Will in the courtyard not far from the gatekeep, speaking to Cyprian and Violet in a low-voiced, tight cluster. She pressed herself behind a jut of wall, out of sight but within earshot.

"He needs you," Cyprian was saying to Will. "But he won't get you."

"We know how to stop him now," said Violet. "Katherine said it. He needs your blood. Without it, he can't release the Shadow Kings. All we have to do is keep you away from him."

"You mean run," said Will.

She had never heard him sound like that before. She couldn't see the expression on his face but desperately wanted to. She pressed herself more closely against the wall, hoping not to be seen.

"The Hall can keep us safe—" Cyprian began, but Violet cut him off.

"Simon knows we're here," said Violet. "We don't have supplies to last for more than a month. It's too easy for him to stake us out. We can't stay in the Hall."

Will was silent.

"Simon's not unbeatable." Violet pressed her point. "Your mother evaded him for years until he found her. Gauthier stayed ahead of him his whole life. If we stay on the move, we can keep you away from him."

It was Cyprian who broke the long, difficult pause. "She's right. We run. We leave England and we get as far away as possible."

"We?" said Will.

"That's right," said Cyprian.

"The Hall's your home," said Will.

"I didn't swear my oath to the Hall," said Cyprian. "I swore it to the people of this world. To remember and protect. That's what I trained to do."

There was another long pause.

Then Will's voice, grimly. "All right. Get your things together. We leave at dawn. We travel light and we stay on the move."

"I'll tell the others," said Violet.

What about me? thought Katherine. *And my sister? Where do we go? Are you just going to leave us? What do we do?*

But just as Katherine was about to hurry back to make sure she wasn't seen, she heard Will speak Violet's name, holding her back.

"What is it?" Violet said.

"The sisters." Katherine stayed very still, fixed in place and straining to hear.

"What about them?"

"I want you to give me your word you'll protect them," said Will as

Katherine's heart beat oddly. "You're the strongest one here. I want you to keep them safe."

"I might not like her fiancé," said Violet slowly. "But that girl risked a lot to come here. For you."

For you. Katherine flushed, the heat scalding her cold cheeks, feeling painfully exposed.

"Thank you, Violet," said Will. "I couldn't do this without you."

"But where do I sleep?" said Katherine, looking at the small room with its five pallets on the floor.

"This is it," said Violet, shoving a roll of blankets into Katherine's hands.

Will had told her as soon as he returned to the gatekeep what he and his friends planned to do. He'd told her it would be dangerous. He'd told her his friends would help her whatever she decided. And she'd said yes when he'd asked her if she wanted to come with them.

"You can have my bed," said Will, pointing to one of the meager pallet beds in the corner. Will was going to sleep on the cold stone floor. "I know it's not much. We'll find better lodgings for you when we're far enough away, on the road."

She saw in her mind's eye her own bed's soft downy coverings and silver bed warmer. "Thank you. I'm very grateful. Elizabeth, let's settle in here."

There was nowhere to wash or undress, so she asked the two janissaries to hold up a blanket while she stood behind it and Elizabeth helped unlace her corset. She went to bed in her underdress and shawl. Cyprian and Will had gone downstairs and only came back when it was dark and she was under the blankets. She tried not to think about the morning.

She thought Will would go immediately to sleep like Cyprian, but instead he came to sit beside her pallet. She flushed, warming at his presence, at the thought that he wanted to see her before bed.

"I came to say good night," he said softly.

There was something wrong. She could see it in him. She was the one who clasped his hand and stopped him from standing up. She looked up into his eyes. "What is it?"

She didn't think he was going to answer. The others were already asleep or too far away to hear. The silence seemed to stretch out for a long time.

He spoke the words quietly. "My mother spent her whole life running."

He rubbed his thumb along the silver scar on his hand. *Simon killed my mother*, he'd said to her, that night in her garden. She'd thought Will a dashing young man of means, until that moment, when the ground had felt like it was scrolling out from under her feet.

"I wish you could have known her," he said. "She was a good person, brave, strong. Sometimes she could seem harsh or distracted, but everything she did—she had a reason. She sacrificed a lot for her child."

It was easier to speak in the dark, words that might not have found their way out in daylight. He'd given her something true, she could feel it. She owed him something true in return, words that could only be spoken in the dark.

"I thought there was a life that I wanted," she heard herself saying. "It was jewels, and gowns, and pretty fashionable things. Lord Crenshaw would have given me that. But I couldn't be with him. Not once I knew what he was."

"No, of course not," said Will, with a strange half smile. "Once you knew what he was—what he really was—you couldn't bear it."

He said it as though he believed in her. As though he had always known that she would do the right thing. But she hadn't, not at first. She had run from the truth he had told her right back to her world of safety and ease. There was something else she owed him, words that were harder to say since the night she had forced him out of her garden.

"You were right about him," she said. "What you told me that night." She drew in a breath. "All of it."

"I'm sorry," Will said. "If it weren't for me, you'd still have that life."

"I wouldn't want it," she said. "Not knowing it wasn't real."

She looked around at the dark, bare gatekeep room, which didn't have wallpaper or carpets or a lady's maid to help her with her hair. The seven of them were sleeping like paupers in a workhouse. It was frightening and uncomfortable, but it felt like the truth. She looked back at Will's dark eyes.

"What's going to happen tomorrow?"

"You'll be safe," said Will, and then with that strange, painful smile, "I promise."

CHAPTER THIRTY

WILL WAITED UNTIL Katherine was asleep and the room was dark and still. Then he rose and quietly made his way out of the gatekeep and down toward the stables.

The words rang in his ears. *Simon is killing the Lady's descendants. He thinks it will return the Dark King.* Simon had killed his aunt. Simon had killed his mother. Simon had killed who knew how many women, in his desire to bring back the Dark King.

Killing one wasn't enough. It had to be all of them.

A sick logic that had caused Simon to slaughter women over decades: the idea that her death would bring him back. And now Simon had what he needed: the Shadow Stone. If Simon released the Shadow Kings from their prison, they would kill, a destructive force that no door or wall could keep out. Harbingers of the Dark King's return, the Shadow Kings would hunt down and obliterate every enemy of their master.

In hushed tones, Cyprian and Violet had talked about how to run, where to go. They thought Simon needing the Lady's blood gave them a chance. They thought that if they just kept Will safe, they could stop

Simon from releasing the Shadow Kings from the Stone.

They were wrong.

Because if Simon needed blood, there was another place that he could get it. And Will knew where. He knew exactly where Simon would go to release the Shadow Kings from centuries locked in their prison.

On the blood-soaked ground where she had looked up at him, fingers still clutching his sleeve.

Bowhill.

It had a terrible rightness to it, the place where everything started. Of course he would have to go back there—back to the beginning of all of it. He had spent all this time running, but deep down he had always known that he would have to return and face the truth.

Simon was going to stand on ground soaked in his mother's blood and release the Shadow Kings. And they would rain down death and destruction, and through them Simon would end the line of the Lady. That was Simon's life's work, the reason he had slaughtered all those women, the reason he had slaughtered the Stewards. He was going to return the Dark King and bring the terrors of the past into their present.

Will knew what he had to do. Who he had to be. The knowledge had grown in him since he had stood in front of the dead Tree Stone and the Elder Steward had told him about his mother. Or, no, maybe he'd known since his mother had died and he'd stumbled away with a bleeding hand and bruises around his throat.

The Lady is meant to kill the Dark King.

He had run from it at first, not wanting it to be true. But there was no escaping it.

You could run from your enemies.

You couldn't run from yourself.

He took a bridle from the tack room and made his way to the quiet horse stalls. The scene of so much recent death, the outbuildings were eerie at night, cast in shadows and moonlight. He moved quickly, keeping silent so as not to alert the others in the gatekeep. Urgency beat in his blood even as his every move was careful. Simon would have left London this afternoon, after receiving his message at Katherine's house. He would already be well on his way to Bowhill. Even with the swiftness of a horse sustained by the magics of the Hall, Will didn't have much time. He stepped into the stables, where the handful of remaining horses were stalled.

"You're sneaking out," said Elizabeth.

She was like a small ambush, standing right in his way. Her frown was two aggressive eyebrows pointed downward, and her legs were planted, unbudgeable. Will felt a burst of both ridiculousness and frustration, to be stymied like this, right on the threshold, and by this girl, of all people.

"I'm going for a ride."

With the bridle in his hand, he could hardly deny it.

"You just came back from a ride," said Elizabeth. "You're sneaking out. I knew if I stayed up I'd catch you." The light in her eyes was triumphal.

"I'm not sneaking out," said Will.

"You're a sneak," said Elizabeth. "You lie to people. You told my sister that you met her on Oxford Street by accident. But I asked Violet what you were doing in London that day, and she said you were waiting in Southwark. That's nowhere near Oxford Street." Elizabeth had the savage jubilance of the successful sleuth. "You came after my sister on purpose."

Will felt silly as he kept his voice reasonable and steady. "I was chased from Southwark to Oxford Street."

"You're lying. You're lying to me. You're lying to everyone. And tonight—you're planning something. What?"

He thought about what he was riding toward. He had to get to Simon in time. Every moment that he spent here was delaying him further.

Logic wasn't going to work, and nor was charm, and nor was reason. Very well.

"Listen, you," he said. "Step out of my way, or before your sister has a chance to go home, I'll tell all of London that she ran away unchaperoned."

He saw her react to that, a sort of shocked hit. Her mouth dropped open, a child's indignant betrayal at an unfair line of attack.

"That—isn't—" She dug her heels in. "She didn't run away for a *man*. She ran away because she learned Simon's plans."

"I could tell Simon that instead, if you like," said Will steadily. "He'll kill her."

This drained the blood from her face. "He wouldn't!"

"He would. That's why she ran. Now step back and let me through."

He looked down at her pale, drawn face, expecting to be on his way now that this business was done. She stared up at him, obviously searching for a way around his ultimatum, her young mind working furiously.

"I want to come with you."

Christ. "You can't and you won't."

"I want to come with you. If you're just *going for a ride*, you won't mind company. I can take Nell."

She lifted her chin. He opened his mouth to answer, found no words coming out, and saw the victorious flash in her eyes. He made himself breathe calmly.

"I'm not just going for a ride—"

("I knew it!")

"—but what I'm doing doesn't concern you. You're going back to the gatekeep. And you're not going to say a word about this to anyone."

"Or you'll spoil my sister's reputation."

"That's right," said Will. "So if you want to save her, you'll go write your aunt and uncle and tell them that you and Katherine have ridden to stay with a female friend. They should tell everyone she's sick, until she returns, which will be shortly. By then I'll be gone."

"You've thought of everything, haven't you?" said Elizabeth.

Her eyes glared at him, and he'd half braced himself for a new argument, but instead her mouth twisted and her small hands became fists.

"All right," said Elizabeth. "But I'll remember this. You might have fooled the others. You haven't fooled me. I'll find you out. Whatever it is you're doing."

It was almost sunset when he saw the first of the rising hills, the unsafe open hills topped with strange rocks. The landscape was like a blast of memory, the boggy, peaty smell of the earth and the difficulty of escape because the terrain was so open. Valdithar had covered in a night and a day what might have taken five times as long on a normal horse, and he was here almost before he was ready. Moving forward felt like forcing himself into a remembered nightmare, the desperation of that night, his stumbling steps and heaving breath, the fear as he pushed himself across stretches of open hillside.

There was a point at which he had to dismount, tie Valdithar in a clutch of trees, and go ahead on foot. He was close now, perhaps five or six miles.

The land here had no cover, only scraps of trees following the lines of the creeks, and occasional low drystone walls. Bushy clumps housed nesting grouse that would give him away if he disturbed them. He knew that too well. A thick bile rose in his throat as he began to recognize places from snatches of memory that night. There was the ditch where he'd dug himself a hiding hole. There was the rotting log where he'd stumbled and tripped. From the edge of the tree line he saw the thatched stone cottage where he had been stupid enough to try to go for help. He closed his eyes, remembering the way the door had swung open under his hand, the naiveté of his calling out "Hello?" and smiling in relief as he saw the man in the hallway, a second before he saw the streak of blood on the wall.

"—something out here—"

His eyes flew open again. That was a voice, too close. He flattened himself behind a tree.

A second voice, harsh and low. "I heard something. If you keep your mouth shut, we might have half a chance to find out."

It was two men searching systematically through the thin strip of trees. They were drawing closer and there was not enough cover to hide in. Will looked around himself desperately. He couldn't be found here. He was still a mile out from Bowhill, where Simon was taking the Shadow Stone.

"I don't like being out here," said the first voice, sounding nervous. "I heard that *it* is out here. That Lord Crenshaw has *it* patrolling the hills." He sounded more than nervous. "What if it sees us and takes us for an intruder?"

It? thought Will. And then, *Lord Crenshaw.* It was proof that he was in the right place. Simon was here, with his men on patrol.

There was a clump of undergrowth to his left. Carefully, he picked up a pebble from the ground under his feet. He weighed it in his hand.

"It won't hurt us; it knows Simon's brand. Senses it somehow. It's proof we're Lord Crenshaw's men."

They were even closer. At any moment they would pass the tree and see him.

Did that mean Simon would see him? Will remembered Leda saying that Simon could look out of the eyes of the men who bore his brand.

Will threw the stone, hard as he could, right into the bushy clump—

The squawk of an indignant grouse with its red-topped head was loud as it exploded upward in a burst of flapping. A shot rang out almost instantly, missing the bird but echoing across the silent nighttime valley. The men had guns—

"It's just a grouse. You've dragged us out here for a grouse, you fool." Will stayed flattened to the tree trunk, trying not to even breathe, the voice a single step away. "Now you will really have brought it here."

"I told you, I heard someone—"

The other man swore. "You heard birds. This is pointless. We need to get back to the house."

The footsteps retreated, and slowly Will let out a breath, his muscles relaxing one by one.

That had been close. But now he knew: Simon was here. Simon might have already begun, might right now be laying the Shadow Stone on the blood-soaked ground, saying whatever words were needed to release the Shadow Kings. He pushed on, toward Bowhill—

In the eerie predawn light, Will heard the sound of breaking branches, something large in the undergrowth.

It.

He could hear hooves and the snort of a horse's breath, a horse and rider moving inexorably, as if making a slow search. And as he plastered his back to the trunk of the tree, he saw its leaves start to wither and curl.

Heart jammed in his mouth, Will forced himself to move—quietly, quietly, with no rustle of leaves or snap of a twig that might send the horse's head jerking up. He heard the sounds circle the area where he had hidden, then turn and make for the nearby stone house. *It's following Simon's men.* He let out a breath; Simon's men crashing through the thicket and leaving tracks behind them had bought him time.

He drew on every piece of remembered knowledge to get himself away soundlessly. There were handholds on the gritstone. That log is rotten, don't step on it. And always the chilling thought: the memory of withering leaves and the heavy breathing of the horse.

When he reached a small rise, Will wasted precious moments scrabbling up the largest of the nearby stone boulders, scanning the countryside, his blood pounding.

Nothing in the valley. He looked up toward the bleak summit of Kinder Scout, the long, high ridge of gritstone tors where the rocks had strange names.

And there against the skyline he saw a dark figure on a horse looking out across the landscape like an ancient sentinel.

A *Remnant.*

His heart clutched in fear—those blank dead eyes looking out at the valley—

He saw the white breath its horse exhaled in the cold night. He recognized its silhouette, a rider with a single armored shoulder piece that had been dug up in the hills of Umbria. If he had wondered how the horse was immune to the Remnant's touch, he saw now that it wore its own ancient armor—the long nosepiece called a chamfron—giving both horse and rider a terrifying blank look.

It, the men had called it, but Will recalled with a shiver that there was more than one Remnant. There were three. One in the woods behind him. One high on the hill. And the other—?

He told himself to keep going. The same rules applied: Stay quiet so they can't hear you. Stay out of the open, they're watching. Don't panic, you'll give yourself away.

But reusing the same hiding places as he had all those months ago was its own horror. The hollowed-out tree where he had hidden, gasping air into his bruised throat. The outcrop of stone where he had crouched, his hand dripping blood. Each step brought him so strongly back to the past that it felt like he was traveling back in time, returning to that single, obliterating moment that he did not want to face.

And then he reached the tree line and was looking out at Bowhill.

Nestled in the dip between hills, out of sight of the village, the farm-house where he'd lived was now a ruin. The roofing had collapsed. The door was a black rectangle that the wind howled through. Nature had begun to reclaim the place and the paths were a tangle.

He took a step toward it and his foot hit unyielding wood. Logs in a discarded pile, grown over with wet moss—his skin prickled. He'd dropped that bundle of logs when he'd heard the first screams and started sprinting toward the house. Drawing in a shallow breath, he looked up toward his destination—

He couldn't avoid the open now, but there was no one in sight. That dark sentinel on the ridge might see him—see a speck break free from the trees and start moving toward the farmhouse—and that thought sent its shiver through him. But instinctively he knew that Simon was there, beyond the farmhouse, on that patch of earth where her blood had run.

All Will had to do was go forward. One step. Another. Back to those last moments, like a door he didn't want to open. The blood soaking his clothes; himself gasping for breath; the terrible look in her eyes as she—

Something crunched under his feet. A strange, unexpected sound, as if he had stepped onto gravel. He looked down.

The ground under him was black, charcoal shapes that crumbled to ash under his feet, the black earth extending around him in a wide circle, scoured like the ground after a firepit.

Beware the dead grass.

In cold terror he spun, and saw a Remnant, its pale and terrible face so close that he could see the thin veins of black that crept up its neck toward its mouth. Its hand reached for him; the black gauntlet reached out for him, and he drew his sword to knock it away, but his blow glanced off the metal without any effect, and he stumbled back.

It was reaching out again. A cold wave of terror passed over him. *Do not let them touch you,* Justice had said. Will had watched green leaves withering before his eyes, dying from a single touch. It was worse—it was so much worse up close. You could almost taste the death, the grass blackening with the Remnant's every step, as if everything the Remnants touched fell to decay and death.

Now it simply grabbed his sword and jerked him forward. *Death grip,* Will thought, panicked, knowing that its touch would rot and wither his flesh. In the next second, its gauntlet closed around his throat.

At once, Bowhill disappeared, and he was somewhere else—an ancient battlefield under a red sky, surrounded by the clashes and cries of fighting. Before him towered a true Dark Guard in full armor, not Simon's poor imitation playing dress-up with a rusty gauntlet. It was the armor the Remnants wore, whole and unblemished. And now he confronted its bearer. A terrifying fighter of immense power, with an armored hand around his throat. They were locked together, the Dark Guard's eyes burning into his.

Will felt its battering power and expected to die in its grip.

But it was the Dark Guard who gave a terrible cry of recognition, letting him go and cowering back.

Will acted on instinct, not knowing much about sword work but remembering Violet saying, *Up and under the plate.* He drove the blade forward.

The vision stopped.

He was panting, sprawled on his hands and knees, on the ground back at Bowhill. The Remnant lay beside him, with Will's sword rising from his chest like a cross marking a grave. A circle of dying grass was spreading outward from the gauntlet. *I killed him.* It felt unreal and sudden. Will lifted his hand to his own throat.

The Remnant's touch should have killed him as it had killed the grass, but there was nothing to show for its grip besides normal bruising: there was no crumbling ash, no black ring of dead flesh. Nothing.

He remembered his fingertips brushing the Shadow Stone, the Elder Steward crying out, *Don't touch it! Even the briefest touch will kill!* But he had touched it. The truth swelled, one more confirmation of the awful knowledge that he hadn't wanted to face. Nausea rose in him and he vomited onto the black earth. It was long moments before he sat back onto his knees.

He looked at the Remnant, and then, before he could let himself think about what he was doing, he reached out, took hold of its gauntlet, and pulled it off.

Nothing happened. Will didn't wither or crumble, nor did the dead man change. The dead man . . . for he was a man, or he had been once. He had lived a life before he'd put on the gauntlet. Will had half hoped that the black tendrils would withdraw from the man's too-pale skin, miraculously freeing him—that he might even come shuddering back to life now that the gauntlet no longer controlled him. But he didn't. He stayed dead. Dead as the grass, staring up at the sky.

Will wrenched his sword free, took the gauntlet, and went on.

He was bleeding from a cut along his ribs, and his thigh, and limping a little by the time he reached the farmhouse. The way was down a grassy slope, across the deep cut of the stream, then up the other bank. He was close now to the place where she had died. He focused with dogged determination on his goal, ignoring the fresh injuries and exhaustion.

The closer he got, the more his mind crowded with terrible echoes, the screams, the smell of blood and burnt earth, the wrenching horror of hands around his throat. *Run!*

The farmhouse looked so familiar, set on the side of a rise, the gray skies overhead the same shade as the stone house cottage with its slate roof tiles. There was the creek where he had hauled water, more like a rivulet cut into the slope, runoff that always trickled down after rain. There was the crumbling drystone wall that he had promised to fix when they had first come here. It was just as he remembered it, except that the windows were dark and the front door was missing.

Inside, it was dead silent. Small animals and birds nested here; dust and leaves covered the floor. But the dark rooms were eerily preserved, the table still laid as it had been, her shawl still thrown over a chair. He shivered, remembering her sweeping that shawl around her shoulders in the mornings, preparing to go into the village.

Walking forward now was like forcing himself through a barrier, toward a place that he did not want to go.

Through the back door, into the enclosed garden.

Every nerve screamed at him not to go out there, but he did, looking out at a view that almost made him dizzy. It was the place that had haunted his mind all these months, where he had run and dropped to his knees by her side, and said, "*Mother!*"

As he had dreaded, as he had hoped, the garden wasn't empty. There was a single figure there. A man kneeling on the earth, and as Will watched, he rose and turned. And they faced each other.

Simon.

He had imagined this meeting so often. He'd thought of it even before he'd known Simon's name, as he'd hidden in the mud and rain, vowing to find out who had done this to his mother. He'd thought of it in London, when he'd learned that Simon was a rich man, and he'd wondered how a boy might take him down. He'd thought of it when Justice had told him Simon was the Dark King's descendant, part of an ancient world, a monster who had conjured a shadow to kill the Stewards, a godhead who inspired so much loyalty in his followers that they branded their own flesh.

But he just saw a man, and that was chilling in its own right: that an ordinary person had done this. Simon was a man of about thirty-seven years, with dark hair and fine, luminous eyes under thick lashes. He wore black, his jacket made of rich velvet, with long black leather boots, and jeweled rings on his fingers. A familiar look. His money and taste had dressed James, Will thought. And Katherine.

And maybe that was the first hint of similarity he had with that dark power from the past: the way he viewed people as objects to be taken, used, or snuffed out, as a housekeeper snuffed a candle.

"Boy! What are you doing here? How did you get past the guards?"

One hand pressed to the cut on his ribs, Will came forward. The other hand clutched tightly to what he held, trophies of his fights. It was hard to put weight on his left leg, and his limp was pronounced.

Will said, "You don't know who I am."

And he threw the three pieces of black armor to the ground between them: gauntlet, shoulder piece, helm. As the armor pieces hit the ground, the grass beneath them withered, until they lay in a circle of black earth.

Simon looked from the armor back up at Will, eyes widening.

"I know you do it all the time," said Will, "but I'd never killed anyone before."

Will could see the thoughts turning in Simon's mind. How had the Remnants been defeated? How could someone touch the armor? How was this boy still alive?

Then Simon looked—really looked—at Will for the first time, and understanding bloomed in his eyes.

"Will Kempen," said Simon, with dark, rich pleasure. "I thought I was going to have to hunt you down."

"You tried," said Will. "You killed a lot of people."

"But instead, you've come right to me."

The land around them felt very empty, as if each living thing had fled, so that they were alone under the heavy black sky, no sound from the fields or the trees, only the wind shifting the leaves.

"I was tired of running," said Will.

His leg hurt, the slice on his thigh painful, and under the hand he'd pressed to his ribs he could feel slick blood. He ignored it, his eyes fixed on Simon. He was breathing shallowly, his goal in his sights.

"Your mother led me on quite the chase. She got away from me in London after I killed her sister. She even hid you from me at first, until I got reports that she might have a child. That was clever of her. . . . She knew killing her sister, Mary, wasn't enough to bring back the Dark King. That I'd need to kill all of you. She kept one step ahead of me for seventeen years."

A burst of anger at that; he had to force it down. Will thought about what his mother had done—what she had *really* done all those years on the run—had tried to do right up to the end—and he drew in a tight breath. "She was stronger than you knew."

"Until she came here. Hiding in these hills. You know, they call this place the Dark Peak. A fitting name for the birthplace of the Dark King."

Will looked around at the green hills rising to forbidding peaks, the closeness of the sky that hung over the valley where the stream cut its path through the undulating earth. And behind him the brown and gray stone of the house where he'd lived until his mother had bled out on the ground under Simon's feet.

"You think he'll be reborn here?" said Will.

"He'll return," said Simon. "And take his throne."

"After you kill me," said Will.

Simon smiled.

"You know, we're similar, you and I."

"Are we?" said Will.

"You're Blood of the Lady," said Simon. "I'm Blood of the Dark King. We're both descendants of the ancient world. Power runs in our veins." Simon smiled in a way that made Will doubly conscious of the blood under his feet that had seeped into the earth while his mother died. Then Simon's smile grew hard and brittle. "Yet with every generation, the blood weakens. Mingled with the blood of humans, ordinariness, mortality . . . our lines have dwindled until we have no power of our own. We're reduced to using objects. Objects! Remnants of a world that should be our own. Magic is our inheritance, yet it has been taken from us."

"You think this is yours," said Will. "That it's owed to you."

"Humans have overrun this world, an infestation, obliterating the great cultures of the past. I'm the one who's going to cleanse it and return it to the way it should have been. Since I was a boy, my father told me about my destiny. The Dark King ruled a better world. And with your death, I'm going to bring it back."

"Bring back a world of darkness?" said Will. "A world of terror and control?"

"A world of magic," said Simon, "where those with the blood of old will ascend and conquer. Humans will serve us as is fitting. The great palaces, the impossible wonders, the treasures that were taken from us— your death will restore it all."

Simon's eyes burned with greedy intensity. "And when He comes, the world will know *true* power. For He is greater than any human mind can comprehend. He will make them all bow down before Him. He is my true father and He will take me as my heir and deliver it to me . . . my birthright."

Will laughed: a dry, hollow sound.

Simon's head snapped around to him.

"Your birthright? You're not the Dark King," said Will. "You're just a pretender to the throne."

Will drew his sword. Long and straight, a sword of the Stewards with a star emblazoned on the hilt. He faced down Simon, and he thought: *The Stewards are dead, and my mother is dead, and all the warriors of the Light are dead.*

But I'm here. And I'm going to do this.

"A sword?" said Simon, with a laugh. "But of course. James told me. They tried to train you, but you couldn't use her power."

"You can't use his," said Will.

"That's where you're wrong," said Simon, and pushed back his coat, reaching for the onyx hilt and in one smooth motion drawing the Corrupted Blade.

It was Death, thirty inches of black steel, and Simon unleashed its full devastating force. Black fire spewed from its blade, and Will cried out at the annihilating blast of it, as if the air itself was made of pain.

Birds fell out of the sky. The ground began to split open. The tearing power of it ripped at Will's clothes, which were in tatters, and he flung up his hand uselessly, driven to his knees as Simon held the sword, barely controlling it as its black fire erupted, killing everything.

And in the haze, Will seemed to see those eyes of black flame. The image filled his mind, overpowering everything; the pain in his head was blinding, he let out a terrible cry, and the whole world was burning. A nightmare unleashed to destroy every living thing, a dark inferno that would scour away all life—

—and then it stopped, as suddenly as it had begun.

Silence; nothing left alive, just cratered earth.

Will opened his eyes slowly, his fingers moving in gritty, blackened dirt. Slowly, he lifted his head.

He was kneeling in a blasted, ruined crater, the valley gouged open, the birds and animals dead, the trees shattered into splinters, the farm-house sundered. For miles in every direction, he and Simon were the only things alive.

Alive. He saw the look of incomprehension on Simon's face.

It was Will's turn to laugh, except that it might have come out as a dry sob, shaky with the effects of adrenaline, his heart-pounding preparedness to die. But he hadn't. He was still alive. The Blade hadn't worked on him.

He knew why. His mother's last words, her last moments, all of it made sense. What she had known all these years he now knew too. The truth, tested and proven in the fires of the Blade.

"Why didn't it work?" said Simon.

Slowly, Will pushed himself up from where the blast had driven him to his knees. He looked right across the flattened landscape at Simon. His chest was heaving. He was bleeding from new cuts, where small rocks and sticks had hit him during the blast.

"You know, I came to London looking for you," said Will.

"Why didn't it *work?*" said Simon. He was staring back at Will in disbelief.

"At first I thought I could destroy your business. I sabotaged your cargo, untying ropes so that your gunpowder would be lost in the river."

"That was an accident," said Simon.

"That was me," said Will. "When your fiancée left you? That was me too."

"What do you mean, left me," said Simon.

"I kissed her in the garden of the house you bought her. She came to me in the Hall."

"Katherine?" said Simon.

"I think you valued James more. You liked the idea that he was Sarcean's favorite. I heard they called him Simon's Prize. He's left you now too."

"How do you know James is missing?" said Simon sharply, real suspicion in his voice for the first time. Will felt a surge of triumph at that; he'd been right, James had taken the Collar and not returned to Simon. His heart was pounding.

"What could I take from you? What is it that you care about? Your wealth? Your lover? Your plans? What's equal to a mother?"

"My God, what is this? Some pitiful boy's revenge?" said Simon. "You think you can stand in the way of my destiny? The plans my father and I have put in motion can't be stopped."

Simon's voice was full of scorn and mild annoyance. Will glimpsed himself through Simon's eyes: a nuisance, an obstacle that he would soon clear from his way. Simon still held the Blade; it was a straight line pointing downward from his hand.

"You're right," said Will. "It's a boy's revenge. Just not against you."

He picked up his own sword, shifting the hilt in his hand.

"Your father was the one who ordered my mother's death," said Will. "That's why I'm here to kill his son."

And he took his sword and drove it into Simon's body.

Simon lifted the sheathed Blade, but the ancient weapon wasn't something he'd ever expected to have to fight with. It was a power to be unleashed, and once it had failed, he didn't know what to do. The sheathed Blade barely glanced against Will's weapon. Simon's look was one of shock as Will's sword went in.

It was hard, but easier than it had been before he'd killed three other men. He knew the resistance of the body, the strength of muscle and sinew that it took to push the weapon in. He knew that men didn't die right away but clutched their wound, the blood pumping out, each pulse weaker than the last, their life fading slowly. Simon was on his knees, looking up at Will in disbelief, but when he opened his mouth, blood and not words came out of it.

"I might not have stopped your father," said Will, looking down at him. "But I think he'll feel this at least a little."

"You're too late," Simon managed, his voice thick with blood. "The Shadow Kings have been released. I ordered them to hunt down the Lady's descendant. . . ." He was grinning up at Will, his teeth red. "Your death will bring him back. You're the final sacrifice . . . the Shadow Kings . . . You can't escape. . . . The Blood of the Lady will return the Dark King."

He still hadn't understood. He'd seen Will touch the armor. He'd seen him survive the Blade. But he hadn't understood what Will had come to realize piece by piece. The truth that his mother had known when she'd died on this very spot, looking at Will with despair in her eyes.

"I'm not Blood of the Lady," said Will, looking at the sheathed Blade on the ground. "The Shadow Kings aren't coming for me."

CHAPTER THIRTY-ONE

VIOLET WOKE FEELING that something was wrong, as if the un-easy remnants of a dream lingered. She glanced over at the place where Will was sleeping.

He wasn't there; his pallet was starkly empty.

She sat upright, her stomach clenching. The pallet wasn't just empty. It looked like it hadn't been slept in.

No, she told herself. *He wouldn't. Would he?* But she was already pushing out of bed and pulling on her boots and tunic.

The girls were still asleep; the sisters Katherine and Elizabeth look-ing oddly peaceful despite the circumstances, while Grace and Sarah lay in a tense sleep of exhaustion. Violet padded quickly downstairs and made for the gatekeep door, only to find it already opening. But it wasn't Will entering the gatekeep; it was Cyprian, back from a morning excursion, and he spoke to her in a low, urgent voice. "Will's horse is gone."

"What do you mean?"

"Valdithar. Will's horse. He's gone from the stables."

The ominous feeling redoubled into a sick certainty, the memory of

Will's untouched sleeping pallet like a terrible premonition. Violet forced herself to stay calm.

"Has anyone seen Will?"

She addressed the others after returning with Cyprian, and waking Elizabeth and Katherine with a few sharp shakes to their shoulders. Grace and Sarah had slept in their janissary uniforms, both waking jumpily at the sound of the door. Now they were a tense huddle in blue on Grace's pallet. Katherine was sitting up at the small table, extraordinarily pretty in her white underdress and shawl in the morning light, her sister Elizabeth frowning beside her, her eyebrows too heavy for her small face.

Violet got blank stares from all of them.

"No one?" she said. "No one's seen him?"

"I talked to him before I slept," offered Katherine.

"What did he say?"

Katherine turned red. "Just good night."

Violet remembered looking up and seeing the two of them together, Will at Katherine's bedside, murmuring to her in the candlelight. Her chest tightened, and she pushed the emotion to one side.

The announcement came from an unexpected place.

"He's gone," said Elizabeth.

"What do you mean?"

"He left. He ran off."

"How do you know that?"

"I saw him ride out last night."

Violet was staring at her. Elizabeth's tone said, *Good riddance.* She looked back at Violet defiantly.

Katherine was shaking her head. "He wouldn't leave us."

"Well, he has. I saw him in the stables. He said he was going for a ride. That was a lie, and I told him I knew it was, and he said if I said anything he'd get Katherine in trouble, so he's a bully as well as a sneak."

"Elizabeth!" said Katherine.

"You know what happens if Simon finds him," said Cyprian in a low voice. *The Blood of the Lady will return the Dark King.*

Violet tried to be reassuring. "If Will went for a ride, it was for some purpose. He wouldn't just leave us, and he doesn't do things for no reason. We wait here for him to return."

Elizabeth scoffed. Violet went to search the grounds to make sure Will was missing, and gestured to Cyprian to join her.

Waiting for him at the door, she saw Katherine looking out toward the gate with a strange expression on her face, her hair shining gold in the morning sun.

Violet turned away. A moment later, Cyprian joined her and they each took a different part of the Hall, splitting up to cover more ground.

They searched for the better part of the day, but Will was well and truly gone. With every silent, empty area of the fort that she checked, the truth was rising in her.

When she finally returned to Cyprian in the courtyard, Violet said what she was really thinking. "Will hasn't gone for a ride; he's gone to fight Simon."

Cyprian paled. In the gray afternoon light, his face looked drawn, and it occurred to her that staying here with all the memories of the dead must be hard on him. He was still dressed like a Steward, in his pristine silvery tunic. She'd watched him wake early the last few mornings to train, a solitary figure performing the Steward rituals alone.

"Why would he do that? His blood is the only thing that can release the Shadow Kings." Cyprian was shaking his head. "You said it yourself, all we have to do is keep Will safe, and out of Simon's hands—"

"His blood isn't the only thing that can release them," said Violet.

She couldn't believe she hadn't seen it sooner. She thought about all the plans they had made last night, and felt so stupid. Will had been indulging her, nodding and listening, and all the while planning to leave on his own.

"I don't understand," said Cyprian.

"Will's mother," said Violet. "Simon killed Will's mother. Will never talks about it, but—"

"But if it was violent," said Cyprian, "there would have been blood."

The Blood of the Lady. She saw Cyprian realize it. Simon already had what he needed. He could release the Shadow Kings any time he wanted. He just needed to harness Will's mother's blood.

Had Will guessed that immediately? Had he heard Katherine's words and understood right then what he had to do? But why hadn't he told anyone? Why had he gone to face Simon in secret, and alone?

"The place where his mother died," said Violet. "Will's gone there to try to stop Simon."

"Where?" said Cyprian urgently. "Do you know where that is?"

Nights sprawled out on their beds, talking until dawn. *My mother and I, we moved around a lot,* Will had said at a London inn. But he'd never spoken about his mother's death. As if there was something in the story that he was holding close, something private that he didn't want to tell. And now he was traveling there and they had no way to find him. *Will, why didn't you take me with you?*

"No," she said. "He never told me."

The truth was that she knew very little about his life. She knew his mother had been killed, but he'd never told her how. She knew they'd moved from place to place, but he'd never told her where. He'd never said what he'd done in the months between his mother's death and his own capture. He'd never talked about what had happened to him on Simon's ship. Or on the run before that.

In all their conversations, he'd sprawled on the bed with his head propped on his hand and asked questions as he teased out her thoughts. She'd been the one who talked, telling him far more than he'd ever told her. For all that they'd fought side by side, she knew almost nothing about him.

"We need to go after him," said Violet.

"We don't even know where to go."

A burst of frustration. "We have to do someth—"

She broke off, hearing a strange sound, almost like the far-off cry of a hawk on the wind. Her body responded like prey sensing a predator.

"Do you hear that?"

"What?" said Cyprian.

"That," said Violet. "It's coming from—"

"—the gate," said Cyprian as the sound rang out again, louder.

Above them, sudden as a firework, the sky flared red. She looked up and saw the ghostly impression of a dome across the sky, shot through with sparking red.

"What's happening?"

"The wards," said Cyprian, an awed fear in his voice as he stared up at the red sky as if this was new to him. "I think—I think the wards are under attack."

The red was spreading. It looked like a great dome was burning, red streaking across its surface, the wards visible for the first time.

"Will they hold?"

"I don't know."

Inside, Elizabeth was in the center of the room, while Sarah was pressed with her back in the corner. "She won't move," said Elizabeth. "She just keeps staring like that." Sarah's eyes were glazed the way they had been when they'd found her and Grace in the devastated Hall. "I'll pinch her if you like." Elizabeth took a step forward.

"No," said Violet quickly, grabbing Elizabeth's small arm.

The chilling sound cut through the air again, louder and closer, and it wasn't the cry of a hawk. It was a scream that came from no human throat.

"What is that?" said Elizabeth.

It sounded like it was coming from outside the wards. As if there was something out there on the marshes. Something old and terrible, scream-ing to get in.

"Don't let it in," said Sarah, her voice sounding strange, "don't let it get inside—"

Violet's stomach turned. It couldn't be. It couldn't. Violet found that she and Cyprian were staring at each other. They had spent the day look-ing for a way to track down Will; they had forgotten the true danger that hung over them all.

"A shadow," said Violet.

The air was colder, she could feel it. Was it also getting darker? Inside the gatekeep, the shadows seemed to thicken until they were tangible. As if they were responding to a presence outside.

She looked at Cyprian. The last shadow who had attacked the Hall had been his brother. She remembered the hollow look in his eyes as he had stared at the burned imprint of Marcus in the Tree Chamber. He had the same hollowed-out look now.

"We're safe in here," said Cyprian. "It can't get through the wards."

"Marcus got through."

"Marcus was a Steward," said Cyprian. "He didn't break through the wards; they opened for him. They recognized his Steward blood even though he was a shadow. Nothing else can get through. We're safe as long as they hold."

The terrifying, uncanny scream rang out again. Outside, something was rending at the Hall's protections, trying to get in. Violet imagined a swirl of pure black in the archway of the gate, hungry for entry.

"Safe from what?" Elizabeth's two small hands were clenched.

Violet looked down at her and felt sick. What could she tell a child? That there were things in this world darker and more terrifying than she could imagine? Things that could slaughter your friends?

"Safe from what?" Elizabeth said again.

Violet drew in a breath. "Simon wants to hurt Will, and has sent a creature here to attack him. I won't lie to you. It is dangerous, with unnatural powers. But this Hall was built to keep things like it out."

"A 'shadow,'" said Elizabeth.

Violet nodded, and tried to look calm, even as a part of her knew it was worse than that. Because if Simon had released it from the Shadow Stone, then—

She looked around at the gatekeep, built centuries ago by a civilization that they knew so little about, and a new thought turned her utterly cold.

Because what was at the gate was worse than a shadow.

She took Cyprian by the shoulder and led him off to one side, keeping her voice low, and out of earshot of the others.

"Are you sure it can't get in?"

"As long as the wards hold—"

"This was their Hall," said Violet. "Before it was the Hall of the Stewards, it was the Hall of Kings."

Cyprian went pale.

As that unnatural scream shattered the silence, she felt the true horror of what lay outside. *This place is theirs*, thought Violet with a shiver. *More than it was ever yours.*

A Shadow King.

Far deadlier than Marcus, it had laid waste to forts far greater than this one. It couldn't be stopped by force or by magic; it was a Shadow King, a commander of armies, forged into darkness by the Dark King himself. And now it was coming home.

Violet forced herself to think. "Cyprian, go and get Grace and Katherine. We can't stay here in the gatekeep. We retreat to the inner fort."

Cyprian nodded and went at once.

"We thought we could run from it," said Sarah, in a too-loud voice. "We went to the inner fort too. And when we came out, they were all dead, Stewards, janissaries, horses, dead just like we'll be—"

There was the scrape of wood on stone as Elizabeth pulled up a chair, stood on it, and, with the benefit of this extra height, slapped Sarah hard across the face. Sarah stared back at her, shocked into silence, clutching her cheek as Elizabeth said, "Shut up. Shut up or you'll bring it. And then you'll be dead first because you're the loud one."

Violet blinked, grateful for the sudden ringing lack of sound.

"All right. Listen. The wards are holding for now. Get food and water. We're going to take whatever we can carry to the inner fort. It's safer there. It has extra protections, and there are places where we can hide."

Elizabeth nodded, scurrying to gather up what she could, with Sarah glassy-eyed. Violet packed up all the provisions she could carry, folding them up in a blanket. But as the awful, echoing shriek of the shadow rang out, there was only one thought in her mind.

Will.

If Simon had released the Shadow Kings—

"It doesn't mean he's dead," said Violet to herself, a hope, a desperate wish, "it just means that Simon found the blood."

Grabbing up packs and provisions, Elizabeth and Sarah were ready in a few minutes, and Violet led them out into the courtyard. There she stopped, and looked up in horror.

The wards were like red fire across the sky. Coruscating like flame, like the tails of dead comets. They lit everything with a strange red light, reflecting against everyone's faces. They were coming down. They were all coming down. It was like the end of the world.

"They're not going to hold," said Elizabeth.

"Go," said Violet.

They ran across the red-lit courtyard. Cyprian and Grace were approaching from the direction of the Hall. Their faces were drawn, and Cyprian was shaking his head. It was his turn to speak in a tense, private voice.

"Katherine's missing. She took one of the Steward horses."

"*Missing?*" Violet's stomach clenched. "How long has she been gone?"

"I don't know. When was the last time you saw her?"

When was the last time any of them had seen Katherine? *This morning, when I told her Will was gone.* Violet's stomach twisted. She thought of the look in Katherine's eyes whenever she looked at Will; the pink on her cheeks whenever she said his name; the fact that she had come here at all, through the mud and rain at night, leaving the comforts of her home on the word of a boy she had met twice.

"She went to follow Will," said Violet.

"We don't know that. She might have just—gone back to London—"

"And leave her sister behind? She knows." Violet suddenly recalled the look of determination she had seen on Katherine's face this morning as the girl rose from the table. "She knows where Will's mother was killed. He must have told her."

The image of Will and Katherine murmuring to one another last night came back to her. She ignored the twinge of hurt that Will had told Katherine about his mother, but not her. How long had he known Katherine? A few days? She tried not to feel the way she had felt locked outside her father's house, knowing she could never return.

"What's this about my sister?" Elizabeth pushed her way into the exchange.

"She's gone," said Violet.

"But—" said Elizabeth.

"She's outside the walls. A Shadow King is trying to get in. Wherever your sister is, she's safer right now than we are."

She immediately regretted saying it. Everyone was frightened, and Elizabeth was a child. Elizabeth's face turned, if anything, paler, as she stood there in a muddy short dress, separated from her family. Violet felt awful.

"We're going to the inner fort," said Violet, trying to temper her message. "We'll be safe there. That thing outside isn't looking for us. It's looking for Will. When it realizes he's not here, it will leave." That's what she hoped, anyway. "We're going to hide and wait it out in the safest place in the Hall."

But she could hear Sarah's voice in her head. *We thought we could run from it.* She could see Elizabeth remembering those words too.

"Can I bring Nell?" said Elizabeth in a small voice.

"What?"

"Sarah said that last time they killed the horses. Can I bring Nell?"

"No. I'm sorry," said Violet. "There isn't time."

Getting to the chamber that held the Tree Stone meant going back into the citadel, something they had all avoided since the attack. Together they climbed the main steps to the immense entry doors that stood unnervingly half-open with the silent citadel behind them. Violet's skin crawled as they entered the first of the ghostly empty hallways that had already taken on the stillness of a tomb.

The red light seeped inside the buildings, and any windows were now rectangles of crimson. Violet saw Elizabeth take in the eerily lit destruction and go pale, but the girl said nothing and even on her short legs kept up with the others as they hurried through the corridors.

The five of them hurried past the halls and the dormitories, entering a more deserted part of the citadel. The chilling screams of the shadow could be heard in the distance, but muffled by the thick stone walls of the Hall they became strange echoes, coming from everywhere and nowhere. The red-lit rooms and corridors became long dark passageways so deep in the Hall that outside light didn't reach them.

Violet stopped at the entry to the chamber that held the Tree Stone.

She had considered taking them down into the vault and hiding them all in the underground rooms behind that heavy stone door. But the vault had held the Shadow Stone, and she had felt the irrational sense that the Shadow King would know if they hid there.

Besides, if a Shadow King could pass through any wall, a stone door would not keep it out. So instead she had brought them here, trusting in the Elder Steward's decision to retreat to the oldest part of the citadel.

But when she looked at the dark, dead branches of the Tree Stone, she couldn't help wondering if she was repeating a hopeless past. The stones of the doorway were cracked and shattered; his sword that she had not retrieved lay discarded. The wall was dark with his dried blood. A thick silence hung over everything.

She was looking at the place where Justice had died.

He was a better fighter than she would ever be, and he had not survived for long. The shadow had only been defeated by the great power of the Elder Steward, and the Elder Steward was gone.

She told herself that the Shadow King was looking for Will. Sarah, Grace, and Elizabeth weren't Lions or Stewards, and there was a chance that when the Shadow King realized that Will wasn't in the Hall, it would leave without killing any of the girls.

She nodded at Cyprian, then looked at Sarah, Grace, and Elizabeth.

"All right. The three of you get in there, and we'll close the doors."

Elizabeth looked up at her. "Aren't you coming?"

"Cyprian and I will be right outside."

"But—"

"Get in," said Violet, giving Elizabeth a push between the shoulder blades.

She didn't push her hard, and she wasn't expecting what happened, a sequence that seemed to play out in slow motion, Elizabeth stumbling forward, her small foot tripping.

Elizabeth cried out and flung out her hand to steady herself, grasping on to the trunk of the Tree Stone.

Violet felt it happening: the scent like blooms in an ancient garden; the shivering impression of bright tendrils running through the Tree like veins; of white flowers opening. Yet she wasn't ready.

Light burst into the room; an explosion of light; a brilliant eruption as the Tree Stone lit up, brighter than a hundred stars. It was blinding; Violet cried out and lifted her arm and pressed her face into the crook of her elbow instinctively.

When she looked up a second later, her blinking eyes opened on a warm and beautiful glow, infusing the Tree's trunk, its branches and leaves and its hundreds of new flowers, each one a new point of light. It lit the expressions of shock and wonder in the faces of the others, and the little girl standing under it.

Elizabeth's hand was still on the Tree, and the light was surrounding her; it was part of her.

"What is it?" said Elizabeth. "What's happening?"

Oh God, thought Violet. She was staring at Elizabeth, her washed-out face, the light in her long, dull hair.

She remembered Will trying to light the Tree Stone, the hours that he had spent gathering all his will trying to stir a single spark. In all that time, the Tree Stone had not given so much as a flicker.

Violet thought of all she knew about Elizabeth. At ten, she was still in short dresses and had the personality of a stump in the road, blocking your way. She lived with her parents—no, not with her parents, with her guardians, her aunt and uncle—who had taken her in after—

"Who was your mother?" Violet heard herself say.

"What?" said Elizabeth.

"You live with your aunt and uncle. Who was your mother?"

"No one you know." Elizabeth stuck her chin out. "What does it matter? She was a respectable gentlewoman."

There was something defensive about the way she said it, as if she'd heard questions about her birth before. Or as though she'd been the one asking them, thought Violet, smart enough even at ten years old to sense that the things her aunt and uncle were telling her weren't true.

Simon had been hunting children. And if someone was hunting your children, what did you do? Did you keep them with you, in danger? Or did you give them away to kind strangers who would pretend to be their aunt and uncle? Wasn't the best way to hide a child to disguise them as one of the thousands of ordinary children growing up in London?

Protect the sisters, Will had said.

Violet felt all the hair on her body stand up as she stared at Elizabeth's plain child's face, and her torn, muddy clothes, streaming with light.

She turned to Cyprian. "She's Blood of the Lady." Violet could see the mix of shock and confusion in Cyprian's eyes. "I don't know how, but she's Blood of the Lady. It's not Will the Shadow King is after," Violet said. "It's her."

The inhuman screams were louder, the last of the wards shredding.

Violet looked around at the ancient doors that would be no kind of protection once the wards were down. Violet had thought they could hide here and hope for the Shadow King to pass them by, but no one could hide this cascade of light.

And if the Shadow King was after Elizabeth, it would not pass her over; it would do everything in its power to find and kill her.

She couldn't let that happen. Justice had trained her to fight for the Lady. And the Lady had come to her, even if she didn't understand how or why. Wasn't a Lion supposed to be a protector? Her strength and Steward training together: she understood what it was for now. What she had to do.

"Cyprian, you have to find a way to get her out."

"What do you mean?"

"The Shadow King is here for one reason: to end the line of the Lady. Elizabeth can't hide or wait it out. The only chance she has is to run." She was thinking it through as she spoke. "It will break through the wards. I'll hold it off in the great hall. You use the distraction to get the horses and go." She looked out at the hallway that was torn to pieces, the walls cracked and the furniture splintered. The shadow had tried to get at Justice and failed. At least at first. Now he was ashes and flame, and the memory of a hand proffered to help her. "Justice held Marcus off for a while."

Cyprian's face was white. "There are only two horses left."

"Then you each ride double."

It wasn't what he had meant; she knew it; she heard him say it, almost as if he was at a distance. "That doesn't leave a horse for you."

She looked at him. She didn't have to speak. They both knew she wouldn't return from this fight. There was no one alive who could stand against a Shadow King. But she might be able to delay them long enough to buy Elizabeth time.

"I won't leave you here," said Cyprian.

"You have to." She remembered the Elder Steward's words to her. "I'm the strongest one here." *You are the strongest fighter the Light has left.* She was a Lion. Grace and Sarah were janissaries, and Cyprian was a Steward who had rejected the Cup. "I'm the only one who can buy you the time that you need."

"Then let me fight with you."

He meant it. She could see that. She looked at his noble, familiar face, realizing that it would be the last time that she would see it. She hadn't thought she'd grow fond of his perfectly ordered hair, his immaculate clothing, the proud upright of his Steward posture.

"You can't leave the others," she said. "They need a fighter with them too."

"Violet—"

"This is what I have to do."

His eyes held the pain of acknowledgment as he looked back at her. "I was wrong about Lions," he said. "They're brave and they're true."

"Go," she said.

They parted ways, with the sky on fire. He went to the stables.

She went to the great hall.

It was covered in refuse. The remnants of the fight littered the ground: the last stand of the Stewards against the dark. Violet remembered her first glimpse of the great hall, walking in dwarfed by its size and awed by its ancient beauty. Now it was a graveyard; the bodies were gone, but the impression of death remained, the silence and stillness that of a tomb. *This is the end of the Hall*, she thought as she walked through its forest of giant marble columns. The Stewards were dead, and once the wards fell, the Hall itself would be overrun.

Above the dais, the four empty thrones took on a frightening significance. *The Shadow Kings are coming home.* They had ruled here once, before the Dark King had twisted them into his servants. It made her all the more certain that it would come here, to the great hall, and that this was the place where she might for a moment or two slow it down.

She closed and barred the giant doors just as the Stewards had done. Unlike the Stewards, she knew that closing the doors was useless. *It can get through the walls. It can get through anything.* She only hoped that extra barrier might buy her a little more time.

And then she waited, her breathing shallow, listening to the inhuman screams of the Shadow King. When they started to get closer, she knew that it was coming. It was the last sound that the Stewards had heard as they stood in their ranks facing the doors, not knowing what was on the other side. But there were no Stewards left to fight what was coming.

She was surprised how much she wanted Cyprian to be with her. Or Will. How much she wanted someone to stand beside her, so that at the end, she wouldn't be alone.

But Justice had been right. How you faced darkness was a test.

She felt the temperature start to drop, the shadows start to lengthen.

And against the cold and rising dark, she drew her sword.

CHAPTER THIRTY-TWO

"SO YOU KNOW who you are," said a voice behind Will.

He turned.

A pale figure was approaching across the blackened landscape, surreal yet somehow inevitable. It was Devon . . . Devon, the last unicorn, arriving like a herald from some ancient battle.

In London, Devon had recognized him. That scene played out in Will's mind, now full of different meaning. The terrible, sickening truth of his own identity made him shiver now that he'd tested it for himself.

Who else could have mastered the dark armor? Or touched the Shadow Stone? Who else could have survived the fire of the Corrupted Blade?

"Tell me I'm Simon's son," said Will. The plea sounded very far away. It seemed to fade like the last of his hopes as the truth rose between them.

"You know you're not," said Devon, "My King."

My King. The horror of confirmation, the truth that he hadn't wanted to face.

Simon hadn't failed seventeen years ago when he'd killed Will's aunt

Mary. He'd succeeded. He'd brought the Dark King back that day, with the Lady's blood.

Will wasn't a champion of the Light.

He was the Dark King, reborn into this time.

He had found his mother bleeding in the garden behind the house, three dead men on the ground and more men on the way, though he hadn't known it then. He'd heard the screams and dropped the wood he'd been collecting, running toward the sound. There had been so much blood, on her hands, on her neck and chin, spreading through the blue fabric of her dress. "What happened?" He was on his knees beside her. "What can I do?"

"The knife," she'd said. "Give me the knife."

She was too hurt to reach it. So he'd picked it up and given it to her. Bloody fingers stroking against his cheek, she had drawn his head down toward hers, as if to whisper some final benediction.

Then she'd plunged the knife toward his throat.

The hand he'd thrown up to protect himself was all that had saved him. The knife had gone through his palm instead of his neck, like a nail through wood. But the cry he'd let out had been drowned out by his mother's scream of frustration. She had let go of the knife, her hands closing around his throat, squeezing the breath out of him. He tried to pry them off, his world narrowing to a black tunnel. He'd thought, stupidly, that she was fighting some specter of the imagination, that she was confused, still struggling with the men who had attacked her.

"It's me!" he'd gasped. "Mother, it's me!" He'd thought if she just knew who he was, she'd let go.

She had known who he was. It's why she'd tried to kill him.

Scrambling backward, he'd pushed her off, gasping in air and clutching his bleeding hand to his chest. He had stared at her from a few paces away, half sprawled in the dirt. She had been too weak to come after him, barely able to move.

"I shouldn't have raised you. I should have killed you." She had had blood in her mouth, the same blood that was all over his clothes and smeared on his neck. "You're not my son. You're not the child I had to give up."

"Mother?" he'd said.

Her eyes were widening as if at some vision. "Oh God. Don't hurt them. Don't you hurt my girls. Will, promise." Desperation in her voice.

"I promise," he'd said.

He hadn't understood. He hadn't understood anything. "I've failed. I've failed. *Damn you*," she said to Will bitterly, and there were men coming out of the house toward them. He could see them carrying knives like the one that he'd pulled out of his palm. Like the one that had cut her open. She'd turned her sightless eyes to the men and shouted to them, "*Run!*"

As though they needed a warning. As though he was the one who was dangerous.

Had his mother found him as an infant? Or had she given birth to him after an unnatural pregnancy? Will didn't know. He didn't remember his past life, or the choices he had made in it. But he had learned enough about the Dark King to know that he would have chosen the most twisted path, the one full of vicious horrors. *That thing is not my son.*

"How did you know?"

He said it to Devon, dully. He had to drag himself out of his thoughts to look up at Devon, and when he did, the boy was only a few steps away, pale and inscrutable.

"I'd know you anywhere," said Devon. "After ten thousand years, I'd know you. I knew who you were the moment you walked into Robert's store."

"Why didn't you tell me—"

He broke off. Devon's pure white hair was stark against the black landscape. His skin was so pale it was almost the same color. He looked at Will as if he knew him better than Will knew himself.

"The last time I saw you," said Devon, "your armies were killing my kind; a thousand unicorns lying dead on the battlefield. Simon thought you'd reward him. What a fool! You're as ruthless now as you were then. You let the Stewards take you into their Hall, then you slaughtered them. The Blood of the Lady was your mother, and you had her killed."

That's not what happened, he wanted to say.

"She wasn't my mother," Will said.

It had taken him months to find his way to London and learn the name of the man connected to the attacks. He had taken on dock work for Simon, planning to find a way to get close to him, and learn what he could about himself and his past. The past had come for him instead. But his mother had hidden her secrets too well. Her old servant Matthew and the Stewards had both mistaken Will for her real child.

The Stewards would never have helped him if they had known what he was. No one who knew the truth could be trusted. He'd learned that with his mother's hands around his neck.

A voice behind him said, "Will?"

It was like seeing a ghost from his past, his mother standing in the doorway of the house. The dawn light was behind her, her hair in a long blond plait and her blue eyes like those eyes that had looked at him from the mirror. He blinked.

It wasn't his mother. It was Katherine.

She was standing there pale and terrified. She had dirt streaked across her face, and her skirts were grimy from hem to knee. She must have ridden all day and all night, as he had. She was staring at him.

The world was tilting out from under him. She'd heard. She'd heard. How much had she heard?

"Is what he said true?"

"Katherine—"

"You killed all those people?" Her voice was small and shocked, and she looked afraid the way his mother had looked afraid.

"I didn't kill them, I—"

He saw Katherine look past him, to the place where Simon lay sprawled out on the ground. Around him the earth was blasted, torn up by the Blade, so that he lay almost at the middle of a crater. Katherine made a small sound.

Simon was dead, unequivocally. A man she had known—had walked with; had taken tea with; had believed that she would marry. Now he lay dead on scoured earth by Will's hand. Will could see all of that in her face, the disbelieving horror as she looked back at Will.

"He killed my mother," said Will. Those were the words that came out, when he could have said, *He killed the Stewards. He tried to kill me.*

"So you killed him?"

"Yes."

What else could he answer? He felt sickly exposed, almost shivering at the thought of what she might have overheard.

"It's not true," she said. "You wouldn't kill someone. You're not—"

The Dark King.

The name hung between them, a splinter from the past. Katherine looked at Devon, and Will knew what she had heard. She had heard everything.

"He would have hurt you," said Will. "He would have hurt the people I care about."

Katherine's face was pale and frightened. "You said the Dark King had to be stopped. That he had to be defeated, and that you were the one who was going to do it."

"I meant it," said Will. "I meant that, Katherine—"

That creature from the past that he felt—that he could still feel—trying to control everything. The Dark King like a hand reaching out of the dark, setting in motion his unstoppable plans, and Will trying somehow to believe the Elder Steward that he could be the one to—

A terrible sound cut through the dawn: the scream of an animal; the shriek of a nightmare. It echoed off the peaks, coming from everywhere and nowhere. The sky began to grow darker, as if something was putting out the dawn.

No—

"What is that?" Katherine's head jerked toward the trees.

No, no, no. It was Devon who answered, Devon who had heard that sound before, long ago. Will could see it on his face, a primal, ancient fear. Devon looked like he was keeping himself in place only through an effort of will.

"A Shadow King," Devon said. And then: "Tell her." In his eye, the hard glint of one determined to see things through to the end.

The truth, laid bare between them.

"It's come to kill the Blood of the Lady," said Will.

Promise.

Sent by Simon on its single mission, to seek out his mother's children and end her line.

Will, promise.

"I thought you said that you weren't the Blood of the Lady," said Katherine. "That you were—"

"It's not here for me," said Will. "It's here for you."

She didn't understand. She looked frightened and out of place, her world one of drawing rooms and elegant clothes and fine manners.

"What do you mean?" said Katherine. "Will, what do you mean?"

Around them the torn, blackened earth marked the place where his mother had died. She was standing where his mother had stood. Everything seemed to come full circle, fate turning.

"There's a tree made of stone in the Hall of the Stewards." Will drew in a painful breath. "It's said that when the Lady returns, it will shine."

The Tree Stone had never responded to his touch. It had stayed dark and cold no matter how much he had wished for it to shine.

"It's her symbol." Will met Katherine's eyes. "A hawthorn tree."

And he saw Katherine remember it: the hawthorn tree coming alive in her garden, its flowers bursting into bloom, the petals swirling around them like snow.

"That was you," said Katherine, shaking her head. "You did that. That was—"

"It was never me, Katherine," said Will.

She had woken that tree out of its winter slumber, her power racing bright through its branches. She'd kissed him, and the tree had streamed with light, starbursts of glowing white flowers, radiant and beautiful. He'd jerked away and stared at her in shock, the horror of realization churning in his stomach. What she was; what she could be—

"Your mother sent you away," said Will. "She did it to protect you. Not just from Simon. But also from me. From what she thought I might become. She raised me as her child, but I wasn't. I was something else."

"It's not true," said Katherine.

"She tried to keep me from my fate. She made me promise—" *Promise me.* He remembered her desperation, her frantic need to protect her child. *Will, promise.* Her knife through his palm, her bloody fingers around his neck. "—she made me promise not to hurt you. And I did. I promised you'd be safe. You're the Blood of the Lady and I'm going to protect you."

The inhuman shriek of a Shadow King rang out again, closer. The sky was darkening, as if ink swirled across it. He imagined them racing toward him, shadows rushing through the air.

"There's two of them coming," said Devon, his eyes hard and bright. "They're going to kill her."

"No," said Will.

He could feel their darkness, their sheer destructive power. He let himself feel it, and he let it feel him. Simon was right; he had no magic of his own, no access to whatever lay inside him.

But he knew what he was now. And if the Shadow Kings were powerful, it was a power that they had from him.

You're mine. Mine to command.

He could hear the screams of the two Shadow Kings echoing across the land. *Kill the Blood of the Lady. Kill her and end her line.* They had their orders, given to them by Simon. And they wanted to do it. They were the harbingers, unleashed to usher in an age of darkness and subjugation and rule over it as its masters forever.

No.

We thirst for destruction. We thirst to conquer. We thirst to kill!

Above him the sky was jet-black. They were coming. They were coming. The wind started to whip at him. His skull was filled with a rushing darkness, as if they were inside his head.

You will obey me.

We will kill the Lady and bring this world to its knees.

And in a flash, he was somewhere else—that ancient battlefield under a red sky, where an army of shadows stretched across the land. They were his to command, on the cusp of victory. The sheer power of it was intoxicating, his steed a giant scaled creature that winged across the sky.

He heard the screams as the Shadow Kings led the charge, nightmares with shadow armies at their back.

In the next moment, they showed him a vision of how it would be. Will saw the destruction of the Hall magnified a thousand times, London in ruins, the rolling countryside of his youth blighted, the sky black and the ground littered with the rotting bodies of any who would stand against him. And above that, four thrones, the Shadow Kings ruling in absolute dominion, with only one power greater, rising above it all.

Him.

All this we will give you. The world that was taken from you will be yours once again.

A world he controlled, where he was safe, where those he wanted would stay by his side and those who he mourned would be brought back to life . . .

"Return to the Stone," he gritted out as a dark wind howled around him, and the two Shadow Kings screamed and lashed at his mind like prisoners thrashing in chains. He forced them back, and in that second, he felt it. He was their maker. He was their master. They *recognized* him, and when he took control, they had to obey him, bound to him by their abhorrent bargain, made when they had drunk from the Cup.

"Return to the Stone!"

They wanted to fight. They wanted to kill and to conquer, to create a world where they could reign. But he was their monarch and he drove their darkness back, chasing it down with every atom of his will.

"I am your King, and YOU WILL obey me."

The whirling black split open in the sky; the shadows on the ground shriveled like singed paper. With a last inhuman scream, the two Shadow Kings were compelled, throwing themselves against his command but unable to fight it, forced down into the Shadow Stone.

Will opened his eyes, feeling shaky, and saw light streaming across the valley. The sky above him was blue and clear. The sun was rising, the dawn revealed, a new day.

He'd done it. He'd *done* it. He wanted to laugh, intoxicated with success, the elation of it, the dark brought under his control.

"I told you I'd do it," said Will. He turned to Katherine, full of exhilaration, looking to see his joy mirrored in her eyes.

She was staring at him, horrified.

His smile faltered as he suddenly saw what she saw—himself, a boy commanding the forces of darkness, the black skies parting at his word. She was looking at him like a stranger, like an enemy out of a nightmare, woken to bring ruin to the world. His stomach sank, a yawning pit opening up between them.

"You are him," she said, as if she saw the truth for the first time. "The Dark King."

"Katherine—"

"No, stay back from me!" she said.

She stepped backward, and as she cast about herself, her eyes fell on the Corrupted Blade. It lay where Simon had dropped it, sheathed in the center of a patch of dead ground.

Quiescent in its sheath, it was death to any human who drew it, and death to all life around it, which would blaze and then die in its annihilating flame.

"Don't!" he said. He took a step toward her, which was a mistake. She snatched the sword up, holding it by the sheath.

If she drew it . . .

"Don't," he said. "You can't draw it. The blade is corrupted. If a human draws it, it will kill them."

He remembered its black fire, tearing open the air, ripping the earth apart, killing every living thing for miles.

"Please. Look at the ground. The sword did that. Not—not me."
Was that even true? It was his blood.

She hesitated. "How could a sword do all that?"

"It was made to kill the Dark King," he said, "but his blood changed
it. Corrupted it. Now it's dangerous."

"You're scared of it," she said.

It was made to kill the Dark King. He'd said those words unthinkingly.
She'd heard them like a bugle call, and he remembered that the Corrupted
Blade had once had another name.

Ekthalion.

The Sword of the Champion. That's what the Elder Steward had
called it. It had carried all the hopes of the side of Light, until the moment
it had failed to do more than draw a single drop of the Dark King's blood.

The Sword of the Champion in the hands of the Lady. His skin prickled at the fated nature of it. That sword; this girl. They were meant to
hurt each other, these events set in motion long before his birth. Katherine
was the Lady's descendant, born to strike him down. Just like his mother.

I cannot return when I am called to fight
So I will have a child

The Lady had loved the Dark King, and she had killed him. She had
been the only one who could do it. Now Katherine stood in front of him
with the weapon forged to do it, and it felt true. Because if Katherine
struck him now, he'd let her. He'd let her run him through.

She was right. He was scared of it. It was his blood on the blade. His
killing blood.

"I don't want to hurt you," said Will helplessly. But he would: if she drew the sword, his blood would kill her. Or maybe it would kill him—

"You're lying," she said. "You've been lying to me this whole time."

Her hand closed on the hilt—

"No," said Will. "Katherine, no—"

Promise me.

"Katherine, don't—"

Will, promise.

"Katherine!"

—and in one single motion she drew the sword.

It hadn't always been corrupted; forged by the blacksmith Than Rema, Ekthalion had once been the great hope, borne into battle by the Champion and raised like a shining light.

The Elder Steward had told another story. *The Sword of the Champion bestows the powers of the Champion.* She had said there was a myth that the Corrupted Blade would be purified in the hands of someone worthy, that it would become a champion's blade once more.

Katherine held the sword triumphant, and for a moment, Will felt his own foolish burst of part fear, part hope.

And then black tendrils began to creep up Katherine's hands where she held the blade out in front of her. "Will?" she said. Veins of black were traveling up her arm under her skin. "Will, what's happening?" She was trying to let go of the blade and she couldn't, as the spidery black webbing raced toward her heart, then up her neck to her face.

He was running the four paces toward her, catching her in the moment that she collapsed, pale and cold. He was cradling her in his arms as he knelt in the mud. Her eyes were two black orbs that were freezing over, the sun eclipsing. Her veins were hard as onyx, as though her blood had turned to stone. "Will, I'm frightened." The words were a whisper, her lips barely moving.

No champion saved her. They were the last words she said.

He held on to her for a long time after, as if his grip could keep her with him. He held on so tight his fingers ached. He felt as if he had been locked in this ache forever. As if the two deaths were one death, the promise that he'd made and broken in the same place, this place that had taken both of them. Mother, and—what? Lover? Sister? Enemy? Friend? He didn't know what she might have been to him. He only knew that the fate that bound them together had brought her here.

He heard footsteps approaching behind him, crunching in the black dirt.

"Now you have everything you wanted," said Devon. "Your usurper is vanquished. The Stewards are dead. The line of the Lady has ended. There's nothing left to stand in your way." Devon spoke as if his business was complete. "Katherine had a sister, but the last Shadow King remains free and will already have found her. That little girl is dead now too."

Will lifted his head, looking up at him and speaking in a new voice.

"No," said Will. "I sent her a Lion."

CHAPTER THIRTY-THREE

VIOLET STOOD WITH her sword outstretched, her eyes fixed on the doors.

Outside, the sky was black. Even the strange red light had faded from the windows. *The wards are down.* It was almost pitch-black in the great hall, the dark of an eclipse, or of being enclosed in a tomb. Only the three flickering torches that she had lit made a small island of light, where the marble columns were pale shapes that disappeared into the dark.

The rest of the light had been stolen, making a shadow world in the middle of the day.

The blast of an inhuman scream—so loud the foundations shook—the stone shuddering—

Outside. It was right outside the doors. Her grip tightened on her sword.

For a moment, silence: the only sound that of her breathing. It was so cold that her breath hung whitely suspended in front of her. And then it got colder. Violet thought she was prepared for it. Grace had described it: a creature of shadows, a formless shape, hard to fight. But then it began to come through.

Darkness; a gaping pit that drew all light into itself. Violet couldn't drag her eyes away. The spreading black felt like standing at the edge of an abyss and wanting to throw herself in. She was looking at death, oncoming, unstoppable; the end of everything.

A Shadow King.

It came alone. A single King was enough to tear down the wards that had protected the Hall for centuries. The Stewards were nothing to it. This world was nothing to it. She could feel the power that could destroy anything it wished, and knew that nothing could stand against it.

The four empty thrones were behind her. She could feel its desire to take its rightful place, to rule, to crush this world into utter subjugation.

"I'm Violet Ballard, Lion of the old world," she said, her voice small in the cavernous hall. "You won't get past me."

She felt its attention slowly turn to her, the swivel of an unnatural eye. Its ancient robes spread out around it, shadowy and grand as a tomb. Its sepulchral crown lay atop half face, half bone. The flickering armor of a king; a sword that burned with cold; armies in its eyes. She could almost taste the worms of the grave.

Lion. The word went right through her, the cold terror of recognition; it *knew* her, knew her power, knew her blood. *I am here for the Lady.*

"I won't let you have her." Louder this time, her grip on the sword hilt tight.

She was breathing shallowly. Thousands of Lions dead on the battlefield, mighty commanders and their armies embalmed in darkness, unicorns lying slaughtered—the enemy in front of her had fought them all, and before that had been a man, who had put his pale hand around a cup. The vast columns of the hall were like an ancient forest, extending out into the dark, a spectral landscape of a vanished world.

Then you will die, said the Shadow King.

A torrent of darkness, it rushed at her with shocking speed, dark sword upraised. Instinct—she dived and rolled, feeling a burst of cold to her left as the King barely missed her. She came up low, just as she'd been trained, and swung, her sword cleaving it from behind—

—and passing right through it as though it wasn't there.

A disorienting sensation like missing a step. It was like hitting nothing, like swinging at a phantasm. Carried forward by her own momentum, she stumbled. And in the swirl of darkness, it seemed she saw a King in ancient armor, and in its eyes the end of the world, a desire to conquer and to rule, all of humanity bound to it, and all she knew turned to ashes and ruin.

As its blade came down to cleave her in two, she desperately pulled up her own sword—

—the sword of the Shadow King passed through her own as though it wasn't there. *Nothing can stop them. Nothing can hold them back.* Her eyes widened and she jerked sideways, too late, the dark sword slicing her cheek and then cutting deep into her shoulder with a sensation of burning cold, and a splatter of blood hitting the stone beneath her feet.

She cried out and gritted her teeth through the pain, forcing herself to keep hold of her weapon, though her arm was burning. Why? Why was she holding a sword if she couldn't fight with it? Her weapon couldn't hurt the Shadow King. Nothing could hurt it, its body as insubstantial as the shadow for which it was named.

The nightmarish truth sank in. The Elder Steward was right. This was an enemy that no mortal could fight. This was the horror each of the Stewards had faced: years of training, strength gained at a terrible price. None of it meant anything to a shadow.

She understood then that she was going to die—she had seen the splintered furniture, the strewn weapons, even the dried blood visible in the last flickering flame from the torches.

And that was the destruction left by Marcus, a single shadow who was as nothing to this nightmarish King, who was more powerful than any Steward, more powerful than any of the great heroes who had ever walked this earth, let alone a single girl.

I can't beat it, she thought. *But I can hold on long enough for Cyprian and Elizabeth to escape the Hall.*

She thought of Justice—of the wreckage that had surrounded his body when they'd found him. Marcus had torn the corridor apart to get at him. *No, not Marcus.* The inhuman thing that had taken Marcus's place. Justice must have realized that he couldn't fight it, and simply tried to evade it as long as he could, as the corridor was destroyed around him. He had bought Grace and Sarah a handful of minutes . . . enough time for the Elder Steward to arrive.

But there was no Elder Steward to come and save her. And not even the Elder Steward could have fought the Shadow King, for it was greater than any shadow, and master of them all.

Justice, I never finished my training. I was never a Steward. But you told me my sword could protect people. And that's what I'm going to do.

Cyprian and Elizabeth would be at the stables, saddling Nell and the last of the horses. Soon they would start their ride across the marshes, riding double with Grace and Sarah. East—Cyprian would know better than to lead them back to London, where a Shadow King's attack would hurt others, the black skies of its arrival terrifying the city.

If she could just hold it off a little longer, they'd have time to reach the gate—

Keep it here, she thought. *Keep it occupied. Let them get away.*

She ran, sprinting for the columns with a torrent of darkness at her back. Her arm was screaming at her, her breath gasping in her throat. She thought she could use the columns to weave and circle, but the Shadow King simply came through the marble, a rushing dark that nothing could stop. A burst of black sent her flying backward to smash hard into the far wall by the thrones.

Blinking to try to focus, dazed. *Get up. Get up.* Her heel slid, her movements clumsy. Pain lanced through her shoulder as she pushed herself onto her hands and knees, collapsed, then tried to push up again. The freezing cold told her the Shadow King was there, towering above her in its horrifying majesty. She looked up at it, barely able to crawl, with her sword missing somewhere in the rubble.

She couldn't stand. She had no weapon. This was the end, and it wasn't enough. She hadn't given Elizabeth and Cyprian enough time.

She saw a dull gleam of metal near her outstretched fingers. Instinctively, she grabbed at it, too wounded to dodge. As the Shadow King's sword descended, she threw it up desperately to cover herself.

It was the old broken piece of a shield.

Useless; foolish; nothing could stop the sword of a Shadow King, which had passed through metal like smoke. She gripped it anyway, a last instinct, a last way to fight. Her thoughts were on Elizabeth and Cyprian. *Please. Please have made it out.* Eyes closed, making herself small behind the fragment she held, she felt the icy cold as the sword of the Shadow King came down upon the shield.

A great clang rang out through the hall, reverberating up through her arm, jarring her teeth. The sword—the sword hitting the shield—striking it like a mallet—

And being knocked back.

Violet opened her eyes and saw the face of a Lion. Etched into the metal, warped and tarnished with age, it was looking back at her from the surface of the shield.

A broken shield, forged long ago, and borne by the Lion whose ancient strength ran in her blood.

The time will come when you must take up the Shield of Rassalon. Do not be afraid.

The Shadow King screamed, a sound of pure rage at being thwart-ed, and brought its sword down on her again—and she met sword with shield and knocked it away.

It worked, it *worked*, the sword flung back, the shield intact.

Breath heaving, she planted her foot on the stone and stood up.

In your blood run the brave lions of England and the bright lions of India. You are the strongest fighter the Light has left.

Rassalon's shield on her on her blood-soaked arm, she faced the Shadow King, staring it down among the broken white columns of the ruined hall.

Around her lay all the signs of her fallen comrades. The Stewards who had fought and died to push back against the dark. Their weapons littered the floor; their blood drenched the stone.

She stood in the center of it all, and attacked with the shield.

They fought in earnest then; she hit out with the shield as the Shadow King screamed in fury and tried to get at her. Her arm hurt; she ignored it. She ignored the swirling dark and freezing cold, and when she saw an opening, she took it, sweeping her shield at the Shadow King's jaw and knocking it back two steps. Another blow, striking its shoulder.

A visceral surge of triumph: the shield could not only block, it could hit. She attacked with it, sweeping away the Shadow King's strikes with ease while it railed and tried to reach her, then hitting it with all her strength.

It reeled: an opening. She ran at it, shield first like a charger, letting out a furious cry of her own. The shield impacted, slamming the Shad-ow King back—and she followed it to the ground—so that she tumbled down above it, among it, the swirling dark all around her.

For a moment she was trapped in it, an endless abyss. But inside the freezing dark she glimpsed its flickering form. Their eyes met, and she was staring down into two chilling pools. She lifted the edge of the shield and brought it down like a blunt guillotine onto the Shadow King's neck.

It screamed and a force blasted outward from it, strong enough to shatter the windows, stone dust raining down around them. She had to pull the shield back up to protect herself from it, covering her face and eyes as she would against a gale. It went on and on, unnaturally long though its neck was severed, until the winds died down and the sound faded.

Silence. She slowly lowered her shield arm, opening her eyes. The Shadow King was dead. It had vanished into nothing from beneath her hands. Only the horrifying black shape of it remained, scoured into the floor.

She looked up. Light was filtering in from the shattered windows above her. She could now see the empty hall around her, illuminated in daylight. Its beauty endured, though columns were smashed, stone paving was cracked, the floor covered in marble dust, coating the strewn remains of an even older fight.

A broken shield. She pulled the shield from her arm and turned it over, looking down at the etched lion that seemed to look back at her. Something inside her stirred, and for a moment she almost thought she saw a real lion, gazing at her with its liquid brown eyes.

Alive; it hit her suddenly that she was alive. The Shadow King was dead. Cyprian and Elizabeth were safe. . . . She had done it. Relief flooded her, and she grasped tight to the shield. She felt her exhaustion now because she could afford to feel it, the pain in her sliced arm, the bruising and ache in her shoulder, the throbbing cut in her cheek. Curling her fingers around the warped metal, she closed her eyes and thought, *I did it, Will.*

CHAPTER THIRTY-FOUR

IT WAS LATE when he reached the inn at Castleton, because he had stayed with her through the night, while the room grew cold.

He had taken Simon's purse, and his jacket, and cut his horses loose from the carriage that waited for him on the road. A pair of restless matched steeds with shiny black coats, they would find plenty of forage on the moors, until they were cornered by a farmer who couldn't believe his luck. With Devon gone and the sun rising, he had made his own way back up over the craggy tors to the thicket where he'd left Valdithar. From there he'd ridden to the nearest inn, where he'd asked for a room, a pen, and ink.

Sitting by the fire in the downstairs common room, he began to write a letter painstakingly to her aunt and uncle. Tomorrow he would find a man of the local parish and tell him where to find her. She would still be there. The body was horrifically preserved like stone. Petrified. Her black marble eyes staring open forever. When he had brought her into his mother's house, she had been heavy like stone too, and cold.

He had sat with her for a long time.

They would find Simon dead. And the three men who had once been Simon's Remnants. And every bird, plant, and animal close enough to be touched by the black fire.

Will tried not to think about the dead.

His room was up narrow stairs of dark wood. Thick stone walls covered with plaster and wash gave it a sturdy, enclosed feeling. At one end was a bed with a wooden frame, and a fire burning low beneath the mantel; at the other end a small table and chair, and a curtained window cut thickly into the stone. Its normalcy was surreal, like his conversation with the innkeeper. *Thruppence for cold meats and ale* and *Weather's holding* and *Our boy put horse in field in back*. The soft dialect of the Midlands seemed to belong to a different world. Will stripped off Simon's jacket and looked blankly at the bed with its coverings of clean linen.

A footstep—but before the sound came the feeling: insubstantial, a shift of air. A figure was emerging from the billowing of the window curtain. *Katherine*, Will thought. It ought to be her, but she was lying cold in a ruined house, and the vital shiver that went through him was a response that he'd only ever had to one person.

"James," said Will.

He was a pale gleam in the dark, with his brushed blond hair over the fitted jacket Simon had bought him, and the face that was like nothing else left on this earth. Will felt the ache of something wrenched out of its time: something that shouldn't be here, alongside his own terrible feeling of gladness that it was.

"You did it," said James, in a quiet voice laced with disbelief and wonder at his own burgeoning freedom. "You stopped Simon from returning the Dark King."

He didn't know.

The choked feeling that pushed into Will's throat wasn't a laugh.

James didn't know. He didn't recognize Will, didn't see in his face the master that he had known long ago. And then came the darker thought: James didn't know but was drawn to him anyway; maybe he felt what Will felt, a helpless fascination, an oiled danger, sliding through reluctance and desire together. Both of them Reborn. Both of them brought here by a Dark King who couldn't let go. All Will could do was look at James and feel that same acquisitive shudder. The desire to step toward him was one that hit him in the throat.

"You shouldn't have come here," said Will.

In a different world, he had put a collar around James's neck and forced him to kill his own people. He had made James do his bidding. And then there were the darker whispers, the accusation that the High Janissary had thrown at him, and that Gauthier had spoken of almost covetously. That James had been the Dark King's plaything. That James had been in his bed.

The Dark King brought you here, thought Will, feeling the knowledge of it trickle through him. *He wanted you, and he made sure that he'd have you.*

That I'd have you. That thought was darkly dangerous.

"It's not a good time to be around me," said Will.

When he looked up, James was closer. James was looking at him like he knew what Will was feeling, and was here with him anyway.

But he didn't know. Not really.

"I know you killed Simon," said James. "I don't think you'll hurt me."

The light from the fire lit the planes of James's face. The trust in his blue eyes was for a savior who he had started to believe was real.

Will wanted to laugh. He had hurt him. He had driven an ivory spike into his shoulder, then killed the man who had raised him. And that was only a pale shadow of what he'd done to him before. Once upon a time, he had been a man who had taken what he wanted, and maybe that was easier than this painful ache he felt. "Won't I?"

The curve of a smile. "I'm more powerful than you are, remember?"

Will felt the whisper of invisible hands against his skin. James was showing off his power. *Look what I can do.* Of course: James's sense of value had always relied on what his abilities were worth to someone else.

It uncurled something in Will, a desire to say, *That's right. Show me. Earn my attention.* He bit down on it, forcefully ignoring the feel of James's ghost touch against his skin.

"What are you doing here?" said Will.

"When I saw you holding the Collar," said James, "I was sure that you'd put it around my neck. I didn't think you'd stop Simon. I didn't think anyone would." James took another step toward him. "I thought the best thing that I could hope for was that I'd find the Collar before Simon did. Instead I'm free to choose my future. . . ." Invisible fingers stroked down his chest. "Can you think of a better outcome?"

"Katherine's dead," said Will.

The invisible touch disappeared, dropping away instantly. Reality settled over the room, as saying the words aloud gave her death the finality that it had not had at Bowhill, when her blood had run black and her eyes had turned to stone.

"I'm sorry. You felt something for her?"

He had barely known her. She'd liked ribbons, and teacups, and fine things. She'd ridden for two days and a night to follow him to the place where her mother had died, and she'd picked up a sword to fight. *Will, I'm frightened.*

James gave a bitter smile. "I thought the Blood of the Lady was supposed to fall in love with the Dark King."

What? That didn't make sense—until Will realized that when James said *Blood of the Lady* he wasn't talking about Katherine. He was talking about *Will.*

Was that how James saw him? As the Lady? As being like James, another obsessional object of the Dark King? The Dark King's paramours: James and Katherine had both belonged to Simon, and before that . . . before that the Dark King had loved the Lady and taken James to his bed. The three of them were intertwined, and it had ended with James twisted out of his time and the Lady dead.

God, James thought that being drawn to Will meant being drawn to *her*—to the Light—to the one who had escaped the Dark King's hold and managed to kill him. He wanted to tell James to run.

"And you?" said Will. "He wanted you. Did you want him?"

James flushed. In the dim orange light from the fire, James's pupils were large, and the blue that ringed them took on the fathomless quality of night water.

"I fell," said James. "Does it matter why? He dragged me across time to be born into a world that didn't remember me. He wanted me waiting, ready to serve him with a collar around my neck. Instead I'm alone, and all that remains of those days is dust. Believing he still controlled me would have given him pleasure."

Will felt the flickering of the past, old selves like shadows. It was difficult to breathe, the air heavy. "You said you didn't remember that life."

"I don't," said James. "But sometimes there's—"

"—a feeling," Will said.

Downstairs, the sounds of the last of the patrons in the inn were distant: the slam of a door, the creak of a board. James didn't hear the admission in his voice. Instead the words seemed to draw them closer, as if they were in a bubble, the only two people in the world.

"My whole life, all anyone's ever wanted was to possess me," said James. "The only one who ever set me free was you."

I haven't set you free, Will didn't say, because the other words were unspeakable. *You won't ever be free of him.* The Dark King's power was control, the ability to draw people to him and warp them into the shape he wanted. The fingerprints of it were all over James, who had run from the High Janissary to Simon, seeking out men with power. "I told you. You shouldn't be here."

"I know that," said James. "Are you going to send me away?"

James said it like he knew Will wouldn't. James was here, like a moth to a flame, not caring if he was burned. And Will wasn't telling him to leave; not even when James took another step forward. Will tried to tell himself that it wasn't because of who James had been, but it was. The past was between them, their histories twining together.

"You killed the Stewards."

"I've done worse than that," said James.

"For him," said Will.

Him. He. As though the Dark King was separate. As though he wasn't inside them both.

Another step. "You said what someone was is less important than what they could be."

He had said that. He'd wanted to believe it. But that was before she'd died in his arms, the turning cogs of the past relentless and unstoppable. The Dark King had set all of this in motion. He'd even brought James here, a gift for himself. Will needed to send him away, but James was a gift he couldn't turn aside, and maybe when he'd ordered James killed all those lifetimes ago, he'd known that about himself.

"What is it we could be?" The question rose up out of some deep part of him. He needed the answer not only for James, but also for himself.

"I may not carry his brand, but he . . . He's burned into me." James's eyes were very dark. "He branded himself on my soul. They called him the

Dark King, but he was a bright flame, and everyone else, everything else is just his pale shadow. I was Reborn, but I lived a half life. It's like this world was a blur. No one else was in focus. Until you."

It was awful, yet Will couldn't look away. He wanted James to keep talking more than he wanted him to stop.

"You made me believe he could be beaten. You make me believe—" James broke off. "The boy savior. I didn't think you'd save me." James's smile was painful. "I thought Simon would bring the Dark King back. I thought the collar would close around my throat. I never thought I'd be free to choose my future. But I am." In the quiet of the room, his words seemed to twine themselves around the beats of Will's heart. "Simon and his father . . . they had a dream of ruling a dark world, and they told me there was a place for me at their side. But I don't want to follow them," said James. "I'm here to follow you." His eyes were bright, his lips smiling, his hair gold in the shifting light from the fire.

Will said, "Of course you are."

ACKNOWLEDGMENTS

I FIRST HAD the idea for *Dark Rise* in the Louvre. There is something so disturbing about museums: all those displaced remnants of forgotten lives. I started to think about the idea of a long-dead magical world.

It was more than ten years of careful world-building and creation before *Dark Rise* was finished, and in that time countless people, books, and institutions have helped me along the way, from the curators at London's Natural History Museum, where I saw my first narwhal horn, to the Castleton locals who served me hot apple crumble after I trudged across the Dark Peak.

Closest to the book have been the Melbourne writers and friends who lived *Dark Rise* with me: Beatrix Bae, Vanessa Len, Anna Cowan, Sarah Fairhall, Jay Kristoff, and Shelley Parker-Chan, all of who read numerous drafts and offered feedback, encouragement, and support. I owe you all a tremendous debt of gratitude. This book wouldn't be what it is without you.

Bea, I first unfolded *Dark Rise* on your table when it was just a roll of butcher paper and a collection of note cards, and I didn't yet know that I was gaining a friend for life. Vanessa, I cherish countless late nights drinking strong hot chocolates and eating cheese toasties "in the style of a club sandwich" while we talked and built our worlds together. Anna, writing days with you at the State Library are some of my favorite memories, as we artfully arranged our desks so that we could leave and get muffins and talk through each other's books. Shelley, your knowledge of monks, mentors, and asceticism was irreplaceable. Thank you also to Amie Kaufman for invaluable friendship, support, and advice, and to Ellie Marney, Penni Russon, and Lili Wilkinson, for all your help along the way.

I've recently come to realize how important early influences are, and I want to thank Rita Maiuto, Brenda Nowlan, Cherida Longley, and Pat McKay for being teachers, mentors, guardians, and family when I needed it most.

Some of the earliest conversations about *Dark Rise* were had with friends, long before the book began to resemble itself. Thank you to Tamara Searle, Kirstie Innes-Will, Kate Ramsay, and Sarah Charlton for indulging those early talks. Particularly vivid is the moment I accidentally woke Tamara up with my shout as I realized that a long-lived unicorn would know the Dark King on sight, and much of the book clicked into place.

Thank you to my incredible agent, Tracey Adams, and to Josh Adams for believing in the book and finding it a home. I am forever grateful to you both. Enormous thanks to the team at Harper, in particular Rosemary Brosnan, and my editors Andrew Eliopulos and Alexandra Cooper. In Australia I had the great fortune to work with Kate Whitfield and Jodie Webster at Allen & Unwin; thank you both so much for your wonderful work. Thank you also to Ben Ball for a piece of early career advice that has helped me more than any other, and to Emily Sylvan Kim for her early career support.

Finally, thank you to Magdalena Pagowska for her stunning cover art, to Sveta Dorosheva for creating a beautiful map of London in 1821, and to Laura Mock and the design team at Harper, who brought all the visual elements together.

Researching *Dark Rise* took me across Europe, from London to Umbria to Prague, into castles and ruins, and deep into the past, pouring over old maps, journals, and artifacts. Over the years of research, I read too many books to name. But I have included in *Dark Rise* a reference to Odell Shepard's observation, "I have hunted the unicorn chiefly in libraries," because that is where I hunted them too.

And found them, perhaps.